★

"Why did you call him a poacher?"

Reed shrugged. "Mr. Avalon's secretary called him that. She said he was poaching poppies. Maybe he was after the secret of Blue Poppy perfume."

Venus bent down, touched the dead man's fingertips. His fingernails were scrubbed clean, but when she pulled her hand back, some iridescent orange dust came off on her fingers. She rubbed them together, studied the dust. She touched the corpse's fingers again. More orange dust, and some metallic silver dust. With her other hand, she fished a notebook from her pocket, rubbed the stuff onto a piece of paper, tore off the paper and handed it to Claudia. Claudia made a quizzical face, then placed it in an evidence bag.

★

"A passionate and knowledgeable environmentalist sensibility..."

—Publishers Weekly

"...an intriguing mix of environmental thriller and police procedural."

—Booklist

SKYE KATHLEEN
MOODY

BLUE
POPPY

W💠RLDWIDE.

TORONTO • NEW YORK • LONDON
AMSTERDAM • PARIS • SYDNEY • HAMBURG
STOCKHOLM • ATHENS • TOKYO • MILAN
MADRID • WARSAW • BUDAPEST • AUCKLAND

With love, for Paul

BLUE POPPY

A Worldwide Mystery/December 1998

First published by St. Martin's Press, Incorporated.

ISBN 0-373-26293-0

Printed in U.S.A.

ACKNOWLEDGMENTS

Special thanks to Washington Department of Fish and Wildlife biologists Ann Potter and David Hays, both for nature lessons and our blooming friendship. Thanks also to Robert Michael Pyle, Ph.D., lepidopterist and author, whose intelligent yet user-friendly writings taught me so many valuable and fascinating things about butterflies; to Daniel Mathews, for his beautifully composed, thoroughly researched works on Olympic Mountains natural history; the Xerces Society, which taught me so much about insects; the United States Department of the Interior, for consultations about their Ashland laboratory and internal structure; to my editor at St. Martin's Press, Kelley Ragland, whose ideas always improve my work; to St. Martin's coolest publicist, David Goldberg; and especially to my literary agent, Pam Ahearn.

Special thanks to my niece, Michelle Speten, for research assistance and collegiality on treks across the Olympic Peninsula; and to actor Michael Su, friend and inspiration.

Many others contributed to this work, and to each of them I am eternally grateful. However, this is an original work of fiction, and if any errors are found within, they are mine.

Note: The butterfly species *Speyeria zerene* is a true species. The subspecies created for this story, *Speyeria zerene dungenessii,* is my invention, although references to the butterfly's feeding, mating habits and process of metamorphosis are based upon accurate records of butterfly behavior.

"The caterpillar on the leaf
Repeats to thee thy mother's grief.
Kill not the moth nor butterfly,
For the Last Judgment draweth nigh."
—William Blake, 1757-1827

"If my first glance of the morning was of the
sun, my first thought was for the butterflies it
would engender."
—Vladimir Nabokov
Speak, Memory

PROLOGUE

THE TERRITORY

KWATEE CREATED the sprites from the sound his footsteps made coming down Mount Rainier. Back then, Mount Rainier was called Takobah. When the Original People walked the earth, Takobah was a wife who abandoned her husband by the ocean and moved a little inland, where she could still watch him, still keep an eye on him. Kwatee, the Changer, came up out of the hole in the top of Takobah, and down Takobah's side. He came to change all things, including the Original People, into new creatures who would worship Tyee Sahale, the Great Chief Up Above.

The sprites' job was making invisible waves to support all flying creatures. Without sprites, the new creatures of the land would all be bound to the earth. Immediately after Kwatee made the sprites, he made Bald Eagle. To reach the high cliffs where Bald Eagle dwelt, you had to pass through a thick rain forest, over steep ridges sharp as wolf's teeth, through a mushroom grove full of witch's butter and death's angel and thickets of giant ferns as tall as the forehead of the first man who walked there, down a steep meadow filled with fragrant blossoms where sacred Bee and enchanted Butterfly lived, then along the River Filled-With-Salmon. Salmon ran so thick in the river that you had to step across their backs to reach the other side. Finally, you had to climb the steep, snowy cliffs that overlooked the whole territory. From here, Bald Eagle guarded the land and all its inhabitants.

Kwatee the Changer created all the creatures of the land and sea, and this territory where they dwelt was made from their collective soul. Kwatee made no creature ruler of the territory. All were equal, all were for the glory of Tyee Sahale, the Great Chief Up Above. From Mount Olympus and the Two Brothers, Kwatee's territory covered a vast ocean, many rivers, snow-capped mountain ranges, glaciers, deep rain forest, lakes and meadows, and endless beaches, all of them traveled by the Chinook winds, and by Kwatee's sprites. Kwatee had made enough room for all who respected the collective soul.

The Changer created Whale, Bear, Elk, Wolf, Rabbit, Eagle, Raven, Thunderbird, and Butterfly, and many other creatures, and he made them all out of the Original People. And out of the Original People, Kwatee created humankind; the Quinault, Makah, Hoh, Quillayute, Queets, Klallam, and other tribes, and Kwatee charged them all to honor the Great Chief Up Above, to live in harmony with their fellow creatures, to take only what was necessary for survival, and to give thanks for every creature, every season, every rain.

The tribes and all creatures, even Raven and Eagle, hunted superbly all along the ocean beaches and in the rain forest. When salmon ran thick up the rivers, Bear came to the river mouths to fish. No one could fish salmon like Bear. No one loved to frolic in the ocean waves more than Bear. Food was abundant in the territory, and sacred cedars made fine dugout whaling canoes and the bark made ceremonial skirts for women of the tribes, and Whale's red blood made fine ceremonial paint. Whatever was taken from the territory was taken respectfully, and only enough for survival was ever harvested from land and from the wide ocean. Tyee Sahale, the Great Chief Up Above, had blessed all creatures of the territory, and His blessings rained down through many seasons, until one day, Thunderbird chased a bad storm off the ocean onto the beach. The storm beached Whale, who was inhabited by wicked spirits.

The wicked spirits spread out across the territory, infecting the shoots and berries and the camas bulbs people used for food. Kwatee's creatures accidentally ate Whale's evil spirits, and began to kill one another, Bear against Man, Man against Wolf, Wolf against Rabbit, until even Raven and Butterfly were no longer safe from harm. Then one day, the whole territory stood still, as every creature watched a new tribe come up out of saltwater and step off strange canoes. The new people came up from the beaches, through the salt-spray meadows, up into the rain forest. With fierce energy these pale-skinned men raised shining blades and attacked the ancient cedar, the old fir, felled them to the ground, and dragged them down the mountainsides to build their camps. They guarded their camps with weapons no tribe had ever seen before. Kwatee's creatures feared the new people's gunfire, and the native tribes retreated deep into the forests, and out along Seal's beach.

One day on Seal's beach, the tribal chiefs held a big potlatch. Braves and women came from every tribe, from the Makah, the Quillayute, Quinault, Queets, the Hoh, and the Klallam. When all the native tribes had arrived, the chiefs sent scouts to invite the white people to join them, to share in a feast of salmon, to make peace. The tribal women put on their cedar bark skirts and the men smeared salmon blood over their limbs. When the white people arrived, Kwatee's people welcomed them with gifts of camas cakes, fragrant baskets woven from cedar, ceremonial masks, whale blubber, and bear hides. The people with big noise also brought many fine gifts to the potlatch, including bright woolen blankets, sweet cakes, and liquor, which Kwatee's people accepted. For a little while, peace prevailed in the territory, but a strange feeling lingered over everything like a dark cloud full of bad rain. The feeling gnawed at the hearts of all the creatures, and their collective soul wept without knowing why, and the sign of the dark cloud was felt when the wind blew through the meadows and the wild violets shivered, and Butterfly slept longer than usual. Kwatee the Changer went back up Mount Takobah, disappeared into the crater, and hasn't been seen since.

ONE

BUTTERFLY

Dungeness silverspot
Speyeria zerene dungenessii

Medium-sized, orange butterfly with distinctive black-
checkered pattern on upper wing surface and bright metallic
silver spots on underwings. Range: NW North America, Strait
of Juan de Fuca, northern tip of Olympic Peninsula, Vancouver
Island. Main habitat characteristic, the presence of salt-spray
meadows and the western blue violet (V. adunca), for this is
the only plant on which its larvae will feed. Believed to be
extinct.

*—Green's Endangered Species
of the Olympic Peninsula*

ONE FOGGY June morning, vagrant sunbeams pierced an opaque
cloud bank over the Olympic Mountains, spilling radiant light across
Hurricane Ridge, comforting the shivering Brothers, dappling the
bald, icy dome of Mount Pluvius. On the mountain's northeastern
slopes, the sun rays tackled a glacial meadow, brimmed over an alpine
ridge, and flooded an ancient rain forest. From there, the sunbeams
radiated along the steep slopes of Yodeler National Wildlife Preserve,
through a subalpine meadow ablaze with wildflowers, spilled across
Yodeler's richly blooming salt-spray apron, and then dissolved into
a dazzling pool of shimmering liquid light on the rolling, churning
saltwater Strait of Juan de Fuca. Soft breezes rode the halcyon light,
inspiring a brilliant dance of pink fawn lily, purple camas, golden
yarrow, pearly everlasting, larkspur, and blue violets.

In Yodeler's meadow, two butterflies emerged from under a blackberry vine, where, drained of energy, they had been waiting for the

sun. Cautiously, avoiding predators, they crept onto a nearby kinni-kinnick bush, spread their mist-dampened orange-and-black wings, and soaked up solar radiation. When the sun had recharged them, the male released a strong seductive scent and performed a short ritual-istic fly-by dance. At first, the female took defensive flight, spiraling upward, then gradually she turned coquettish, fluttered back down to the kinnikinnick branch, and curving her abdomen, invited the male's attentions. The male swooped down, and on the first brilliant attempt, penetrated the female. Locked in pro genitive posture, they remained immobile for a very long time.

The sun disappeared, then came back again, a brighter shaft this time, hot. The butterflies broke free and fluttered together along the sunshine path, through the deep meadow. When they had flown about two-thirds the distance of the meadow, the male banked on a wind-swell and bobbed off toward Dungeness Spit. The female dallied, seduced by a sweet, familiar scent.

The western blue violet grew close to earth, its whimsical petals and deep green, hairy leaves in their prime. Fluttering near the ground, the butterfly laid several hundred eggs among the delicate hairs on the underside of the violet's leaves, where in all good time, the eggs would hatch and little black larvae with orange-striped backs and beady green eyes would gorge on tasty greens. Her task com-pleted, she basked a few minutes, then took off, sailing across the meadow in search of nectar. Some days are busier than others.

She hadn't traveled far across the meadow when Jonathan Willow netted her. She didn't die immediately when her captor's fingers grasped her ebony body and pressed it up against something hard. A moment passed, then a great heat pierced her abdomen and she died quickly—still, she died—pinned securely to Jonathan Willow's but-terfly board.

The butterfly catcher grinned, for he had just captured the most beautiful creature he'd ever seen. This was no ordinary butterfly, he realized immediately. Might it possibly be...but, no, it surely isn't... For it seemed to Jonathan Willow, though he dared not believe it, that he had just netted *Speyeria zerene dungenessii*, the Dungeness silverspot butterfly, thought to be extinct. He would take it to Budge immediately. Budge could identify the specimen. That is, if she was still speaking to him. Of one thing Jonathan Willow felt certain: He'd netted a precious creature, really the catch of a lifetime, certainly the answer to Jonathan Willow's prayers, had he been the type to pray.

Willow was examining the rare specimen, applying a preservative to its corpse, when he heard a rustling sound. He looked up. A few yards from where he stood, in the highest reaches of the meadow, Peter Avalon's blue poppy fields ran along the forest edge, full of long green stems swaying in the breeze. Each tall stem supported an axle near the top, and each stem on the axle bore a partially opened green pod. Any day now, these thousands of pods would fully bloom, transforming the forest edge into a dazzling blue ribbon, and then the perfume harvest would begin. From the abundance of pods, Willow guessed this would be a fabulous season for Blue Poppy perfume, the famous "Fragrance of Tibet" improbably concocted right here in the Pacific Northwest.

Willow heard the rustling noise again. He looked down at his feet. Might he be trespassing on Avalon's leasehold in the federal wildlife preserve? Or was that the sound of a ranger, coming to arrest him for chasing butterflies on protected government land? Did he really hear a noise, or was he just imagining it?

Jonathan Willow's several questions never got answered, unless you count the bullet that punctured his sternum, pierced his heart, and laid him flat on the fragrant meadow, where he died, one hand clutching his fatal wound, the other gripping the special butterfly. A man who recently inhaled the sweet bouquet of love, a man who truly appreciated virginal landscapes, could not have died better. Unless, of course, it was a case of mistaken identity. Then, too, the butterfly might have gone free, to die later by Nature's unstudied hand.

TWO

RHODODENDRON

THE LANDLADY WORE two wigs. On a typical day, like today for instance, she donned the dusty rayon artichoke model. It fit like a swimming cap. She wore the other wig, an orange bubble-shaped affair, approximately once every six months, on special occasions, like when she lapsed into a good mood. Whichever wig she wore lay crooked on her head.

Like her hair, Clara Gasgcoyne's house perched on a slant, on the brink of Queen Anne Hill in a neighborhood that breathed nouvelle Pacific Northwest zephyrs and mourned a grand old past tainted by the conversion of genteel Victorian mansions and noble estates into mazes of cubicle-sized, trendy apartment dwellings. Clara Gasgcoyne owned several of the restored properties in Cedar Lane, including the upscale Rhododendron Arms, next door to her own abode. This steep corner precipice on Queen Anne Hill embodied Clara Gasgcoyne's world, and she ran it like a prison camp.

She kept her money in cash bills in a heavy steel box, stashed somewhere inside her house. She kept her husband the same way, except when she let old John out to tend light fixtures on rafters and perform other precarious duties, where his two feeble legs struggled up rickety stepladders or coupled like bent toothpicks under his Black & Decker toolbox. Clara Gasgcoyne was merciless.

The sky over Seattle drizzled this Friday morning in June, and a steel gray Puget Sound wore angry whitecaps. At half past eight, bumper-to-bumper traffic rode Queen Anne Avenue's roller-coaster slide into downtown, and a nefarious breeze wafted exhaust fumes upwards into the ozone. This was the year of Seattle's famous Spring Drought, when for three glorious weeks, freak El Niño winds transformed the drizzling Emerald City into an astonishing arid desert, and a stunned citizenry rationed water and walked around acting like beached salmon. But all that had changed this morning, when a robust nor'westerly blew into town. In spite of drizzling skies, Clara Gasgcoyne's steep lawn on Cedar Lane bathed luxuriously under a giant, arcing aluminum sprinkler, placed carelessly on the edge, where half the water fell wasted over concrete sidewalk. She wasn't a conservationist.

Venus Diamond waited for the sprinkler to arc onto the grass and slipped past to the landlady's front porch. Wearing civilian dress on her first day off in two months—black jeans, black T-shirt, and a slick new Patagonia anorak—Venus felt energized this morning, in spite of nor'westerlies and drizzle. If she had a choice, she'd be back in Singapore, swimming in Raffle's pool, sipping Slings, soaking up tropical sunshine. A Pacific Northwest native should never go to the tropics. It divides your loyalties right down the middle.

Some giant had built the porch stairs, and Venus felt her leg muscles stretch. The stretching felt good, in a Zen way, adding spring to her legs. Short legs, like the rest of her, small-boned, in superb physical shape. Most people, when first meeting Venus, were put in mind of an asexual wood nymph, or Peter Pan, and she despised these fairy tale references to her size. Her boss, Oly Olson, at the regional headquarters of the Department of the Interior, described Venus as a miniature androgyne. Olson refused to recognize her female aspect. As if Venus could defy Nature's whimsy. Not surprisingly, Olson had personally taught her how to shoot a gun, how to drop a two-hundred-pound opponent with an arm lock, how to track big game poachers in the wild, and generally, how to act tougher than she was. Work like hers demanded a bulletproof facade.

She had deep-set, startling green eyes, and fragile features that fooled her prey. She kept her blond hair in a slick Jimmy Dean, not to play up the androgyny aspect, but because Richard, her fiancé, liked it that way. Richard never mentioned androgyny. But this was delving into intimate territory. The thought of Richard caused her mind to wander, her legs to weaken. She stumbled on the landlady's porch steps, her shin bone sharp against the edge, and catapulted across the porch. Sprawled akimbo, the chagrin rankled more than her shrieking shin.

Laughter, high-pitched like a bird's voice, mocked her prone position. She looked around. To the right of the front door, an aluminum rocker couch, green and white paint peeling off silver bones, swayed gently, creaking in the chilly breeze. Above the rocker couch, one beam of the porch's roof housed a nest, where a red-breasted mother robin lived with her five tiny hatchlings. They seemed amused, in a superior species sort of way. Birds don't often trip.

Near Mrs. Gasgcoyne's front door, a fat brown nipple with a black button invited touching. Venus punched it. It clanged like a fire drill bell.

A voice answered right away. Venus knew it was the landlady because no other human could imitate Clara Gasgcoyne's *patois poulet*. Two stories up, a dirt-filmed window released her cross, clucky inquiries.

"Eh? Who is that?"

"Your favorite tenant from the Rhododendron Arms," Venus answered sardonically. "The 'gell with crazy eyes'."

Clara Gasgcoyne stared at the creature below, this Venus Diamond. She knew too little about this particular tenant. You can never know enough about your tenants. Especially young women with chartreuse eyes. The landlady said, "Oh, it's you, is it? So wait already."

Minutes ticked by. While she waited on the porch, Venus studied her own left hand, the engagement ring on her finger, the way pale sunlight caught the facets in the huge, flawless pear-shaped diamond. Her small hand and delicate short fingers just barely supported the rock. It felt heavy, burdensome. Richard's grandmother had accepted the boulder from a Viscount Someone-or-Other, Venus couldn't recall his name right now. Right now, all Venus could think about was Richard, and she wondered for the hundredth time since breakfast if their engagement hadn't been too hasty. Two months isn't a very long courtship, but then, you can't predict when love will tiptoe into your life and caution flee.

Footsteps sounded inside the house. Floorboards creaked. The front door shivered, rattled, and the grinding sound of two locks being undone and chains clunking against the door frame announced Clara Gasgcoyne. The door slowly opened about four inches.

She was wearing the dusty artichoke wig and a brutal frown. Her bleak eyes smoldered. Her Captain Hook nose made unsavory snuffling sounds, and her fish lips, smeared siren red, worked nervously. She clasped a loud muumuu tight to her bosom, stretching a field of magenta zinnias across a heaving belly. Her thin bare legs segued into swollen feet that ballooned from pink-flecked polyurethane house slippers, six sizes too small. She reeked of stale body odor and something else Venus didn't care to identify.

Clara Gasgcoyne barked, "What do you want?"

Accusatory. Venus breathed through her mouth and spoke. "It's my special day, Mrs. Gasgcoyne."

The landlady grinned broadly then, all friendly, lipstick spreading between rayon tendrils, crooked as the wig. "Oh, you want to pay your rent?" She said "rant" for "rent."

She held out one flaky hand. Into this flytrap palm, Venus placed a good check drawn from a good bank against a generously endowed trust fund. Clara Gasgcoyne's arthritic digits snapped shut, molding the smooth rectangular sheet into a fan, thrust it somewhere underneath the muumuu, and pulled out an old-fashioned receipt book labeled RHODODENDRON ARMS. Leafing through worn pages, she stopped halfway through the book.

"You have a pencil?"

Venus handed her a Pelikan broadtip. Mrs. Gasgcoyne wrote out a receipt, carefully curling the tails of her squared-off cursive, tore the pink copy off the pad, and thrust it at Venus. She studied the pretty Pelikan, then reluctantly handed it over. The exchange ended without further event, and Venus had reached the sidewalk when the landlady cried, "Wait!"

Venus glanced back at Clara Gasgcoyne. The dollar signs had almost faded, but the scanners flitted around, agitated now. Money had not satisfied Her Landladyship. Something else was bothering her. Venus went back up on the porch. Mrs. Gasgcoyne said, "Okay. Now we talk. Come."

She brushed past Venus and headed for the aluminum rocker couch. Venus sat at a safe breathing distance, their combined weight straining the vehicle's springs, creaking a loud warning to the fugitive robins. When Mrs. Gasgcoyne rolled her eyes upward toward the nest, Venus asked, "What's up, Mrs. G.?"

Her gaze dropped just in time. She hadn't detected the squatters. Clara Gasgcoyne said, "Tell me, please, why don't you work for a living?"

"I do work. I'm a special agent for the Department of the Interior. Fish and Wildlife Service. That information is on my lease application."

"Maybe you was lying. Maybe you don't even have a job."

Venus sighed, reached into her pocket. Even in civilian dress, she carried identification. You never know when you'll need it, especially if your landlady is a paranoid. She fished out her badge, aimed it at the landlady's hungry eyes. This might be a ritual of some significance, for all she knew. She'd only been Mrs. Gasgcoyne's tenant for five weeks. This was their third actual exchange of legal tender. The landlady examined Venus's badge, running her arthritic fingertips over its polished, embossed surface. She thrust it back at Venus. "Okay, so tell me please, why are you never at home?"

"What, are you spying on me?" Venus's strategy was to make light of the landlady's snoopy repetitive mantra.

"I am your landlady. I have to know these things."

Venus laughed. "What else do you know about me?"

"Don't laugh at me. A landlady needs to know her tenants. About you I know very little. I know that your mother is that famous movie actress with royal bloods. A beautiful lady, beautiful. You don't remind me of her at all." She sucked in some air and added, "That is all I know."

Venus stood up. "That's more than enough."

The Gasgcoyne pressed on, adding a fresh barb to her repertoire. "And I know something else. I know that you are getting married. What kind of a man would marry a queer gell like you?" The old woman harumphed indignantly. One pink slipper made dull thumps against wooden floorboards in time to the rocker's rhythm.

Rain fell softly, nattering at the landlady's madrona trees. It was barely nine o'clock Friday morning. Already, Clara Gasgcoyne had dropped a damper on Venus's three-day weekend. Through small, evenly spaced, clenched teeth, Venus said, "Anything else?"

Clara Gasgcoyne sighed and folded her gritty, gnarled hands in her wide lap. That's when Venus saw the crude tattoo. She usually covered it up, but today she had on the sleeveless muumuu, and she'd forgotten the Band-Aid she usually wore over the grim reminder. Venus had known, but this was the first time she'd actually seen the tattoo. She averted her gaze.

Mrs. Gasgcoyne said, "I need advice. I have troubles with my John. He is very ill, but he won't see a doctor."

"Sorry to hear that. May I ask what's wrong with him?"

"He is stubborn, that's what's wrong. Grouchy old men are always stubborn."

"I mean, what's his health problem?" Venus didn't have much

more patience. Anyway, why would the landlady confide her troubles to a tenant?

"His prostrate. At least, I think so. But he absolutely refuses to see the doctor."

"Maybe he's scared. And by the way, it's 'prostate'."

"Scared, schmared. He has to go. How do you spell it?"

Venus spelled the word. Mrs. Gasgcoyne nodded, comprehending. "Now, tell me, please, how can I persuade John to see a doctor?"

"Trick him. Tell him you're taking him out for clam chowder, then take him to the doctor's office."

"He hates clam chowder."

Venus read her Swatch.

Mrs. Gasgcoyne sighed. "God, so give me my health, my husband is ruining me."

"How's that?" Venus glanced furtively at the robins' nest. One brilliant eye poked over the woven walls. She thought muffled laughter leaked from beneath a maternal wing. Clara Gasgcoyne snapped, "That is none of your business. And you give terrible advice. Now, go away. I have had enough of you for one day."

She was swinging on the rocker couch studying the wood beam where the robins squatted when Venus left her that dreary morning. Venus waited for the sprinkler to arc off the cement, then slopped through the puddles dribbling down Cedar Lane. It might have been the compassion she felt for Clara and John Gasgcoyne, haunted Jewish immigrants who, as children, had been scooped off the streets of Paris and deported to Auschwitz, where they'd barely survived a horrific childhood. Or it might have been the robins' mocking song, or the bruised shin obtained in the clumsy fall. But something occurred that morning which heightened Venus's senses, causing her to sniff trouble in the drizzling spring air.

Back at the Rhododendron, she turned on Benny Goodman, whipped up a Kenya roast double tall skinny, and drank it, staring out wraparound picture windows that framed Puget Sound, the Olympic Mountains, a sliver of the Cascade range, and the ever-changing Mount Rainier. This morning, Rainier's snow-capped dome reflected a soft peach hue, like perfect sorbet. Richard liked this peach shade better than all the other sorbet shades of Mount Rainier.

Beginning with the old World's Fair grounds, the Opera House, and Space Needle, the view from her windows swept across downtown Seattle's architectural salmagundi, panned the old Pike Place

Market with its quirky vendors, including the fish mongers who throw the fish to thrill their clientele. Then came the steep Hillclimb, spilling chic cafes and boutiques down to the waterfront, then the ever-changing Puget Sound, the ferry boats and shipping traffic. Beyond Puget Sound, the Olympic Mountains cut a jagged white border between water and sky, and on a clear evening you could watch a copper-toned sun sink into the Olympics' snow caps, tinting them vermilion, turning Puget Sound to liquid gold. When ferries plowed through the golden waters, deep scarlet lines appeared in their wakes and sea gulls breaching the wakes screeched their evening lullabies. Mount Rainier stood watch over all this splendor, its snow-capped dome changing constantly with the light, from blue-white to the sorbets, to rose, then deep moody purple.

Right now, it was what? Four, five o'clock in Stockholm. Richard's first lecture was probably just into the discussion stage. What a funny picture, Richard lecturing to the World Academy of Forest Conservation. If she'd gone with him, sat in on the lecture, she'd be there now, making faces at him from the back of the room, trying to make him laugh, crack up, in the middle of all the academic hoo-ha.

Back in the dark ages, when he was a businessman, Richard never lectured. He sold trees and made pots of money. His swift conversion to conservation cost Richard the lucrative timber ties. Now he had a new life, a new identity. Just a few weeks ago, he became chief officer of a forest conservation trust fund. That was ducky with Venus, but Richard's new mandate to protect the world's forests meant he had to travel frequently, lecture, and raise funds. Richard wanted Venus to go along on these junkets, but her boss wasn't sympathetic. Olson would say, "No way. We're understaffed as it is."

Richard wouldn't return for three weeks. She was solo for a while, and the weekend suddenly seemed a little lonely. A visit to the family castle on Magnolia Bluff usually proved diverting, however painful at times, and right now she needed diversion. She picked up the phone, punched in Bella's number. Stephen, her mother's personal assistant, came on the line.

"Your mother is sleeping in," intoned Stephen. "She and young Timothy arrived home very late last night."

"Where from?"

"The Napa Valley. Your mother has taken another film role."

"What's the film?"

"*Chateau* something or other. I can't recall. It is one of these

sweeping epoch films, a blockbuster, of which I do not approve. I
sent Burden along, more as baby-sitter than anything else. Young
Timothy needs more discipline than Lady Bella can manage in the
midst of filming."

"You and Timmy aren't getting along?"

"Whatever gave you that idea?" Sarcastically.

"You only use 'Timothy' when you're ticked off at him."

Stephen sniffed. "Timothy is insufferable, and far too intelligent
for an eight-year-old. I don't care if he is Asian, he shouldn't be so
bright."

"He's still adjusting. He's had a lot of trauma in his short life. So
what's the problem?"

Stephen sniffed again. "I don't know if he can ever adjust to this
household, or us to him. He's only been here, what? Six weeks, and
already he calls me names."

"Such as?"

"Freak. Fuddy-duddy. Demeaning epithets. My temper's running
very short."

"Hmmm." A seagull flew past the window, screeched. Venus
watched it ride an updraft, bank toward Puget Sound.

Stephen said, "I should ring off. The grocer is standing here waiting for me to select three dozen fresh asparagus. Will you be joining
us for dinner?"

"Maybe. I'll check in later."

Venus paced, musing over the mentally unstable landlady. Maybe
next time she should mail her rent check, avoid the Gasgcoyne ex-
perience. Or maybe she should find another, less meddlesome landlady. She'd hate to give up this snazzy art deco pad with its wraparound corner windows, the panoramic view. Even in the rain, this
view of Oz caused her heart to leap. If only the landlady weren't so
flaky.

The Kenya roast went down smooth, perked up her spirits. She
was staring out the window at the dancing whitecaps on Puget Sound
when the phone rang.

"Put on your uniform and comb what's left of your hair," Oly
Olson barked. "Then get down here."

Venus touched her hair. It felt slick, the way she liked it. She said,
"What's up?"

"A man was shot to death up on Yodeler Preserve. It happened in the subalpine meadow, near the Avalon leasehold. He might have been stealing poppies from Peter Avalon's leased portion.''

"Poaching nonnative blue poppies?''

"That's the implication. Avalon's security office called in the report. And the sheriff called in, too, but he's not keen on getting involved. He's got other fish to fry. Sheriff's name is Needles. He was elected last fall, while you were in Asia pretending to work. Needles is right, too. It's our baby. I want you to go up to the preserve, then once you've scoped out that scene, stop by the Blue Poppy perfume factory. I've called ahead. They're expecting you. Have a talk with Peter or Troy Avalon. And for the love of Mike, please try to behave professionally, will you? It might just be a simple mugging that went wrong, I don't know. In any case, don't forget your diplomatic airs at Avalon's perfume factory.''

"They don't call it a factory. It's a *parfumerie.*''

"Maybe I should just send Louie up there.''

"I'll be good. I promise.''

Olson growled, "Then hurry up. I'll meet you at the office. The team can meet us on the chopper pad. Sweetwater's pilot on call. He's already here, waiting for you. Take Louie Song with you, and Paganelli, if she's available. Sparks is trying to locate them right now. That's all the help I can spare. And we have the body to bring back. Contact me soon as you've scoped things out.''

"Cell, fax, or e-mail?''

"Don't be snide,'' Olson snapped, then added, "Wear your uniform this time. I want you looking civilized when you meet Peter Avalon. So lose the black leather, do you understand?''

"I never wear leather between Memorial Day and Labor Day.''

"Come to think of it, I'm going to personally escort you to the chopper, to be sure you're in uniform.''

She winced, said, "Before you hang up, who's Troy?''

"Peter's younger brother. I think it goes like this; Peter and Troy Avalon are Conrad Avalon's nephews, and heir apparents to the Blue Poppy fortune. Conrad retired earlier this year and left Peter at the helm. Troy's of lesser importance. I think that's how it goes. Now, scram.''

Olson was signing off when she said, "Who's Mike?''

"What are you talking about?'' whined Olson.

"A minute ago, you said 'for the love of Mike'. I was wondering who Mike is.''

Maybe she was holding a hot iron instead of a telephone receiver. Steam blew across the line. She held it far from her ear until the surge and sputter quit, then said, "Before you hang up, what other fish is Needles frying?"

"You know the Inn at Raven Point? That chichi spa up past Agate Beach?"

"Uh-huh."

"Chef up there dropped dead this morning. Botulism, Needles thinks. That's all I know. Nothing we need to worry about." Olson rang off.

The sky turned a shade grayer. Raindrops spattered the window. She rubbed her bruised shin and went to change clothes. If Olson was lucky, she might even comb her hair.

On the way out, passing the coffee table, she noticed her laptop, decided to check her e-mail. You never know what a person in love will find on e-mail. Jackpot. A note from Richard. She stared at the screen and read:

"Venus, this is no way to end an engagement, but I just couldn't say it in person. I've met someone else. I'm sorry. Please forgive me. Richard."

The Rock of Gibraltar slipped easily off her finger. She stood frozen for a moment, holding the engagement ring in a fisted palm. She opened the fist and the ring dropped at her feet. With one regulation hiking boot, she stomped on the dazzling stone. Nothing happened. She stomped again, and again. The bloody thing was indestructible. She knelt down, plucked the ring off the carpet. Intense heat seared her chest, but before it could truly be defined as pain, the cast-iron casing she kept in reserve enveloped her heart until all she could feel was a secure numbness. On the way out the door, she paused at the refrigerator, opened the freezer door, tossed the viscount's legacy in the freezer section. Then she headed out to examine the corpse up on Yodeler Preserve, vowing to store up the pain and the rage, hold it hostage in the iron prison. In a few weeks, she might fire it all at Richard. Then again, she might not bother.

She'd been right about today's ominous beginnings. Maybe she should have been a channeler, or a hermit. Hermits don't need anyone.

THREE

SALT-SPRAY MEADOW

> Excessive land development, herbicide/pesticide applications
> on land adjoining reintroduction efforts, and the introduction
> of nonnative plants have also contributed to the butterfly's ap-
> parent disappearance...
>
> —*Green's Endangered Species*

IT WAS ONE of those charming spring mornings on the Olympic Peninsula when rain swells off the Strait of Juan de Fuca inspire ennui,
and suicide notes. Adding to the exuberance, a thick fog blanket
draped the broad saltwater strait that divides Canada from the United
States at the northern tip of the Olympic Peninsula. The fog clawed
at Dungeness Spit and poured southward into foothill meadows,
creeping up the mountainsides through dense rain forest to timberline,
until all the Olympic Mountains disappeared from view. From the
Bell Jet Ranger's passenger seat, Venus looked down and through a
rent in the fog, saw the swollen Elwha River raging towards its mouth
at the saltwater strait.

Already a hundred inches of rainfall had drenched the Olympic
Peninsula's northwestern coastline between Cape Flattery and Port
Angeles, and this was only June. Below the sullen fog, Venus knew,
the one hundred and first inch now fell. Yet, by some miraculous
quirk of Nature, the Olympics' northeastern slopes, in the sun-kissed
"rain shadow" of the mountains, boasted remarkably clear skies, and
even now, as the chopper made a sharp turn across Dungeness Spit,
a brilliant sun beat down.

On the northeastern slopes of Mount Pluvius, an ice cap crowned
a snow-laden glacial meadow, and below that, a thick rain forest
caught the snow melt in its primordial thrall. Below the rain forest,

a flower-laden meadow ran steeply down the mountainside and, if not for a tiny stretch of Highway 101 just before the curve at Deer Park Road, the mountain would have cut straight down through Yodeler Valley and touched the cobbled beach somewhere between Dungeness and Port Angeles. Here on the sunny side of the mountains, in the peaceful valley where Lassie passed her retirement years, here among Edenesque country estates and simple cow pastures, DOI agent Eric Sweetwater brought the agency's Bell Jet Ranger down on Yodeler Preserve, landing in the subalpine salt-spray meadow, a few yards from the windblown highway and rocky, driftwood-strewn beach. Venus unbuckled her seat belt and jumped onto the grassy meadow.

She wore her DOI badge pinned to the pocket of her summer uniform. They had to custom-make her uniforms because standard issue didn't fit miniature persons. In today's world of giants, Venus stood like an insect among thriving dune grass, which is precisely how she had felt two hours ago, when Oly Olson had dragged her onto a crowded elevator in Seattle's Bumbershoot Building, where Interior maintained an eagle's-eye view of Puget Sound and some offices. In that acrid steel jungle of sweltering fragrance-laced bodies crushed together, boxed for the ride, Venus had held her breath until the fifty-first floor; by then most of the crowd had cleared out and it was just herself and Olson riding to the helicopter pad on the roof. This is how her first day off in two months ended, like all the others, before the day's first real sun break. In spite of the thin sunshine up here on Yodeler Preserve, this wasn't her idea of a fine spring morning.

Venus helped Sweetwater and the others unload equipment, then began the long hike up above the steep meadow into the heart of Yodeler Preserve. Claudia Paganelli, Interior's regional forensics officer, followed Venus. Tall, bony, Norwegian Paganelli-by-marriage carried her physician's black bag of forensic tricks and a Nikon digital camera. Then came Eric Sweetwater, the chopper pilot and rookie agent, still wet behind the ears. Sweetwater was a slim, chiseled Quinault of few words. Beside him, walking up the meadow, was Louie Song, Amerasian, early thirties, with jet black hair and Ray Bans tattooed to his face. Song was Interior's regional crime scene expert. Sweetwater and Song brought a canvas body bag, some lab equipment, and another camera that reminded Venus of the one-eyed monster in *Godzilla, the Final Scream.* The foursome trudged up the deep meadow toward a cluster of people about a quarter of a mile above them.

Carpeted in brilliant wildflowers, as if someone had shaken out a Van Gogh, the virgin salt-spray meadow formed a distinct break in the surrounding evergreen forest, covering about fifty acres of grassland starting at the saltwater strait and sweeping up the Olympic foothills to meet a wide band of partially opened blue poppies on Peter Avalon's leasehold. East of the poppy field, on adjacent private land, you could glimpse Peter Avalon's new home, a contemporary glass and concrete structure the size of a football stadium but more tasteful. Avalon's villa, designed by a cutting edge Seattle architectural firm, sprawled over several wooded acres, an Alvar Aalto knockoff, futuristic, a technologically informed monolith-on-a-cliff, soaring above the saltwater strait and set conveniently adjacent to his poppy field leasehold on Yodeler Preserve. Surrounding the Avalon estate, embracing Yodeler National Wildlife Preserve, the Olympic National Forest rose to glacial peaks where even in July you might need chains on your tires.

A few ancient Douglas firs dotted Yodeler's meadow, but the land mostly supported woody plants, saw grass, wildflowers, and herbs. Here and there, generous clumps of low bush kinnikinnick and salal offered abundant refuge for small wildlife, and the meadow blazed late spring color, from the most delicate pink fawn lily blossoms to bright purple camas, wild larkspur, buttercups, and early Shasta daisies, forming a fragrant pastel panorama, better than Disney and real to the touch.

Trudging up the meadow, Venus surveyed Peter Avalon's blue poppy field. It covered the upper third of this federal wildlife preserve, a parcel leased to the perfumer for cultivation of a rare and delicate species of *Meconopsis betonicifolia*, the Tibetan blue poppy. Not yet in full bloom, the five-foot-tall, brilliant green stems—each crowned with five partially opened pods—performed a swaying dance in the breeze, Olive Oyl in multiples. On the still-virgin meadow, a few yards below Avalon's poppy field, three men stood in a circle, arms hugging their chests, talking earnestly. When the federal agents arrived, one of the men turned to greet them, but Venus didn't notice him right away because something sinister had caught her attention.

The corpse lay face up among the meadow's ambrosial blooms, pale blue eyes bulging, an astonished expression on a once-handsome face. He wore a thin nylon navy blue vest, white T-shirt, and faded blue jeans. His hiking boots had seen better days. His hands were large, ringless, with slender fingers, and one hand clutched a few stems of blue poppies, recently uprooted. He had a lot of fine blond hair in a Dutch bob. He'd been shot once, with a small-caliber weapon. The bullet had entered cleanly on the left-central portion of the chest, passed through the rib cage, pierced the heart, then made an unusually flamboyant exit through the back before he fell into a clump of Shasta daisies.

"Oh, he's dead, that's for sure," chirped one of the men standing near Venus. His colleagues grunted in agreement. Their sheriff's deputy uniforms had arm patches with small silver chevrons. Venus stood up. The deputy who had spoken, barely taller than Venus, proffered his hand. "Officer Ronnie Reed," he said. "We're Needles's deputies."

The men stared. They weren't offering anything besides that tiny shred of information. Venus would have to drag it out of them. Behind her, Paganelli, Sweetwater, and Song waited. Venus said, "Who found him?"

"I did." Reed. "Maybe two hours ago. On a routine patrol."

"Sheriff been here?"

Reed might have nodded. "Sheriff Needles said this here's federal land, so it's none of our business. I guess he might've radioed you folks down in Seattle, but he didn't seem too interested in the whole thing." Reed lit a cigarette, blew out smoke, said, "Sheriff's on another case, see? The chef down at Raven Point, at the inn down there? He croaked. Wasn't murder, though. Food poisoning."

The other deputies guffawed. Apparently a private joke. Venus said, "Needles contacted us. Or one of his deputies."

"That was me," offered another deputy, taller than Reed, with a thick mustache that hid his mouth. He spit on the ground, mottled brown spittle, rotated his jaw, his cheek bulging where a tobacco chaw lodged. He said, "Reed called in. I took the call. Then I called Sheriff Needles, and he told me to contact the feds." He hitched up his trousers. "That's you, huh?"

Venus nodded. To Reed she said, "Tell me how you found him."

Reed scratched his head. It didn't go with his wiry body. It was too big, with a broad forehead shaped like the meadow, but pale, liver-spotted. "Well, it was like this, see. I come up here this morning to the poppy fields." He gestured over his shoulder. "Just a routine security check. I do that every morning, every evening, too. Walk the perimeter, just in case of vandalism. So here I come down along this side of the field, and what do I see but this poacher lying here dead on the ground." Reed shrugged. "That's all."

"He was dead when you found him?"

"As a door nail."

"You move him?"

Reed frowned quizzically. "Course not." He had a nasal, resonant voice. "I'm a trained officer of the law. I'd never touch a corpse, except maybe just to feel its pulse. No sirree bub, he's just exactly how I come across him."

"Including the poppies?" Song interjected.

Reed spread his hands. "Like I said, I haven't touched him."

Venus said, "What time was that?"

"When I found him? Eight-fourteen a.m. It's on the phone log at the office."

The tobacco-chewing deputy nodded, verifying Reed's version of things. To Reed Venus said, "Why do you patrol the poppy fields?"

Reed shrugged. "Sheriff likes to keep an eye on the Avalon properties. We do it for other businesses in the county, too. Standard procedure."

In the dead man's rear jeans pocket, Venus found a wallet. In the wallet, a Canadian driver's license, a Visa gold card, an AAA membership card, a library card for the Vancouver Library of Natural Sciences, and fifty-three dollars in cash. In his other pockets she found a red Swiss Army knife, a small clear plastic box containing a few dozen silver straight pins with black heads, a tiny bottle with its top screwed on tight, a packet of Kleenex, a box of lemon Ricolas, the chewy variety, like Jujubes, a dog-eared map of Olympic National Park and Coastal Marine Sanctuary, and a sterling silver key chain with three brass keys and one silver Isuzu ignition key.

The man's name was Jonathan Willow. He would have turned twenty-seven next month. His address was Number Four, Penwell Mews, Victoria, British Columbia. A Canadian citizen.

She opened the tiny bottle, sniffed. Formaldehyde. She handed it to Song.

Reed said, "In case you're interested, Sheriff Needles said the feller's Isuzu Trooper is over on Raven Point, in the inn's parking lot."

"How did the sheriff figure that out?"

Reed shrugged, nodded at the corpse. "He took the wallet out, got the name and driver's license info. Then he radioed a deputy. Didn't take long to locate the Trooper 'cause the inn complained to the sheriff's office about it being illegally parked in their lot. They're pretty uptight over there. It's one of those high-end resorts.''

"So Needles has already been up here?" She repeated the question.

Reed nodded.

Venus said, "Why did you call him a poacher?"

Reed shrugged. "Mr. Avalon's secretary called him that. When I told her about these here poppies clutched in his fist, then Mr. Avalon's secretary called him a poacher. Said he was poaching poppies. Maybe he was after the secret to Blue Poppy perfume.''

Every Pacific Northwest native knew the legend of Blue Poppy perfume, the claim made for nearly a century that some secret formula, or flower essence, provided Blue Poppy's mysterious scent. They called Blue Poppy perfume "the Fragrance of Tibet," and no one had ever cracked the Avalon family's jealously guarded secret. Scores of celebrated, prestigious women, including Lady Bella Winsome-Diamond, Venus's mother, coveted their Blue Poppy perfume. No one else could afford it.

Venus bent down, touched the dead man's fingertips. His fingernails were scrubbed clean, but when she pulled her hand back, some iridescent orange dust came off on her fingers. She rubbed them together, studied the dust. She touched the corpse's fingers again. More orange dust, and some metallic silver dust. With her other hand, she fished a notebook from her pocket, rubbed the stuff onto a piece of paper, tore off the paper, and handed it to Claudia. Claudia made a quizzical face, then placed it in an evidence bag.

While Song photographed the scene, Claudia bent over the corpse, carefully removing the ragged nosegay from the clenched fist, placing the flowers, roots and all, in an evidence bag. Sweetwater and Song bagged the body and carried it down to the chopper. Claudia sat on the grassy meadow, fished a laptop computer from her bag, set it on her folded legs and punched in her report, or maybe a love letter to her perpetually amorous husband. Venus wrote down the deputies' names, told them they were free to leave. They waded downhill through the meadow to where their patrol cars idled on the shoulder of Highway 101.

Before Peter Avalon cultivated the poppy field, this meadow facing northeast toward the Strait of Juan de Fuca was one of the few virgin stands left anywhere on the Olympic Peninsula. In spring, the whole mountainside bloomed, forming a carpet of wildflowers that supported a panoply of species, including the bobtail rabbit, badgers, Olympic marmots, the jumping mouse, gold-mantled squirrel, and black bears. Migratory birds joined native species pecking at fresh seedlings, hummingbirds nose-dived into succulent nectar blooms, and several rare butterfly species flitted brilliantly against the sun-splashed splendor.

In autumn, the rare Roosevelt elk grazed high up in the glacial meadow until winter, when the sleeping alpine ridges wore a thick blanket of snow beneath a lacy frost overcoat that glistened cheerfully, but never entirely melted. The higher ranges lay so deep under snowdrifts that it made grazing impossible. The snow cover formed a fatal backdrop for the Roosevelts, and hunters illegally shot the rare elk for their antlers. Trophies.

During heavy storms, windswells off the strait tossed saltwater spindrift over the rocky beach into the lower portion of the meadow, which everyone called Yodeler's apron. A virgin salt-spray meadow, a rare species today. Salt-spray meadows are an important part of the Olympic Peninsula's ecosystem. Most of the salt-spray meadows had been bulldozed to build private homes, condos, and commercial malls that serviced the burgeoning human population. The meadow on Yodeler Preserve was unusual because of its huge size and its virginal quality. Even though the salt spray didn't actually touch the meadow's upper reaches, it was by definition all a salt spray meadow, a congruent ecosystem in symbiosis with the rain forest, the alpine ridges and waterfalls, the glacial meadows, and the mountain's ice-capped dome. The key to all this lushness, all these thriving life forms, was the unusual combination of moist salt air, the multitiered climatology, and the rain shadow's generous sunshine.

Like northwestern China and the mountain meadows of Tibet, like certain regions of Scotland, the climate, combined with Yodeler's unique rain shadow factor, made this meadow a perfect site for cultivating the breathlessly beautiful, exotic sky blue Himalayan poppy. Too bad it was a nonnative species, an intrusion, like Scotch broom, a menace to the ancient, fragile ecosystem.

Venus recalled that the poppy field deal was struck during Congressional budget cuts, when an anticonservation majority decided that protecting the nation's coastal salt-spray meadows didn't fit their version of balancing the budget. The Department of the Interior had been politically and financially coerced into leasing a third of this fragile federal preserve in order to maintain the remaining two-thirds. Peter Avalon, heir to the Blue Poppy fortune, had leaped at the chance to acquire the lease.

Jonathan Willow. Not a familiar name. Venus didn't recall this name appearing on Interior's list of the federal conservation laws' chronic violators. She studied the man's showy deathbed. From the corpse's position, Willow might have just stepped out of the poppies into the virgin meadow. An inspection of the peaty soil around the poppies turned up no signs of footprints, but the soil responded like a wet sponge to her touch, so if he had come out of the poppies, or through them, say, from up in the forest, the springy soil would have already given up his footprints.

No signs of the body being dragged, or even moved. No sign of a struggle, but the meadow in late spring formed a resilient carpet of fresh bear grass, woody plants, and flowers that, like the peaty cultivated soil, would spring back fast. The corpse could have been moved a few feet, but she doubted it, because its position on the ground suggested he fell where he lay. And, too, Willow's fingernails were pristine. He hadn't uprooted these poppies. Someone else had.

The ground felt damp, spongy, the rich black earth barely visible under the dense woody meadow growth. If a stray bullet lay in this meadow, it might never be found. Combing the area produced nothing of interest. From the steep slope Venus paused, looked north to the little straitside town of Fern, home of Blue Poppy Perfumery. She could see the paved highway going east to west, and beyond, the stark beaches and the saltwater strait. Anyone looking up into the meadow might have seen the murder happen, but from such a distance, the murderer and the victim would have appeared the size of ants. Unless someone used binoculars, the event may have passed unwitnessed.

She was trudging downhill towards the helicopter, when she noticed a particularly fine clump of *Viola adunca*. She knelt down, carefully examined the leaves. Something had chewed them. She summoned Claudia, borrowed the Nikon and a macro lens, photographed some of the ground and the undersides of the leaves. Claudia laughed. "You lepidopterists are all weird."

Eric Sweetwater said, "I never knew Venus was a butterfly person."

"She studied them at Oxford," whispered Claudia, making a face. "Along with Shakespeare."

Sweetwater's eyebrows shot up, but he didn't say anything. He just revved up the chopper while Venus rolled her Harley out of the cargo hold. Song yelled something at her, but she didn't understand him through all the whirring. He said it again, and she thought it was "Romeo," but she wasn't sure. She decided to humor him, nodded as if she'd caught what he yelled. She watched Sweetwater take the chopper up, waved as the Bell Jet Ranger banked and disappeared, headed southeast to Seattle. She walked the Harley half a mile along a dirt path that led to Highway 101, got on 101, and rode a half mile to Fern, Washington.

FOUR

PERCOLATOR

Meconopsis betonicifolia (Blue Poppy)

Rare plant from Tibet, flowers 3" across, freely borne, grow in partial shade. (Several subspecies.) Best started in a cool greenhouse. Recommended for experienced gardeners only.

—*Butchart Gardens Seed Catalog*
Victoria, British Columbia

FERN, WASHINGTON, belonged to the society of depressed nineteenth-century logging camps until 1926, when a former Scottish Highlanders paratrooper by the name of Conrad Hinge landed in town with a handful of exotic seeds and an idea. The idea first came to Hinge quite unexpectedly during the Great War, one spring afternoon on a Normandy hillside, as the young Highlander admired a fragrant French crocus field.

It was widely known that a Scotsman could produce the very finest whiskeys. But what about fragrances? Conrad Hinge thought about this for a few minutes, then dismissed it from his mind. The idea didn't surface again until years later, when, on a visit to the western Canadian provinces, Hinge paid a social call on family friends, the Butcharts of Victoria, who as it so happened were world travelers like himself, and who unlike himself, had brought back exotic plants and flower seeds from their global forays. Among the Butcharts' treasures was the Tibetan blue poppy, and one fine Canadian afternoon, as young Conrad Hinge stood among Mrs. Butchart's carefully tended, delicately fragrant blue poppies, Conrad remembered France's crocus fields and experienced a sort of mental ressurection.

It was 1926, the era of the entrepreneur. Employing just a tiny bit of subterfuge, young Hinge diverted the attentions of Mrs. Butchart and several of her guests so that whilst they pried the skies for any sign of the silver-throated red banana warbler that Hinge had invented in a pinch, he plucked and pocketed several healthy poppy seed pods.

Some weeks later, after prudent research, Hinge crossed the Strait of Juan de Fuca into the United States of America, where a seed poacher might escape the flamboyance of a Canadian Mountie's red jacket. Finding sleepy, bucolic Fern to his liking and the rain forests and verdant rain shadow meadows a perfect environment for the pilfered seeds, Hinge acquired a small plot of land and overwintered. In the spring he planted his rows, tended them scrupulously, and waited. On midsummer's day Hinge's own blue poppies bloomed, and the perfume the young Scotsman created from their light, pleasurable scent could swoon the burrs off a thistle. Only one thing was wrong. Nobody wished to purchase perfume from a Scotsman. Thus, Conrad Hinge made the weighty decision to change his name to Conrad Avalon. The rest is legend.

When the founder's son, Conrad Avalon the Second, inherited the perfumery, he strictly conformed to his father's practices. The younger Nose had his father's talent for detecting fragrances, from the most exotic spices to the lightest, most delicate floral scents. Blue Poppy perfume embodied the latter, a fresh top note of *Meconopsis betonifolia,* the mysterious blue poppy, balanced with an abundance of crocus, and pulling the scent together into its beguiling cachet the incomparable ingredient that remained a closely guarded family secret. When Blue Poppy's founder suffered an attack of gout and died, the younger Conrad Avalon took over, and like his clever father, personally tested all batches of flowers and oversaw the manufacture of the base scent, to which he alone added the final secret ingredient. As for the business end of things, Conrad was a shrewd risk-taker who, immediately upon his coronation, created the Miss Blue Poppy advertising campaign. No one ever understood how Conrad's razor-edged brain functioned, but the entire family agreed that his astute business acumen—combined with his flair for fragrance—resulted in soaring sales figures and a sterling reputation among the world's grandest ladies. The title "Miss Blue Poppy" soon fueled the ambitions of millions of young ladies around the world, for with the title came fame and fortune, and, too, a lifetime supply of Blue Poppy perfume.

Time passed and Conrad Avalon produced no heirs. And so, on the brink of the millennium when retirement beckoned, Conrad turned

over the day-to-day business of perfume manufacturing to his nephews, Peter and Troy Avalon. But Uncle Conrad was no fool, so when
his nephews accused him of spurning the year 2000's cutting edge,
Conrad decided to watch over his flamboyant heirs like a hawk over
carrion. Uncle Conrad simply didn't trust the Pepsi generation.

Blue Poppy Perfumery was reached by driving north on Highway
101 as far as Dungeness, coasting west a few loopy miles, turning
right at the sign that said FERN, POPULATION 354, onto Fern's main
drag, Salamander Street, and after two lazy yellow lights, turning left
off Salamander onto Orca Lane. The Blue Poppy facility, including
the old family estate, occupied all of Orca Lane and then some. The
main house contained corporate offices, a research and production
facility, and Uncle Conrad's private digs. Judging from its elegant
facade, Venus thought it might not be a bad place to punch a time
clock. She showed a security guard her badge, scooted past a Japanese
Zen garden, past an employees' recreation area complete with swimming pool and tennis courts, past an English rose garden, to the
perfumery's main entrance. From there she followed discreet signs to
Peter Avalon's private offices.

He was locked up behind eight solid oak doors, like a CEO should
be. A perky secretary with perky eyes and a perky smile and a polished perky appearance welcomed Venus in the reception room. A
brass sign on her Louis the Sixteenth desk identified the eyeful as a
Miss Perkins. Also on Miss Perkins's desk sat several flacons of Blue
Poppy perfume and a Steuben vase loaded with fresh Mrs. Bowser
roses. When Venus gave her name, Miss Perkins got that dismayed
look on her face that is supposed to tell you something is wrong.

"What's wrong?" Venus asked.

"Oh! Well, it's just that Mr. Avalon had a sort of emergency come
up." She reached into her desk drawer with perkily painted fingernails on slim little fingers and pulled out an envelope. She handed it
to Venus. Smiling, she said, "Mr. Avalon asked me to give you this.
With his apologies."

Venus said, "Okay if I sit down?"

Miss Perkins nodded, indicated a sleek blond leather sofa, and
resumed her work, which consisted of sitting behind the big desk
looking smart. Venus sank into the couch and opened the envelope.
It was freshly sealed, the glue not yet dry. It opened smoothly without
a tear. The note inside, scribbled on Blue Poppy Perfumery stationery,
had been penned carelessly.

Dear Agent Diamond,
Unfortunately I cannot meet with you just now. Some urgent business has come up. Miss Perkins will fill you in. Perhaps later this afternoon? Meanwhile, Miss Perkins has a little surprise for you.

Sincerely, Peter Avalon.

P.S. You aren't by any chance related to Lady Bella Winsome-Diamond, are you?

Miss Perkins was staring down a Mrs. Bowser. Venus went over and broke the trance. "So what's the scoop?"

"Scoop?" Miss Perkins squinted. Maybe she wore contacts.

Venus said, "On the shooting, up in the meadow."

Miss Perkins went limp like a silly rag doll and laughed. "Oh, that. I thought you meant something else. Tsk. I really and truly think Mr. Avalon is turning paranoid in his old age. Not that he's that old, really. I mean, forty-five is hardly senile. But suddenly he's gone paranoid on me. I mean, really, can you even fathom anyone poaching a bunch of flowers out of someone else's field?"

"Yes," said Venus. "I can."

Miss Perkins curved a slim hand around an oval flacon of perfume. Etched in the frosted crystal were the words BLUE POPPY, FOR LOVERS. The stopper, exquisite and functional, was an enameled blue poppy sculpture. Miss Perkins said glibly, "Oh, you think somebody's trying to discover the secret formula?"

"What are you talking about?" Venus had trouble following Miss Perkins's train of thought.

"You know. The secret ingredient in Blue Poppy perfume. That's the whole cachet, the mystery. Ever since this place opened, back in the nineteenth century or something, the perfume has contained a super-secret formula. To this day, no one's ever discovered what it is. But they sure try hard enough, stealing our precious crops. Maybe that's why that man trespassed on Mr. Avalon's poppy field. Well, he certainly got what he deserved, didn't he?"

Venus said, "Poaching a poppy crop?"

"Poppy crop!" Miss Perkins giggled. "Now, that's funny. Poppy crop. Hee hee. I really like that. Poppy crop. Sounds sort of like..."

"Nothing else?" Venus cut her off.

Miss Perkins thought it over. After a turn through her memory banks, her eyes lit up and she said, "There was one more thing. Mr.

Avalon felt you should know about this, since the man had been shot. There have been threats."

"Threats against Avalon?"

She tilted her head. She looked better sideways. Miss Perkins said, "Have you heard of Zora?"

Venus said, "Maybe. What's her last name?"

"Tsk. She doesn't have a last name. I mean Zora, the fashion model."

Venus rubbed her neck. A tension had set in. The muscles ached. She said, "Never heard of her. So where does this Zora fit in?"

Miss Perkins sighed, moved a hair closer to Venus, said, "This is confidential information. Mr. Avalon gave me permission to tell you, but it can't go any further. If there's a leak, we'll know who it came from." She lowered her squeaky voice and said, "Zora was recently chosen as Blue Poppy's official spokesperson. She's scheduled to launch our big ad campaign next week. But Cookie, Peter's wife? Cookie's opposed to Zora. So then Mr. Avalon, I mean, Peter, had second thoughts. Not as a final thing, but he was thinking about choosing a 'different image' for the product. When he told Zora, she went ballistic. I swear to God, I myself heard her threaten to kill Peter if he dared to cancel her contract. Of course, Mr. Avalon is a single-minded man, and nobody tells him what to do without getting an earful. So he gave Zora an earful and then she threatened to kill him."

Venus said, "Go on."

"Well then, when this poacher turned up this morning, I personally put two and two together. I believe the poacher and Zora were in cahoots, trying to steal the secret formula. For the Blue Poppy fragrance? And—this is my own conjecture, mind you-possibly Zora murdered her partner to silence him. I saw a program like that once on *Crime Cops*. I shared this thought with Mr. Avalon. He said the idea has merit, and that I should share it with the authorities. I guess you're the closest thing to an authority. I mean, with a badge and all."

Venus said, "Anything else?"

Miss Perkins stared at Venus. "Isn't that enough for one day?" she quipped smartly.

Venus said, "I'd like to leave a note for your boss. Have you got a spare sheet of paper?"

"I could put you through to his voice mail."

"No, thanks. I prefer to write a note."

Miss Perkins tore exactly one sheet off the message pad. She had no spare ink, but Venus always carried a pen. She wrote Avalon a note saying she certainly was aware that he was a busy bee, but that this was a murder investigation and he should make himself available at once. Meanwhile, she wrote, she would park on the buttery blond couch until he granted an interview. She handed the note to Miss Perkins.

Miss Perkins unfolded the note, read it, blanched, and gave Venus a good view of her backside as she flounced through a big door.

While Miss Perkins was gone, Venus studied the portrait behind the secretary's desk. A photograph transferred onto canvas. It passed for portraiture, if you like photo-realism. Here stood Peter and his wife, the socialite Cookie Charmeaux Avalon, amidst their blue poppy fields. Peter's eyes were cast demurely downward, as if gazing upon his poppy crop, or perhaps down Miss Perkins's blouse when she sat at her desk. Cookie Charmeaux Avalon had Texas hair, big and zesty red, probably natural, a reedy figure, like the poppy stems, smoky dare-you eyes, and a sulky mouth. She wore a Gucci sheath in carnival colors and spoiled her high couture style by cuddling a ball of white Pekinese with a froufrou pink ribbon tied on its tail. In spite of the pouting expression on Cookie, Venus mused, the couple made a handsome portrait, especially when you tossed in Peter Avalon's natural good looks and subtracted the froufrou caress.

Miss Perkins was taking a very long time behind the big door. Maybe the secretary had disappeared out some secret exit. Venus ambled over to the corridor. Across the hall from the boss's office, a door stood slightly ajar. A sign on the door said TROY AVALON, CFO. A pleasant male voice floated out of the office, apparently speaking into a telephone. He sounded excited, like a Wall Street broker in the pit. Venus eavesdropped.

"No, no, no, no, no. We can't renege on the contract," said the voice. "Yes, I'm aware of that... What? I disagree, Cookie. I think Zora's a natural for the Miss Blue Poppy role. Besides, we can't go around reneging on our contracts. What? Frankly, I don't care what Peter says behind my back, we're going with Zora. And remember, Peter discovered her in the first place, so he hasn't any right to grumble." A pause, then, "Yes, yes, yes, yes, yes. I heard about the dead man, and to be frank with you, Cookie, I don't think the guy was stealing our poppies. That's just my personal opinion. What's that?"

A pause, then, "Now, why can't you get off that hobbyhorse of yours?"

Someone tapped on Venus's shoulder. She whirled around. Miss Perkins's mouth twisted sourly, and she squinted darts. Her blouse seemed a little ruffled around the buttons, but that might have been Venus's imagination. Miss Perkins tried turning the twist into a smile but the corners would not rearrange themselves, so she stuck with the twist and growled, "Mr. Avalon will see you now. If you'll step this way."

"I almost forgot," said Venus, "the boss said you have a surprise for me."

Miss Perkins had forgotten herself, and smacked the side of her head for it. "Oh, I mean, I completely forgot. Well, it doesn't matter. You hardly look the type to appreciate flowers." She had that squinty, prissy, catty face on. "You see," she continued, "we offer a complimentary blue poppy to every, er, lady who visits Mr. Avalon's office. From the fields. Since they aren't yet in full bloom, we've been giving out Mrs. Bowsers." Her eyes toured Venus's forest green uniform, the short-sleeved shirt, the tailored trousers. She pinched her nostrils together and whined, "Would you like one?"

"No thanks," quipped Venus. "The hot air in the next room might wilt it."

FIVE

MR. NOSE

THIN AND HAWKISH, physically fit and tan, Avalon came striding forward with an outstretched hand. Venus pumped it, and a few sparks crackled in the grip. He had tall, blond, and handsome nailed down, the hungry look of the rich, and a thick crop of straight blond hair tinged silver at the temples, understated, with luster. His clear blue eyes sparkled, and his pampered skin's healthy glow played down the bigness of his crooked nose and emphasized the clarity of his eyes. He must have liked carrots as a kid. When he smiled, his nostrils flared and the smile went straight across his cheeks, lips taut against perfect teeth. There were laugh lines around his eyes that didn't show up when he appeared on television in a rare public viewing. They softened his face. If he was over forty, he hid it well.

He said, "Agent Diamond, is that what I call you?"

Venus nodded. Let's keep it professional. Her hand still burned from the hot-wired grip.

He wore a pale lavender Polo shirt, starched khakis with knife pleats, tan bucks with no socks. His hands were slim with trim nails and long fingers that danced on the desk top when he sat down in his executive's wing chair. He leaned over to adjust the louvered blinds, gave Venus a view of his profile. Some people were too gorgeous for their own good.

Venus sat on the other side of the desk, on a chair made for giants. Her feet dangled slightly off the ground. She scooted forward in the chair so that when she angled her feet downward, her feet would appear to be actually touching the floor. Giants ruled the world. Leaning forward like this, she caught a glimpse of the screen on his laptop IBM. He had a custom-designed Blue Poppy perfume screen saver.

Avalon said, "So what about this shooting in my poppy field? Fellow died, didn't he?"

She nodded. She liked how he didn't mince words. She said, "Sheriff's deputy reports the man was dead when he found him. The body wasn't in your poppies but in the meadow, about three yards below your fields."

The smooth blue bedroom eyes blinked slowly. "Oh, I see. I'd understood that he was actually in my poppies when Reed came across him. I guess I got mixed up."

"If it makes you feel any better, he was clutching a bunch of your poppies."

Avalon stared. Then, "Oh yes, Reed mentioned the poppies. That's funny, because they aren't even in full bloom yet." One of the beautiful hands came to stillness against the desk top. Then, gradually, discreetly, the index finger and thumb began massaging each other, moving lightly in counterpoint, the way they teach you in self-hypnosis to imagine a grain of sand there. He said, "Did Miss Perkins tell you her theory?"

"She did."

"What did you think of it?"

Venus shook her head. "Prime-time material, maybe. Not reality based."

Avalon smiled appreciatively. "She's something, that Miss Perkins. Really quite a gal."

Venus said, "What's your theory?"

Avalon shrugged. "Don't have one, really. But one thing does bother me."

"What's that?"

"Reed tells me the man who was killed resembled me. What do you think?"

She mulled it over. Both Avalon and Willow were tall, slender men, both wore casual clothing this morning, unless Avalon had changed clothes already. They were approximately the same height and build, their hair identical, except for the slight graying at Avalon's temples and the victim's Dutch bob. They could pass for each other, especially if the killer had poor eyesight. The murderer, if not too close, could have mistaken Willow for Avalon.

She said, "Maybe from a distance."

Avalon said, "So do you think someone was really after me, and they shot this poor fellow by mistake?"

Venus said, "Too soon to tell. What about Zora?"

"What about her?" Avalon blinked rapidly a few times.

Venus said, "Your secretary mentioned something about a disagreement between you and Zora."

"Oh well, it's really just your typical case of rampant narcissism. Representing Blue Poppy is a big honor. It's been the launching pad of many a young woman's career. I offered this year's title to Zora, so it's my own fault." He shrugged. "Anyway, I've resigned myself to the whole thing. It's too late to find another Miss Blue Poppy."

"So you're keeping the contract with Zora?"

Avalon said, "Yes, it's in writing. But, you know, when we signed the contract, I had no idea she was such a little...twit. And when we did the test shots, she just didn't fit the image. But I was so certain she fit the role, I'd already signed her, and now it's too late to change course. The fields will be in full bloom in the next few days. Those poppies, with Zora bathing in them, is the centerpiece of our campaign."

"She angry with you?"

His hands folded into a church with people and a tall, elegant steeple. He worked his nice lips a couple times and said, "This is confidential, you understand—I'm afraid that Zora might be carrying things too far, might actually be out for revenge. I share this confidentiality only because you're a federal agent. I really think she could have shot that young man, having mistaken him for me."

"But you said it's all smoothed over now."

He shook his head sadly. "There's one more thing." He pressed his lips together, grimaced. It hurt him to say what he said next. "Zora made an advance towards me. Of course, I put her off. That is, I didn't reciprocate the gesture."

"What gesture?"

Avalon reddened. "She came in here yesterday, wearing a sexy dress. She stood right over there." He nodded to the center of the room and continued, "She peeled off her dress. She was stark naked underneath. She said she wanted to, ah, go to bed with me."

"Exactly those words?"

Avalon cringed. "She has a foul mouth. She used obscene language, but that's what she meant. As I said, I didn't return the favor. If that's what it was. I told her to put her dress back on and get out. I was pretty harsh. I told her that if she ever behaved like that again, in public or in private, towards myself or anyone else besides her boyfriend, this contract would be immediately terminated. We can't have Zora or anybody else tarnishing the Miss Blue Poppy image.

On her way out, she threatened to kill me if I told anyone what she did. At first, I took it as metaphor, nothing more, but now I'm not so sure. Maybe she was serious.''

"Why?"

He made a futile gesture. "Who knows? Maybe her boyfriend's the jealous type. Maybe she's worried about her reputation. I gather men don't usually say no to Zora."

"Anybody else see this happen?"

He made a face. "God, I hope not."

"Where is she now?"

"Over at the Inn at Raven Point, incognito, until after the public announcement. We always keep the identity of Miss Blue Poppy a secret until we release the first photos of her in our fields. Maybe you already knew that."

He studied the tips of his graceful church. Something worried him. Now his eyebrows purled and looped, looped and purled. "I know this sounds totally paranoid, but just bear with me. I think Zora really means to kill me. This wasn't the first time she's made an advance towards me. It's been a chronic problem ever since we met last summer. I'm a married man. She doesn't seem to respect that. She's probably certifiable. I've seen her throw tantrums that put the fear of God into me. And another thing, Zora knows that I usually walk up along the field most mornings.''

"Were you and she ever intimate?"

He smiled, said, "Unfortunately, no." Then he laughed uncomfortably. "I'm joking, of course. I've got a terrible sense of humor."

The finger church collapsed. Avalon stretched his arms in a relaxing gesture, added, "That was a stupid thing to say." He rubbed the back of his neck, sat forward at his desk. "So I really don't have a clue. Anyway, I feel lucky today."

"Why's that?"

"I didn't go up there this morning. To check on the field. I had a meeting with my secretary."

Venus studied her ring finger, the one that had briefly worn the marvelous engagement ring. Now her hand felt lighter, normal. Still, something gnawed at her heart, sickened her stomach. She dropped her hand back to her lap and looked up. She said, "Can you think of anyone else who might want you dead?"

He frowned. "Not really."

"What about your wife?"

"Cookie?" Avalon laughed. "My wife's a redhead with a matching temper. But she wouldn't harm a flea. And she adores me."

"Marital bliss, eh?"

He grinned ironically. "More like a roller-coaster ride. I'm slightly hotheaded myself. Cookie and I thrive on contention. But I shouldn't discuss my wife's sexual fetishes." He squirmed in his chair. Maybe aroused by some private fantasy.

Venus said, "Anyone else? A relative, maybe? Or a friendship gone sour?"

"Not really, no. Unless you count the old MacGregor woman. Aggie MacGregor. She's a fixture in Fern. Our families have been feuding since Scotland. My grandfather was from Scotland. So was Aggie MacGregor's grandfather. Some bad blood between them. The feud goes back even further than that, back to the clan wars. Anyway, Aggie's a zany old lady. She never particularly liked me. But she's fond of Troy. My brother, Troy? She's fond of him."

Venus nodded. She knew zany Aggie all too well. She said, "How long will Zora be staying at Raven Point?"

"Soon as we finish shooting, she's out of here. She hates the Pacific Northwest. Too damp for a Valley Girl. We're shooting all the ad copy and television spots in the next few days, so she won't be here much longer. Once the poppies bloom. Which brings up another subject."

Venus stared at Avalon. Something about his tone of voice raised goose bumps on her arms. Her sour stomach did a somersault. Intuition athletics.

"We still have to import some poppies from Tibet. We'd rather grow them all domestically, of course. There's been a problem lately with the Chinese. What with all the trade sanctions going back and forth, the Chinese have refused to sell us any more flowers. We have a sufficient supply for this year's production. But next year, we're out of luck. Unless we grow them all domestically."

"Are you growing poppies anywhere else, besides on Yodeler Preserve?"

"Just that small stand, domestically. We're growing crocus down near Marysville, and some rose varieties here on the estate, but poppies require a special setting. The land where my grandfather and uncle used to grow poppies was returned to the Klallam tribe by the government. That was seven years ago, just a few months before we leased the Yodeler parcel from Interior. If we hadn't acquired that leasehold in Yodeler Preserve, we'd now be totally dependent on the Chinese. Tibetan blue poppies are an extremely sensitive issue"

"Why are you telling me this?"

"I just want you to understand why we're taking the meadow off your hands."

"What are you saying?"

"Oh, I'm sorry," he said. "I thought you knew. My brother and I are in discussions with the Interior Department about purchasing the whole meadow. Not the entire preserve, just the meadow. But don't worry. We'll keep it in poppies. We won't develop it. I know how much national forest land means to you guys."

Venus stood up. Coolly, she said, "You'll never get Yodeler's meadow."

Avalon grinned, showing all his teeth. "I like a woman who stands her ground."

Venus said, "I'm telling you right now, Avalon. That land holds the last remnants of several endangered species. It's not for sale."

Avalon shrugged. Softly, he said, "That's not what your boss in Washington tells me."

"Returning to the issue at hand," said Venus. "The murdered man's name was Jonathan Willow. Ever hear of him?"

He cocked his head, thought about it. "He wasn't one of my employees. I'm sure of that. Although, if you'd like me to double check?"

"Sure. I'd like that."

He pressed a discreet button on his desk. Five seconds later, Miss Perkins poked her perky nose through the door. Avalon instructed her to check the employee roster going back three years. She went away. While they waited for her to come back, Avalon studied Venus. She could almost see the wheels of his brain meshing and turning, and she wondered what was on his mind. Right now, her mind was on fire. No one had told her about the meadow being up for sale. Did Olson know?

They sat in silence, keeping their separate thoughts private. On the desk top, Avalon's fingers drummed a soft tattoo. His gaze met hers. He studied her wide green eyes, the pale complexion free of makeup, revealing some nicely placed freckles, the thin mouth sporting just a trace of color, maybe natural. Her facial features were small, like the rest of her, nicely put together, but too boyish for his tastes. She had no breasts to speak of, just a hint of collarbone showed where her uniform shirt was unbuttoned at the neckline. He made a mental note to tell her later that he thought her collarbone was her best feature. He liked to compliment women. He cleared his throat and said, "Will you be staying over in Fern tonight?"

"Maybe." Noncommittal.

"How would you like to have dinner with me tomorrow night?" Venus said, "I wouldn't."

Avalon laughed. "Oh, this isn't a come-on. I'm not that kind of guy. It's a perfectly legitimate business invitation. I'd really appreciate your input before I make a formal offer on the meadow."

"I'm not the right person..."

"Humor me?"

Venus thought it over. She had nothing to lose, except maybe her self-respect, and besides, Avalon might have some more interesting tidbits hiding up his short lavender sleeve. Venus said, "Where do I meet you?"

"Do you know the Inn at Raven Point?"

"You really want to eat there?"

"Why wouldn't I? They have a swell restaurant." He blinked his powder blue eyes.

She told him about the dead chef.

He appeared shocked. "What? You don't mean Otto Lux?" Avalon placed a hand over his mouth and the blue eyes went traveling. "God," he whispered. "My cocktail party." He grabbed the telephone, punched in a number he knew by heart. After talking into the phone for a few minutes, after a lot of sympathetic clucking, he hung up and said, "It's all right. The inn's made arrangements to fly in Slava from the Olympic Hotel in Seattle."

He brightened, rubbed his hands together. "I'm giving a small cocktail party at the inn tomorrow evening at eight. Just a few people involved with the Miss Blue Poppy campaign. Zora and her chaperone are camped out there already, and the rest of her entourage is arriving momentarily. It's going to be a pleasant little gathering. Zora herself won't attend, naturally, since she's incognito until the poppies bloom. You might like to join us for cocktails. Then afterwards, you and I can have a late dinner in the Fiddlehead. I'll have Miss Perkins make reservations for ten o'clock." He glanced down at his tan bucks. "Oh, and don't worry about dressing up. We're pretty casual up here in Fern."

Miss Perkins came back, her blouse all neat, freshly glossed lips sporting a sneer. "Here it is." She sniffed coolly. She made a few passes at Avalon's computer screen and something resembling a roster popped up. She explained it to Peter Avalon, then made a haughty face at Venus, and huffed out.

Avalon took a minute to glance over the roster. "Like I said, the fellow didn't work for me."

At the door he said, "Are you by any chance one of Lady Bella's brood?"

"I'm the middle child."

"Well, give your mother my warmest regards. She's a friend of my Uncle Conrad, you know. And our family's favorite client. Your mother's a terrific actress. I'll bet you're really proud to be her kid."

It's amazing how people of a certain social status, upon learning who her mother was, immediately changed their style of communication. A few minutes ago, she was just another individual seated on the poor side of his desk. Now she suddenly ranked as his peer, and his whole attitude changed. He might as well have been her long-lost cousin.

She said, "Now that your uncle has retired, who's your nose?"

He stood beside the door, holding it open. "I am, of course. It's a talent, a genetic trait, with which my family is blessed. The normal human nose is able to detect just a few hundred scents. Members of my family, particularly the males, are able to detect thousands of scents, and identify them as well. There are no hired noses at Blue Poppy. Now that Uncle Conrad has retired, I am the official nose. In case you haven't heard, the townsfolk call me 'Mr. Nose'." He laughed good-naturedly. Maybe it didn't bother him.

Miss Perkins was away from her desk. Across the room, the Mrs. Bowsers invited sniffing. Venus went over, inhaled the heady fragrance, dizzying at first, until she got used to it. Then she sat down at Miss Perkins's desk, took out her digital phone, and punched in the office number.

Olson came on the line in his usual brusque manner, a little like Miss Perkins, only Olson's voice had a deeper bass with brass knuckles riding the high notes. A strict low-fat diet can trigger this condition, and worse.

Venus said, "I just heard an ugly rumor."

Tiredly, Olson said, "Okay, I'll bite. What?"

"The Avalons want Yodeler's meadow. Purchase, not lease.

They're talking business with our D.C. office. Probably with Wexler himself.''

Olson grunted, said, ''Figures.''

''What do you mean, *figures?*''

''Didn't I tell you yesterday that Ebert's arriving Monday morning? Put two and two together. What do you get?''

''This can't happen, Olson. That meadow is virgin land, at least two-thirds of it is still virgin. We'll lose some species. Like the Dungeness silverspot, for instance. Yodeler's meadow is not for sale.''

Olson said, ''The Dungeness silverspot hasn't been sighted in fifteen years. True, the last sighting was on Yodeler Preserve. But the Dungeness silverspot is probably extinct by now. At the very least, it's extirpated from that area.''

''Maybe it's making a comeback.''

''You don't come back from extinct.'' Olson grunted. ''Let's wait until Ebert shows up. We don't know anything for sure yet.''

''Wait?'' Panic. ''How can you wait? We need to call Wexler, get this all out in the open right now. They can't do this. They're supposed to notify us well ahead of time...''

Olson coughed. ''Actually,'' he said, ''they did, in a roundabout manner. Wexler told me about two months ago that Yodeler Preserve had made the short list. I didn't mention it to anyone here because, at the time, it was way down on the list; there was no need to be concerned.''

''Well, there is now.'' She was almost shouting. She dropped her voice and said, ''Call Wexler right now. Or else I will.''

Livid now, Olson shot back, ''I will not tolerate you shouting commands at me, do you hear me, Venus? Neither one of us will phone Wexler, or fax Wexler, or e-mail Wexler until we've heard what Ebert wants. Ebert is Wexler's emissary, remember.''

''Stick Ebert. This is an emergency. Besides, they can't sell off a piece of land when it's the site of a murder investigation.''

''Right,'' Olson said placatingly. Anything to coax her off the subject. ''Maybe you'd like to hear what we've found out about the dead man.''

''Go ahead.'' She was pacing now.

''Weapon was a little .38-caliber hand gun. Not exactly a hunting rifle. But the killer was a good shot, or lucky, and fired from low to the ground at a distance of maybe twenty yards. It was definitely murder. I want you to stay up on the peninsula until you've got a handle on this thing."

"Stupid..." Muttered.

Olson snapped, "Just what do you mean by that?"

She could see Olson now, sitting in his office in the Bumbershoot. She guessed he was staring out the window at a fog shroud, or rain. Olson's moods didn't just hang on the low-fat diet regime. They also swung with the weather, which meant that maybe once a week or so, when the gray skies rolled back and a sun break unveiled a heart-breakingly beautiful view of Puget Sound and the Olympics, Olson would look out his office windows and actually smile. It definitely wasn't one of those Mount Rainier moments. She guessed one pudgy hand was rubbing his bald head, the other might be stuck inside a box of Frango Mints. Oral ecstasy. Cheating on his diet.

Olson repeated his question. "I asked what you meant by that."

"I meant people in general. Especially land grabbers."

Olson made a scoffing sound, dismissing her worries. "Now, listen here, Venus, we've found out a couple interesting things about this fellow."

She glanced around. Still no sign of Miss Perkins. She moved closer to the Mrs. Bowsers. To Olson, she said, "Shoot."

"Willow was an assistant professor, a doctoral candidate at the University of British Columbia, in Vancouver. You'll never guess what his thesis was about."

Venus said, "Rare butterfly species."

"Why the hell would you say that?" Olson. Irritated.

"Just a guess. Am I right?" She ran a hand through her hair.

Olson said, "He was a biologist. But not a lepidopterist. His doctoral studies were related to the attractant qualities in insect pheromones."

"Natural aphrodisiacs?"

Olson said, "Maybe. Now, I got this information from the university, from an administrative secretary. She told me Willow taught a couple courses there, but he spent most of his time working on the thesis. He lived in Victoria, with a woman."

"Next of kin?"

"London. University's contacting them now. I gather they're distant cousins. The woman, his fiancée, is a Mimi Budge, also Canadian. She's a clothing designer, high couture stuff. The university's also contacting her."

Venus said, "Why would a fashion designer live in Victoria?"

Olson growled, "How am I supposed to know the answer to that?"

"Anything else?"

"According to the university secretary, Willow's fiancée, this Mimi person, is Anson Budge's daughter."

"Canada's Olympic diving champion?"

"That was thirty years ago. Now Anson Budge plays golf, parties, and spends money. From what I hear, his daughter doesn't really need to work."

"Bella says the same thing about me."

"What does that have to do with anything? Anyway, she's apparently very-up-and-coming. In business for herself. I think you need to consider her a suspect."

"Check."

"Why do these things have to happen on our land?" Whining. "Why can't they kill one another in their own homes?"

Venus said, "I need Song back up here, to go over the Trooper." She winced, waited for his reply.

Surprisingly, he said, "That's not a bad idea. Tell the sheriff to impound it, then I'll send Song back up tomorrow morning."

"Check."

Olson grunted. That was as close to a collegial noise as he got on foggy days. "Now, I want you to get a handle on this situation. Nip it in the bud. Do it fast."

"What's the hurry?"

"The hurry?" Olson mocked her. "Maybe you haven't heard that this is an election year. Maybe being off in Asia for three years has affected your memory. Election years mean our preserves become political footballs. We have a congressional football team coming to inspect regional next month."

"Venus thought she saw Miss Perkins poke her saucy head around the corner for an instant, then disappear. "What does a congressional inspection have to do with Willow's murder?"

"Oh, now I remember," Olson said sarcastically. "You skipped Tuesday's staff meeting, didn't you? Well, if you'd been at the meeting like you were supposed to have been, you would know why the congress*persons* are coming to inspect Yodeler Preserve. They're considering cutting all of its federal funding in the next budget bill.

And the president needs these congress persons' votes. Need I say more?'' Olson hung up.

On the way out, she plucked a Mrs. Bowser from the vase, left it lying on Miss Perkins's chair, thorns and all.

SIX

COOKIE

ANOTHER DAMP, melancholy morning. Cookie Charmeaux Avalon pulled a bed pillow over her head and muttered to herself, "I don't care what they say about rain shadows, this place reeks of mold." In the distance, a ferry boat tooted. How could you live this close to saltwater and the damn rain forest and not have mold on everything? This whole town reeked of mold and rotten fish.

What time was it anyway?

Reaching one slightly misunderstood arm out of the down comforter, Miss Blue Poppy nineteen seventy-never mind fumbled for the bedside table, grasped a small Tiffany and Co. alarm clock with Roman numerals, and squeezed tight, as if she could read it by braille. When that failed, Cookie pulled the arm back under the covers, including the hand with the clock. She held it against her breast, feeling it tick, and meditated on her unfortunate arms.

Bat wings.

Sprawled face down across the bed, Cookie clasped the down pillow tighter around her glorious red locks, like a helmet, and plotted her next move. She might get up. Then again, she might not. When your dreams play better than your reality, why get up at all? She couldn't summon enough energy to open one eye and read the clock face. Why not just go back to sleep?

It must be noon, or thereabouts. This was what? Tuesday? Friday? God knows. A weekday in June. She knew that much, if you please, and anyway, the exact date hardly made a difference. If Death's fingers reached for her right now, she'd go willingly, begging to be taken. Suicidal fantasies had gnawed at her for months, or was it years? But she was always too tired to construct such intricate plans.

Maybe another fifteen minutes. Then she'd rise and face the weather. For now, she'd just lie in bed and meditate on things.

Cookie had already risen once this morning, like every dutiful Junior League wife, at six o'clock with her husband. All Junior Leaguers do that in the first few years of their marriages. The habit stuck with Cookie, though. She'd been doing the wife bit every weekday morning for, what? Twenty years next month.

On a normal day, which today wasn't by any stretch, Cookie rose with Peter, then performed her yoga salute to the sun. As if a sun existed in Fern, Washington, and I don't care what the weatherman says, that isn't a real sun out there. It's a pale imitation. A real sun sends heat, tropical heat. Pacific Northwest sun, which she had endured these two decades, radiated nothing stronger than a chameleon's breath. You might as well have perpetual rainfall, because even the sun shone damp. Why did she have to go and marry a northerner?

Following the salute to the pseudosun, she'd slip into something fresh and pretty and join Peter for breakfast. On what they called mild mornings up here in Fern, Washington, like this morning, Cookie and Peter would breakfast on the terrace, where inevitably, Cookie would catch a chill. Peter found the fresh air exhilarating, and so she begrudged him that, breakfast on the terrace, in season. She'd begrudged Peter a lot more than that, but did he notice?

So then, Imogene, the family's cook, would carry breakfast out to them while Peter scanned *The Wall Street Journal* and Cookie stared at the croissants, hating Peter for ignoring her. She had dressed and groomed, and she always presented such a fresh, pretty picture.

Still Peter ignored her. This had been going on for four or five years now, and Cookie had tried numerous times to confront Peter about the problem, and other issues as well. In fact, just this morning when the alarm went off and Cookie dragged herself up and out of bed, her marital duty as she saw it, the first thought on her agenda had been confronting Peter with the fact that he chronically ignored her. Their marriage was obviously in trouble, and it was time they talked it out. But this morning, when Cookie turned around to say good morning, Peter wasn't in bed.

Cookie heard her heart pound. Her stomach felt heavy, sour. She inhaled deeply, but that only made her eardrums throb.

How many times was this now? She'd lost count after the double digits. Once again, Peter had spent the night somewhere else, most certainly, she felt, with another woman. And this morning, Cookie was pretty sure she knew the identity of his latest conquest.

Zora. Sex goddess *du jour*.

Peter appeared late at the breakfast table, acting as if nothing was wrong. She pounced on him with all her pent-up rage, all the accusations she'd held inside her for months now. Peter denied everything. He wasn't in love with Zora, definitely not. No, he loved Cookie with all his heart and soul. He had worked late at his office, he must have fallen asleep.

Cookie screamed, pummeled Peter's chest, sobbed. Peter stood his ground, waiting for the rage to subside. Then he folded Cookie in his arms, held her to him, pulled his fingers gently through her hair, whispered in her ear. "Darling, darling Cookie. You've got to put a lid on your fantasies."

"I try, Peter. I really do try."

Peter left for the office. At which point, Cookie had…what had she done then? Of course. She had gone straight back to bed. And that was all anybody needed to know.

Cookie lay in bed, her eyes open now. Still grasping the clock to her breast, she rolled over, stared at the ceiling. Had Imogene seen anything? Had any of the house staff heard the quarrel? Thank heaven the girls were off in Europe. Their father could do no wrong. Thank God they weren't around to hear the spiteful things she'd said. Yelled. Screamed.

And what about the gardening? Had Imogene wondered about her digging in the foxgloves while wearing her best summer dress? Did it matter if she had? Well, yes, it mattered. You just don't want your house staff witnessing personal stuff.

Not that anything had really been resolved. Cookie thought back to the first time Peter had mentioned Zora. It was last August, in Rome. The new, glossier, sexier Miss Blue Poppy campaign was in the early planning stages, and Peter was scouting for the right image to promote the fragrance. Nothing sells like sex, Peter had commented that first morning in Rome as he and Cookie breakfasted on their terrace overlooking the Piazza Navona. Cookie took issue with Peter's remark.

"Isn't it true, darling," she'd said to Peter that lovely summer morning in Rome, "that Blue Poppy's image has traditionally been more, well, mysteriously romantic?"

"Hmmm," was all Peter said.

"I mean," pressed Cookie, "when I was Miss Blue Poppy, back when we met? The title represented a sort of polished, intelligent woman. You know, charming, alluring in a secretive sense, only hinting at sex."

Peter merely smiled. Like she was naive or something. She pressed her point. "Didn't your grandfather Conrad always intend Blue Poppy for the genteel woman, the sort of lady who knows innuendo goes so much further than raw sex appeal?"

Peter smirked, so Cookie pointed out that once upon a time, certainly long before she was born, Blue Poppy had been the sovereign property of only the world's most discriminating women, had graced the dressing tables of queens and society ladies and such. Civilized ladies. And hadn't that been the path Peter's Uncle Conrad had wisely followed when he inherited the perfumery? Now, here came Peter and Troy, third generation Blue Poppy noses, trying to put a vulgar connotation on the family fragrance. How could he even think of sexploitation anyway? It would ruin Blue Poppy's good name.

Peter replied simply, "You are dead wrong, darling. Just wait and see. You are dead wrong."

That ended the discussion.

And so commenced the search for Miss Blue Poppy. And whom do you suppose just happened to cross the Piazza Navona below their terrace the very next morning? That tall, pale as milk, raven-haired aspiring young fashion model Zora, holding fast to the arm of her sturdy mother as they dodged a flock of pigeons flying at the bread crumbs Cookie had tossed over the balcony. Peter's quick, brilliant response proved startlingly effective. He called out to the mama in clumsy Italian, "Gorgeous lady! Leave your daughter, and come away with me. I am in love with your hair, your eyes, your Valentino dress. Give up your daughter for me, and I will give up my wife for you."

Of course, this had caused Zora's mother to giggle. Especially since Zora's mama hailed from Studio City, California, and didn't speak a word of Italian. How could she not giggle at such a hunk of Americana? She waved up at Peter. He shouted, "Wait! I am coming down to speak with you." And due to the extent of Peter's inimitable charm, the lady waited, her dazzling daughter still safe on her arm. That was Cookie's memory of how it happened. The rest was history, and next week, thought Cookie darkly, the world will wake up to this year's Miss Blue Poppy, the sexy, exotic Zora.

There was nothing mysterious about Zora. Nothing at all romantic. She was pure Hollywood and all wrong for Blue Poppy's image.

Everything the perfume wasn't. Why hadn't Peter seen that before it was too late?

Cookie needed nicotine. Rummaging through the bedside drawer, she found a stale pack of Tiparillos, lit one, inhaled, blew out smoke, inhaled again, slower this time. She picked up the phone, punched in the kitchen code. The housekeeper's voice came over the line. Cookie said, "I'm getting up now, Imogene. Have you got tea made?"

"Yes, madam," came Imogene's voice back, "but I thought you had gone out."

"No, no, no, no, no. I haven't moved an inch. Why would you think that?"

"I must have been mistaken, madam. I thought I heard you go out earlier. And the picnic basket is sitting here on the counter..."

"Never mind the picnic basket," Cookie snapped. Then catching herself, she purred more kindly, "Bring in some tea, will you, dear?"

"Yes, ma'am. I'll be right there."

Cookie fumbled with the phone, punched in Peter's number. Peter's simpleton secretary came on the line. "Miss Perkins, is my husband there?"

"He's out," Miss Perkins lied smoothly. "I don't know where." Without even crossing her fingers.

"Oh!" Cookie acted surprised. "In that case, would you kindly locate him for me? I need to know our dinner plans."

"Oh!" mimicked Miss Perkins rudely. "I suppose I could try to locate him. Meanwhile, Troy just walked into my office. Maybe he'd speak with you."

"Put him on," snapped Cookie, not nicely.

"By the way," said Miss Perkins smoothly, "I really don't mean to present a threat to you, Mrs. Avalon. I'm not interested in your husband, and besides, I am a feminist..."

Cookie heard some muffled laughter, then Troy-boy came on the line, smooth as ever.

SEVEN

NOTHING NOUVELLE

THE OLYMPIC COASTLINE winds westward from Fern, beyond Pysht, Seiku Point, and Neah Bay to Cape Flattery's primitive jaws. Here, the Pacific roars into the Strait of Juan de Fuca. Here among the orcas and porpoise and ponderous octopi, fathoms below the crashing surf, doomed shipwrecks languish in a kelpy museum of maritime that legends are made of: ancient dugout canoes; splintered clipper ships, their exotic cargo still aboard; unlucky Coast Guard vessels from rescue missions gone awry; even the occasional enemy submarine; all sunk deep in a merciless watery grave, wrapped in barnacle shrouds, their lost souls and fabulous treasures haunting the unwary beachcomber, plunging the whole territory into its legendary saturnine vapor. In the midst of it all, Tattoosh Island rises triumphant, echoing the last prayers of stymied Makah sailors, salty Britishers, and Europe's Don Quixotes of the seas.

The Makah, the cape people, say that before the Changer came to change the Original People into other forms, Tattoosh Island was a woman, married to Destruction Island in the south. But Tattoosh and Destruction quarreled constantly, and finally, Tattoosh loaded their children into her canoe and sailed north. When she got to the Point of Arches, near Cape Flattery, she noticed the children behaving exactly like their father, so she dumped them overboard and sailed on alone. The rugged peaks jutting out of the ocean between Destruction Island and Tattoosh Island are the children of that bitter union. Yes, this was God's Country, created from copious tears.

Halfway between Cape Flattery and Fern, the beach at Raven Point is stark, dank, driftwood strewn, a desolate stony outcropping that faces north across the strait, enjoying little protection from frequent Pacific monsoons. There's an automated lighthouse on the point to guide the vessels that survive Cape Flattery's caprice toward the Ediz

Hook light, which guides them to the light at Dungeness Spit, and so on into Admiralty Inlet, where the trough feeds Puget Sound's protected inland ports. All this shipping traffic provides endless entertainment for beach dwellers along the strait and for guests of the Inn at Raven Point.

The sky drizzles here most days of the year, and the word "dry" is utilized by the locals only in the context of martinis. If you go there intentionally, it's because you're hiding out from something, or someone, or because you're delivering supplies to the posh Inn at Raven Point, or you work there. It's a tony health spa, secluded, full service, with a four-star chef and discreet personnel. People come to the Inn at Raven Point from all parts of the world, for various reasons. Some come to take seaweed cures, others to recover from nasty divorces or insufficient alimony judgments. A robust number of guests are fugitives from plastic surgery clinics and other hazards of the elite. There's no other reason to visit Raven Point, unless you're on the trail of a murderer.

Apparently, the swish clientele had never heard the Olympic tribes' dark Raven legends, because when Venus rode onto the inn's lush grounds, the place was buzzing with activity, and even in this godforsaken rain-soaked backwater, she couldn't find a vacant parking space. When she started to park in the valet zone, a sheriff's deputy materialized and waved her over to a narrow space near the inn's service entrance. She parked, removed a backpack from the fender case, and wound through a riot of hot pink geraniums toward the front door and the deputy.

His name was Houck. Houck said, "Mortifying. A chef drops dead from his own food."

He had clamshell lips like a kid she once knew down in Ozone Beach. The Heard boy. Only Heard hadn't been a sheriff's deputy. Heard had been a novice criminal. Houck might have the same shellfish lips, and he might be somewhat of a smart aleck, but he probably wasn't dangerous. To Houck, she said, "What happened?"

Houck squinted. Maybe nearsighted. "Chef died of food poisoning this morning. Isn't that why you're here?"

"Actually, I came to check out an Isuzu Trooper."

Houck's brow cleared. "Oh, that." He pointed across the parking lot. "It's over there. I thought you came about the chef keeling over."

"You sure it was food poison that killed him?"

The deputy nodded grimly. "Coroner says so. They found some

mushrooms in him. Pretty sure it was death's angel. He said Lux, that was his name, died within half an hour of ingesting them. Coroner said the only other time he ever heard of the death's angel actually killing anything was when some goats up on Mount Pluvius had some for dinner and croaked the next day."

Venus nodded. "That's how it usually works. Usually takes around fourteen hours to kill. I'll bet it wasn't mushrooms that killed Lux."

Houck flushed, said, "That's all I know, what Sheriff Needles told us."

He led Venus to Willow's Isuzu. Almost apologetically, he said, "Since the owner's body was found up on Yodeler Preserve, we didn't touch it. Called you folks instead. Figured you could get up here soon enough." He scratched the side of his neck. He said, "You think they're related?"

Venus shrugged. "Probably not. And yet, this is Willow's Trooper, parked at Lux's place of employment. Right now, the only thing that connects them is this vehicle."

Houck said, "Weird isn't it? Two guys keel over the same day, within hours of each other, only a few miles apart, and one of them parks his vehicle in the other's parking spot?"

"This is Lux's parking spot?"

Houck nodded. "According to Mr. Price. He's the inn's manager. He said Lux had to park his Bronco in the guest parking lot because this Trooper had taken his place."

Venus said, "Maybe coincidence."

Houck sucked air through his teeth. "Maybe," he said, dubious, "but it strikes me as totally weird." He went away then, leaving her with the Trooper.

The tires had seen a lot of highway, but were clean, like the rest of the vehicle. The doors were unlocked. Willow must have been a trustful soul. Or careless. She took a few photographs, poked around the interior. It was neat and tidy, clean as a whistle, and exuded a new-car odor. She read the odometer. Thirty thousand, three hundred forty-three and a half miles. Not exactly brand new. Willow must be a clean freak like herself. She was poking around the glove compartment when she remembered something. No ignition key. It had gone to Seattle with the chopper.

In the glove compartment she found the owner's manual, vehicle registration in Willow's name, and auto insurance documents. Willow belonged to AAA and had liability insurance. There was a yellow hard-rubber frost scraper for the windows, another small carton of Ricolas, a felt-tip pen, black ink, and a note pad with nothing noted on it. On the front seat, a silver foil cardboard box of Kleenex Boutique tissues, opened, with one clean white tissue poking out. Nothing else. On the floor, the rubber mat on the driver's side was slightly soiled where Willow's left foot had rested when he drove, but otherwise the mats were as clean as Bella's kitchen counters. She wondered how it felt driving an automatic four-wheel-drive vehicle. Willow definitely hadn't been the backwoods type.

On the backseat lay a stack of student quizzes, filled out. The subject was insect pheromones. Somebody else would have to grade them now. In the rear compartment, Willow had packed a thermal picnic box with some energy bars, an unopened box of Wheatabix, an unopened carton of skim milk, the expiration date three weeks distant, no longer cold. There was a stainless steel spoon and some bottled water, also untapped. Beside the thermal picnic box, a wooden wine crate held his neatly folded rain gear and rubber galoshes. Beside that lay a black umbrella, furled and snapped, the handle made of cheap plastic. He'd been a frugal man, she guessed, with no great need for aesthetic accouterment. Unlike his haute couture fiancée, Willow wasn't invested in style.

A second wine crate held several butterfly boards, a bottle of ether, and a violet pastilles tin. Venus shook it. It didn't contain violet pastilles. She opened it and stared at the excellent collection of butterfly pins. A thrill pierced her senses. She plucked out one of the black-headed pins, rolled it between two fingers. The gesture and the closeness of Willow's butterfly equipment instantly transported her ten years into the past, to a verdant meadow in southern England.

She was a student at Oxford, out chasing golden fritillaries on a sunny English afternoon. Alone in the meadow this midsummer day, she'd stopped to examine a flowering host plant for signs of larvae feeding, or pupae clinging on their silk patches to the leaves. Kneeling in the meadow, she felt a presence behind her, a dark shadow cast long across the host plant. The shadow moved slowly to her right. In her left eye's peripheral vision appeared the largest, flabbiest badger she'd ever seen. It had wandered up out of the Thames, probably a purely accidental meeting. Badgers can be nasty, but this one just seemed officious, like a security guard with a trespasser. Venus made a clicking sound with her tongue. The badger blinked but otherwise didn't react. She tried staring him down, but he won the contest. Then he turned and waddled toward the river bank. He kept peering over his shoulder, pausing, as if waiting for her to follow him. Finally she did, and he led her to a thick tuft of lycinae near the river bank. On the leaves of the lycinae, she found the strange chrysalis. She returned every day thereafter for three weeks to witness the metamorphosis, and every day the badger showed up to watch with her. Finally one warm but overcast morning, the chrysalis cracked open, and wiggling slowly out of the pupa appeared a glorious *Parnassius phoebus oris*. She waited one, two, almost three hours, until its wings had completely broken free of the chrysalis, until its body had emerged entirely, until its golden wings had dried. When it began fluttering, in preparation for its first flight, she reached out with her net to capture the rare beauty. Just then the badger cast its shadow over her. Obediently, she dropped the net on the ground, then she and Badger watched as the golden apollo took flight, fluttering across the meadow, pure joy riding the wind. Badger gave her one more stern warning glance, then slipped down the river bank. When she shared the exciting news with her professors, they chided her for not capturing the rare species, then they all ran for their butterfly nets.

The ping of the pin against the violet pastilles tin interrupted her reverie. She pocketed the tin and the pins, and went in search of Houck. She found him near the inn's entrance, instructed him to impound the Trooper at the county lot. Then Houck led her inside, into the lobby, remarking over his shoulder, "People shouldn't eat just any old thing they come across, no matter how tasty it looks. Lux, he was an experienced chef. He really should have known better. Anyway, we've moved the body over to the morgue, so now he's in someone else's fridge." He chuckled at his own joke.

The lobby was posh for a beach resort, and the fashion plates adorning the premises, wearing their money on their backs, resembled aliens from Rodeo Drive. Consider, for instance, the two Thoroughbreds lingering over a couple long snorts of flavored O_2 at the Oxygen Bar. Both wore plush white terry robes that fell casually open, revealing million-dollar legs. Both had attenuated fingernails, curved like eagle's talons, French manicured, and their coiffures wrapped up against the elements in playful turbans. One of these forty carats had let a few jet black tendrils slip out the sides and back so you knew she had length and an attitude. She was young, exotic. She had bone-white skin, top shelf cheekbones, wide, slanted baby blues with heavily fringed black eyelashes. Maybe false. She was too young to be so sultry. Then again, probably she was Zora.

The other turban was slightly riper, thirty-something, working on a double chin, with sharp, petite features, and a bright copper fringe tickling her eyes. She wasn't smoking, but her right hand clutched a fat cigar, still in its cellophane, which she twirled between her fingers. As Venus followed Houck across the lobby, she overheard the turbans' chatter.

Aerobics had been too boring, but the seaweed wraps had worked wonders, and that bust-firming treatment Alvin gives really, really works. The swim just now had limbered them up in certain strategic spots. Then, let's see, this evening, for the Coppertoned only, cocktails with Peter and Troy Avalon at six sharp. Later on, Poopsie, and maybe Troy-boy, if he's lucky, for dinner in the Fiddlehead. No wait. The black-haired beauty would be dining alone in her suite this evening. Like last night. And tomorrow night. Well, Cinderella was fed up with dining solo in her suite, but she was incognito, you know, and they were paying her a fortune, so don't complain already. Another snort of O_2 would purge that stress factor, and might even set the right mood for an afternoon siesta. Not much to do in this Shangri-la, is there?

The turbans paused, watched Venus move across the carpet, studying her gait as she rounded a corner. One of them made a clucking sound. Then some low murmuring before the chatter resumed.

The Fiddlehead Restaurant faced west, commanding a sweeping view of the cobbled, driftwood-strewn beach and the saltwater strait. The place was closed, the dining room deserted, but someone had set the tables for dinner with the menu, handwritten in neat calligraphy on Japanese rice paper, lying neatly beside each place. Venus picked one up, read it.

Hamma Hamma Oysters
Olympic Mountain Morels in Cream
Poached Chinook Salmon
Native Camas and Herbs Cake
Asian Pear and Ginger Chutney
Sautéed Fiddlehead Ferns with
Raspberry-Hazelnut-Thyme Glacé
Chateau San Michelle Beaujolais Sauvignon
Cloud Berry Gelato or Frango Mint Mousse

*Accompanied by Your Choice of
SBC Espresso or Murchie's Tea
Remy Martin*

Houck said, "I'll leave you here. Sheriff wants me standing by out front." He went away. Venus looked around. To her right, a pair of stainless steel swinging doors had port hole windows so you could peek through if you were over six feet tall. One foot shy, she guessed there was a kitchen on the other side. Maybe a new chef in there, working on the hamma hammas and camas cakes. She skirted the dining tables, put a palm against one of the cool silver doors, and pushed. It swung inward into the Fiddlehead's kitchen.

EIGHT

LUX

DAZZLING LIGHT blinded her. Venus blinked a few times and the kitchen came into focus. Fluorescent lights bounced off gleaming stainless steel, and at first glance, the kitchen seemed as white and pure as new snow. Then her olfactory senses kicked in and she detected death's putrid odors.

Before the chef's painful final writhings had spoiled the atmosphere, this kitchen had been as hygienic as an operating room, with highly polished stainless steel walls, ovens, sinks, counters, and a white tile floor. A long wood butcher-block counter formed an island in the kitchen's center. On the counter top sat a colossal stainless steel bowl filled with wilting fiddlehead ferns. Beside the fiddlehead ferns was a pile of vomitus. Some of the vomitus had landed in the fiddleheads, ruining tonight's salad. A thin stream of bloody bile ran down the side of the counter onto the floor. It had dried, but still emitted a sour odor. On the floor was a puddle of loose feces, also bloodied. Beside the puddle of feces lay a chef's high flanged hat. The chef's body had fallen here.

Presumably, the coroner had taken samples of the offal. She rummaged in her pack, found some sterile disposable plastic gloves. She fished them out, along with a few sterile evidence bags. She took samples of the vomitus, bile, and feces, placed these in separate sterile bags. In the freezer, she found some dry ice, made a neat package with a nearly empty gelato carton. Rose petal flavor. Like eating perfume, she thought, ditching the dregs. She put all the evidence in a plastic trash bag, tied it securely, looked around some more. She studied the paper chef's hat, where it lay, how it lay. She was diving into the huge refrigerator when someone coughed gently. She turned around.

A small round young woman, probably Japanese-American, said, "Looking for something?"

She was short, like Venus, but chunky, pushing twenty-two or -three, with a stern, businesslike aura. She wore a navy blazer, crisp white shirt, navy skirt an inch or two above chubby knees, and sensible black oxfords with glossy black stockings. She'd lined her lips with black eyeliner, gone over that with a black currant gloss. Her small, rounded fingernails were painted frosted forest green. She'd had her nose pierced, but apparently didn't wear the ring to work. It wouldn't go with the tailored uniform. She spoke with a lisp.

"I'm Beatrice Yamada," she said. "Front desk manager. Is there something I can help you find?" Tactful. Her handshake felt damp, like squeezing a wood's ear mushroom, and she pumped lightly. Venus showed Ms. Yamada her badge. She explained about Willow's murder. Ms. Yamada listened patiently, her baffling lips dancing across her moon-shaped face. When Venus finished her story, Ms. Yamada said, "Well, I can tell you right now, Otto Lux's death is not related to that stuff. He died from eating wild mushrooms. The county coroner has already been here. And he just called us about five minutes ago, to verify that."

Venus nodded. Ms. Yamada added, "If you want any more information, I suggest you consult our general manager." She reached into her natty blazer, fished out a business card, held it between her thumb and index finger, like a communion host. "This is Mr. Price's card. If you'd like to make an appointment, call this number. There's a house phone in the lobby."

The card was translucent, engraved in gold, showy but understated. Venus said, "Thanks. I'll do that. But first, maybe I'll just finish up in—"

"First you will speak to Mr. Price," snapped Beatrice Yamada assertively. She held open a stainless steel door. As Venus passed her, Beatrice wrinkled her nose and said, "Pee-eeuww. It smells like a sewer in here."

Venus carried the nauseating samples out to the parking lot, locked them up in the Harley's rear compartment. On the way back in, she passed Houck, who said, "Find what you're looking for?" Friendly, collegial.

"Not really," she said, and went inside.

On the house phone, she asked the operator for Price, and waited. Over in the bar, the Coppertoned turban had a little Motorola phone riveted to her ear. The one who must be Zora was sucking bubbles. There are two ways to ingest oxygen: via the nasal passages, from tubes placed in the nostrils, or by mouth, delivered in little vaporous liquid bubbles that you suck up through a tube. Apparently, Zora was a sucker.

Mr. Nathan Price emerged from the wine cellar, where he'd been turning the cabernet sauvignons and maybe doing some other things. He couldn't be over twenty-five, but had a patina as slick as his inn's marble floors. Price said, "Beatrice found the chef's body in our kitchen. She screamed and screamed. We couldn't get her to quit screaming. Then Dr. Abel came down from his room and gave Beatrice something for shock." He glanced over at the desk clerk. Beatrice stood behind the reception desk, apparently awake and competent. Price added, "These new drugs are amazing. A few hours ago, her aura was all out of whack. Now it's back to normal, and hey, the guests never even knew what happened. I've got a great staff here, really terrific guys. Still, it hasn't exactly been my idea of a quiet morning at the hacienda." Price chuckled inappropriately.

Venus said, "Do you realize that every day up here in these rain forests, a bear, or a Roosevelt elk, or a woodland caribou is shot dead just so some macho hunter can boast a rack?"

"What's that got to do with anything?"

Venus shrugged. "When a bear or an elk gets shot, nobody screams."

"It's a species thing." Price. Coolly.

"Think so?"

"Anyway," intoned Price, "those are dumb creatures, lacking free will. Here we have a human life, and a very talented one. Lux was the best chef in the Pacific Northwest. And we only had him on a temporary basis, for just a few months. He'd been here just eight weeks, and now this terrible incident."

"What time did he come in this morning?"

Price had the information on the tip of his tongue. "His usual time. Five a.m. Then I think he went out—that is, I know he went out again, to pick up some fresh produce. It was a little after six when he left here, and he got back about seven, seven-fifteen. I saw him cross the lobby here with a couple huge paper sacks of stuff, go through the restaurant into the kitchen. Right through those doors. That's the last time I saw him alive."

Venus said, "Anybody in the kitchen when he went in there?"

Price shook his head. "Lux has several assistants who come in at five-thirty, set up the breakfast buffet. They do a little lunch prep, then they leave and don't come back again until eleven-thirty, just before the restaurant opens for lunch. Then they're joined by the maître d' and wait staff. But no, Lux was alone in there when it happened. I guess if someone had been in there with him, he might have survived the attack. But food poisoning can work fast, y'know?"

"Where'd he go for the fresh produce?"

Price smiled. "The lettuce and so forth come from Fern's fresh market, up in the town center. But the special items, the mushrooms and herbs, and the wild berries, came from Lux's secret sources. He never told anyone where he bought his morels and garnishes, but he always used the freshest herbs and berries. And camas bulbs, for his camas cakes. That was his specialty." Price frowned. "So you share the coroner's opinion, then? You think he got ahold of some bad stuff, like poison mushrooms or something?"

Venus said, "Maybe."

Price shook his head. "Well, he brought in more than fiddlehead ferns this morning. I mean, he was really loaded down."

"You sure it was produce he brought in, and not something else?"

"Like what, for example?" Price turned slightly hostile.

Venus shrugged. "The hamma hammas, or fresh salmon, something else for tonight's menu. He might have brought in more than fiddlehead ferns and mushrooms. What else would those paper bags contain?"

He pursed his lips. "Oh, now I get it. You're thinking he might have swallowed a bad oyster or something like that." He spread his hands, showed her empty palms. "Well, I can't help you there."

High-pitched laughter streamed from the Oxygen Bar into the lobby. The turbans, laughing hysterically. Maybe too much O_2. The stuff has a way of sneaking up on you.

To Price, Venus said, "Did Lux have a family?"

The innkeeper shrugged. "Depends how you define family. Up here he lived alone. There's no mention of relatives in his employment records. I already looked. I know he spent his days off in Seattle. He's got a condo there. And, er, a friend. But when he's working for us, he stays here at the spa, and he's always alone. Which makes sense. He took this position so he'd have solitude to write. It was a nice setup for him."

"What was he writing?"

"A cookbook, of course. All Native American recipes." Price sounded impatient. Maybe the merlot needed twirling. Maybe something else was on his mind. His eyes darted around the lobby and he shifted on his feet.

Venus said, "Where's the manuscript now?"

Price stroked his smooth, prominent chin. "I've never seen it, myself. Sheriff Needles just gave Lux's private room here the once-over. I asked him if he found the recipes, but Needles said he didn't see anything like recipes in there. The strange thing about it, he didn't find any of Lux's personal effects in there. Not even his razor, or a toothbrush. And I can't let you in there until Sheriff Needles gives me an okay. But you can talk to Needles yourself."

More laughter dribbled from the Oxygen Bar. The turbans now slouched nearly horizontal in their chairs. The younger turban's dangerous legs were propped up on a coffee table, knees bent, terry robe splayed open. From this angle you could see too much. Across the table, the elder turban had succumbed to temptation and puffed on the fat cigar. If you were advertising the House of the Rising Sun, here was your tableau.

Venus said, "What about his car?"

Price flinched. "His car? I don't think he owned a car. His friend, or roommate, or whatever, from Seattle? He usually dropped Lux off, then came back to fetch him on his days off."

"Then how did Lux go out this morning?"

Price fidgeted. "Bicycle. He always rode one of the spa's bicycles, with a little basket for his purchases. I bought him the basket."

Venus smoothed her short hair back toward the nape of her neck. A shock of blond fell across her eyes. She pushed it back again. Time for a haircut. She said, "What about the friend, in Seattle?"

"What about him?" Price spoke acerbically, rocking on his heels.

"Have you contacted him yet?"

Price frowned, confused. "About what?" His train of thought had obviously derailed. Maybe the turbans had distracted him.

"Lux. About Lux. Did you contact the dead man's friend in Seattle?"

The innkeeper's face flushed deep crimson. "Actually, I forgot about that. I'll take care of that right away."

He was turning to leave, when Venus touched his arm. "What's the friend's name?"

Price reached inside his navy blue blazer, fished out a little digital device, consulted it, said, "Oscar Sundborg. He's a commercial photographer in Seattle. I think he was Lux's boyfriend." Price fumbled, at loose ends, unable to complete his train of thought. Maybe homophobia.

Venus said, "What about the Seattle address?"

"Of course, I have the address right here. I have all my employees' addresses." He punched a couple buttons and waited until a paper printout popped up. He tore it off, handed it to her. He put away the remarkable digital toy, wiped his hands carefully with his breast pocket handkerchief.

Lux lived in Seattle's trendy Belltown, adjacent to the Pike Place Market and the new marina on the waterfront. There was a phone number, too. She pocketed the little paper printout. She said, "What about tonight? You find a chef for tonight?" Double-checking.

Price let out a full balloon of air. "Slava from the Olympic Hotel in Seattle is flying up right now. We closed for lunch, but we'll be back open for dinner this evening. Right now, I'm waiting for my crew to get in there and clean up. Sheriff finally just gave us permission to go in there."

Venus said, "Mind if I go in and look around first?"

From the front desk, a distance of about thirty feet, Beatrice piped up. "She's already been in there."

Price shrugged. "Well then, go for it. Needles is finished in there. I certainly want nothing to do with the place, at least until they've sanitized it."

Before Price went away, she said, "Was Jonathan Willow registered here?"

Price nodded. "The man who was shot up on Yodeler Preserve? He checked in late last evening. But there is nothing to see in his room. It's already been cleaned. He didn't leave anything in it, and he checked out before dawn this morning. I don't know why he parked in our employee lot." He took one giant step sideways. "Is there anything else I can do for you, before I go back to my wines?"

Venus said, "Maybe you can tell me why this inn was built outside the rain shadow. They could have gone five miles east and had twelve inches of rain, instead of twelve feet."

Price grimaced. He didn't like stupid questions. Drolly, he said, "Personally, I find the atmosphere enchanting." The innkeeper retreated, gliding across the marble foyer, disappearing into the wine cellar. Maybe he'd phone Sundborg from there. Whatever Price did in the wine cellar, he missed the big hoopla a minute later when God's gift to Valley Girls entered the lobby.

Troy-boy Avalon, the Pacific Northwest's most eligible bachelor, advanced on the turbans, a *GQ* natural with nicely articulated muscles and range-roving hazel green eyes. The turbans spotted him instantly and their talons ejected. The copper fringe set down her oxygen tube, stood up, adjusted the sash on her terry robe, and glided toward Troy-boy.

Beatrice motioned Venus over to the front desk. She whispered, "That copper-haired babe is Shelby Warlock, Drake Warlock's old lady?"

Venus said, "Warlock Shipping Lines?"

Beatrice nodded. "And that girl with her, do you recognize her?"

Venus said, "Let me guess. She's an aspiring fashion model. Name's Zora."

Beatrice giggled. "Hey, you're good. Even the turban and no makeup didn't throw you off. I think she's in town because—this is just a guess—she's been chosen as this year's Miss Blue Poppy. It's all top secret, you know, until the ads come out. That's when everyone finds out who's been chosen. Zora's keeping a pretty low profile around here, too. This is the first time I've actually seen her, and she checked in yesterday morning. Hiding from the paparazzi."

"What about the Warlock woman? She her chaperone or something?"

Beatrice said, "I think so. And that hunk who just walked in? That's Troy Avalon, of Blue Poppy Perfumery. I wonder what he's doing here. He really shouldn't be seen with them before the ads come out. He'll spoil the secret."

Venus watched Shelby Warlock snag Troy, draw him up to the bar. The bar served other things besides oxygen, and Troy-boy ordered a draft Pyramid. He wasn't the oxygen-sucking type. Drake Warlock probably wouldn't like the way his wife stroked Troy Avalon's tan, muscular arm, or the way Troy took Shelby's hand in his, pressed his lips into her palm. Beatrice whispered, "Aha. I see Mrs. Warlock has landed the second biggest fish in Fern."

Venus played the gossip. "He's the younger Avalon, right?"

Beatrice flared her nostrils. "And if you think Troy's cute, you should check out Peter Avalon. Troy's older brother? He's ten times better looking than Troy-boy. But that's only my opinion. I mean,

you have to see Peter in person to totally appreciate his magnetism.
Now, if I had Zora's face and figure, I'd go after Peter Avalon myself." Beatrice swooned. "But then, he's been married to the same
woman for like, twenty years. One of those delicate Southern belles.
I think she was a Miss Blue Poppy when they met. She's beautiful,
really beautiful. Not like these model types, more natural. I hope I
look as good as Cookie Avalon when I'm her age."

"What's her age?" Small talk.

Beatrice flicked her bobbed hair. "Around forty. Peter has affairs
with younger ladies, though, at least that's the rumor. I did hear
through the grapevine that Peter and Zora were an item in L.A. last
winter." She licked her blackberry lips. "It's going to be one fascinating week around here."

Beatrice went back to work. Venus went back into the Fiddlehead's
kitchen. There was nothing else interesting in the foul-smelling room,
unless you had a sheepskin from the Cordon Bleu, or a fetish for
Swiss pastry implements. In the refrigerator's crisper, mounds of
smooth baby butter lettuce and...what's this? Edible flowers.

Pansies, fresh. Nasturtium, wilting. Violets. *V. adunca* variety, native to the Olympic Peninsula. Venus placed the flowers in an evidence bag. The coroner's crew should've done this earlier. Back in
the refrigerator, poking around, she located some wood flats of cloud
berries and a small carton of fresh gooseberries, took samples from
each. The hamma hammas had been piled neatly in stainless steel
bowls. She hadn't noticed any empty oyster shells around the kitchen,
but she might have missed them, or the coroner might have taken
them. She took several hamma hammas. Besides the berries and oysters, there were freshly grilled camas cakes, each wrapped in waxed
paper. She added several cakes to her specimen collection. Below the
camas cakes, on a separate rack, lay thick slabs of Chinook salmon,
beside them, a mass of butter patties, stamped with "RP" for "Raven
Point," and a quart jar labeled APPLE-GINGER-CHUTNEY MAYO. In the
freezer section, a half-dozen Dungeness crabs stared back at her, pin-
cers intact. On the meat side of the freezer were New Zealand lamb
cutlets and a short stack of Beefalo filet mignons. That was all.

There was nothing else to find, not even a recipe book. Like Jonathan Willow, thought Venus, Lux had been a minimalist.

NINE

UNCLE CONRAD

UNCLE CONRAD AVALON stepped out of the Washington Athletic Club into Seattle's dreary morning mist. Turning north on Sixth Avenue, the tall, distinguished, nattily attired country gentleman popped open his black silk bumbershoot with the hand-carved bear paw handle, paused on the curb, and when the streetlight finally blinked green, crossed Union Street under the hostile gaze of three adenoidal punks. One of them, Conrad could see from quite a distance, was an illustrated man. The second would have had a rather becoming crew cut if not for the stubble's fierce blue color, and, lower down, the fully exposed rippling abdominal muscles that bulged below a high-cut, torn black T-shirt and a couple of navel rings. The third young man was engaged in the rude process of blowing his nose with his fingers, so that Conrad was forced to avert his eyes and didn't immediately get a good look at his features. But Avalon had noticed the blackjack instrument in the nose blower's other hand. These young chaps, thought Conrad charitably, might simply be your perennial loiterers. One thing Conrad did not wish to consider as he approached their vicinity was the possibility that the three might be ruffians lying in wait of a victim. Should that be the case, they could be very sure that their victim wouldn't be Conrad Avalon the Second. It took more than three young Nosey Parkers in unkempt clothing, a blackjack, and a severe case of bad manners to intimidate Conrad Avalon. You don't live to seventy-something without a keen survival instinct.

The three youths watched Avalon approach along Union Street. Through the fine misty rain, Conrad thought he noticed a silver ring clinging to one chap's mouth. Then the lip ring nudged the illustrated man and the illustrated man nudged the blackjack, and then Conrad witnessed the unthinkable. The blackjack chap transferred his lethal weapon from the (relatively speaking) clean hand into the nasal mucous-contaminated hand. The blackjack started swinging.

Horrors, thought Conrad, has the fellow received no sanitary training whatsoever? Now the blunt instrument swung slowly, as if winding up for an attack. Conrad tightened his grip on the umbrella's paw and glanced around the street. A few pedestrians waited at the next corner for a light to change. Across the street, two elderly, elegantly dressed Bellevue-type ladies had taken cover from the rain in the entrance to a chic boutique, so he wasn't entirely alone; should the gang strike, surely someone would fly to his aid. The moment of discomfort passed and Conrad, knowing what he had to do, reached into his trousers pocket, relaxed his other hand's grip on the umbrella, and continued walking toward the three menacing youths. When he got within striking distance, the punks shifted laconically and stepped into Conrad's path, blocking his way.

The illustrated man snarled. The blackjack fellow raised his weapon threateningly, and the rippling ab muscles lad started to say something when suddenly the elderly gentleman produced a fine linen handkerchief from his pocket. Holding the starched, neatly folded white square out to the nose blower, Conrad said with some authority, "Here you are, young man. A runny nose can surely be a nuisance, what?" With that, Conrad Avalon sidestepped the startled punks and tripped breezily on his way.

He hadn't gone far when up ahead Gunderson Jewelers came into view. Conrad had reached his destination sans handkerchief but unscathed. Pressing the doorbell beside Gunderson's discreet front door, he hummed lightly to himself. Presently the door buzzed open and Conrad entered the small jewelry shop, making sure to shake his umbrella before stepping onto the lush carpet. The shopkeeper greeted the elderly Mr. Avalon like an old friend, for, of course, he was.

"So, Mr. Avalon." The shopkeeper smiled. "How are you enjoying retirement?"

Conrad harumphed. "A Nose never retires, chap. We just leave the actual day-to-day perfumery business to the younger, less-talented noses."

The two men enjoyed a hearty laugh. Although Conrad had intended to stop at Gunderson's only to pick up a new watch battery and to have his gold wedding ring polished, once inside the shop, his usual fiscal discipline suddenly failed him. For on the display counter, in a black velvet tray, sat the most exquisite lady's brooch he had ever seen. And what a marvelous coincidence; the brooch seemed to be waiting just for Conrad Avalon. Who else but an Avalon would really appreciate the mysterious beauty of a Tibetan blue poppy?

Conrad peered at the brooch through the magnifying glass he always wore on a gold chain around his neck. Four large pear-shaped sapphires formed brilliant blue poppy petals around a diamond pavé seed pod. Two generous emeralds formed leaves on a straight platinum stem. Even the safety clasp was a work of art, being two platinum butterflies joined together at the abdomen. The shopkeeper, a thin, balding California import with no blood ties to the original Gunderson, demonstrated the correct angle for pinning the brooch, borrowing his female assistant's convenient lapel.

Marvelous. Were Dolly alive today, Avalon wouldn't hesitate to purchase the brooch for his wife's generous bosom. Alas, a widowed man of means can't acquire a piece like this for just anyone. Has to be someone special, very special. Just then, as if lightning had pierced the gray wool Seattle sky, bolted through Gunderson's show window, and struck Conrad square on the cranium, an idea formed in the not-quite-retired perfumer's mind. Indeed, there existed just one woman in all the world—besides Dolly, God rest her soul—whose natural beauty could withstand the competitive placement of such a marvelous brooch in the vicinity of her face.

"I'll take it," Conrad told the jeweler, and reaching into his deep pocket he pulled out a book of bank drafts and proceeded to write the exact amount the jeweler had quoted under his breath. While the jeweler wrapped the brilliant blue poppy brooch, Conrad hummed contentedly to himself and glanced down to admire his favorite pair of Italian loafers. That was when Conrad noticed something near his right foot. He leaned over, more nimbly than most septuagenarians, and plucked a piece of paper off Gunderson's carpet. He didn't recognize the small folded scrap, but noted a thin layer of navy lint on the paper. It must have fallen out of his pocket when he pulled out the checkbook, yet he didn't recognize it. Setting his umbrella carefully against a gilded Venetian chair, he unfolded the paper scrap and read a neatly typed message:

"Avalon—Hands off Yodeler Preserve. Unless you want to die badly."

Conrad glanced around Gunderson's showroom. Outside the window, pedestrians walked past, and occasionally one paused to admire something in the window, but no one noticed Conrad. He read the note a second time. This time, he made a sort of whistling sound, then carefully folded the note and tucked it back into his pocket with the checkbook. When the jeweler returned, the client's face reflected nothing more than sheer delight over his dainty acquisition. Conrad tucked the little gift-wrapped brooch in the breast pocket of his jacket, replaced his wristwatch, examined the newly polished wedding ring, and slipped it neatly on his left ring finger. As he exited Gunderson's, bumbershoot first, the face Conrad Avalon presented to the Emerald City was one of supreme satisfaction with himself. Only later would the dapper country gentleman admit that the nasty note had insinuated more than a minor annoyance into his easy spirits and graceful footstep.

Back at the WAC, safely ensconced in the Pioneer Suite, Avalon ordered up a couple stiff shots of Ushers and a corned beef sandwich. Outside, the rain fell heavier now, the midday sky dark as night. He bolted the first shot of scotch, then picked up the phone and called his nephew Peter in Fern. Peter came on the line full of his usual confident brio. Conrad said, "Peter, what the devil is going on up there?"

"Nothing much, Uncle Conrad. The field's about to bloom, so we'll have the film crew up in the meadow in a day or so. Everything's set for launching the new ad campaign. Other than that, it's status quo."

Avalon told his nephew about the note. Peter seemed downright nonchalant, Conrad thought, his only comment being a dismissive, "The world's full of crackpots, Uncle Conrad."

Conrad remarked, "I just don't know what this world is coming to. Even Fern, Washington, isn't safe from crime anymore. Just last week, Sigrid Chin's veterinary hospital was held up at gunpoint. The Crocker boy was beaten up by a gang of nomads the week before that. These things didn't happen in my day. The world's gone sour."

Peter made a noncommittal noise and said, "When are you coming home?"

Conrad harumphed. "When I'm ready. And it's none of your business, my comings and goings. You know where to find me, if necessity arises." He hung up the phone, bolted the second shot of scotch, and finished his corned beef sandwich. Outside, rain beat relentlessly against the windows, and even in the climate-controlled Pioneer Suite of the Washington Athletic Club, Conrad Avalon thought the air held dampness, and the scent of trouble.

TEN

RADIO

MURDER SHOULDN'T BE SO pretty. Now that Jonathan Willow's corpse had been removed, the meadow once more felt gloriously alive, buzzing with energy, in the height of its life cycle. Venus sensed a presence, like sprites or forest nymphs, could almost see them dancing in the warm breeze in the upper meadow, near the edge of Peter Avalon's poppy field. If this meadow could talk, what would it tell her?

From the birth of these mountains, born on glacial melt in a collision of water and stone, to the epoch of trans-Siberian migration, when northern tribes followed their reindeer across the legendary Arctic land bridge and trickled down into this milder climate, from the first discovery of these Olympics until today, how many deaths had occurred in this glorious mountain meadow? Not just humans, all creatures. Discounting the natural death of seasons and survival instinct, how many deaths from unnatural causes? Surely hunters had stalked this meadow for food. But before this morning, before this man was gunned down in cold blood, had other murders occurred on this magnificent carpet, this fragrant sanctuary?

Speak, meadow.

There was a trail on Yodeler Preserve leading from the stark beach across the highway, to the salt-spray meadow, then up through the meadow where it reached the poppy fields, skirted them on its climb up to a magnificent waterfall, and from there to timberline, where the path ended abruptly on a rocky promontory above the falls. The trail had been carved out a hundred years ago by an old logger named MacGregor, a Scots timberjack who, according to legend, had made a fortune selling cedar logs off Mount Pluvius. The eccentric MacGregor, so the legend went, had stashed his wealth in a bank vault in Seattle and lived out his old age in utter simplicity up on Mount Pluvius, scouring the forest for mushrooms, edible roots and berries, and medicinal herbs. He trespassed on government land, on the wildlife preserve that included Yodeler's and the surrounding forests, but no one ever arrested him. He was old and had gone deaf, and he lived entirely off the land. What little cash he earned from selling the roots and berries and such, the old man used to purchase a few dry goods, candle wicks, and wax. After the Native Americans, old man MacGregor was the first professional wildcrafter on the Olympic Peninsula. Now his granddaughter, Aggie MacGregor, already a senior citizen and just as eccentric and wild-eyed as all her ancestors, maintained the old trail.

The Forest Service let Aggie MacGregor alone; she'd lived up here all her life, and what she scavenged from the forests she took respectfully, without greed. Aggie never harmed anything. When Interior took over management of the preserve, they, too, left Aggie MacGregor to her wildcrafting and trail maintenance. Aggie kept the trail neatly manicured and she had carefully preserved the ecological purity of the only cleared trail down Mount Pluvius. The locals had come to respect this trail, officially named MacGregor's Trail, and scrupulously avoided trampling on the wild flowers or disturbing the native species in any way whenever they made this climb. Only during summer tourist season did the path suffer, when hikers strayed off the park trails into the off-limits wildlife preserve. Then the fragile plants and their flowers were crushed by careless trespassers, for no one was supposed to enter this protected rain forest, or the blue poppy leasehold below it, or the salt-spray meadow sloping down to the saltwater strait.

Peter Avalon had implicated Aggie MacGregor, suggesting she had shot Willow by mistake, meaning to kill Avalon. Their clans had feuded for centuries, he'd said. The MacGregors had a reputation for making their own laws. Even Aggie, in this day and age, with her indoor plumbing and electricity, with her cell phone, fax, and computer, disdained the law. She lived by the law of the land, a techno-hermit who believed government interfered too much in people's private affairs. Her land adjoined Yodeler Preserve on the western side. Maybe she was home today.

As Venus followed the steep hiking trail, she watched for bears. This was foraging season. They might be around, she might hear a stomach growl. Then, too, up here above the meadow she might pick up the scent of the killer, Willow's killer.

There was a deep, raging waterfall in the forest up along the climb to timberline, where bald eagles nested, and there were caves. Behind the waterfall, Venus knew, a family of black bears hibernated each winter. The fog rarely crept as high as the waterfall curtain that hid their dwelling from the outside world.

Now Venus could hear the waterfall, and when she finally reached the base of the falls, she paused, sat on her haunches, and drew up some water from the cold, clean pool formed by the engorged falls when the plunging liquid shaft hit the ridge and ricocheted into the Elwha. Through sun-dappled giant ferns, she spotted a Roosevelt elk, rubbing its molting rack against an ancient cedar. It hadn't sensed her presence, and she moved softly across the ridge, then up deeper into the forest, where she knew a shortcut to the top of the waterfall. Maybe Aggie was up there. Or the bears.

The mother, Sunbeam, was named for her favorite activity. She loved nothing more than discovering a beam of sunlight shooting through the ancient cedar stands, washing the forest floor, and lolling in its golden warmth. Sunbeam was one of the most beautiful, and therefore desirable, females in the territory. They called these bears cinnamons because their coats were slightly lighter than their cousins over in the Cascades. Still, to the untrained eye, their fur looked sleek, velvety black.

Sunbeam's twin female cubs, Berry and Roe, were sighted more often than other family members. Berry was named after the cranberries that were her obsession. In summer she went around with a scarlet-rimmed mouth and apparently thought this made her more attractive. Roe, Berry's twin, was the bear most often spotted by climbers up here. Venus had seen Roe often, and knew that her favorite spot for fishing was the mouth of the Elwha River. Roe got her name from the part of salmon she favored. She was more beautiful than Berry, more exotic, but she had a foul temper. Both twins were naturally flirtatious and were shameless beggars at the tourist sites in the nearby national park. Their reputation preceded them, and hikers kept a special watch out for the twins.

Two winters ago, Sunbeam, the twins' mother, gave birth to a male known as Skookum, after the Chinook jargon word meaning "especially good." Just after the cub's birth, Skookum's father, Arrow, was massacred by poachers on Dungeness Spit. They took his paws and his genitals and his gall bladder. They left the rest of the corpse on the rocky beach to get picked over by seagulls. The following spring, Sunbeam mated with Radio, the tribal elder, and Radio moved in behind the waterfall.

Radio had inherited a boom box some campers left in the national park one summer. He'd dragged it to the den up behind the waterfall. The bear family enjoyed, or suffered from, hours of nonstop entertainment. Then something went wrong. It ceased playing. Radio kept the instrument anyway, and occasionally autopsied the plastic carcass. Radio was big and burly, and when he snarled he could scare the bravest man. Only the rangers knew how gentle Radio was toward his family, especially toward Sunbeam. In hiker lore, Radio was the most feared creature on Mount Pluvius.

It was no surprise that Radio would mate with Sunbeam; he'd always admired her from a respectable distance. So now the bear family numbered five, at least at last count. Venus hadn't been on Pluvius in over three years, but the park rangers had carefully documented bear activity on the mountain. According to their reports, Sunbeam's family was healthy and thriving, and one hiker claimed to have sighted a fourth cub trailing Sunbeam.

Sunbeam's offspring were excellent fishers, living off salmon from the mouth of the Elwha River, where the Elwha met the Pacific just west of the village of Fern. No one can fish like Olympic Mountains bears. They also forage along the stark ocean beaches and in the rain forest for berries and shoots. Their world is Paradise, or was, once upon a time.

AGGIE MACGREGOR drove a beat-up CJ-4, and she meant business when she did. Aggie's favorite pastime whenever she went in to town was terrorizing the tourists on Highway 101's hairpin loops. Like her home computer setup, Aggie took special care of her Jeep. She trusted machines more than she did people.

Aggie's one true friend was Sigrid Chin, the local veterinarian, married to Fern's mayor. As youngsters, Sigrid and Aggie sometimes played together, but in later years Sigrid got an education, entered society, became a successful society matron and a vet. Nonetheless, Aggie and Sigrid remained close, and often Aggie brought wounded creatures from the forest to Sigrid's veterinary hospital in Fern.

There was an oft-recited local tale about Aggie and a bear named Lilac. Lilac ate some poison camas bulbs someone had dug up and left to rot. Aggie found Lilac just in time. Lilac rode in Aggie's CJ-4 to Sigrid Chin's hospital. Sigrid pumped out Lilac's stomach, and the bear recovered quickly. Still woozy from tranquilizers, Lilac rode back to the forest with Aggie. Some tourists visiting the national park saw old Aggie barreling down the highway with a black bear slumped beside her in the front seat. The tourists drove off the highway, rolled over on the beach, and ended upside down in the strait. They survived the crash, but never forgot that hirsute highway encounter. Even though she was tranquilized, Lilac, too, probably still remembered that ride. For the natives, the point of the story was, tourists better watch out when they invade Paradise. For Venus, the salient point was what the tale said about Aggie MacGregor.

Venus found the trail head and climbed up through the rain forest until at last she reached the mouth of the waterfall. Pounding out of million-year-old granite, fed by thousand-year-old glaciers, these crystalline waters flushed the melting snow off Mount Pluvius and sent it thundering over the rocky ridge where it plunged to solid earth twelve hundred feet below, then spent its power in the clear pool before joining the Elwha's gathered forces to feed salmon with wanderlust into the Strait of Juan de Fuca.

Radio and Sunbeam weren't home, nor were the youngsters. Venus had hoped to sight the new cub, but this wasn't why she came all the way up here. She'd climbed up here to gain another vantage point on the upper meadow where Willow's body had fallen a few hours ago. She found a flat granite slab and sat down, surveying the panorama below. From the rain forest's timberline where she sat, the saltwater strait appeared calm as lake water, and between occasional wispy cloud trails, she could see Vancouver Island and imagined she could actually see Victoria itself. Over there, the land appeared misty purple, but she knew that when you got up close, Vancouver Island was an idyllic emerald forest with that quaint jewel of civilization, Victoria, thrown in for fun.

She stood up, inhaled the marvelous pure air, and focused on the meadow below. This panoramic perspective seemed to offer little useful information. From here, if a hiker witnessed the shooting, the hiker might spot figures in the meadow, but they would be too small to identify. With binoculars, or a telephoto camera lens, the hypothetical hiker might make out some identifiable details. Maybe a witness would report something.

The sounds of the forest, the fragrance of moist cedar, the sumptuous air elevated her spirits. There was a reason to live after all, in spite of the shredded heart beating dully in her chest, in spite of untrue lovers, forsaken promises, shattered dreams, and a general plunge in self-esteem. The rare thrill of being alone among Nature was salve on an aching heart, and when an exquisite pink lady slipper appeared on the path, she stopped, knelt to examine its pale, innocent color, its softly erotic shape. It might belong to a lady, but it wasn't her slipper. This close to the trail's pine needle covered floor, Venus noticed an indentation in the earth. Hiking boot, with a heavy, old-fashioned waffle sole. Then another, and another, barely discernible but definitely imprinted in the damp ground. She stood, followed the footprints along the trail, moving quietly, cautiously. She followed the waffle-soled footprints about thirty yards, where whoever left the prints apparently paused in a cedar grove. The footprints led to an ancient cedar tree that soared two hundred feet into the sky, but Venus's eyes didn't get that far, because something froze them on a spot about six feet off the ground, an object on the rugged red cedar's trunk; a baby bald eagle, nailed through the throat into the old cedar tree.

Half an hour later, carrying the eagle's fresh corpse, Venus followed the waffle footprints to the edge of Aggie MacGregor's homestead. She spotted the roof of Aggie's two-story Victorian clapboard, set below the MacGregor meadow in a wooded grove on a bluff overlooking Highway 101. This was Nine Fingers Ridge, where the preserve and Olympic National Forest met the MacGregor property in a triangle.

Aggie's immediate family included the black lab, Tina, a friendly, frothy thing; a nasty, temperamental, and utterly imperious feline named Pearl; a few ornamental chickens; one milk cow; and a gaggle of mean-spirited geese. Other than a weekly visit from Sigrid Chin, Aggie mostly kept to herself.

Venus crossed over a small brook, walked through the grassy meadow, past a billy goat and its mother, past the coop where Aggie raised fancy bantams with feathered feet. She came to a low cedar-log fence, lifted the gate latch. Remembering the black lab's skittish-ness, and Aggie's, too, Venus walked gently toward the front porch. This slight motion sent Tina into a tailspin, and out the window, Pearl the cat hissed.

Aggie didn't answer the door when Venus knocked. Pearl lounged in the window hissing, and Tina whimpered at Venus's side, but Aggie didn't appear. Venus went around to the back of the house to the shed up on a knoll at the edge of the property, where the

MacGregor homestead met the rain forest. The shed was built from granite boulders cemented together, its earthen roof coated with bright emerald moss. If you didn't look carefully, you'd miss the shed altogether, so well did it blend into the mountain side.

She found Aggie MacGregor inside the shed.

Filtered light from a single dusty windowpane shone across Aggie's shoulders as she bent over a long table piled with herbs and mushrooms and roots. Her fine hands were protected by canvas gloves as they sorted yarrow from tansy. She had on her working clothes: heavy hiking boots, thick woolen stockings, a pastel cotton summer dress, and a heavy canvas three-quarter-length coat. Her yellowed white hair poked out around her ears beneath a summery Panama secured to her head with a dangerous-looking hat pin. Venus knocked lightly on the shed's partly open door. Aggie didn't look up, kept her back to the door. "Okay, Bert," said Aggie, "this batch is ready for market." She had a high, happy voice, like a lark, or a society matron.

Venus said, "It's me, Aggie. Venus."

Aggie whirled around. Her face caught the light from the window and glowed, her pale skin taut, luminous. Her small blue eyes glittered like a couple of dancing forget-me-nots, her lips were thin red lines, her mouth wide, full of strong yellowed teeth like old ivory. She had heavy black eyebrows and a pert sunburned nose. She laughed, a tinkling sound, and said, "Well, bless my soul. If it isn't Miss Stick-in-the-Mud." Then she laughed again in that bird song.

Aggie might be seventy-five years old, but she had a youthful spryness and a spring in her gait. She pulled off the canvas garden gloves and came outdoors, met Venus in the yard. Tina came tearing around the house and barked a greeting to Aggie, who pointed one crooked, freckled finger and sent the lab obediently back to the porch.

Venus showed Aggie the dead eagle. The older woman touched the eagle's feathers, as if hoping it would revive. It didn't. Aggie said, "It's those illegal hunters again, poaching off the preserve."

Venus said, "Maybe disgruntled loggers."

Aggie shook her head adamantly. "Can't be."

"Why?"

"Because," said Aggie with certainty, "this forest preserve hasn't been one of their targets. The loggers are all down south and over in Grays County now. They never come up here, not even to make a point. Wouldn't dare, as long as I'm up here."

Aggie went inside the shed, came out a minute later with a plastic garment bag. "This is all I've got."

Venus wrapped the dead eagle in the plastic, made a loop, hung the bag on her shoulder. "Why do you say hunters, Aggie?"

The old woman shrugged. "Who else would do that? An ordinary hiker wouldn't be that mean. The tourists are all too lazy to come up this far. Who else would take the time and effort?"

Venus said, "The footprints end at your meadow. Whoever it was must have left the forest through your land. The eagle hasn't been dead longer than a few hours."

"Well, I've seen nary a soul on my land today. Except for you. And Sigrid. Sigrid came up early this morning, about dawn, to bring me some udder balm." She shook her head. "I might have missed him, though, if he came through the meadow before daylight."

They stood in the yard, on the forest's edge, talking of this and that, catching up on news and gossip. Venus told Aggie about her Asian adventures, the malaria, and her brief but passionate courtship, the engagement, and the way it ended so suddenly, so cruelly, by e-mail. Aggie listened intently, her head cocked, favoring her best ear. When Venus finished, Aggie patted her on the shoulder and said, "Now maybe you'll quit being such an acerbic little scamp. That's probably what run him off."

She told Aggie about the body found in Yodeler's meadow. A mistiness clouded the old woman's eyes, like a painful memory returning. After a minute, Aggie said, "It's a shame, truly a shame." She sat down wearily on an old garden chair. In her lap, her fine freckled hands rested in the folds of her summer dress. Venus pulled up another garden chair, sat facing the old woman, and said, "Did you know him?"

"Sure. All the wildcrafters knew Jonathan Willow. He was a bright young man, very amiable but not too intrusive, the sort of chap I like. He's Canadian. He'd come up here with his lady friend, oh, about once a month. After butterflies, so they said. All the wildcrafters knew them. They never bothered us, they rarely went up further than the meadow."

Venus said, "When his body was found, his hand was clutching a bunch of poppies from the Avalon leasehold."

Aggie's brows knitted and she pulled at the tip of her nose. "Now that's a mystery, for sure," she said. "I never saw him go into that poppy field. Never. He's been coming around the preserve for three or four years, and all that time I never saw him or his lady friend pick the poppies.''

"Did they come only in summer?" Venus watched the old woman's eyes. Something flickered in the forget-me-nots, like a hard rain dashing their petals.

Aggie said, "They came all year round. Except winter. I don't recall seeing them in winter."

"You ever talk to them?"

Aggie shook her head. "Nothing more than idle chat. We don't even talk among ourselves during the harvests. Sure and now, we'd not converse with strangers."

"What about his companion? Did you ever speak to her?"

Aggie laughed sharply. "The girlfriend? Never. But I know who she is. She comes from the Budge family. She's Anson Budge's oldest daughter. They call her Mimi. I don't know what 'Mimi' stands for. Maybe Miriam. But she's too clumsy to be a Miriam."

"Any other wildcrafters working Yodeler Preserve? I mean, besides yourself?"

Aggie shook her head emphatically. "They don't trespass on my territory. The others keep to the national forest. They've got permits, you know, to harvest there. They'll be out two nights from now, in the forest, every one of them. Midsummer night. And this year, we've got a good moon. Now, if the fog will just cooperate and stay out at sea, we might have a record harvest."

"What time of night?"

"Always around midnight. When it's pitch dark, with nothing but the moon and our flashlights to guide us. It's the traditional time."

Venus said, "You'll be up in Yodeler's meadow then?"

Aggie nodded. "The others will work the national forest. I've got Yodeler to myself. Meadow and forest both."

"You anticipate a good harvest?"

The wildcrafter shrugged. "Can't predict that. Ever since the Avalons took that leasehold, my harvest has been spotty. It's an invader, that poppy; it isn't native, and it spoils the natural ecology. Now the meadow's overwatered from the Avalon's irrigation system. And then, that chemical fertilizer they use on the poppies, and all that peat, that's a strain on the meadow. You fellers ought to take back that lease. Peter Avalon can get by on imports. He doesn't need to grow Tibetan poppies on this virgin meadow, that's for sure."

The poppy controversy had been raging for years, since the first day the leasehold agreement took effect. Most of the natives wanted Yodeler Preserve to remain virgin. They'd fought the parcel lease to Avalon, and no manner of explanation about Interior's budget cuts would satisfy them. Venus had grown weary of explaining the lease-hold arrangement, especially since she, too, disapproved.

Before she left Aggie, Venus asked, "Do you ever pick the western blue violet?"

Aggie shook her head adamantly. "I know what I'm doing is just as forbidden. And I know the rangers wink at my puny harvests, and I appreciate that. But I would never harvest an endangered flower just for selling on the market, now, surely and then, you know that's the truth. *V. adunca* is the host plant for the Dungeness silverspot butterfly. I wouldn't harvest it, for sale, no I wouldn't."

"You ever see the Dungeness silverspot?"

Aggie nodded. "Sure, and didn't all the MacGregors back fifty years ago. We saw huge colonies every midsummer, fluttering like pieces of evening sky dropped from heaven. In twilight, they shine bright silver. The most beautiful sight you'd ever want to see."

"Seen any recently?"

Aggie made a funny face and shook her head. Venus had seen this expression on Aggie's face before. Distrustful. The elder woman stood, walked Venus to the front gate. Leaving Aggie's land, Venus turned to wave good-bye. Over the woman's shoulder, she saw the cat, Pearl, lolling on the windowsill, licking her paws, preening.

AT THE EDGE of the dense forest, ancient cedar trees and Douglas firs cast a deep shadow over Peter Avalon's poppy field. Without this critical afternoon shadow, the delicate Tibetan plants couldn't mature. Venus plunged into the field, parting the willowy green stems with their pregnant seed pod crowns, looking for anything that might sub-stantiate her memory of that red thing she'd seen this morning, flut-tering among the poppies.

Cultivating blue poppies is an art only a handful of horticulturists have perfected. Tibetan blues are among the most difficult poppies to cultivate and require the skill of an emerald thumb, which Peter Avalon apparently wore into this world along with the special nose. The splendid Tibetan blues were nonnative plants, and in that sense, desecrated the virgin meadow, interfered with the delicate ecological balance of native wildlife. Although confined to a narrow band run-ning across the upper meadow's border with the forest, the immigrants had already altered the meadow's ecology. The poppies attracted alien insects, invaders among a two-thousand-year-old community that had an established order. The new arrivals had bollixed up the ecological balance it had taken thousands of years to create. Change might be good for progress, but there's a difference between natural metamorphosis and the "progress" created by horticultural management practices.

Hiking down toward Highway 101 and the rocky beach, she emerged on the road's shoulder at a sharp bend, where the western blue violet grew close enough to the tideline to bathe in salty spindrift. When a breeze caught the strait's surface and spun off briny effervescence, the violet soaked up the nutrients and thrived. Venus knelt beside a clump of violets, examined its flowers, the undersides of its leaves. Something had obviously chewed on these thick, hairy, nutritious green leaves. Searching among the stubby plants, she was about to give up when she found the little caterpillar, munching voraciously on a violet leaf.

Carefully, she removed the violet clump, roots and all, the fuzzy hitchhiker still gripping the leaf. She tore off part of the plastic garment bag that shrouded the dead baby eagle, placed the caterpillar and the plant in a temporary cocoon, then crossed over the highway to where the Harley basked in the afternoon sunshine. She packed up the shrouded eagle and the busy caterpillar, straddled the bike, and drove west toward Raven Point.

ELEVEN

LILY

WHENEVER Peter Avalon needed to ruminate on the more difficult aspects of his complex life, he fled the family perfumery, leaving business in the care of his able brother, Troy. Secure in the knowledge that with Miss Perkins's lively competence Troy could handle any problem that might arise, Peter frequently fled to his poppy fields up in Yodeler's meadow. But today, although he dearly wished to be alone among this season's spectacular new crop, to cleanse his mind, perhaps even to reach a certain decision about his personal life, this proved impossible. Already, news of a dead man's body discovered near the fields had attracted gawkers, and in the wake of various and sundry murder rumors came a tidal wave of curious townsfolk, seeking the thrill of morbid gore. But the amateur hearse chasers found little to feed their adrenaline at the crime scene.

Avalon realized with dismay that he could hardly hope to find solitude in Yodeler's meadow today. Oh well, a set of tennis sounded good, and Raven Point's Golf and Tennis Club beckoned from the short distance of a twenty-minute drive. The weather looked perfect for a drive just now, the strait had been fairly calm last time he looked, and only a light mist seemed to be falling outside the rain shadow. Avalon called the club and requested his favorite tennis pro, who was serendipitously available. If you thought about it, you'd realize that much of Peter Avalon's life ran on serendipity. So it was with a brief nod to Miss Perkins on the way out that Peter Avalon fled the Blue Poppy tedium and drove his Rolls-Royce Silver Cloud up Highway 101, taking the fork at Highway 112, alongside the Strait of Juan de Fuca, to secluded Raven Point.

Avalon played tennis the way some people drove cars, with ferocious aptitude. Following the match, which Avalon won 6–2, 6–love, he performed his ritual half-mile crawl in the club's indoor swimming pool, showered, dressed, and ordered a light lunch, which he enjoyed while lounging on a chaise, poolside, on the indoor terrace. Overhead, through the pool atrium's glass ceiling, thin sunlight shone down, bathing him in a soft glow and shimmering across the swimming pool. A sun break.

At last he could think clearly, and now his mind emptied all the riffraff of a day where everything seemed out of kilter. Take the killing in the meadow, for instance. A stupid, unnecessary accident. Then the body being found so quickly by the sheriff's deputy, then the sheriff and the federal Fish and Wildlife agents. All this and Zora besides. A man didn't need these headaches. He was wiping the last bits of lunch from his lips when a tiny splashing sound caused him to glance up.

Avalon gasped, placed a hand on his chest. He could do nothing else, for before him, appearing out of nowhere, or possibly out of the swimming pool, walked the most beautiful creature he'd ever laid eyes upon.

When she crossed the patio, wearing an exquisite jade bathing suit, she swayed gracefully, her tan flesh quivering just barely, like youthful flesh does. But truly, she must be a goddess, Avalon told himself. Only a goddess reflected sunlight like this; only a goddess possessed such magnificent curves. And to think, only moments ago, he'd been feeling wretched. Now, as she turned to reach for a bath towel, he felt his heart flutter. Could this be...surely not...but it felt like...oh, no, could she be the one?

The young woman passed the towel across her perfect face, and when it reappeared, a wide smile crossed her full lips and her teeth appeared in two perfect gleaming white rows. He noticed the slight gap between the front teeth, a seductive space. She had a fawn's eyes that twinkled now at some distant memory, or perhaps at some future plans. Her glossy earth-colored hair rippled across her shoulders, stopping abruptly just before touching the most glorious...well, never mind. He was no prude, but he did respect women. Now he struggled to suppress sheer animal instinct. He was good at guessing people's ages. She couldn't be more than twenty. Same age as his oldest daughter Colette, only this creature was more beautiful than Colette. Not to disparage his own daughter's beauty, but this vision now standing only yards from his chaise longue, still lost in her private smile, surely had no equal upon Earth.

Avalon raised a limp index finger and Darin, the maître d', rushed to his side. He ordered a Dewars with Perrier chaser. While Darin was gone, Avalon watched the young beauty towel off, recline on a nearby chaise, and close her eyes, stretching her head like an offering toward the poor sunshine leaking through the atrium's crystalline ceiling. When Darin returned from the bar, Avalon reached for the scotch and said casually, "Who's the young lady?"

Darin glanced around. Four or five ladies of varying ages lay supine on chaises at poolside, and he knew all their names. He also knew which had captured the Nose's notoriously roving eye.

"That's Miss Budge."

"Tell me more."

He might have wanted a pedigree, or maybe just her phone number, Darin wasn't sure. He said, "The youngest daughter of Mr. Anson Budge. The Canadian diving champion?"

"That's Anson's daughter? Really?"

Darin nodded. "That's Lily. He has another daughter, but Lily's by far the better looker. You might have heard of her sister, the older one? Mimi Budge, the fashion designer."

Avalon rolled scotch around in his mouth. "No," he said. "No, I haven't heard of the sister. But I know the father. I know Anson. Will you bring me the telephone, Darin?"

Darin went away, counting to himself. This made five times already this month that he'd played a role in matchmaking. He kept statistics on these things, and right now, he'd bet anyone a thousand dollars that Peter Avalon would walk out of the club with the young lady hanging on his solid gold arm. That's what money gets you: the Lilys of the world.

Avalon surreptitiously watched Lily. He wanted to go over there, fall to his knees, and proposition her. Gad, how could Anson Budge let this child out of his sight for one minute? On the chaise, Lily turned over onto her stomach, like she was on Kuhalani Beach, tanning. She folded her arms, made a cradle for her head, shut the heavenly eyes. The smile, now a serene grin, remained on her face. From the silken hair falling across her softly rounded shoulders, Avalon traced her body's curves to the small of her back, across the firm buttocks, down the perfect thighs to the strong, nicely muscled calves, the slim ankles. Even the creature's feet took exquisite form.

Darin reappeared, slow walking his way into manhood, his grubby postadolescent hand clutching a cell phone. Avalon tipped him generously and waved him away again. He loped back to the bar, holding the tip limply, like it meant nothing to him. He was maître d', after all.

Avalon punched in the office number, got Miss Perkins on the line.

"Zora's entourage has arrived," announced Miss Perkins. "It's the size of Tacoma, and they brought along a 737 cargo hold of luggage. I bet they're all her relatives."

"You're sure no one's identified Zora with Blue Poppy?"

Miss Perkins said, not humbly, "I promise you, sir, no one knows but myself and Troy. Now, don't worry. I've got it all under control. Zora's safely ensconced at the Raven, along with her friend Mrs. Warlock. Zora's in the Snow Crab Suite, just as you specified. I guess you have that number."

Lily, restless, turned over onto her back again. Avalon's heart leaped like a bullfrog. Into the phone he said, "Yes, I have the number. Are they satisfied with the arrangements there?"

Miss Perkins snorted ever so slightly. "So far so good. But I gather the manager spent all morning trying to find a chef to replace Otto Lux. Gawwwd, that was brutal. The poor guy ate his own food and keeled over. I guess you already knew that, huh?"

"Yes, Miss Perkins. Everything else in order?"

"Your wife called."

Avalon swallowed scotch, chewed on some ice. "What did she want?"

"To know your dinner plans. She says you never tell her anything, so she decided to ask me. I didn't know what to say, so I put her on hold a minute ago, but she hung up."

"Call Cookie back for me, will you, Miss Perkins? Tell her I'll be home late this evening. Office work. And, Miss Perkins, will you mention tomorrow night as well? Tell Cookie she's welcome to join us at the cocktail party for Zora's entourage."

"Yes, sir. Should I say you want her to join you?"

"Just say she's welcome to join us."

"What about dinner afterwards? You made reservations for yourself and that federal agent. What about Mrs. Avalon?"

"Don't mention the dinner, just the cocktail party. She'll be too tired anyway, to sit through a business discussion."

"Got it."

"Fine. Now look up Anson Budge's private number. It's in my personal phone file."

He was about to ring off when he thought of something else. He said, "And, Miss Perkins, since when have you addressed my brother by his given name?"

"Since a few minutes ago, when he told me to, sir. He insisted. Troy says he wants to encourage a certain new informality around here. But if you don't want me calling Troy, Troy, I'll quit now, sir. After all, you're the boss." She giggled. Avalon clicked off the line. Miss Perkins seemed annoyingly cheerful this afternoon. He liked her better snippy.

Anson Budge came on the line full of bluster. The Budge men always blustered. It was a family tradition, the blustering Budges. The Budge men blustered and the Budge women stammered, in a coquettish way. Avalon fervently hoped that young Lily lacked this family trait.

"Avalon," shouted Anson Budge over the phone, "where the hell have you been, old buddy? I'm up for the ninth hole so I can't be long. What's up? Don't tell me it's Stanford reunion time already?"

"You're at the Raven?" asked Peter.

"Came over with my daughters last night, just for a couple days. Why? Are you here, too?"

"Er, no, that is, yes, I am. I'm in the, ah, lobby, at the bar," he lied. "I won't keep you long, Anson. I understand that your elder daughter—Mimi, isn't it?"

"Fantastic memory, Peter. Fantastic."

"I learned recently that your Mimi has gone into the couture business."

"She designs this saccharine fairy tale fluff, but she's a success with it; she's making waves across Canada." Anson added, "Our Mimi's an odd duck, and it's an eccentric lifestyle. But she's got some chap on the hook, maybe that'll settle her down, heh-heh."

"I'm entertaining some fairly influential ladies tomorrow evening, Anson. One of them is Mrs. Drake Warlock. You might know Shelby?"

"Sure, sure," blustered Budge. "She owns several chichi boutiques in Paris and Milan, places like that. I know Shelby."

Peter said, "The other young lady is a very hot model by the name of Zora. I thought your Mimi might like to meet her."

"What did you call the second one?"

"Zora."

"Oh, I thought you said Zorro. Well, Mimi just might go for it. I'll ask her when I catch up to her at the end of this godforsaken course. She's at least two tees ahead of me. And it looks like rain again.''

While Avalon waited for a return call, he folded his hands, made a church with a steeple, and pondered. He was in no hurry to see Zora, as long as Lily lay supine before him. He ordered another Dewars, some cheese and fruit. Lily had fallen asleep. Now only four sunbathers remained around the pool. There was Lily, and here was Peter, just three chaises apart. Across the pool two matronly women with frosted bobs and thick middles dozed contentedly. One had telltale bandages on her chin, around her earlobes. He didn't recognize her as a local, so she must be an import, hiding away in the boondocks, while traces of the cosmetic surgery healed. The smart ladies did that. Avalon turned his attention back to Lily.

Here lay perfection, and if he was not mistaken, here lay the perfect replacement for Zora. If only he could figure out a way to drop Zora. Zora was all wrong for Blue Poppy's ad campaign. On the other hand, this enchanting maiden, this Lily, embodied everything Blue Poppy stood for. Maybe it wasn't too late to dump Zora. An idea flirted with his brain cells, then the phone rang, jolting him.

''Hello, Mr. Avalon. It's Mimi Budge here. W-why, it's been s-simply years, hasn't it, since you last saw me.'' Avalon cringed. She stammered like the other Budge females. ''How are Colette and Claudine? I hear they're in Europe for the summer. Lucky ducks.''

Avalon cut right to business, cleverly exaggerating Zora's importance in the stellar ranks of fashion. He added, ''It's very hush-hush, mind you. Mustn't tell a soul. I thought maybe you'd like to join us for cocktails tomorrow evening here at the Raven?''

Mimi gushed, ''Gad, this is intense. A real supermodel in Fern, Washington. Should I bring along a portfolio, samples of my designs, fabric swatches, or would that be presumptuous?''

''Maybe a bit premature. Just bring yourself this time, then once Zora knows you socially, I might fix up a business meeting.''

''This is totally impressive. I'm ever so grateful, Mr. A.''

Smoothly, he said, ''I understand your sister...ah, Lily, isn't it?''

''What about Lily?'' A hostile edge to her voice.

''Why don't you bring her along? I know Cookie would love to see her.''

''Your wife's going, too?'' A trace of envy, or was it disdain?

''That's right. I know Cookie would enjoy seeing both of you.''

A small puncture to her balloon, but nothing fatal. Mimi Budge said, "Are we to dress?"

"Maybe dressy casual."

"You're speaking to a fashion designer, Mr. Avalon. Now, if I dress down, that is, as you say, 'dressy casual,' may I include a hat without offending anyone?"

"Oh yes, I love hats. Now, don't forget to invite your sister."

He heard Mimi's golf partners calling her to the greens. He rang off then, smiling to himself. Tomorrow couldn't come soon enough.

Minutes later, a telephone rang at poolside. Avalon watched Lily reach down with a languid arm and pluck the burring telephone out of her tote bag. He heard Lily's sweet unstammering voice say, "Count me in, sis." He bolted the Dewars, tucked the Perrier in his pocket to drink later, on the trip home.

Over at the bar, Darin mixed a cocktail and watched glumly as the Nose exited alone. Darin had lost the bet to himself. He heard a splash and a moment later, watched Lily's head and shoulders emerge from the shimmering turquoise water.

ON THE GOLF COURSE Mimi Budge chalked up a par 4 and then slipped into the ladies' locker room to shower and change. The elder Budge sister boasted thick auburn hair styled in a severe Dutch bob but otherwise possessed nondescript features—medium everything. In convent school, they'd dubbed her "Medium Mimi," just to set her off. Yes, it was true what they said about Medium Mimi, except for her splendid hair and fierce ambition. Mimi had copped early on to the realities of life, viz. beauty can be had through the art of trickery, and by age thirteen the Budge had learned all the tricks of the trade. To compensate for her mediumness, Mimi developed a studied flair, cloaking her blandness with artful costumes and eccentrically brazen cosmetic tricks. No one ever called her a fresh beauty, as so many called Lily, but they noticed her, and the subterfuge got her through the Sorbonne, and a few other strategic places. By twenty-six, Mimi had created a persona so engaging, so attention-getting, that beauty barely came up. In just five years, Mimi Budge had built a successful couture business, owned two boutiques in British Columbia and another one in Toronto, and had a runway show scheduled in New York next spring.

Lathering her hair, Mimi smiled at the thought of meeting Zora. The past couple days had drained her emotionally, starting the night before last when she'd quarreled with Jonathan. It began as a silly little row over the way Jonathan touched another woman's shoulder at a party. But the quarrel had escalated into one of those dreadful previolent things, and once again Jonathan had threatened to report Mimi to the authorities, whereupon Mimi deftly reminded Jonathan that secrets between fiancés ought to be held sacred, and Jonathan, in his supreme meekness, agreed. But he'd aroused her ire by bringing up uncomfortable subjects again, and when it was over, Jonathan left her condo with all his personal belongings and all his scientific equipment, leaving Mimi shrieking in the lonely darkness. The night from hell.

Now, after a great golf game and this Zora invitation, life's hue took on a rosier glow, and the Budge actually hummed in the shower. When the phone in her handbag rang, she heard it but chose to ignore it. Whoever it was could just wait until a more civilized moment. Ten minutes later, in the midst of her elaborate makeup routine, the phone rang again. This time, Mimi answered.

"This is Professor Robert Burke at the University of British Columbia in Vancouver." A grave tone, softly delivered. "I am trying to locate Miss Mimi Budge."

She remembered Burke. He was Jonathan's colleague, a bug man or something at UBC. She said, "This is she," and her voice echoed through the locker room.

Professor Burke coughed lightly. "I regret to inform you, Miss Budge, that Jonathan has been killed."

"What?" A flat, atonal voice.

"It happened this morning on the U.S. side, in a mountain meadow near Fern, Washington. The investigating officer reported that his body was found just after eight o'clock. Jonathan had been shot through the heart. It was instantaneous, thank God; he didn't suffer. I am sorry to be the bearer of such tragic news." Burke sounded distraught. "I've lost a close colleague," he added forlornly. "I share your grief."

"Oh." Mimi fumbled for a coherent thought. She hadn't expected this development.

Professor Burke broke the silence. "I realize that you must be very much in a state of shock, Miss Budge. If there is anything I can do...he hadn't any family, really, as you probably know."

"Yes, yes," said Mimi, trying to organize her brain. "But I can't really think straight just now..."

"I understand. Would you like me to go down and claim his body? They've taken him to Seattle for an autopsy. It's mandatory, of course, when a crime may have occurred. They don't seem to have any idea who killed him, or why."

"No. No, I'll go, Professor Burke. I'm already over on the American side. I'll go ahead by myself."

"The school will want to hold a memorial service. He was a respected member of faculty..."

"Yes, certainly. Oh, I really need to just sit down and think."

"I know. I think perhaps you should know that the United States federal authorities are conducting the investigation. I believe their Fish and Game unit, something like that, has jurisdiction over the land where they found him. I gather Jonathan was chasing butterflies on a wildlife preserve. Hardly reason to shoot a man. The officer in charge of the investigation, a Mr. Olson, will meet you in Seattle. He'll want to interview you. Are you sure I can't go along with you, just for moral support?"

Mimi sighed heavily. "That's quite all right. I might take my sister along. I...I'm really fine. Just please give me the Seattle address."

Alone in the locker room, Mimi slid to the cold tile floor. Gradually came silent sobs, then louder, more heartfelt sounds, that anyone passing by the locker room was certain to hear, and remember.

So it was over. No more Jonathan. No more horrid rows. Without warning, a nasty little voice whispered in Mimi Budge's ear: "What about tomorrow night? Are you still going tomorrow night?"

"Damn," Mimi blurted aloud. "Double damn." She stared blankly at her crouched image in the wall mirror. "It just wouldn't look right right now, would it?"

TWELVE

FISH MAN

AT THE Oxygen Bar, Venus ordered a MacKenzie's cream stout. She carried it out to a broad flagstone terrace that adjoined the lobby, overlooking the wilderness beaches and the Strait of Juan de Fuca. A fine mist fell, and she shivered slightly from the damp chill in the air. On the terrace were six wrought-iron tables and twenty-four chairs, all vacant. On each table was a tiny laminated card with the message, "In consideration of our natural environment, please limit your cell phone calls to three minutes." She chose the table closest to the beach, fished out her phone, dialed. Dottie answered.

"Olson's gone out," said Dottie cheerfully. "We're having a big celebration here."

"Celebrating what?"

"Olson's absence. He's in one of his darker moods today."

"Well, where is he? I need to speak with him."

"My, aren't we touchy today?" Dottie sniffed over the phone. Lately, Dottie had lost interest in her job. Maybe a personal problem. Maybe apathy generated by the federal budget cutbacks. None of them enjoyed working twice as hard to preserve endangered species only to feel Congress's political guillotine chop off their good intentions. Whatever caused the apathy, Dottie wouldn't say. Olson was an inch away from firing Dottie, and she didn't seem to care. Dottie said, "He's at the gym."

"You're joking."

"Negative. It's his new weight reduction regime. His personal trainer told him this morning that from now on he needs to go to the gym and work out instead of eat lunch. He's probably still there."

"What's the gym's number?"

"Gosh, I don't think he mentioned that."

"What gym?"

"I don't remember the name. He said it real fast like, when he left."

"Think, Dots." Exasperation.

Dottie thought a while, then, "Maybe I should ask around here. Maybe someone else knows."

"Good idea." While she waited for Dottie to come back, Venus nursed the stout. It felt good going down, frosty, full-bodied. She wasn't supposed to drink on duty, but stout is a food, she rationalized. Stout makes a nourishing lunch. Dottie came back and coughed into the phone.

"Sparks says it's Belltown Body Boys."

"Sounds terrific. You got the phone book there?"

"Somewhere." She could hear Dottie rummaging around her desk. This wasn't the Dottie she'd known and trusted, the Dottie who trained with her on the target range, in the forests. This new Dottie behaved like a helpless, hare-brained ditz. Dottie said, "Belltown, Belltown. Belltown Barber Shop, Belltown Cleaners, here it is...no, that's not it, Belltown Flicks...gotcha. Belltown Gym. Here's the number..."

Venus wrote the number down. Before she hung up, she said, "I thought you said the place was called Belltown Body Boys."

"Oh! Wait, let me double check."

"Forget it, Dots. My three minutes are almost up."

"What three minutes?"

"I'll find it myself. Now, listen, Dot. In case I miss Olson, tell him I need Song back up here. Got that?"

"Got it," said Dottie unconvincingly.

On the strait, a loaded cargo vessel pushed northwest toward Neah Bay and the Pacific. *Pandora.* She flew a Liberian flag. The vessel, Venus knew, carried paper pulp from the big mill in Port Angeles. Pulp made from trees felled in the Olympic Peninsula's rain forest. The pulp would be pressed in Japan, formed into sheets of paper, sold on rolls to publishing houses to produce fine coffee table books. Some of the pulp would end up as fancy wrapping papers or origami cranes. A lot of it would return to North America by ship and be sold in Canada and the United States. None of this made sense to her. But then, she wasn't an economist.

The receptionist at Belltown Body Boys couldn't interrupt Olson in the middle of his training session. Venus left a message. While she waited for him to call back, she walked down a steep flight of redwood steps to the beach. A typically gray Pacific Northwest beach, rocky, driftwood-strewn, with abundant green algae, seaweed, and kelp flung over the rocks, and a bracing breeze blowing in off the Pacific. There was a small boat launch, two ancient iron rails embedded into the ground, now caked with barnacles. No longer the ideal place to scoot your skiff into the waves. Unlike the ocean beaches a few miles to the west, the waves here didn't slam onto the beach, except when a bad storm blew in off the Pacific and down the strait. Here in the saltwater caverns off Raven Point lived a panoply of whales, porpoise, octopus, Dungeness crabs, sea urchins, and harbor seals; abundant sea life, threatened now by a human influx, shipping traffic, fishers and crabbers, and tourists. Like the three people now walking across the terrace, headed down to the beach toward the tideline.

A small wiry man, a fat woman, and a fat boy. The woman and boy wore sweat suits and wind parkas. The man, apparently the spouse and father in the trio, wore a wet suit and carried a pair of rubber fins that dwarfed him. The woman stood in attendance to the little man, his land wardrobe and a fluffy towel draped over her arm. The boy stood beside the woman, holding the man's hiking boots. Over the wind, the little man shouted some instructions at them, put on a snorkel and some goggles, and waded into the icy saltwater. The woman and boy shaded their eyes and watched their hero wade deeper, deeper into the frigid water. Up to his knees now, he attempted to don the flippers, but each time he leaned down, a wave came and bowled him over. He tried again and again and just when the boy had bowed his head in dismay, or disillusionment, the man succeeded in pulling on the flippers. Suddenly this was no longer a mere little man, husband and father. Here now was great Fish-Man, amphibious conqueror of the elements, as much lord of the sea as he was king of his castle in Edmonds, or Lynnwood, or maybe Bremerton. Fish-Man waved triumphantly to his disciples and dove under water just as Venus's phone rang.

"What do you want?" Olson barked.

"Working off the Frangos, chief?"

"I am not allowed to eat chocolate on this diet."

Fish-Man appeared, bobbing on the water's surface. The woman and boy waved excitedly and then Fish-Man went under again. Venus said, "I wanted to inform you of the situation here."

"I'm listening."

She told him about the baby eagle. Grimly, he said, "Those loggers again." She told him what Aggie said. Olson grunted. "Then maybe it warrants looking into. But please, do me a favor, Venus. Don't try tying this in with Willow's death. You'll only complicate things. Anyway, it can't be related."

"Why not?"

"It just doesn't seem related. But bring the individual in and we'll send it down to Ashland for necropsy. And by the way, I want you to go over to Victoria tomorrow morning. One of Willow's colleagues from UBC is coming over from Vancouver. He's going to meet you at the Victoria dock. He's expecting you on the first boat."

"Why?"

"His name's Burke. Robert Burke. He called the office a while ago, said he had just been notified about Willow's murder. Said he was Willow's friend, and he has something to give us."

"Hostile or friendly?"

"You know Canadians. Even if they're planning to slit your throat, they're polite. He was polite. I think he means well."

Venus sighed. "I was going to head back to Seattle this evening."

"Your plans have changed."

"I could always take the hydrofoil from Seattle..."

"Forget it. They're going to put you up at the National Park Service. The ranger's cottage on the way up to Hurricane Ridge?" He chuckled meanly. "Maybe you'll learn something from those Smokeys."

"Great. Just great." Sarcastic. She added, "Also, I may have come across a poaching operation."

"Poaching what?"

"Wildflowers. Maybe other things, too."

"For example?"

"I'm not ready to say just yet."

"Say."

"Lepidoptera. But before I say more, I need to hear Claudia's test results."

Olson said, "She left a message for you at the office. Dottie has it."

"I just spoke to Dots. She didn't mention a message from Claudia."

Olson snorted. "Par for the course. I think Paganelli's message said to call her ASAP. She's down in Ashland. At the lab."

Venus had turned her back on Fish-Man and his family. Now she said to Olson, "Willow wasn't alone in the meadow this morning."

"Of course not. His murderer was also there."

Venus said, "I mean, someone else who died this morning was probably in the meadow around the same time as Willow. The chef, Lux, might have gone to the preserve to harvest edible wildflowers and mushrooms and so forth. I found some sprigs of *V. adunca* in his kitchen. In this part of the peninsula, the only place you can still find them is on that preserve. He might have gone there to pick them. He might have witnessed the killing. Then he might have been murdered because he saw the killer."

Olson said dryly, "So you're suggesting that the same individual who shot Willow then fed poison to the inn's chef? And then, toss in the baby eagle business. Don't you find all that far-fetched?"

"Maybe I'm jumping to conclusions."

"On the other hand, I'm willing to cut you a little slack. If Needles's deputy found Willow's Isuzu parked at the inn, maybe he and the chef had some connection. Anything else?"

"I almost forgot," she said. "Here's another interesting tidbit. Guess who's this year's Miss Blue Poppy?"

Olson thought a minute, then said, "You."

"Very funny."

"Anyway, it's always a secret. You can't know who's Miss Blue Poppy until it's officially announced."

"I do. Your favorite pinup girl. Remember the little picture you showed me from *Playboy?* In the up-and-coming section? Zora. She's got it wrapped up."

"She'll sell product, that's for sure." Matter-of-fact. "Just out of curiosity, what color's her hair now?"

"Jet black."

"Ah." Satisfied now, Olson said, "What does this have to do with the Willow thing?"

"Nothing, I suppose. Just thought you'd like to know what's going on up here."

"You okay, Venus?"

"Sure. Why?"

Olson said, "I mean...especially now that...what with..."

Venus stared at her bare ring finger. "Word sure gets around fast," she muttered.

"Winters is a bloody fool if he lets you go," Olson declared hotly.

"Now, just hang in there. Do you want me to pull you off the investigation? Maybe you need a few days off."

"I'm fine." Swallowing the hard lump in her throat.

Olson said, "All right. I'll see you Monday morning. And don't be late to the office. We're being graced with Ebert first thing."

"The Grim Reaper."

"Like I said, don't be late." Olson hung up.

She called Ashland, asked for Claudia. Claudia had gone out to lunch, the receptionist said, so call back later because she didn't have time to take messages, she had other things to do.

The waves tossed something at Venus's feet. She crouched down, inspected it. A frilled dogwinkle, *Nucella lamellosa,* about three inches in length, orange, the color of orange marmalade, or a marmalade cat, its frills and spines strongly sculpted. Dogwinkles feed on barnacles. The dogwinkle has three teeth it uses to drill holes in the shells of barnacles, mussels, and other prey. The dogwinkle's role in Nature's grand scheme is to control the northern spread of mussels and the southern spread of the acorn barnacle. We all have a job to do, even the frilled dogwinkle.

Fish-Man emerged from the deep, tossed up by the waves head first onto the rocky beach. He crawled to his feet, raised his arms high over his head, clasped his hands together and bowed toward his little family, and bowed to the saltwater strait. He accepted a dry towel from his beloved, and the three joined hands and headed up to the spa.

Fish-Man and the woman were probably engaged once. Only, unlike Richard Winters, Fish-Man had probably gone through with it. Even if Fish-Man had broken off the engagement before the little boy came along, Fish-Man probably would never have done the dastardly deed by e-mail. Unlike Richard.

THIRTEEN

BLACK BALL

LIKE FERN, the city of Port Angeles faces Juan de Fuca strait. Like Fern, the Olympic Mountains occupy its backyard. Unlike Fern, Port Angeles is an international port, and has been for two hundred years. Shrouded in time-warped legends of salty British and Spanish sailors turned landlubbers, the old logging community had in the twentieth century metamorphosed into a thriving mill town and pulpwood producer.

There's a beach in the middle of town, called Hollywood Beach, but it has nothing to do with cinema. Twice daily, spring through fall, at the ferry dock adjacent to Hollywood Beach, you can board a ship ferry across the strait to Canada. The Black Ball Lines ship crosses in ninety minutes each way. The ferries dock at Victoria, the provincial capital of British Columbia. Canadian immigration at Victoria is no piece-of-cake border patrol; the officers are thorough, precise, and follow the rules. If you don't pass muster, they'll send you back where you came from and it goes on your record next time you try crossing.

The morning after Jonathan Willow's murder, Venus rose early at the park rangers' station and drove to Port Angeles. At the ferry dock, she bought a ticket for the *M.V. Coho* ferry. It sailed at eight a.m. She read her Swatch. Seven-fifty. She joined a long line of summer tourists in diverse vehicles. The ferry's signalman directed Venus to the parking deck. She parked the Harley, checked the lock on the gear box, and climbed three flights of steep iron stairs to an outdoor passenger deck.

The strait wore a rippling briny cloak that turned emerald when the *M.V. Coho* cut through a bounding surface into the icy fathoms. Overhead a cloudless sky promised smooth sailing. From the shady port side, Venus watched a school of porpoise hop the ship's broad wake and ride it, then dive, then hop the wake again. Sea collies herding the *M.V. Coho* across the briny meadow. The air out here on the strait held the single scent of saltwater. Nothing complex, nothing fancy, just pure unadulterated saltwater air, an eternally intoxicating perfume that natives like Venus thrived on and preferred above all others. Even Blue Poppy.

When the United States and Great Britain negotiated their boundary lines, the land on the south shores of the strait went to the U.S. By the time the territory was finally designated as Washington State, the Olympic Peninsula's timber camps had burgeoned into huge operations, shipping timber around the globe, making fortunes off the rich, abundant land. The American dream realized.

Aggie MacGregor's grandfather was one of those timber barons. More than a century earlier, Arlo MacGregor had brought a little bit of Scotland, including a wife and ten children, across the seas to settle in Pysht, a thriving timber camp on the rainy side of the Olympics. He soon ran the most prosperous timber camp in the territory, and left his family wealthy. His son, Aggie's father, Johnny MacGregor, married a Norwegian woman, and they produced one child, little Aggie, who was raised in the logging camps, home educated, and not at all like the rich girls down in Seattle.

Aggie's father invested his one-tenth MacGregor inheritance into a timber business of his own, and before long, Johnny MacGregor was the wealthiest man in Northwest Washington. When he died, Aggie MacGregor inherited the fortune and reportedly became the wealthiest person on the Olympic Peninsula. No one knew what she had done with her father's money, or if she had ever touched it.

As a child, Aggie played alone along the desolate beaches and up in the rain forests near her father's timber camp, but her favorite spot was what they now call Yodeler's meadow. Before that, according to county documents, the land had been just another virgin meadow that somehow had escaped the ravages of logging and development. It got its name back when Aggie was just a girl of five, when Aggie and her friend Sigrid played up in that meadow. The young girls frequently hiked to the very top of the meadow, up into the forest and above the waterfall, to the huge granite outcropping. There Aggie would stand facing the sunny side, and yodel into the valleys of the rain shadow. The old people who remembered it said the beautiful sound of little Aggie's yodel would fill the logging camps and the whole town of Fern. Some people said Aggie must have had a spot

of Swiss blood, she yodeled so well, but that just showed their ig-
norance. Norwegians can yodel.

The *M.V. Coho* tooted its horn. A fishing boat headed toward Port
Angeles had drifted too near the big ferry. The big belching horn
warned it off in good time, but the ferry listed slightly until it com-
pleted its cautionary swerving turn. Venus went inside the ship's
cabin, found the restaurant, ordered a cup of Murchie's Prince of
Wales blend, found an empty booth, slid into it, and drank the tea
until her phone rang.

"Venus," cried Bella, "where on Earth are you now?"

"In the Strait of Juan de Fuca. Canadian side. On the *M.V. Coho*.
What's up, Mother?"

"There's trouble brewing, and I need your help."

"What's the matter?" Venus felt a cold chill tickle the back of
her neck. Something in Bella's vocal arrangement rang dissonant. The
chimes didn't peal as richly as usual.

Bella said, "I am at home, snug as a bug, mind you, without a
care in the world. Timmy is here at my side. He and Stephen had
another small quarrel this morning. This makes two rows in two days.
I'm frantic."

"I heard about that. Timmy called Stephen a nerd again. Or something like that."

"No something about it. He said nerd and he meant nerd. Honestly,
sometimes Stephen is just plain oversensitive. After all, Timmy is just
a child. And coming from such a disadvantaged background, really,
Venus, what are we to expect? Now, I've asked Timmy to apologize
to Stephen—"

"Mother, pardon me, but we're docking in Victoria Harbour in
five minutes. Can you cut right to the point, or should I ring you
back?"

"Venus, you are not to cut me off. Now, I want you to speak with
Timmy. See if you can convince him to apologize to Stephen. Then
I wish to discuss another matter with you. Post haste."

"Okay. Put Timmy on. Then after I talk to him, I'll hang up. Then
I'll telephone you from the dock as soon as I clear immigration."

"Fine, dear. Are Auntie Jo and Uncle Rollo meeting you?"

"This isn't a social visit. I'm here on business."

"Have we run out of tea again?"

"Put Timmy on, Mother. Then I'll call you back." Venus started
down the ship's passage toward the stairs. People were heading down

the stairs toward their vehicles. Timmy came on, a hoarse, seething little voice.

"Hey, Tim," Venus said cheerfully. "How's my favorite little brother?"

"I'm not your little brother," snapped Timmy angrily. Venus could see the boy's face screwed up in one of his snarls. "I am adopted, and my last name is unknown. I only use Winsome-Diamond for convenience."

"What's wrong, Tim?" She thought he sounded particularly grumpy for a kid who stood to inherit a few jillion from his new stepmother.

"There is nothing wrong with me. I wish all of you would just leave me alone and let me concentrate on my project."

She was running down the stairs now. The ship sounded its signal to the harbormaster, and the harbor pilot pulled his tug alongside. They'd be docking any minute now, and she still had two decks to go. Into the phone she said, "You're working on a project? That's swell. What's it all about?"

"I am creating a new face cream."

"Oh, really?"

"Yes. And Mother won't permit me to use items from her cosmetics case. Things I need for my experiment."

"Hey, Tim," she said, "I need to ring off now. I'll call you right back."

Timmy snorted over the phone. "You're just like the rest of them. Adults simply don't care about anything important." She heard the old-fashioned phone receiver slam.

Fifteen minutes later, she'd cleared immigration and customs and emerged into the pale Victoria sunshine, squinting through a pair of Serengettis, looking for a professor type among the crowds greeting the ship. Her eyes focused on the ancient stone Parliament building, then the imposing copper-turreted Victorian landmark, the Empress Hotel. A flood of childhood memories engulfed her. The tortured silence at afternoon tea. Spotless white gloves, the family kilt, the Empress's, the heavy maroon velvet drapery and snooty butlers, the ladies with pinched noses sipping Queen's Choice brew, and the rotund jolly gentlemen snacking lustily on scones with lemon curd and whipped cream. And, too, she recalled the slogan so often whispered from Bella's authoritative lips, "Children should be seen and not heard." Those were dreary, disagreeable afternoons, but if Dagny and

Rex and Venus behaved, Bella and Father always rewarded them with a trip to Crystal Gardens, a swim in the Crystal's Olympic-sized pool, and later, fish and chips with vinegar, and a barley sugar candy.

Professor Robert Burke came forward tentatively, offered a slim cold hand. He had lively eyes and an amused drollness around the mouth. In one hand he held a tennis racquet and in the other, a rust-colored accordion file folder tucked up under his arm, the way a pelican tucks up its flight wings.

Burke led Venus across the street from the pier, left three blocks, right on a narrow, tidy cobblestone lane to a place called the Tea Stain. They found a table looking out on Government Street, Burke dropped about fifty sugar cubes into his tea cup, slurped the syrupy brew, and smacked his lips.

"This isn't easy," he said. "Jonathan was my friend. So this isn't easy."

He handed the rust accordion file across to Venus. She opened the accordion folds. There were twelve sections, each containing a neatly labeled file. Venus glanced up at Burke inquiringly.

Burke said, "Jonathan had apparently been working for the Blue Poppy Perfumery across in Fern. I didn't know that until yesterday morning, when I found this." He indicated the accordion file. "It's against university rules for faculty to accept outside employment. Jonathan was apparently working as a consultant for Blue Poppy. I shouldn't have peeked at the file, but a paper fell out, and then, well..."

Venus said, "Where'd you get it?"

"In his office. Jonathan kept a spiffy office. Shipshape, eh? He never even put pictures on the wall, just kept them plain painted surfaces, boring, if you ask me. He had a library, but he kept most of that at his home here in Victoria. He did all his paper work on a laptop. So it was just his desk, eh? His few desk necessities and one drawer. I found this in the drawer."

"Where's the laptop?"

Burke shrugged. "Don't know. He usually carried it with him everywhere he went. You didn't find it then, when you found him?"

Venus said no, and rifled the files. They had been arranged alphabetically, each of the twelve pockets neatly labeled:

Analysis
Breakdowns

Chemical Components
Financial Aspects
Floral
Herbal
Mineral Compositions
Pheromone Analysis
Pheromones—Comparative and Synthetic
Process: Harvest to Bottle
Roots, Berries and Other Specific Organic Material
Simple Synthetic Components
Spices

Venus pulled out the file labeled ANALYSIS. Inside was a single sheet of paper, a title page from a longer document, it seemed, titled "Blue Poppy Corporation." The document itself was missing.

Next, she pulled the CHEMICAL COMPONENTS FILE. Empty. She went through the entire accordion file, one section at a time. All the files were empty, except for the one cover sheet and under financial, a copy of an invoice Jonathan Willow had prepared for issue to the Blue Poppy Perfumery. The invoice was dated one week earlier, addressed to Peter Avalon in care of the perfumery in Fern. Willow stated on the invoice that he had performed one hundred seventy-eight hours of work, and billed Avalon at several hundred U.S. dollars for each hour. His return address was listed as his home address in Victoria. That was all.

Venus said, "What was Willow doing with a file titled MINERAL COMPOSITIONS?"

Burke shrugged. "Got me. Maybe he collected rocks. A lot of naturalists collect rocks as a hobby."

"You don't know what happened to that file?"

He shook his head. He said, "I didn't show this accordion folder to anyone at the university, eh? Didn't want to cause trouble for Willow, even though he's gone from us. I decided to contact the authorities, and the county sheriff across in Fern referred me to your office. A Mr. Olson asked me to meet you here at the dock with the files, so I came on the way to my tennis match. In fact, the game is about to start."

He said "a-boot" for about. He finished his tea, gave Venus his calling card, told her she could ring him any time, he'd be glad to cooperate. On the way out, Burke said, "Jonathan was a super chap, really. He just got mixed up with that girl, and she was hell bent on ruining him."

"Ms. Budge?"

Burke nodded. "Yes. Mimi Budge, the girl with pots of money and no ethics at all. Have a good day." He went away, twirling the tennis racquet. She watched him head back toward the Empress until he disappeared behind the grand hotel's Victorian stone facade. She ordered another cup of tea and punched in Bella's number. Some things were more pressing than others.

Burden, a recent addition to Bella's household staff, answered the phone. In his crisp British accent, Burden said, "Young Timmy is right here, Miss. If you will kindly speak to your mother when you have finished with the boy."

"Sure, Burden. Put Timmy on."

"I am not a beach ball," snapped Timmy, "to be tossed around from one adult to another."

"Hey, Tim, let's talk about the face cream experiment."

Timmy sniffed over the line, an eight-year-old snob who'd already suffered more heartache and trauma than any one lifetime should. In the few weeks Bella had been Timmy's legal parent, the boy had transformed from a bright but paranoid, finger-biting, terrified child into a fairly secure and cheerful boy with an overload of brain power and a hair-trigger temper that popped up on rare occasion but wreaked havoc whenever it did. The temper was how he dealt with the heartache of losing to violence all the adults in his life before Bella adopted him. You don't forget trauma. It grows up with you, it affects every stage of development. You have to devise mechanisms to cope. Timmy had devised an overactive distrust of adults-in-general, and a temper that flared as flamboyantly as a fandango dancer's skirts.

Timmy growled, "I do not want to discuss my experiment. I want to get on with it, and that means I need some stuff from Mother's cosmetics case. It's as simple as that."

Venus rubbed her jaw. "Okay. If you promise to be very kind to Mother, and to Burden...and Stephen, I'll coax the cosmetics your way."

Timmy thought it over. "All right," he said finally. "I promise. But this has probably been the most boring day of my life. Can't you come home now?"

"Pretty soon. Now, put Mother on, Tim. I'll see what I can do."

"Here I am," chimed Bella. "Now what is it?"

"Mother," said Venus cautiously, "I think I know what to do with Timmy."

"A good spanking would go a long way," retorted Bella. "Unfortunately, I am out of practice in that department, and anyway, I don't believe in spankings."

"I wish you would've decided that twenty-five years ago." Venus felt her backside. There was a small indent from an old bullet wound, but otherwise it was smooth and taut, and it retained the memory of Bella's deft open palm.

"Don't call up the past, Venus, unless you are prepared for a firm indictment against the five little Diamonds who—"

"Here's the thing, Mother." Venus steered Bella back to the present. "I'm on a job right now. I'm not in a position to negotiate this face cream deal. But if you will share some gooey things with Tim, I promise to replace them soon as I get back to Seattle."

Bella sniffed lightly. "My cosmetics case is not a toy."

Gad, Bella could be stubborn. Venus tried another tactic. "Okay, how's this for a deal? You send Timmy downtown with Burden. Let them scour the cosmetics department at Magnin's. I'll reimburse you for the whole works."

"Reimbursement is not the issue here," Bella retorted. "The issue is a child's feeble attempt at a power play. I have never let my children walk all over me, or my cosmetics case, and I don't plan to start at this late date."

Venus wiped her brow. Sweat had formed there. Before the malaria, she had never broken a real forehead sweat, except aerobically. Now, six months after the initial attack, the fevers struck intermittently, but often. More and more, she thought Bella might have something to do with the fevers. To Bella, she said, "Okay, Mother, I give up. You and Timmy will just have to solve this one without me. And in case you're interested, I'll be back in Seattle late tonight."

That brightened things up. Bella purred, "Oh, and lest I forget. The urgency in contacting you concerns your sister Echo. Echo is giving a reading of her poetry next week, in some beatnik parlor down in Pioneer Square. When I told Dagny that Echo was coming home for a few days, of course Dagny wanted to be here as well. And when I mentioned the reading, Dagny immediately made airline reservations. You know how Dagny always feels so left out of things."

Venus's older sister, Dagny, lived in Sherman Oaks with her steeplechase jockey husband and their brood. Venus couldn't keep count of the offspring. She said, "That's nice. What's so urgent about this?"

"Honestly, Venus, you have no sense of protocol. I believe those years in Third World countries have impaired your sense of priorities. There are arrangements to make. Echo will arrive sometime tonight, and then on Tuesday, Dagny is bringing John and the children. We shall have to make a house plan, who goes in what room, etc., etc. Then there is entertainment for the children to consider. Also, I have asked Rex and Bart to come home for the occasion. You know how much Echo's poetry means to them."

"Mother, stop, please. Listen very carefully. I work. I have responsibilities. These things take up my time. Unlike certain siblings, I do not sit at home popping out babies every other year—"

"Venus! I won't have you speaking like that about your sister. Dagny suffered terribly in her formative years, and the least we can do is thank God that she tossed off the remnants of grunge mysticism and settled down."

"With a steeplechase jockey," Venus added, studying the tips of her fingers.

"Never mind steeplechase. John is from excellent stock, and I might add redundantly, he is a prolific man."

Venus wiped some more sweat off her forehead. She had overstayed her welcome in the Tea Stain. She placed some coins on the table and moved outdoors into the lane. She despised portable conversations, and Bella wasn't in a hurry to ring off. Anyone but Bella would have been cut off long ago. Venus had never learned how to hang up on Bella. "All right, Mother," she said finally. "I'm going to hang up now. I hope you and Timmy work things out. I have to get back to work now—"

"You don't work, Venus. You dabble. You never worked a day in your life."

Bella often confused Venus with herself. She continued, "When you stop by Jo and Rollo's, give them my best regards. And tell them about Echo's poetry reading."

She hung up then, and Venus was sorely tempted to toss the digital phone into Victoria Harbour. Instead, she tucked it inside her jacket, went back to the Harley, and drove a mile and a half to the condo where Jonathan Willow reportedly had nurtured a stormy romance with Mimi Budge.

FOURTEEN

CHRYSALIS

NO ONE ANSWERED at the condo. Venus drove back into town, purred along Government Street. The Harley looked slick, a polished chariot, a postmodern Joan of Arc's off-duty wheels. She put on the Andrews Sisters full blast, sailed around the corner at Humboldt Street. On the sidewalk, three senior citizens saw the Harley, heard Venus crooning "Hearts of Stone," and applauded. She turned right on Douglas Street, drove one block, pulled over to the curb in front of the Crystal Garden.

In recent years, the Crystal Garden had replaced its famous Olympic-sized indoor swimming pool with a botanical garden, and while the gardens made a nice setting for afternoon tea, the absence of the swimming pool, in Venus's opinion, ruined the Garden. But memories still radiated from the ancient building.

It had two diving platforms, a low dive and a high dive. To reach the high dive, you had to climb two stories on a wood ladder and when you reached the platform, the pool below looked about a mile away, and you couldn't recognize the people in it. It was that high, that daunting, especially for a four-year-old.

One morning long ago, Venus, along with her older siblings Dagny and Rex, were breakfasting at the Empress Hotel, where the family was staying on holiday. Across the egg cups, Rex, age five, announced that today he would dive off the high platform at the Crystal Garden pool.

Venus idolized Rex. He was only a year older than she, and yet he could do all these cool things, like read books and construct ham radios, and now Rex was going to dive off the high platform.

At the breakfast table, Father had painted a perfect Humpty Dumpty face on her soft-boiled egg. The egg was slightly runny, so she added more than the usual amount of toast bits into the cup. You have to butter the toast bits first, then tear up the toast, otherwise the egg doesn't taste right. Besides the soft-boiled egg, she'd ordered a stack of hotcakes, like Rex, and two glasses of milk, like Rex. As Rex described how he planned to execute his first high dive, six-year-old Dagny, the eldest child, sniffed. "You'll probably die. Not that I wish you to die. But you probably will."

This suspicious cautionary comment only strengthened Rex's resolve to go for it. Dagny, who had determined to perfect her breast stroke over the holiday, buttered a scone, lathered blackberry preserves over it, and took a bite, when suddenly she was struck by a fit of giggles. So distracting were Dagny's giggles that Mother's left eyebrow, shaped every bit like Mount Kilimanjaro, shot up with deadly force, causing Dagny to choke. The entire dining room heard Dagny's ghastly choking sounds. Bella pretended to ignore the barking seal performance. Father, the cool, scientific-minded spaceship designer, took charge then, grabbing little Dagny in a perfect Heimlich. Bits of berry-stained scone projectiled from Dagny's mouth and struck an elderly gentleman at the next table. He wasn't a friendly neighbor, and venomously snapped his linen napkin at Dagny, which sent the extrasensitive child into fits of bawling.

Bella stepped in then, shooting a decent-sized sugar cube at the old man. He retaliated with one of his own, and war was declared. Father and Dagny never witnessed the battle, Father having compassionately removed the child from the scene. Rex, on Mother's side, pelted the old man's wife with bits of soft-boiled egg dipped in pancake syrup. The woman shot back a half glassful of grape juice, instantly staining Rex's little striped seersucker shirt, the one he despised. Upon witnessing this desecration, Bella assumed her most regal ire, stood straight and tall, walked over to the elderly woman and poured a Wedgwood pitcher full of cream down the lady's red silk dress. This, apparently, signaled other diners to join in, and the next thing Venus knew, the melee in the Empress's stately dining room swung into high gear.

Butter pats and ice chips flew, syrup poured like water over heads, tomato juice splattered on the flocked silk wallpaper, the burgundy velvet drapes wore eggs Benedict, tables flew over, spilling breakfast cuisine across the Kashmiri carpets. Venus absorbed all of this while finishing her soft-boiled egg with toast, then the short stack of hotcakes. Rex and Mother had disappeared into the fray, so Venus took herself upstairs to the family's suite, where Father and Dagny were watching Minnie Mouse cartoons. Venus went into the bathroom, changed into her green Jantzen bathing suit, slipped on her Keds, and left the suite unnoticed.

From the Empress Hotel to the Crystal Garden was only a short walk. Venus arrived just as the doors were opening for the day. She rented a towel, showered, and entered the swimming pool area. Only three or four swimmers occupied the huge body of water, swimming quietly, peacefully, the gentle lapping sounds echoing in the four-story-high chamber. Tepid steam wafted upwards from the heated pool as the late summer sun beat on the glass roof, warming the outdoors. No one noticed Venus enter the pool area, and the lifeguard hadn't yet come on duty.

Venus walked over to the wood ladder, placed a bare foot on the first rung, and started climbing. When she reached the first platform, she paused just long enough to verify that no one was watching. Children under ten were not allowed on the high dive. She climbed and climbed, until the world beneath her shrank to irrelevance, except for the tiny body of water shimmering below. When at last she reached the thirty-foot mark, two stories off ground zero, Venus paused to pull on her Speedo swimming cap, then stepped out onto the diving board.

She knew how to dive. She swam like a fish. She could do this. Raising her arms high over her head, she formed her hands into a perfect aerodynamic nose, just how Father had shown her. She curved her abdomen, bent her knees. Push. The diving board sprang, sending its cargo up, up into the steam clouds, sailing through the air. "I've done it," she told herself proudly. "Now, for the landing."

She couldn't recall the next few seconds, she'd blocked them from her memory, but the actual landing would be indelibly burned into her abdomen, for she made a critical error in timing and landed belly down on the water's hard surface. A perfectly executed belly flop.

Never mind. She'd done the high dive, and could prove it to Rex. Her aching, burning, purple abdomen bore the proof. Most of all, Venus wanted Father to know that she had conquered the Crystal Garden high dive. When she told him, Father didn't admonish her. Father blew on her little lobster belly, soothing it. Even today, she could remember his breath on her belly. Because it soothed her, and because it was his last living breath. When he clutched his chest and fell to the carpet, she couldn't get him to breathe again. She ran for help. Half an hour later, Father was pronounced dead. Two months later, Bella gave birth to the twins, Bart and Echo.

MIMI BUDGE'S tony Chrysalis Boutique was across the street from the Crystal Garden. The shop door was locked, but Venus could see a shadowy figure in the depths. She buzzed. A young woman came to the door, peered out. She had snappy hazel eyes, thick sorrel hair caught up in a snood, a mountain of sterling silver jewelry around her neck, and a bad case of anorexia over which she'd draped a skinny black tube dress that covered London and France just barely. She unlocked the door and let Venus in. She moved like a caterpillar across the pickled white hardwood floors, her chunky platform shoes advertising each step with a dull thud rivaling King Kong. If she swayed any harder, she'd probably break at midriff. Her name was Cleo, she had two boyfriends, both golf pros, and a glorious future as Mimi Budge's personal assistant. Any day now, Cleo informed Venus on their trek across pickled terrain, Mimi's Chrysalis collection would explode upon Parisian runways and in a single chic wink, transform the very definition of haute couture. Cleo truly believed this, and she held up a set of vamped fingernails to show how long this all would take.

Venus said, "Months or years?"

"Months, of course. Mimi's on the very precipice of superstardom."

Cleo left Venus near a clutch of gowned mannequins and went off to answer a telephone. While she was gone, Venus studied Budge couture. The Budge had a flair for gossamer, pure silk tulle, wispy, floaty, innocently sexy wood nymph gowns in bright pastels, iridescent yellow, dewy blues, seafoam greens. Mimi's signature papillon, brushfoot and monarch designs, sported huge gossamer wings set between the shoulder blades. The mannequins wore wire headpieces designed to mimic butterfly antennae, golden stems tipped with little knobs, so that no one would mistake these painted ladies for mere moths. There was a *Parnassius phoebus,* a *Polygonia interrogationis,* a *Nymphalis antiopa,* even a west coast lady. Mimi Budge knew her butterflies.

Cleo came back. "That was Jerome," she explained. "The hole-in-oner. Now, what may I show you?"

"I wasn't interested in a gown." Slightly apologetic.

Cleo knitted her brows. "Oh, oh, I see. Did you just wish to borrow the W.C.?"

Venus leaned casually against a glass display case full of golden antennae. "Actually," she said casually, "I'd hoped to see Ms. Budge. Is she in?"

Cleo frowned. "If you're another one of those butterfly collectors wanting to see Mimi's collection, you can't. For one thing, Mimi isn't in the shop today, and I'm not authorized to show it. For another thing, she never shows that collection to her rivals."

"Rivals?"

"Other butterfly collectors. That's what you are, aren't you?"

"Who does she show it to?"

Cleo parted her wide lips, showed off a mouthful of dazzling teeth, said, "Like, when a client wishes to mimic a particularly rare species. Then Mimi will bring out the collection so that the client can be sure what she's ordering. It's a brilliant concept, don't you agree?"

Venus nodded. Anything to please Cleo. This was going to be tougher than she'd expected. "How about if I ordered a gown? Could you show it to me then?"

Cleo brightened. "Oh. In that case, I'm pretty certain Mimi wouldn't mind my showing you the collection. What sort of gown did you have in mind?" She thrust a hand out suddenly. "Stop. Don't say it. Let me guess. Yes, that's it. A wedding gown. Am I right or what?"

Better let Cleo be right. Venus said, "Uh, sure, that's it. Wedding gown."

Cleo clapped her hands. "This is going to be such fun. You're so, well, so petite. Just like a little wood nymph. Oh, we're going to have such fun putting you together. Now, first things first. When is the wedding?"

"Er, this coming autumn. It's an autumn wedding."

Cleo led Venus to the triptych mirrors. "That's going to be tough," she said. "I mean, you really need to order your gown at least a year or two in advance." She winked at Venus. "One of these quickies, eh?"

"Right. Quickie."

"Early autumn or late autumn? God, I do hope it's late autumn."

"Late autumn."

"How late?"

Venus ran her hand across her mouth. "Pretty late. Say, like, uh, December. December thirty-first."

"Why, that's winter already," remarked the bright Cleo. "That changes everything." She shook her head, trying to rid it of all the autumn colors and flora and fauna. "Now, let's think cool, floaty winter. Snowflakes. Sugar plum fairies. That sort of theme."

"No butterflies?"

Cleo made a perfect Martha Stewart face. "Silly. Butterflies don't come round in wintertime. They're all sleeping then, or doing something besides fluttering about in the meadows. But now, you see, this is perfect. I have my own designs which I created based on *The Nutcracker*. Very Russian princessy. So this is perfect for me."

Venus argued. "Some species winter over in their butterfly stage. Like, mourning cloaks and question marks, for example. You can see them sometimes in the snow, these bright yellow and black..."

Cleo pouted. "But this really works for me, this *Nutcracker* theme."

Cleo placed the tip of her index finger between Venus's eyebrows, a bull's eye to the sacred spot. "Right here," said Cleo, "is where the last pearl teardrop will fall from your veil. I do hope you won't make the mistake of choosing high heels. The ballerina slipper is the perfect choice. Oh, sweetie, your fiancé is going to melt when he sees you coming up the aisle. Or is it down the aisle?"

"Up first. Then down."

"Is your father giving you away?"

"No."

"Who, then?"

Pause, then, "My brother, Rex. He's just a year older than I."

Cleo put a hand to her mouth. "Omigosh. I completely forgot to ask your name. Tell me."

"Venus."

"Your last name is..."

"Song. No, I mean Stillwater, that is, Sweetwater. Sweetwater's it."

Cleo shook her head. Something rattled in there that didn't belong. Venus hastened to cover up her clumsy faux pas. "See, my fiancé's last name is Song. And I'm a Sweetwater."

"Who's Stillwater?"

Venus smiled weakly, pointed at her tongue. "It gets all twisted these days, what with the wedding bells."

Cleo looked doubtful.

Venus added, "And the drugs. I mean, prescription drugs. It's all making me so crazy, my doc gave me some Prozac, then a little Valium to sleep, and some Xanax for anxiety."

Cleo nodded knowingly, fetched a yellow tape measure, and began taking measurements. When she was down to the wrists, she said, "I know what you mean. I'm on Prozac, forty milligrams, and then you add in the Trazedone to help me sleep because the Prozac keeps me awake, and then you're talking twisted tongue. But Prozac is fabulous, though, don't you think?"

"Brilliant." Venus wiped sweat drops off her brow. Better speak only when absolutely necessary, let Cleo do all the talking. Somehow, she had to convince Cleo to bring out the butterfly collection. She was pondering this when Cleo, who now was entering all her information into a laptop computer, said, "What's your home address, darling?"

Venus gave Bella's address, but used the name Sweetwater.

Cleo said, "Seattle, eh? We have many clients from Seattle. In fact, we have a very famous client there, whose address is similar to yours. I can't mention her name. Our client list is strictly confidential. But I am allowed to say that the lady is a film actress and she has the most gorgeous pair of legs I have ever seen on anyone, including a mannequin. In fact, she's famous for her legs. They're insured by Lloyd's of London, and they should be."

Bella.

Cleo said, "Phone number?"

Venus gave Louie Song's home number.

Cleo set the laptop aside, placed one hand palm down on her knee, and with the other hand picked up a book of fabric swatches. "Now, let's talk about colors, shall we? Keeping within the winter pastel range, of course." She began leafing through the winter pastels. "You're going pure winter white, aren't you?"

"Actually, I'd prefer—"

"Perfect. Winter white for the bridal gown. Now, what about the attendants? Maid of Honor? Bridesmaids? Flower girls? We can fill in the penguin suits later." She was going full tilt now, adrenaline charged, ready to close the sale, after just a few more details.

Venus said, "Just one attendant. Maid of Honor."

"Small wedding, eh? Well, that's all right. We've done one or two small events. What color is her hair?"

"Whose hair?"

"The Maid of Honor. We need to know her hair color in order to select the color of her gown."

Venus scratched her upper lip. It always itched when she lied. "It's, ah, well, it's sort of..."

"Red? Brown? Black? Blond?" Impatient.

"Jet black. It's jet black."

Cleo nodded. "So black that it's blue?"

"Right. Black, with a blue sheen."

Cleo inhaled deeply, let out the air slowly. She chewed her lips thoughtfully. "Her skin color. What's her skin color?"

Gad, thought Venus, this might go on forever. "Pale white. Almost Casper white."

"Casper white?

"The ghost. White as a ghost."

Cleo grimaced. "This is going to be very, very difficult. We really oughtn't do pastels on this girl. Of course, I'll need to see her in person before any final judgment can be fixed."

"She's not really the pastel type," Venus explained, thinking on her feet. "More the iridescent midtones."

"Midtones?" Cleo seemed confused.

"Like, rich iridescent blues, or golden. She looks great in orangey gold. In fact, I was really surprised how fabulous she looked the other night. She was wearing this iridescent floaty thing..."

Lesson One in the Psychology of Information Extraction: Always mimic the other person's behavior.

Cleo smiled. "Of course. She's a Puget blue. Or, or..."

"A silverspot. A Dungeness silverspot. That shade of orangy gold."

Cleo snapped her fingers. "That's it. You know, I do believe you are correct." She stood, smoothed her skinny black tube dress. "Let me go fetch that collection," she said, inspired now, "and we'll have a look at the Puget Blue and the Dungeness."

While she was gone, Venus stared at her naked ring finger.

Cleo returned, hauling a black portfolio case the size of Winnipeg. "Ooof," she said. "This thing weighs a ton."

"I'll help you." Venus gripped the portfolio. As she helped Cleo place the portfolio on a sturdy cutting table, her fingers not more than three inches from the case's zipper, Cleo suddenly snatched it away.

"Oh dash it all," she exclaimed. "I just can't do this. I don't have

Mimi's permission. I mean, she's very close to these specimens, they're like her children. I really shouldn't..." Cleo took off with the butterfly collection, oofing back into the depths where she found it.

"Don't worry, though," she called over her shoulder. "I know what your wedding gown should look like. I'll take care of everything. Oh dash it all, there goes the telephone again...."

FIFTEEN

ROMEO, ROMEO

TRANSLATED FROM the Latin, *lepidoptera* means "scaly wings." Moths, skippers, and butterflies belong to the order of ledidoptera. Butterfly wings are actually clear, but covered with thousands of colorful, light, reflective scales, one hundred and twenty-five thousand scales per square inch. A fresh butterfly, just emerging from its pupa, or chrysalis, has a perfect set of scales. If you touch a butterfly's wing, the scales will rub off on your fingers, cling to body oils. They wash or wipe off easily.

During basking, a butterfly's scales absorb sun rays, providing energy for flight. The patterns formed by the scales ward off predators. And, too, butterflies' wings contain ultraviolet colorations, which humans can't detect, but are seen by the butterfly's talented eye. The ability to see ultraviolet colors allows the butterfly to zero in on nectar plants and to choose a compatible mate. Routine flight causes a butterfly's scales to peel off. If you see a tattered specimen, you can be fairly certain the butterfly is already a senior citizen.

"The thing is," said Claudia, "you were right. That iridescent dust on his fingers came from *Speyeria zerene dungenessii*. The Dungeness silverspot. How in God's name did you know that?"

"I'm one of those weird lepidopterists, remember?"

Venus cradled the phone between her shoulder and chin, sat down in Yodeler's wide apron near a spray of wild violets, facing the beach. Beside her, on a white paper napkin, she spread out a McDonald's fish sandwich, a small order of french fries, and a medium Diet Coke. She took a bite of the fish sandwich. It tasted like every other fish sandwich from McDonald's.

Claudia sniffed. "All I can say is, you hit it right on the button. I can't believe it. That species has been declared extinct."

"Just goes to show you."

"Show me what?"

"Humans make mistakes."

Claudia said, "I sent the hard copy up with Louie. And those samples you overnighted? I'm working on those now. You think the chef's death is related to the other one?"

"Don't know. Your test results will help me decide."

Claudia said, "Well, those results are going to take a few days. Especially narrowing down the toxin. I'll keep you posted. Louie hasn't turned up yet, huh?"

"Song? No. Not yet."

Softly, Claudia said, "Hey, Venus, I'm sorry about you and Richard."

"Thanks, Claud. I'm not ready to talk about it."

After Claudia hung up, Venus watched a cargo ship plow through the strait on its way to the Pacific. More sturdy old disciples of the forest gone to ground, felled spirits, like herself. For a minute, she wished she was on that cargo ship, until she remembered it was probably heading for Asia. Even Asia—especially Asia—held memories of Richard, just weeks ago, in Singapore.

She was sitting on a rattan chair in the garden at Raffles, basking in Singapore's sunshine. Timmy was there, too, splashing in the swimming pool. It was Saturday, in Singapore anyway. Richard had just kissed her. First kiss. She was still swooning from the kiss when a waiter came over, handed her a telephone. It was Wexler, from Washington, D.C. Wexler explained his rude interruption. She could barely concentrate on Wexler's words, but later on she remembered the chief had said something about corporate sponsorship, and something about land sales. That was the first time she'd heard Ebert's name.

Ebert, DOI's land broker. The Grim Reaper. Wexler sounded worried, she remembered that. And insistent that she return to the States. As Wexler droned on across the Milky Way, he couldn't know that right then she was making out with the man of her dreams. Wexler couldn't possibly have planned to ruin that special moment, when Richard, still embracing her, raised his hand, took the phone away, ditched it, and led her into Raffles' orchid garden.

Wexler thought she'd hung up on him, and later on she had to explain that Richard actually hung up the phone, because Richard had something more pressing on his mind than Wexler, or Ebert, or corporate sponsorships of national parks, whatever that meant, and land sales. Richard found a private spot in the orchid garden, kissed her again, longer this time, said, "This is forever, Venus," and slipped the Alhambra Teardrop on her finger.

That was its name, the Alhambra Teardrop, the famous Moorish diamond. Of course, she returned it immediately. Too soon. Richard's divorce had barely been finalized. She didn't want him doing anything on the rebound. And she was terrified of the idea of commitment. So they had waited, what? They'd waited a full month before making the engagement official. Gad, what a month.

Richard taught Venus how to eat vegetarian without gagging. How to create her own Web site. He gave her flying lessons, and on their first aerial kiss, he gave her a gold charm bracelet, with a gold biplane charm. Since then, he'd added other charms, all from Gunderson's, the most discreet jeweler in Seattle. Bella's jeweler. There was the Neptune charm, to celebrate a particularly cozy ferry boat ride. There was the golden bear with diamond eyes, and the pelican charm, to celebrate the arrival of migrating brown pelicans on the Washington coast. There was the charm bracelet, yes, but most of all, there was Richard's kind heart, his gentleness, his fine moral character. Then, too, there was a certain chemistry between them. Magnetic pheromones, powerful as Super Glue. They'd known each other less than six weeks when they became officially engaged. Now that she thought about it, she hardly knew Richard Winters.

Venus felt her face. It felt hot. Richard might be joking about meeting someone else. He had that prankster element. Was the e-mail a big joke?

She glanced down at the fish sandwich. Her stomach churned sourly. Someone had once told her that McDonald's fish sandwich is the fattiest item on the menu. Now the cold, congealing french fries disgusted her, the fish reeked. She drank some Diet Coke and her stomach felt better, but still queasy. No, it wasn't a gag. Richard would never joke about their relationship.

Had she done something wrong before he went to Stockholm? They hadn't quarreled, hadn't even snapped at each other. Richard had wanted her to go along, but she'd declined the invitation, or rather, Olson declined it for her. So she sends him off alone, and look what happens. He meets somebody else.

A deep shadow fell across the McDonald's picnic, across the sun itself, plunging her into murkiness. Somehow it felt right. The sun had been too bright, too cheerful. She looked up. Louie Song, Ray

Bans and all, blocked the sunlight as he dropped down on the grass beside her. Without speaking, he reached out an arm, hugged her. "Go ahead," he said, "let it out."

"I'm alright," she lied.

He ruffled her hair and pulled her closer. "I know," he said gently.

"I'm really okay, Song," she insisted. But she didn't push away. She buried her face in his chest.

Half an hour later, they were walking along the shoulder of Highway 101, heading for the Harley, when Song opened his palm, said, "Got the key?" Puzzled, she handed him the key to the Harley. He straddled the bike, revved it up, turned it around, and said, "Better get your stuff out of the gear box. The Alfa Romeo's down around that curve. Want a ride there?"

Then it all came back. In the throes of heartbreak she'd forgotten about the trade. Not exactly a trade. She'd sold the Harley to Song. She'd bought a new Alfa Romeo from Song's dad, a car dealer. Today was Saturday, trade-in day. Just when she needed her familiar companion, she was losing it.

Why had she decided to sell the Harley? Something about Richard. Richard asked her to give up the bike because he worried about her safety. The day they became officially engaged, she'd sold the bike to Song, who had coveted it for years. Now, she'd lost Richard and the bike.

"Thanks, no." She unloaded her gear, carefully repackaging the caterpillar cocoon, leaving the dead baby bald eagle for Song to ship to the lab in Ashland. "I'll walk."

The silver Spider had a black leather top, black leather interior. A curly maple dashboard, all the bells and whistles. She slid into the dark cradle, adjusted the seat to accommodate her short legs, raised it slightly for better visibility. The top was down, and she liked it that way. In the gear she'd pulled from the bike's bag, she had a few CDs. She found Sibelius, *The Lemminkäinen Suite, Op. 22,* popped it in the CD player. The Kalevala's hero sprang to life on the orchestra's chromatic trembling.

"Then the lively Lemminkäinen
Guided to the isle the vessel
To the island's ends he drove it
Where it ends in jutting headland."

And the maidens of the island all came forth to gasp longingly over the hero's "comely brows." Some heroes are lucky in love. Then again, some suffer miserably.

She adjusted the rearview mirrors, double-checked the controls, and slid off the road's shoulder onto Highway 101. The Spider hugged the road. In the driver's seat, she felt total comfort, total control.

"There comes a time when a Harley head needs a change, however temporarily, to a different mode of transport." Spoken by Richard, pre-e-mail. She'd chosen an Alfa Romeo. Why? A Spider was useless on back roads, in mountain snowdrifts. Forget tire chains. This baby was built to be coddled, protected from the elements, except rain, of course. It would have to tolerate rain. Now, with Richard out of the picture, the little jewel of a sports car might not be good for much. On the other hand, she mused, it might help salve a wounded heart. Now she remembered why she'd chosen the Spider. It had that je ne sais quoi. Character, personality. Cool on wheels.

Turning onto the highway, she let Song pass her, and when he was out of sight, she tried smiling. The corners of her mouth actually curved. On the steering wheel, her ring finger tingled. She might live after all.

Song was waiting at Agate Beach, halfway to Raven Point. He looked good on the bike, like he belonged there. She pulled off the highway, turned off the Spider's purring engine, got out. Song said, "Let's get our act together, before we show up at Raven Point." She followed him down to the beach, and they began walking along the tideline. They both possessed that habitual Pacific Northwest beachcomber's habit of holding their eyes downcast, in case Neptune tossed up some spectacular shell, or stone, or bottle with a message in it. Besides agates, this beach had white quartz rocks, peridotite, granite rocks embedded with fool's gold and fool's silver, and smooth mudstones with rings around them. Over the years, Venus had collected scores of fine specimens. There was the flat taupe rock shaped like a Chinese perfume bottle, with thin black veins like a calligraphy drawing. There was the monkey face gabbro, the fossilized clamshell, and then, too, the agates. There were more rocks in her collection, and all of them came from Olympic Peninsula beaches.

Song said, "Olson wants you back in Seattle."

"Why?" She kept her eyes downcast, her voice steady.

"He thinks you haven't been back from Asia long enough. He

said he's noticed erratic behavior. He thinks your malaria may have caused some brain damage; that you need a rest."

"Now tell me the truth."

Song put an arm around her. "The Richard thing. Olson thinks you're probably too strung out to handle the situation up here. Anyway, it's a fairly straightforward case, as we see it. But the point is, you need some time off."

"Who's 'we'?"

Song jabbed a finger at his chest. "I guess just myself. Olson thinks I can handle this one alone. It would be my first solo case—"

"Forget it, Louie," she broke in. "This is my case. And it isn't as simple as you think." A little too harsh, too defensive. She added, "Still, I could use help. Can you live with that?"

Behind the Ray Bans, Song squinted. He stopped walking, stooped over, focused on something at the tideline. "Look," he said. Venus stooped beside him, inspected the stone. A small yellow nugget. Song plucked it off the beach, held it close to the Ray Bans. "It's gold," he said. "Real gold." He looked at her.

Venus laughed. "Well, prospector, what about it? You going to help me out up here?"

Song flicked the nugget at the incoming tide. It broke the water's surface soundlessly and disappeared. He said, "Okay, I'm yours. But if I notice anything funny about your emotional state, I'm calling Olson."

Venus turned around, headed back up the beach toward the Spider. She didn't have to look back. She knew Song followed.

TWO HOURS LATER, at six o'clock, Song entered the Inn at Raven Point, sauntered up to the reception desk where Beatrice Yamada stood waiting for something to do. Song had on his favorite black leather jacket, a nice pair of blue denims, and the Ray Bans. He had "Mr. Mysterious" broadcast across his persona, a little too exaggerated for Venus's tastes. Beatrice noticed him right away, felt her heart stop momentarily, her breath catch. When she could finally speak, she said, "Good evening, sir. Are you just checking in?"

Song, in perfect character, nodded and gave his name. Beatrice couldn't find it in the computer. She desperately wanted to find it, but it wasn't there. After much delving, Beatrice explained that no reservation had Song's name on it. Song scowled, pursed his lips. "That's funny," he said to Beatrice. "I could swear my secretary called in a reservation last week. Is, ah, is Mr. Price available? I'm sure Mr. Price could smooth things out."

Beatrice's eye widened. "Oh. You know Mr. Price?"

Song smiled, half nodded.

"Well, in that case," said Beatrice efficiently, "I can certainly locate a suite for you."

Song leaned over the counter, close enough to inhale a whiff of Beatrice's perfume. Nice, he thought. Very nice. He hadn't counted on that. He said, "Don't you want to check with Mr. Price first?"

Bea waved a hand. "Oh, he went home hours ago. He's very punctual about quitting time. Now, here's a very pleasant space. The King Salmon Suite. I think you'll like it." They exchanged the necessary information, and Beatrice handed Song the suite's key. "I guess you know how to swipe these things?"

Song nodded.

Bea said, "I'll have the bell captain take up your luggage."

Song grinned and shook his head. Bea desperately wanted to see behind the Ray Bans. Song said, "Thanks, I can manage it myself. Just a little briefcase and an overnight bag."

Beatrice flushed for no reason at all. "Would you like someone to show you to your suite, Mr. Song?"

"That would be lovely." Song.

Bea flubbed around on the phone for a few minutes, then apologized. "Nobody's available right now. I suppose I could take you to your suite."

Song smiled, showing his teeth. "That's very kind of you, Miss…"

"Yamada." She came swiftly around the counter. "Beatrice Yamada. We don't wear nameplates anymore. It isn't safe. Just follow me, if you please, Mr. Song."

Venus glanced up from her chair in the Oxygen Bar and watched the pair step into the elevator. Song held the door for Bea.

SIXTEEN

INSTAR

The larval stage of *Speyeria zerene dungenessii* passes through six instars, or periods between skin molts, before developing its pupa, or chrysalis, wherein metamorphosis occurs.

—*Oxford Lepidoptera Encyclopedia*

ON MIDSUMMER night's eve, which also happened to be two days after Jonathan Willow's mysterious death in Yodeler's meadow, not everybody was in mourning. Conrad Avalon, for instance, was dining at the posh restaurant Canlis, in a party of seven which included a salmon magnate, two Russian ballerinas, the Drake brothers (shipping scions), and that divine British diva, Lady Bella Winsome-Diamond. Somewhere between the shrimp Louie and chateaubriand, Lady Bella leaned across the table and whispered to Conrad, "How's your love life, Connie?"

Conrad flushed crimson. Did Lady Bella know his little secret? But no, that was impossible. The actress merely wished to encourage conversation. Conrad put on an innocent face and said, "No love life to report, thank you very much."

Bella smiled wryly. "Why it's ever so obvious, Connie, dear. Love is engraved on your countenance. Now, I'm not one of those gossipy old hens, so do tell. Who is the fortunate lady?"

Conrad actually felt a bit relieved. He hadn't shared his secret with another soul. Even the object of his affections had no idea that Conrad was preparing to launch a fervid courtship. It might feel rather comforting to share his secret with the ever discreet Lady Bella. At this point, Conrad fished out the little gift box. "Promise not to tell a soul," he murmured, handing the box under the table to Bella. He leaned in close then and whispered the name of his beloved in Bella's ears.

Bella's smoldering Wedgewood eyes sparkled. "You don't mean it, Connie!" she exclaimed in a whisper. "Why, I've always thought you two were a natural." Opening the little jewelry box, Bella smiled. "A charming piece, Connie. Charming." What she really thought was that the blue poppy brooch was a garish, ostentatious eyesore, the sort of piece no true lady would pin on under any circumstances. But Bella made it a life rule never to interfere in matters of the heart. Conrad was her bosom pal, still, Bella never offered advice to the love struck. Too messy.

It was after the figs *en creme* and just before the Grand Marnier, when Conrad again spoke to Bella. "If you have a moment or two after dinner," said Conrad, "I have a tiny problem I'd like to discuss with you."

When the party had dissolved into Seattle's dribbling darkness, Conrad ordered more Grand Marnier and showed Bella the threatening note. Bella's flawlessly arched eyebrows shot up when she read the message.

The caterpillar of *Papilio cresphontes,* the giant swallowtail, resembles a bird dropping. This clever disguise protects the caterpillar from being eaten by birds. *Papilio cresphontes* has a fierce-looking dragon's head with two glittering false eyes and a wide, grim, white mouth. If the caterpillar is startled, it ejects two bright red antennae which emit an odor that repulses a predator. Bella possessed a similar talent, a set of detection antennae which popped out instantly upon sensing danger. Bella's antennae had no discernible odor and were invisible, but when her antennae ejected, her state of alertness resembled the *Papilio* around the dragon eyes and mouth.

"Why, Connie," she exclaimed, "this wasn't meant for you at all."

"It has my name on it. And it mentions Yodeler Preserve."

Bella nodded thoughtfully and said, "That's exactly why I believe this note was meant for another member of your family."

"You think it was meant for one of my nephews?" Bella nodded. "But how did it end up in my trouser pocket?"

"Connie, I want you to tell me everywhere you've been in those trousers recently."

"That's easy. I just retrieved them from the dry cleaner two days ago. The first time I put them on was yesterday."

"Very well then, please proceed."

"Let's see," said Conrad. "I brought the trousers from Fern to Seattle in the dry cleaner's plastic garment bag. Hung them up in a closet at the WAC."

"Which suite?"

"Pioneer."

Bella nodded. "Proceed."

"Yesterday morning, I put them on—"

"Did you check the pockets?"

Conrad scowled. "Of course not. I may be obsessively tidy, but I don't do pocket checks." Bella nodded, and Conrad continued. "I went down to breakfast and back again to my suite, then out to Gunderson's. That is where I found the note, when it fell out of my trouser pocket in Gunderson's showroom."

Bella's slim fingers paced back and forth across her strong chin. The antennae buzzed, crackled. Finally, she said, "How many dry cleaners are there in Fern?"

"Just one. That's all we need. Just Singh's Dry Cleaners."

Bella snapped her fingers. "I've got it."

Conrad sat forward. "Oh, do tell."

Bella patted Conrad's flushed cheek. "Someone's trying to protect that meadow."

Conrad looked puzzled, so Bella elaborated. "You just finished telling me, over the figs, I recall, that your nephews are trying to purchase that meadow. Whoever wrote the note is opposed to the sale. The note clearly warns a certain Avalon to keep hands off the meadow. The public knows you've always disapproved of poppies being cultivated in Yodeler's meadow, that your nephews cooked up that land lease. The note probably wasn't meant for you. It was meant for your nephew Peter."

"But...well, why not Troy?"

Bella's mouth curved into a tiny smile. "Because Peter is the king-pin here. He would be the logical target. And because, Connie, Troy is much shorter than you. Peter, on the other hand, inherited your height and build. Someone placed that note in your trousers at the dry cleaner, mistaking your trousers for Peter's."

Conrad stared. "But why? Why would Mr. Singh do that?"

"I didn't say it was Mr. Singh, darling. I merely said it happened at the dry cleaner. Now, you've nothing to worry about, as long as you stay out of the land purchase business. Peter, however, should run for his life.''

"Really? That serious?"

Bella nodded. "I'm afraid so, Connie. If Peter goes through with that land deal, someone is very likely to retaliate. All the evidence points to murder. Now, shall I have my driver drop you at the club?"

BEATRICE WAS going off duty when Darin slid up beside the reception desk. The maître d' gripped a toothpick in his mouth, or a Stimudent; she wasn't sure, and she really didn't want to know. Beatrice tried her best to ignore the grease ball, but Darin blocked her path. In a smooth drawl, Darin said, "Got any plans tonight?"

"Yes."

Darin said, "Oh, really? Like what?"

Busybody. As snippily as she could manage, for she wasn't the snippy type, Beatrice said, "A date with a sex manual."

That stopped him in his tracks, temporarily at least, and allowed Beatrice to slip past him, car keys in hand, and head for the door. She huffed out, ignoring him, but in a moment of inspiration, she turned on the pesky Darin and bragged, "If you really want to know, I am going to have dinner with a very handsome, ver-r-r-y sexy gentleman."

Darin watched her go, rotating the toothpick on his tongue, appreciating the rear view. He liked roundness, nubile roundness. He called after her, "I could instruct you." But she didn't hear him. When she had disappeared into the parking lot, he sauntered across the lobby, through the Fiddlehead Restaurant, through the stainless steel doors with the round windows.

In the kitchen, the famous Slava was transforming rose petals into a pastel gelato and simultaneously barking orders to his staff. Darin didn't like Slava nearly as much as Lux. Lux had never barked. Lux cooed. But Darin had to admit that the line chef and salad handlers, the dishwashing crew, and the pastry chef were all hopping to Slava's goose-step bark. There was really nothing for a maître d' to do in here, so Darin went to check on his waiters, now serving the Avalon private party in the Totem Room.

When he entered the Totem Room, Darin smiled to himself. He'd won the bet after all. Here was the Nose standing over by the sliding glass doors, his powerful arm steering the luscious Lily Budge onto the terrace. Lily's eyes were swollen, like she'd been crying, Darin noticed. He felt certain he knew why Lily had wept. Nothing escaped Darin's keen observation.

There was music playing, a sanitized Pearl Jam imitation. Darin knew his bands. What with the loud music and all the people in the room trying to outshout each other, Darin couldn't hear what the Nose was saying to Lily, but he guessed it was something suggestive, seductive. Lily seemed so sad, a tragic figure, really. Darin smirked. Just wait until Cookie catches them.

Meanwhile, there stood that Shelby Warlock person in her Calvin Klein cocktail dress, totally inappropriate for the occasion, chatting up that snippy secretary from the Blue Poppy Perfumery. What was her name? Oh yeah, Perkins. She used to work for Mayor Chin over in City Hall. And get a load of her outfit. Rayon, of the Fred Meyer ilk, cheap, frowzy, perfect for the Fern environs, but a disaster in this swishy crowd. At least the Calvin on Mrs. Warlock had class. I mean, thought Darin to himself, aside from Fern, Washington, that dress on Mrs. Warlock could go anywhere: New York, Paris, Rio, Monte Carlo. All places Darin would arrive in after his slow ship docked. He couldn't wait to blow this burg, this backwater full of clamheads and carbuncles. Darin smiled to himself, thinking of the rich future he had in store. He could taste it, but no, it was cautious time, too soon to show his superiority to all these snots. Darin knew his day would come. Not even Mom and Dad knew yet. He'd have to tell them something before he moved out, moved away. Darin grinned, and a thrill visited his chest, swelling it. Darin's bright future lay just around the corner.

Speaking of fashion, over there by the hors d'oeuvres Troy Avalon was chatting up that fashion designer, Mimi Budge. The butterfly lady, they called her. She drew inspiration for her creations, Darin heard somewhere, from the butterflies she captured and pressed under glass. A butterfly fanatic, thought Darin admiringly, who brilliantly turned her hobby into a source of inspiration. Sort of like himself. An amateur spelunker whose sense of adventure had finally paid off. But wait a minute. Hadn't Darin understood that the Budge's boyfriend had been murdered just yesterday morning? Darin made a disgusted face and hoped the coldhearted Budge would see it. How dare she party on while her beloved lay freshly dead in somebody's morgue. Women can be so cold, so cruel. And here was Troy Avalon, about four inches from Budge's so-so body, his own body language shrieking seduction. For a moment, Darin tried imagining Troy Avalon and Mimi Budge in an intimate pose, but the image in his mind was so perverted it made him nauseous, and he almost got sick to his stomach. He gazed around the room, soliciting cleaner entertainment. Women have no common sense when it comes to men.

Except for Cookie. Darin pretended to be checking on his waiters' efficiency while he surreptitiously studied Cookie Avalon. Now, here was true feminine beauty. Cookie Avalon wore her flamboyant locks swept high in a tight French twist. Very chic, very appropriate, including the simple pink silk sheath and the delicate strappy gold platform sandals that permitted tactful views of her excellent toes. Darin was a foot man, no doubt about it, and Cookie's feet, so slender, so tiny, with the platinum frosted toenails, the little sandals, so excited him that for a moment he swooned and nearly fell backwards into a person now entering the room. He broke his fall against the champagne table, rattling it something awful, and nodded to the individual he'd nearly bowled over.

Gawwd, thought Darin, a miniature officer of the law. Now, wait a minute. Is that a state trooper's uniform? Of course not. That's a forest ranger, or maybe one of those Interior Department agents. What's this? Since when did federal agents drink champagne on duty? She's probably crashing this little function, and Darin himself would be obliged to remove her from the premises.

Darin approached the small ranger. Officiously and in his most priggish tone, he murmured, "I am sorry, miss, but this is a private party."

Venus smiled and walked straight toward Mimi Budge. She hadn't heard what the maître d' said. She had other things on her mind. Mimi Budge, for example. Budge and Troy Avalon were deep in conversation. She kept a polite distance and lip-read what Troy was saying to Mimi Budge. Venus's older brother, Rex, had taught her to read lips, and over the years, she had perfected the skill.

"Oh, yes, I've seen them myself," Troy said. "I saw a couple actually mating this morning, and I was sorely tempted to capture them. But Nature slapped my hand, and I just watched them go at it, then left them alone."

Mimi Budge replied, "So take me there. I want to see for myself."

Troy was shaking his head when the maître d' came up and sputtered in Venus's face. "I am Darin, the maître d'. I must ask you to leave the premises. As I said before, this is a private party."

Venus smiled at Darin. "Don't worry," she said. "I won't do

anything to embarrass you." She left him standing there, one hand on his chest, his jaw hanging open.

Troy and Mimi had changed subjects. Now it was food poisoning. Troy said, "You heard about Lux?"

Mimi made a grim face. "Sickening, isn't it? I never trusted oysters."

"Oh, I didn't understand it was mollusks," Troy replied. "I heard it was a poisonous mushroom. Death's angel. The sheriff said it was death's angel."

Mimi nodded. Now it made sense. "He probably was buying from those wildcrafters. I don't trust them. Most of them are career failures, Vietnam vets and such. They don't know about herbs and shoots and berries. They just pick whatever looks interesting and call it something. I'd surely never do business with them. In fact, a few weeks ago, Jonathan—" Mimi stopped. Her hand flew to her mouth. Her shoulders heaved slightly. Venus saw one tear roll down Mimi's cheek. Troy saw it, too, and put an arm around her, cloaking her sorrow, sparing her the embarrassment of a public display. Troy stroked Mimi's stylish hair, whispered something into her ear, then gallantly ushered her out of the Totem Room, maybe heading for the Oxygen Bar. The Budge looked like she could use a good shot of O_2. Venus wanted to follow them out, but it would only draw attention, and besides, she'd heard all she needed to hear from them, so when Darin approached with a tray of champagne flutes, Venus deposited the empty one, plucked a fresh flute off the tray. Darin sniggered.

"Drinking in uniform, are we?" He couldn't resist.

Venus nodded absentmindedly and went outdoors to the terrace. The early evening air hung damp and a light mist drizzled over everything, still, the magnificent view of the strait astonished her. But not as much as the little scene down on the beach.

A couple, walking the tideline. The woman wore a long caftan, its hood concealing her face, but her legs appeared in silhouette against the sky, and their shape was unmistakable. Zora. The man wore a familiar black leather jacket and a pair of Ray Bans. Venus smiled to herself. Song had pulled it off, though she hadn't expected him to work this fast. Already, Song had landed the big fish. Zora, obviously upset about something, was gesturing, as if relating an emotionally packed tale. Song's head was bowed, looking for more gold nuggets, maybe, or just listening to the model's woes. They disappeared down the beach, heading west, toward Pysht, though Venus doubted they'd walk that far. Pysht is interesting if you like old logging legends and Native American lore. Song and Zora weren't exactly in that league.

She had turned to go indoors, when on the terrace she noticed Peter and Cookie Avalon, and a young woman seated around a table. Cookie wore a sour expression, but her husband appeared jubilantly hypnotized by the younger woman, a fresh-faced virginal type, out of place in this jaded crowd.

"That's Lily Budge."

The voice came from behind her. Venus turned around. Darin stood about two feet from her on the rocky beach. Venus said, "Who is she?"

Darin sucked in his cheeks. "A spoiled little rich girl. Canadian."

"She related to the Olympic diving champion?"

Darin nodded. "Anson Budge is her father. Mimi's the sister. Anyway, why are you so interested in things around here?"

Venus joked, "I found some gold down here on the beach this afternoon. I'm searching for the hidden cache." She leaned in close, whispered, "I'm a treasure hunter."

Darin blanched, stared at her for a few seconds. He said, "Where do you think it is? This buried treasure."

Venus laughed. "In my imagination, that's where." Darin scowled, went up the terrace steps, crossed the terrace, and went into the lobby. Venus resumed eavesdropping.

Peter Avalon was relating a humorous incident to Lily. Lily was laughing softly, a forced, polite laugh, as if she'd rather be crying. Cookie wiggled her chair closer to her husband's, reached an arm up and fiddled with a wisp of Peter's hair. Lily continued laughing, and now Peter laughed with her.

"Oh, Mr. Avalon, you are the funniest man," declared Lily. "I never thought you would have a sense of humor." She explained, "I mean, I'd see your picture in newspapers and magazines, and I'd always say to my sister Mimi, 'That's the kind of man I want to marry. So sexy.' And now I discover you have this great sense of humor. That makes a man all the more desirable. Someday, I'm—"

Cookie snapped, "Why don't you just straddle him, right here in front of me?"

Lily made a sobbing noise, jumped up, fled inside, leaving the Avalons to play out their interpersonal drama. Venus slipped down the steps to the beach, stood under the terrace, listened.

"God, that was embarrassing, Cookie." Peter, mortified.

"Well, Peter, just think how you have embarrassed me time and again. Is a wife supposed to stand around looking normal while her husband practically gets a hard-on over another female? I don't think so. It isn't easy being married to you, Peter. Hey, have you ever thought about my feelings? No, Peter. All you ever think about is your damn libido..."

"Stop it, Cookie." Angry, bitter.

"I will not. I have every right to defend what's mine. And this diamond on my finger says it all. And you know what? This is the last time I will go through this, Peter. It's too humiliating. I'm not made of iron. I can't take it anymore. I gave up my professional life to marry you, and here twenty years later, I'm suddenly being shut out in the cold with nothing to show for myself. I gave myself to being your wife, the mother of your children, Peter. And what have I got to show for it?"

Cookie began sobbing.

Peter said, "There, there, Bitsie. Stop crying. I can't take the crying."

"Then you stop philandering."

"But...I haven't been unfaithful, Bits. You know that. Where's your sense of propriety? You just don't go around accusing people of things you fantasize about. Have you stopped your therapy sessions again?"

"That's not the point." Cookie, her voice quivering.

"What I meant was—"

"Shut up, Peter. Just shut up and let me say something for once." Silence.

"Now listen up, Mr. Testosterone, because this is absolutely the last time I will say this. If you ever...again go near another woman— and I am not speaking of this little Budge child, I am speaking in particular of Zora—I promise you, Peter, your life will be ruined. I'll ruin it for you. I mean it, this time. The last time I brought up Zora, you just laughed at me. And now this Budge girl. Peter, she's younger than Colette, your own daughter! So now this is your conscience speaking, Buster Brown. I am giving you one last chance. You screw up and I'll destroy you."

"Don't threaten me, Cookie. I'm not afraid of you."

"Well, I know some things about your family, Peter, and they aren't pretty. So you better be afraid. I could destroy the whole family business in one puny news conference. Or maybe I'll write a book. An exposé of the Avalon men. I could do a lot of things to scare you, Peter.''

A long, loud sigh. Peter said, ''All right. I give up. You've got me where you want me, Cookie. I won't have you dragging my family through your fictional mud, publicly or privately.''

Another silence. Then Cookie said, ''I'm thinking about returning to modeling. I want my career back.''

''Good for you.'' Peter. Sincere.

''You'll support me then?''

''Darling, I'll do whatever I can to help you succeed. I only want you to be happy, Bits.''

''I suppose we should go in and circulate.''

Venus heard the chairs scrape against the terrace floor. Iron on stone. Footsteps, Peter's soft padding footsteps, Cookie's clicking platform heels. Then silence. Venus moved toward the cedar steps. She heard the air whoosh, saw starry darkness, then nothing.

She awoke to a familiar fragrance. Blue Poppy perfume. She was lying on the beach, beside a set of stairs. Her forehead felt numb, cold. Someone was staring into her face. Miss Perkins said, ''It's about time you came around. My hand is frozen.''

Miss Perkins stopped rubbing the ice cube on Venus's forehead. ''I knew this would work,'' she said. ''I've seen it work in movies. Did you faint or something?''

Venus sat up. Miss Perkins flung the melting ice cube onto the beach and stood up. ''Now, I am going to get a fresh drink. You want a doctor or something?'' She didn't really want to be bothered.

''No thanks,'' Venus mumbled. ''I just tripped on the stairs. I'm fine.''

Miss Perkins said, ''That Mrs. Bowser trick wasn't funny,'' and sloshed back into the reception room. Venus got to her feet, brushed damp, caked sand from her uniform, felt the place on her skull where a hard object had struck. Gad, what a goose egg. But no blood, no broken skin. At her feet, a zillion rocks, a whole beach full of rocks. Had it been a rock? Probably. And it hadn't just fallen from the sky. She climbed the cedar stairs, crossed the terrace to the lobby, went inside. She was halfway to the Oxygen Bar when Song and Zora, still loosely disguised in the caftan, came in off the terrace, crossed the lobby, and entered the elevator. Some people have all the fun. She ordered a eucalyptus O_2 bubbler, sucked it down.

FERN'S REXALL DRUGS had plenty of aspirin, ice by the cup. Venus sat in the Spider in the Raven's parking lot, nursed the goose egg, swallowed four Bayers. Maybe it hadn't been a rock, after all. Maybe the wing flap off an overflying plane, or the butt of a gun. No. She'd heard the whoosh when the air stirred, and the object hadn't been sharp, or particularly cold, like steel. It must have come from above, on the terrace. Had Cookie seen her, thrown the rock at her? Or had someone else been on the terrace, maybe hiding, maybe eavesdropping on the Avalons, like she had been doing? Maybe the rock hadn't been meant for her at all. Maybe someone was aiming for Cookie. Or Peter.

Sleep overwhelmed her, even as she fought to stay awake. Maybe a slight concussion. She shut her eyes, setting an internal alarm for a quarter to ten. She made a lounger out of the Spider's passenger seat, lay back and dozed off. An hour later, she woke up, read her Swatch. Nine forty-five exactly. From the console, she removed her gear bag. From the gear bag, she removed her holstered .38 Smith & Wesson. She strapped it on. She dragged herself inside the Raven, located the ladies' lounge. It was called the Mermaids Room. She went into the Mermaids Room to clean up.

In the mirror she noticed a small scrape on her cheek, then two more scrapes on the palms of her hands, where she'd broken her fall. Her pupils were pinpoints, her eyes like two streetlights on Go. She washed the scrapes, tossed some water on her disheveled hair, slicked it back into shape. She was studying the result when Mimi Budge walked in.

She was carrying the black portfolio. She ignored Venus's reflection in the mirror, walked to the farthest lavatory door, went in. Venus could hear her in there, making the usual noises and apparently rummaging in her handbag, then beeps, then her voice, apparently speaking into a telephone.

"Oh, hi, Daddy. What? Yes, I'm all right. I had a little cry, though. But Mr. Avalon, Troy, that is, was very kind and understanding. He took me out of the party to spare me the humiliation of, you know, crying in public."

Pause. Venus took out her comb, pretended to arrange her hair. Budge's voice again: "You know, I didn't think it would be this hard, Daddy. I mean, Jonathan and I had broken up, you know. We hadn't been getting along for months, and it was inevitable, really. I shouldn't feel so utterly devastated. I really thought this cocktail party would, you know, cheer me up, but I feel worse than ever. I wish you would've joined us. Did you have a nice nap?'' Pause, then, "Yes, of course I realize it looks bad, but everybody knows Jonathan and I...just a minute, Daddy.''

Flushing sounds. Rustling, maybe struggling with pantyhose. In the space between the door and the marble floor, Venus could see the portfolio's bottom edge. So close. Then Mimi's voice again. "The reason I called, Lily's left the party, and I can't find her anywhere. Has she called your room?''

She was still in the stall, opening the door. Venus ran tap water, listened harder. Mimi said, "She hasn't? Well then I'm really worried. I mean, something must have happened. Lily was there one minute and gone the next. I haven't seen her for over an hour. She's not in our suite. You know how she hates walking alone on the beach. I checked every facility here at the club, and she simply isn't here. What? Oh, I guess she might have gone out with a date, but she never told me about any plans. Lily always shares those things with me. Well, if she isn't back at the inn by eleven o'clock, I'm going to call security.'' Pause. "I am not a worrywart. There's nothing wartish about me. All right, I'll try to relax. It's the Jonathan thing, I guess.'' Pause, then, "Okay, Daddy. I love you, too. Bye.''

Mimi came to the basins, washed her hands, held them under the blow dryer, turning them, wiggling the fingers. She leaned into the mirror, studied her eyes. Not very bloodshot for a devastated ex-lover. Her eyes went roving, found Venus in the mirror. She said, "I'll bet you heard every word I said,'' then focused back on herself and waited for a reply.

Venus shrugged. Avoiding a direct reply, she said, "Aren't you Mimi Budge? That terrific couture designer? I'd recognize you anywhere.''

Mimi Budge smiled, pleased to be recognized. "Why, yes I am. And you are?''

Venus was introducing herself when Cookie stormed into the Mermaids, a hurricane force driving her toward landfall. In this instance, Mimi Budge was land. Venus stepped gingerly out of Cookie's path.

Close up, Venus noticed, Cookie had a lean, taut, fat-free physique and good bones. Slightly anorexic, very youthful. She'd had a face lift that took ten or fifteen years off the top. Everyone's thirty at heart. She had that hair, that glorious flame whipped up in a smooth French twist, like her head was on fire, and close up, her eyes sparkled like

the gold nugget Song had picked up on Agate Beach. The only problem was, the expression on her sultry mouth exactly matched the
French twist. She held up one strong, diamond-studded hand, pointed
one manicured finger at the Budge, and said, "That is the last time
you bring your sister to one of our affairs, Mimi."

"Lily?" The Budge seemed surprised. "W-what happened?"

Cookie shifted on her feet, like sparring before the bell. "She went
straight for my husband. Fawned all over him. Constantly touching
him in a familiar way, like this."

Cookie demonstrated on the nearest arm, which happened to be
Venus's.

Beginning at the shoulder, Cookie's hand made an exaggerated trip
down the arm's length, slowly, pausing midway to stroke the arm,
then completing the lap, started again from the top. On the second
tour, Venus jerked her arm out of Cookie's caress. Cookie didn't
notice. Her mind was on Mimi, and Venus might as well be a cat
post. She stepped backwards, farther out of Cookie's reach. Now
Cookie pushed up in Mimi's face. "Thank God my daughters didn't
turn out like you Budge girls."

"M-M-Mrs. Avalon..." Mimi stammered.

Cookie snapped, "Don't Mrs. Avalon me. You might be Mimi
Budge, all famous and accomplished, but that doesn't give you permission to Mrs. Avalon me. Now, I like your dresses, I really do, I
admire your creative talent, and I might even like you if you weren't
so...so...Northern. But I don't like your sister, and I never want to
see her come near my husband again, is that clear?"

"W-w-w-well, sure, I mean, yes, I mean, of course, Mrs. Avalon.
I'm sure Lily didn't mean anything by it. She's just naturally affec-
tionate, like a child..."

"That...that seductress is no child. She knows exactly what she's
doing. Now you put a leash on her, or I'll speak to Anson about it."

Mimi nodded enthusiastically. Anything to get Cookie out of her
face. "Of course, Mrs. Avalon. I absolutely understand."

Cookie deflated then, and the flush left her face. She had the door
open and her platform sandals on the threshold when she turned back
to face Mimi Budge. Her voice rode a higher octave now. "Call me
sometime. I'd like to show your work to a friend of mine. A buyer
for Barneys."

Mimi opened her mouth, or maybe her jaw just dropped, Venus
wasn't sure, but before anything came out of the cavity, Cookie was

gone. Mimi turned to Venus. "Still enjoying this tawdry soap opera?"

Venus shrugged. "I wanted to ask you about your butterfly collection."

Mimi shook her head. "Not for sale," she said firmly. Grasping the portfolio's handle, she huffed out of the Mermaids.

Funny thing about jealousy, Venus told herself in the mirror, it always seems to backfire.

SEVENTEEN

COOKIE'S IMAGINAL BUDS

> The caterpillar possesses growth centers, or, imaginal buds, which contain the "program" that drives metamorphosis from larval stage, through the chrysalis stage, and eventually transforms it into a butterfly. This process is triggered once the larva's juvenile hormones switch off.
>
> —*Oxford Lepidopterist's Manual*

UPON ARRIVING IN Seattle from St. Petersburg, Russia, via a cargo ship from Vladivostok, secreted in a shipment of beluga caviar, Slava Simonyinski fell instantly in love with Walla Walla onions. So enchanted was the chef de nouvelle cuisine with the simple Eastern Washington onion that he now included it in practically every dish he prepared. There was Slava's venison Walla Walla, his Walla Walla *creme champignons,* his Walla Walla salmon mousse, even Walla Walla sorbet. When the darling of Seattle's culinary corps prepared his first professional meal in Seattle, he dedicated it completely to the Walla Walla onion. It was Slava's way of saluting his new motherland. Thus, the great Russian chef turned his broad back upon traditional Russian cuisine and created his own unique version of nouvelle Russian-American cuisine, a sort of blending of nations or empires (Slava never quite grasped the difference), a coup de grace de la cuisine, or as they say in Russian, "ochin, ochin harascho oozhin," a little ditty Slava often hummed to himself at work. In short, Slava Simonyinski, once upon a time a humble Russian peasant from rural Petrograd, now reigned over the Seattle restaurant scene, the darling de cuisine of Oz.

A tiny side trip to the Inn at Raven Point wouldn't hurt Slava's reputation one kopeck, in fact, this brief holiday in the enchanting rain forest might add a certain luster to Slava's curriculum vitae, viz. "Slava has even cooked in the American rain forest, for the Avalons of Blue Poppy fame." So it was with great care that Slava prepared the dishes for the Avalons' evening meal. Slava himself would serve the main course at tableside.

The Avalon party of two had burgeoned into a party of three, and Slava didn't appreciate such thoughtless last-minute changes, but the irate chef was made to understand that the newly added member to the Avalon reservation was, in fact, Mrs. Peter Avalon. But then, who was the second figure in this important trinity? Peeking through the round glass window, Slava saw Mr. Avalon enter with his wife, Cookie—preposterous name—and a tiny fairy dressed in a sort of military uniform.

The fairy seemed oddly out of place with the larger-than-life, utterly glamorous Avalons, like a Muscovite in St. Petersburg, although if pressed, Slava would guess that the tiny person in uniform possessed a slightly larger brain than the celebrated hosts. At any rate, the maître d', Darin, showed the trio to the very finest table in the house, and of course every diner in the restaurant, which was full to capacity, stared as discreetly as possible when the Avalons were led to their table. These were celebrities after all, and Slava had to admit that Mrs. Avalon appeared quite lovely, although Slava had never been particularly fond of red-haired women.

Slava sighed, recalling his little Lydia, heart of his heart, soulmate and wife. Sooner or later, Lydia would find her way from Vladivostok, perhaps in beluga, or vodka, and would come to Slava. The first thing Slava would do, after taking her to bed that is, the second thing Slava would do, is introduce his Lydia to the Walla Walla onion. Da, kaneshna, ochin harascho.

Peter Avalon held the chair for Cookie. Darin materialized beside Venus's chair. He waited until Venus had pulled her chair out from the table, and as soon as she sat down, he shoved it in forcefully, so that its arms actually knocked the table, making noise. Darin bowed, smirked, and intoned vacuously, "So sorry, miss." Avalon ordered double martinis for himself and Cookie, a tonic with lime for Venus. He didn't like the idea of virgin tonic, but Cookie chimed in, "If she wants a faux cocktail, darling, let her have it. It's none of our business what—what did you say your name was?"

"Venus."

Cookie nodded. She might retain it this time. "It's none of our business what Vanna drinks. Besides, she's obviously in uniform, and therefore must abstain from alcoholic beverages. Am I right?'' She made a saccharine face and Venus thought for a minute her lips might break, so tightly were they drawn across her mouth.

The goose egg throbbed. Venus said, ''Something like that, Mrs. Avalon.''

Cookie waved a hand. ''Oh, call me Cookie. Just everybody does.'' She laughed, a damp suction, like in the dentist's basin. ''Peter has told me whose daughter you are, Vanna. Lady Bella is the greatest thing on cellophane.''

''Celluloid,'' murmured Peter.

''Now what are they serving us for dinner? I hope it isn't baby quail again. I adore baby quail, but I'm just so tired of it, you know?'' Cookie took up the menu at her place, squinted at it. ''Don't you just despise handwritten menus? Can anyone read this dreadful scrawl?''

''Where are your glasses?'' Peter, obviously annoyed.

Cookie employed the saccharine, high octave. ''I don't wear glasses, darling. I've never worn glasses.''

''Well, you need to.'' Peter lifted the menu from Cookie's helpless hand, pulled a pair of reading glasses from his jacket pocket, read the menu out loud. Cookie leaned forward, hanging on his every word.

Venus watched her. This wasn't the same Cookie she'd eaves-dropped on outside, the fierce, quarreling, gravel-voiced Cookie. Nor was this the Cookie she'd watched clawing the eyes out of Mimi Budge in the Mermaids. Here was a different Cookie, with an ex-aggerated Southern accent and a disconcerting vocal lilt. Here was a fragile, kitten-soft, cuddly creature, a bit too helpless. She couldn't even read the menu herself, for crying out loud. Could she really be so vain as to forgo eyeglasses? Hadn't she heard of contact lenses?

Darin poked Venus's shoulder. ''Pardon me, miss. You have a telephone call.''

''Well, bring the phone to the table, Darin, darling,'' purred Cookie smartly.

Darin shook his head. If there was anything he hated to do, it was to deny Cookie Avalon her request. ''I am very sorry, madame. We do not permit telephones at the table.''

''And just why is that?'' Cookie squinted at Darin.

''It spoils the mood, madame.'' He yanked Venus's chair out roughly. Venus excused herself, followed Darin into the lobby, across the lobby, down a long, dimly lit hallway. Darin made a sharp left turn and Venus followed him into a small, deserted gym. Darin went over to the barbells, touched a fifty-pound weight, caressed it. He said, "You work out?"

"When I have time," said Venus. "Where's the phone?"

"There isn't one. I mean, there's a phone, but nobody called you. That was an excuse. See, I want to talk to you."

Venus leaned against a mirrored wall. She studied Darin's reflection in the mirror, compared it to the real-life Darin. Some people are totally unrecognizable from different angles. But Darin was Darin, from any angle. She said, "About what?"

"I saw what happened to you. Out there on the beach."

Venus didn't say anything. Darin fondled the barbell. In the background, a clock chimed eleven times.

"I saw the rock hit you," continued Darin, "and I saw you fall. Did you see who threw the rock?"

Venus shook her head.

Darin nodded. "Well, I did. It was Mimi Budge. I saw her go out through the lobby onto the terrace, down to the beach. I saw her pick up a rock and throw it at you. After you fell, she ran back inside."

"Why would she do that?"

Darin shifted from one foot to the other, throwing his body around autistically. His mouth worked, but words wouldn't come out. Venus chewed her lip, studied Darin's contorted mouth, twisted body, its language shrieking of anxiety, and probably something else. Finally, the words came out in dribbles, but clearly enunciated.

"Jonathan Willow deserved to die."

"Why?"

"He molested a girl."

"What girl?"

Darin wriggled more anxiously. "She was there tonight. At the party in the Totem Room. She was there."

"What's her name?"

"You know who I'm talking about."

"Maybe. Describe her."

Darin sighed, pursed his lips, then blurted, "That babe, you know, the quiet one? Mimi Budge's little sister."

Lily. Venus said, "How do you know?"

"I saw it. I saw it happen."

"When? Where?"

Darin said, "Yesterday morning. About six o'clock. Up in Yodeler's meadow."

Venus thought for a minute, then said, "Will you sign a statement
to that effect?"

"Hell no. I shouldn't've been up there. The rangers have warned
me to stay off the preserve. They said if they catch me up on Yodeler
again, they'll fine me."

"So why'd you tell me?"

Darin shrugged. "Just trying to help you. You're looking for his
killer, aren't you? Well, now you have a motive. Whoever killed
Willow was defending Lily. It might have been Mimi who killed
him. Or Lily's dad, Anson Budge? He hunts up in that meadow. I've
seen Mr. Budge up on the preserve a few times."

"Why won't you sign a statement? What are you afraid of?"

Darin smiled crookedly. "Nothing. I just don't believe in signing
my name to anything."

"What about your pay check? Do you sign your pay check?"

He twisted again. When he finished, he said, "I have to get back
to work." They walked back down the long hall, through the lobby,
past the Oxygen Bar. When they reached the restaurant entrance,
Darin went in first.

Venus said, "What were you doing up there so early in the morning? When you saw Willow and Lily, and the killer?" Testing him.

Darin turned around. Proudly he said, "I'm a spelunker. Know
what that is?"

Venus nodded. He'd skipped right over the bait.

Darin said, "Well, I'm one. And another thing," he added, almost
as an afterthought, "it's pretty dangerous on the preserve. Bears.
Hunters. You shouldn't go up there."

"It's illegal to hunt on a preserve."

Darin shrugged. "Don't say I didn't warn you."

Slava had personally removed the menus from the Avalons' table.
Darin should have taken care of that, but Darin had disappeared. The
Avalons should never have been given menus, and the fact that Darin
had let that detail slip annoyed the chef. People like the Avalons
aren't supposed to read menus. People like the Avalons are personally
pampered by the chef himself.

Slava stood beside the Avalons' table, preparing hamma hamma
oysters and Walla Walla onion blinis. He hand-fed a blini to Cookie.

Perching forward to receive the morsel, Cookie tasted, paused for effect, and performed an elaborate swoon, limp hand to the forehead.

She swallowed, patted her full lips, and declared, "Scrumptious. To die for."

Venus sat down.

By the second double martini, Cookie had loosened up. She liked to talk, especially about Cookie, and about a certain mirror in her house. She called it the Yocum mirror, named after the Natchez wing of her family. "You can't trust the Yocum mirror," Cookie said. "It shows you things like ghosts and spirits of the dead. Even your own image can become distorted in the Yocum mirror. And, another thing about my family..."

Suddenly, an impenetrable glossal surge seized Cookie, animating her baby-doll face, igniting a sparkle in her nutmeg eyes. Maybe she was on antidepressants, or maybe the martini clashed with her brain chemistry. Avalon made feeble attempts to gag the drone. No luck. Cookie slid the martini glass up to her lips.

"Darling," Peter cut in, "why don't you let somebody else get a word in?"

Cookie giggled, placed a hand over her mouth, mocking him.

Peter leaned across the table, gently pried Cookie's hand from her mouth, and kissed her lips lightly. He said, "Cookie's wearing my perfume this evening."

"I wear it every evening." She belched lightly.

"I noticed the fragrance." Venus dove in behind Peter. "I grew up with that scent wafting around the house."

"Oh, yes, of course, your mother has worn our fragrance for decades. Can you notice any difference when Cookie wears Blue Poppy?"

Venus inhaled. "Now that you mention it, on your wife the fragrance seems a bit sweeter."

Cookie giggled and tackled her entree.

Peter said, "Very good. A fragrance reacts differently on every person who wears it. The body oils mix with the perfume and combine to create a unique signature. Now, Cookie, for example, brings out the high notes of the fragrance, whereas your mother, as I recall, inspires the more sultry notes." Peter reached into his pocket, fished out a small flacon, a replica of the one she'd admired on Miss Perkins's desk, with the hand-cut crystal blue poppy stopper. He placed it on the table in front of Venus. "Your personal Blue Poppy. Try some on. Let's see how it reacts to you."

Cookie squeaked, "But, sweetie, I mean, here? At the dinner table?"

Peter waved his hand. "Venus can go into the ladies' lounge, if she prefers."

He obviously liked establishing his authority, his dominance, early in a relationship. As he'd done with Cookie, and possibly with Zora. Now what did he have in mind for Venus? She'd play along a little, until she had a better read on his game. Besides, she'd never owned her own bottle of Blue Poppy. She opened the bottle.

A mysterious blend of florals wafted from the flacon like a magic genie, scenting the air. Diners nearby pumped their nostrils, looked around for someone interesting. Venus dabbed a drop on her wrists. Impatiently, Peter said, "Here, give me that." He snatched up the flacon, reached across the table, dabbed some behind Venus's ears, down her neck, across her collarbone, that nice collarbone he so earnestly admired, stopped short of her chest, where no cleavage existed. "There," he said, "Now let it settle for a few minutes."

"As I was saying, Vanna...it is Vanna, isn't it?" Cookie fluttered her eyelids.

"Venus."

"Yes. As I was saying, before my husband changed the subject, my next goal in life is to revive my modeling career. I still have the body for it, don't you agree?" A rhetorical question. "Back before Peter came along, I was a Ford girl. On my way to the top." She leaned into Peter. "Then, when Conrad Avalon selected me as a Miss Blue Poppy, I met this hunk of charm. I completely renounced my career for Peter. I just simply plu-u-unged into being a wife and mother. Not that I have one tiny regret, mind you, I'm proud of my accomplishments. It's just that with the children going off to college and with Peter working so much, I'm thinking of doing something for myself for a change. Of course, I'll have to update my portfolio..."

Rudely, desperately, Venus interrupted. "It's been five minutes. What's your take on the fragrance?" To Peter.

"Ah, yes. Let's consider the results." He leaned across the table and performed his favorite physical act. He inhaled. "God, what perfection. A fragrance for Aphrodite. On so many women, so many different skins. Perfection. Thrilling. You should wear it always."

"Not to change the subject or anything," said Cookie, glowering, "but didn't you tell me that the reason for this dinner was a business discussion?"

"All right then, if you'll hush, Cookie, I'll tell Venus what's on my mind."

"It's Vanna, darling."

Peter said, "Shut up, Cookie." Whispered, but Venus heard it. "My family wants to buy Yodeler's meadow. It's no secret. I've been putting out feelers for a year or so."

"We haven't heard about it." Better play it straight.

"Maybe not in your regional office." Avalon smiled. "I'm dealing with Interior's Washington office. They haven't discouraged my advances, I should say that right up front. But they'd naturally be reticent if, say, you or someone else at the regional office raised objections. So, I'd like the opportunity to address your regional staff about my plans."

"I told you before, I don't have the authority to make any sort of agreement or arrangement with you. If you want to address regional on any subject, you need to contact the regional director."

"That would be Oly Olson?"

Her pulse throbbed in her neck. "That's right."

Avalon shook his head. "God, there's just so much bureaucracy in government these days, doesn't it just make you crazy?"

Cookie polished off a plate of fiddleheads, had the martini refreshed. She made little guzzling sounds. She was getting drunk, and fast. Avalon poked at some sautéed ferns that didn't interest him. His interests were grander. He said, "We need that entire meadow for our poppies. If we don't acquire it before this coming winter, we won't have a harvest next June. That's never happened at Blue Poppy, except way back in 'fifty-four, when a particularly mild winter threw off the flowers' timing. That's the only year since my grandfather founded Blue Poppy that we've failed to produce the perfume. It's absolutely critical that we acquire a leasehold on the lower portion of that meadow, or better yet, purchase the land."

Venus sipped the lime tonic. Tonic contains quinine. Quinine is one of several products used to treat malaria. She'd forgotten about the quinine when she ordered the tonic. It's amazing how a taste can revive memories. She could almost feel a malaria fever coming on. She heard Cookie saying something.

"I'm sorry," Venus said. "Would you please repeat that?"

"I said, nobody named Vanna is going to seduce my husband right smack in my line of visshon."

"Now, look here, Cookie..." Peter's face reddened.

Darin appeared at Cookie's side, the spirit of dessert arriving to save Cookie's bejeweled neck from the wringer. He served Cookie some rose petal sorbet. On top of the sorbet lay several tiny wild violet blossoms. *V. adunca.* Darin droned, "For you, madame, and may I say that you are the loveliest lady in the dining room this evening?"

Cookie lapped it up. Venus saw Peter's hand go behind Cookie's chair toward Darin. Maybe a c-note attached. Whatever it was he handed Darin, Darin deftly slipped it into his pocket. Then he went to find the other two desserts. Cookie, martini in hand, located a spoon, somehow connected the spoon with the sorbet, somehow drew a spoonful up toward her mouth, somehow hit the target. Tiny dribbles slid down her jawbone. She giggled, patted her drool. She plucked a couple wild violets off the sorbet, muttering, "Precious little things."

Later, on her third double martini, Peter snifting cognac, Cookie made the announcement. Cozying up to Peter, she addressed Venus across the table. "Peter gave me the most wonderful gift this evening, Vanna. I'd like you to be the first to know." Puzzled, Avalon squinted at his wife.

She lifted her martini glass, sipped, licked her lips for a beat, and said, "Peter has selected me as this year's Miss Blue Poppy."

When the brandy snifter hit the carpet, it bounced. The precious fluid spilled across Avalon's lap, staining his nice trousers. What got the attention of the house, though, was Peter's choking. Holding his dinner napkin over his mouth, he coughed violently. Cookie watched him, sipping her martini, a satisfied little curve on her mouth. Venus handed Avalon a glass of water, while Darin rushed to the table and fussed over the spill. Avalon flushed purple, the veins at his temples bulged, throbbed. When the cough subsided, he smiled weakly.

"Went down the wrong pipe." Apologetically.

"Poor darling." Cookie giggled.

Venus studied the thin foam layer on her cappuccino.

Avalon stood abruptly, excused himself, mumbling something about taking care of the bill. Cookie gestured toward him, conferring her blessings. He fled, the vivid purple flush still plaguing his face. Cookie smiled at Venus. "Really, isn't he just as cute as a bug?"

Venus read her Swatch. The "business dinner" had proved a total waste of time.

Cookie drawled, "Isn't it wonderful? About my being Mish Blue Poppy? I was once before, you know, some years ago. Imagine everyone's surprise when I'm publicly announced. Of course, you mustn't tell a soul, it's a secret, you know, until the ads appear. But isn't it just so romantic?"

Venus said, "So what's the secret ingredient?"

Cookie laughed slyly. "Now you know that's an Avalon family secret. Not even I am privy to that information. Although I have my ideas."

"What's your best guess?"

Double martinis are wonderful concoctions. The first one feels marvelous. The second one truly relaxes, and the third usually wields the force of a sledge hammer. Cookie was on her fourth. Her head lolled lazily on her shoulders, her fine red hair fell from the sleek twist, across one eye. Her body had as much starch as a used dish rag, and her mouth slurred the words when she held up a limp violet and said, "Blue violets. From over in Yodeler's meadow. Know where that is...?"

Darin caught Cookie, breaking the fall from her chair. Slumped in Darin's convenient arms, she belched softly before vomiting. Slava wouldn't appreciate the result.

Later, in the Mermaids, Cookie overhauled her face. Venus tagged along, just to prevent Cookie from crashing into something breakable. They made it across the lobby without incident. Inside the Mermaids, Cookie had another heave.

"I'm just so mortified," Cookie said through her lip pencil. "I mean, I've never in my entire life been so completely mortified. Do you think anyone saw me?"

"Naw." Only everyone in the dining room.

"Well, thank God for that." Cookie struggled with a Chanel lipstick, finally separated the top from the tube, but couldn't manage the twisting part. Venus took the tube from Cookie's helpless hands, twisted the metallic pink lipstick up, handed it back to her. Cookie swathed a ribbon across her mouth, jumping the lines in a few places, then pressed her lips together for the smeared effect. She smiled thinly at her reflection, said, "There, now I'm all put back together." She stumbled on the way out, but her general sense of direction had authority, and she made it across the lobby without falling over.

In the lobby, Avalon waited in an armchair, chatting with Mimi Budge, who sat across from him on the couch. The black portfolio rested against her knees. The butterfly collection. Mimi's fingers firmly grasped the portfolio's handle. When they saw Cookie approaching, Avalon stood, took his wife by the arm, steered her toward the door. Halfway there, Cookie stopped, turned around.

"Vanna? I just want you to know that Jonathan Willow was a really sweet young man. He really and truly was."

EIGHTEEN

FULL COOL

MIMI BUDGE jammed a Virginia Slims the length of a drinking straw into a faux tortoiseshell cigarette holder, stuck it between her eggplant lips, and sucked. Mr. Butts would have admired her smoke, how she inhaled then disdainfully emitted little puffs, insulting the air. She didn't care who the hell called this inn a no-smoking zone, when you've lost your beloved, particularly to murder, you inevitably do things you wouldn't otherwise do. Perching forward on the tapestry couch, pulling and puffing on the gasper, her ho-hum knees supporting the black leather portfolio, Mimi imparted a distinct impression of grief and suffering. Silent, but suffering. She might have been concentrating on private thoughts of Jonathan Willow as Venus approached her, or she might be focused on the smoke patterns, Venus wasn't sure until she got up close and realized the Budge was staring at the newsstand across the lobby.

Willow's murder had made the front page of the *Straits Times*. There wasn't a photograph with the story, but Mimi squinted to read the headline from across the lobby. Venus went over, put fifty cents in the coin slot, fished a newspaper out of the rack. She carried it across the lobby, sat down beside Mimi, handed her the newspaper. She watched Budge's reaction.

The Budge held out a pale limp hand, accepted the rotten news. Setting her portfolio on the couch, carefully, so not to disturb its contents, Mimi read the short piece about the incident in Yodeler's meadow. When she finished reading, she dropped the newspaper onto the carpet listlessly, the way she rubbed out her cigarette in her portable ashtray.

She put away the cigarette holder, leaned forward, placed her head between her hands. Her body heaved, and the heaving gained force. Venus didn't actually see tears, only the body language. Soft sobbing noises set off the tableau, like the right piece of jewelry sets off a well-cut dress.

She let the Budge sob into her hands for about three minutes, then said, "You want some oxygen?" Mimi apparently didn't hear Venus, so she repeated the question. This time, Mimi ceased sobbing, but kept her head buried in her hands. Maybe listening. Venus watched the second hand on her Swatch rotate one full circle, another half circle, then the Budge raised her head, stared into the far, far distance, and in a dreamy voice said, "Why would I want that?"

"Might help ease your blues."

"These aren't the blues. These are sobs of grief. Maybe you don't know it, but that man who was murdered was my boyfriend."

"Sure, I knew that," said Venus. "I handed you the newspaper, didn't I?"

Mimi sat up straight, smoothed her hair, her dress; everything that would smooth, Mimi smoothed. "Oh," she said tonelessly. "I thought you were just being kind to a stranger in distress. How did you know?"

"I'm a federal Fish and Wildlife agent. Willow's murder is the case I'm working on. I was hoping we could talk about it."

Mimi turned her kohl-smeared, tear-stained puffin eyes on Venus, studied her uniform, the badge, the face, the slick hair. In the final analysis, it was the hair that convinced Mimi to talk. Mimi liked slick hair, and if she wasn't careful how she handled herself in this situation, with this attractive stranger, she might make a fatal mistake. But she could play along with Slick. Mimi said, "I've never had oxygen before. I mean, pure, unadulterated oxygen. I'm always afraid to try it."

Venus stood. "Come on. Let me introduce you to an oxygen cocktail."

They sat side by side at the Oxygen Bar. They both selected mouth tubes, Venus inhaling little bubbles of spearmint-enhanced, carbonated O_2, Mimi giggling over a bubblegum-flavored hit. When you suck, the bubbly moist oxygen ripples upwards, tickles your throat, and passes into your lungs, delivering pure O_2 to the bloodstream. One hit was enough for Venus, but the Budge proved an addictive personality and went back three times. Taking Budge by the elbow, Venus led her out onto the terrace. Mimi floated like a circus balloon, her footsteps barely touching ground. She talked a blue streak and her voice was high pitched, squeaky, like leaking helium.

"Gawd, this is just so cool. I can't believe how cool this is. Why haven't I tried this before? It's like floating on a cloud, you know? Gawd, this is just so cool." And so forth. On the terrace, she deflated enough to be seated and stay there. Eventually her vocal cords relaxed and lay normal in her throat. Mimi sighed. "That was just the coolest thing I have ever done. It's much better than weed, you know? And it's legal, is it?"

Venus nodded. "Can you talk about Jonathan yet?"

Mimi stared. "Did I leave my portfolio in the Oxygen Bar?"

"It's okay in there. Everyone's gone to bed. Desk clerk will keep an eye on it."

"No. I must have it with me. I mustn't lose track of it like that. That portfolio contains my entire future." She leaped to her feet and rushed inside, returning a moment later clutching the black portfolio. "There," she said, "now I feel much more secure." She placed the portfolio on the wrought-iron table, sat back in her chair. "About Jonathan. What do you want to know exactly?"

"Where he stood with you, for starters." Venus didn't want to rush her. If she could feel comfortable, she'd reveal more.

Mimi made a face, studied the fingernails on her left hand, then turned the hand palm down and held it out so Venus could see it was ringless. "We had this awful quarrel. The night before he was killed. We were on the brink of a formal engagement. He even bought me a ring, at least I heard through mutual friends that he had done. I never saw it. The last time I saw Jonathan, we had this horrendous quarrel, just horrendous. Have you ever quarreled with someone you loved?"

Venus shook her head.

Mimi went on. "Well, it's devastating, truly devastating." She brought a fist to her mouth, sobbed lightly. "I'll never forgive myself for that."

"What did you quarrel about?"

"It's really too personal."

"Was it about someone else?"

Mimi stared at her. "How did you know that?"

Venus shrugged. "It happens all the time. Lovers invaded by a third party."

Mimi chewed her lip, made a little tsking sound and said, "I am somewhat of a celebrity. I can't afford to have my personal life dragged around in public. I am a very private, somewhat eccentric person. The artistic temperament, you know, and I do things my way, not like other people, but my way. That includes my grieving process."

Venus let that disintegrate into thin air, watched Mimi's sobbing routine again. After a while, Venus said, "Was it Lily?"

The sobbing ceased. Silence. Venus heard the waves slap against the rocky beach. Slap, swoosh, slap, swoosh.

"Oh, God," cried Mimi suddenly. "Oh, God. How could he do this to me?"

Venus left her sobbing at the terrace table, went inside, ordered a couple cognacs, paid for them, carried them back outside. Mimi was bawling now. She reminded Venus of an injured seagull, screeching at the tide. The night manager appeared on the terrace. "Please, Miss Budge," he pleaded. "We have guests who are trying to sleep. Please stop making all this noise. Otherwise I shall have to call your father."

Venus handed Mimi a cognac. "This should help." Mimi ran her anguished eyes over Venus's face, accepted the cognac, sipped. Venus said, "Feel better?" The Budge nodded and self-consciously rearranged herself so that she resembled a mannequin. The manager went away.

Venus said, "Now that you've gotten it out of your system, tell me what happened."

"We quarreled Wednesday evening. At my condo in Victoria. I have a condo there, and Jonathan lived with me. Not in the biblical sense, mind you. I'm saving that for...and we officially broke up. That's what happened."

"Over Lily?"

"Over Lily."

"Have you and Lily talked about Jonathan?"

"Lily's my little sister. I love her dearly. Jonathan hadn't even told her how he felt. Lily's too good-hearted, too innocent to understand these things. No, I haven't spoken to Lily, and I don't plan to, either."

She said *eye*ther, not *eee*ther. She probably said *tomahto*, too, and *aboot*.

Venus said, "So what happened in the morning?"

"You mean, like, where was I, and all that?" Venus nodded. Mimi said, "Jonathan left my condo Wednesday night. I didn't see him, nor did I hear from him after that."

"What about Thursday? What did you do on Thursday?"

"On Thursday morning, Daddy brought Lily and me over here

from Victoria to spend a few days. We checked in about two o'clock that afternoon, had dinner in the Fiddlehead. Then the three of us walked down along the beach out here. It's a summer ritual we have. Mother never comes along. She hates the United States."

"Did you know Jonathan was also registered here Thursday night?"

Mimi blinked. For a minute she seemed caught off guard, but she came back smartly. "Of course, I knew Jonathan was here. He and I often stayed here when we went out hunting butterflies. I wasn't at all surprised when I heard that Jonathan had checked in. It's the height of butterfly season. In fact, I was out on one of my own expeditions when—"

Pause. Reflection. The vamp lips clamped shut. Venus watched Mimi through the darkness, the soft light from the lobby barely revealing her features. There wasn't a moon, or if there was, it was hiding behind thick clouds. The stars had disappeared and you could almost taste rain in the air. Gently she said, "You went out chasing butterflies yesterday morning?"

Mimi nodded grimly.

Venus said, "Where'd you go?"

"Oh...just...that spit, you know? Dungeness Spit." The lie rolled smoothly off her tongue.

"Dungeness Spit?" Venus seemed surprised. "What species were you collecting there?"

Mimi scowled, maybe trying to remember. "Oh, I guess, uh, well, you know I'm just a hobbyist. I was just looking for anything interesting. Not monarchs or anything boring like that."

"Anyone go along?"

Mimi shook her head. Negative.

"Anyone see you out on the spit?"

Another negative.

"What did you capture?"

Mimi swallowed some cognac, took her time replying. "I know it's not legal. I mean, I know I was on government-protected land and all. And the species, well, it's a pretty special butterfly."

"Whulge checkerspot?"

Mimi's jaw dropped. "How in the world did you know that?"

Venus said, "I'm a lepidopterist. My thesis was on Pacific Northwest butterflies."

"Really?" Mimi perked up then and suddenly everything was all right. Two lepidopterists equaled kindred spirits in Mimi's vivid imagination.

"Cooool," said Mimi. "Cooool."

"Can I see the specimen?" Testing veracity.

"The whulge, you mean?" Squirming.

Venus nodded. Mimi squirmed some more, her quivering lips trembled, the face fell into the cupped hands, and the sobbing commenced. It wasn't bawling this time, just sobbing, a noise level the management could live with. Venus yawned.

It was twelve miles to the ranger lodge, where she had arranged to meet Song. After that, she could sleep at the lodge for a second night, on a stiff cot in a damp room. Or she could aim the Spider south, drift on down to Kingston, catch the last ferry to Edmonds, slide into Seattle, be in her own bed—alone—by two a.m. She was pondering which way to go when Mimi Budge stood, snatched up her portfolio, and sobbed off dramatically, crossing through the lobby to the elevator. She didn't have to share her pretty butterflies with anyone. And if anybody tried to take her butterflies away from her, Daddy would soon step in and put a stop to it.

THE RANGER COTTAGE was tucked in the woods adjacent to the Olympic National Park Visitors' Center. The Harley was already parked behind the small stone lodge. Song was sprawled out on the couch in front of a stone fireplace where embers glowed. He wasn't wearing the Ray Bans and Venus could see through the dim light that his eyes were half shut, a dreamy expression on his face. When he saw her, he sat up slowly, waved her over to the couch. She went over, sat beside him.

Song said. "There are a couple rangers asleep in the bedrooms upstairs. Your cot's taken, too. If you want to stay over, they said you can take the couch. I'm heading back to Seattle in a few minutes."

Venus said, "Me, too. So, how did it go?"

Song grinned. When he smiled he kept his mouth closed, even though he had perfect teeth. Song said, "She's a fantastic woman."

The glint in Song's eye reminded her of Richard when he got amorous. She said, "Go on."

"It worked just like you said. I checked in, made goo-goo eyes at the desk clerk. Bea Yamada. What a killer sense of humor. Anyway, she showed me to my suite. I took her out to dinner at a place called the Alibi. Lousy menu, but Bea was a howl. After I got back to the inn, having cleverly secured Zora's suite number from Bea, I went to Zora's suite, knocked.'' Song grinned some more. "She came to the door, asked who was there. I told her I was hotel security, and then maybe she looked through the peephole and saw me. She must have liked what she saw, because she unlocked all the locks and opened the door wide, like welcoming me. The rest was easy.'' Song chuckled. "You were right. Zora's a sucker for Amerasian men. Then, too, maybe it's the pheromones, I don't know, something about Valley Girls lights my wick. We had this instant attraction going right off. She's a babe, all right. I could fall for her.''

Venus said, "Don't call her a babe." Irritably. "Anyway, Zora's all exterior. Not a shred of substance. All bosom, no brain.''

Song grinned, amused. "Now who's being politically incorrect?''

"Get to the point, Song.''

Song stared at her, like he could penetrate her brain cells, read her private thoughts. After a moment, he said, "So we walked out on the beach, and it's only a guess, but I think she's been holed up too long in that suite by herself. She spilled her guts. Where should I start?''

Venus said, "At the beginning, but do me a favor. Leave out the gushy, boy-meets-babe details.''

"So anyway, Zora's got a thing about Peter Avalon. She has this love/hate thing over him, like really strong. She told me all about his discovering her in Italy, doing the screen tests, offering her a contract, ad nauseam. Then later, he decides she isn't right for the product. The younger brother—Troy, isn't it?''

"Right.''

"Troy smoothed things over. But Peter's acting suspicious. Now she's wet henned at Peter. She believes in her heart that the title of Miss Blue Poppy is her destiny. She's afraid Peter's going to pull a fast one at the last minute.''

"What do you think?''

Song shrugged, put a cigarette between his lips, lit a match, cupped it to the cigarette. He smoked Player's, unfiltered Navy Cut. He plucked a tobacco shred from his lip, inhaled, blew out smoke, watched it rise in the dimly lit room. After a minute he said, "She's a determined lady. My opinion doesn't matter.''

"Tell me anyway.''

He shrugged. "I'm not familiar with the fragrance, so how would I know?"

Venus leaned over, pointed to her neck. "Put your nose right here. Take a whiff."

Song leaned over, inhaled. "Hmmmm. Nice. It's got class."

"How about on Zora? Think you'd like it on Zora?"

Song shook his head. "Not Zora's type. That's too light, too fresh. Zora might be young, but she's the sultry, exotic type. It's not her whiff."

Venus said, "You don't think Blue Poppy's exotic?"

Song considered. "It's mysterious, but Zora's more the sultry, heavy frangipani type. Some people have that aspect in their skin, like musk. She's got that kind of skin, that natural musky scent. Blue Poppy isn't Zora, if that's Blue Poppy you're wearing."

"I'm surprised you could smell her skin underneath all that Opium she wears."

"Meow."

She watched the embers pulsing in the fireplace. Maybe a ghost had passed, stirring the air, reviving the embers' glow. A heart is a lot like an ember. It waxes and wanes, depending on what stirs it. Some hearts turn cold, to stone. Like the Andrews Sisters said, "Hearts of stone will never break." Doodley-wop, doodley-wop.

Song said, "Where are you?"

She shrugged, said, "Go on. Tell me more."

Song cupped the cigarette. He knew it was illegal to smoke on park property. He bent the rules, and the ashtray on the coffee table suggested he wasn't the only one who did. He said, "That's about all I could tease out of her in the short time we were together. But I'm meeting her again tomorrow, for a swim."

"In the strait?"

Song scratched the side of his neck. Maybe that's where he kept his brain. "Maybe. We'll see."

"Bet you end up in the indoor pool."

"What're we betting?" Song glanced up.

"The Harley."

Song grinned, broke out laughing. "No way. It's mine forever."

"Okay, how's this. You go swimming in the strait, no wet suit, just your swimming trunks, and I'll fix you up with Echo."

He sat up straight. "Echo's in town?"

"She's flying in from New York tonight."

Song took a deep breath, exhaled slowly. He's a man with problems, all of them female. He said, "You've got a bet." He walked over to the cottage door. "I'm out of here," he said.

"Why not stay at the inn tonight? You've got a suite all to yourself."

Song shook his head. "Gotta get back, see someone."

"Oh, I get it." Wryly. "The Seattle love interest who's about to take a fall. Am I right?"

Song didn't answer right away. He walked back over to the fireplace, took the brass poker from its stand, worried the embers. She watched him, his back to her. He was medium height, a weight lifter, the kind who wear white T-shirts with the short sleeves rolled up, a pack of cigarettes rolled into one sleeve. The slick black hair, the cool Ray Bans, and black leather jacket all fit Song's personal style. She said, "Why didn't you show up in uniform this afternoon?"

Without turning around, Song said, "Olson said you might refuse to turn the case over to me. Uniform's in my pack. Lucky, huh?"

"Yes," she agreed. "And it better stay there for a while."

THE SPIDER HUMMED along the highway, caressing the hairpin curve at Agate Beach. A full moon flirted with the cloud cover and a light, misty rain fell. The air hung cold and damp, but she hardly noticed. Cradled in the Spider's kid leather seat, the heater on purr, Peter Duchin's lush riffs tickling her ears, she savored the comforts. "Go ahead, coddle me," she told the Spider. "Be my best pal. Make me forget."

You don't just suddenly decide to forget and then it happens automatically. Doesn't work that way. What you do is, you drive over the next high cliff, plunge screaming into the deep saltwater abyss, bury your aborted dreams in a grave of kelp. It's easy, especially if your vehicle cooperates. The Spider felt pliable, flexible, obedient under her deft direction. Teasing it over a cliff would be a piece of cake. You die, you stop feeling. Simple. Just put lead into the gas pedal, floor it. Let's see...she floored the Spider, her headlights barely penetrating the thick fog, took the next curve on two wheels, sailed about fifty yards that way, then leveled out. Nice rush. Nothing really suicidal. More like a dress rehearsal. She took Duchin off the CD player, put on Benny's "String of Pearls." Her head bounced to the rhythm, her fingers danced across the cool leather steering wheel. She was wondering why weed never appealed to her when she saw the blue flashing lights, slowed down, and pulled off the highway onto the road's narrow shoulder.

Sheriff Needles pulled his car up behind hers, got out slowly, and walked toward her. She stepped out of the Spider, stood beside it. The closer Needles got to her, the more she understood why he was sheriff. He was the size and shape of Goliath, and he walked like Wyatt Earp. He kept his right hand on the butt of his pistol and his hips rotated a full circle with each long stride. She raised her hands to show they were empty. When Needles saw the small bare palms, he moved his right hand from the butt of his gun to his breast pocket. He fished out a ball-point pen and clicked it. Venus lowered her hands. Needles got out his ticket book, poised the pen for action, and said, "Got a driver's license?"

If a human head could be a pine cone, Needles would be an alpine fir, the hatless crown steeply domed, the surface packed with tight, sharp features, symmetrical in a troubling way. Venus handed him her driver's license and the Spider's papers. Needles's sharp eyes glistened in the moonlight as they scanned the documents. When he saw her name, he glanced up momentarily, then he went back to the documents. Venus's mouth puckered into a dry, soundless whistle.

Needles was taking a long time. A logging truck strained up the highway and passed the scene; Needles and Venus were illuminated by the sheriff's rotating blue lights. The truck eased around the next sharp curve, and Venus got a good look at the load. Toothpicks. That's what they called logs these days. Toothpick facsimiles of the once-grand Douglas firs felled by the original lumberjacks in this territory. Back then, the logs were seven feet across in diameter. A man could lie down on the stump and stretch out. But now, the depleted forests only gave up these skinny poles. That truck just rounding the corner had three or four dozen trees, each about eight inches in diameter, maybe a foot at the outside. Progress.

Needles handed back the papers. "New car, eh?" Maybe Canadian, maybe a transplant.

Venus said, "Just today. By the way, I'm the DOI agent—"

"I know who you are." Needles cut her off. He walked around the Spider, checked under the hood, in the trunk, under the seats, checked it thoroughly. If he was thinking, it was to himself. When he finished studying the vehicle, he wrote a ticket for reckless driving, handed it to her, and said, "Your pal Song picked up the Trooper."

Venus nodded. Needles said, ''Houck says you went into the kitchen.''

Houck, the deputy.

Venus nodded again. Needles chewed his lip. His eyes scanned the two-lane highway. Forests on one side, on the other, a steep cliff over the water. The moon came and went, bathing the strait intermittently, when the clouds let it. The chilly dampness clung to everything, including Venus's mood. Needles said, ''What'd you find in there?''

Venus tucked the reckless driving citation in her pocket. Out of sight, out of mind. She said, ''A lot of fancy produce. Some stinking evidence. But I guess you saw it all first.''

Needles shrugged noncommittally. He pointed at the Spider. ''Brand new, eh?'' He licked his lips.

She handed him the keys. He went over and shut off the patrol car's engine and lights, locked it up, then came back and slid into the Spider's driver side seat, moved it back as far as it would go to fit his long frame. She got in the passenger side. Needles fed the Spider some juice. It purred as he guided it off the road's slim shoulder onto the highway, headed east. Once round the hairpin curve at Aggie MacGregor's place, Needles pushed his foot to the floor. The Spider responded, still purring, only faster. Nothing passed them on the road. If it had, it would have screamed off the road, because Needles was driving down the broken yellow line like he owned the road, and she guessed he did. He handled the vehicle expertly, gently, but demanding its best performance. The Spider liked how Needles massaged the accelerator, how he gave it full reign on the outside of the curves. Venus watched the serendipity between Needles and the Spider. By now she'd completely forgotten about the ticket in her pocket.

When they reached Fern, Needles took the main street flying, then tried one of her maneuvers on two wheels around the corner. No one saw the performance because Fern was all asleep. Needles navigated the town square going eighty on the straightaways, sixty on the curves. He took Orcas Lane flying, raised gravel at Blue Poppy's front gate. The guardhouse light flicked on, but they were gone before anyone saw them. He sailed back onto the highway, heading west. Needles didn't talk, he just drove. When they reached the patrol car, he climbed out of the Spider. Venus slid across into the driver's seat, adjusted it to her own size. Needles turned the patrol car around. He let the window down on the passenger side, nodded at the Spider, said, "Full cool." Then he peeled off.

She turned the Spider around, swung onto the road, heading back toward Oz. Toward civilization.

NINETEEN

PHEROMONES

"VENUS, whatever are you doing at my breakfast table?"

"Eating breakfast, Mother."

Bella slid into her throne. Stephen had set a sunny table on the upper terrace. A soupy fog spilled across Bella's fish-eye view of the Cascade Mountains, Puget Sound, and Mount Rainier. The Sunday morning air held promise, though. Bella's unwarranted optimism could pierce fog shrouds, could even trigger burn-off, or a sun break. Bella was imagining a gloriously blue noontime sky, ardent sunshine beating down upon her gardens and her perfect skin. Right now, all Venus could imagine was gloom. Death, and gloom. Life is a slug, she decided. Nasty, oozing slime.

Bella plucked a yellow linen napkin from its silver ring, spread it neatly across her comely lap, and said, "Life is full of tiny surprises. And all along I thought you had your own breakfast table, in your own home." Her lovely hand flew to her mouth. "Oh dear, I almost forgot. Of course you had to come here, darling."

"Sorry I didn't phone first. It was very late, about two o'clock this morning. I just slipped in through the lower terrace door and went to bed. So as not to disturb you."

"Of course, you are always welcome, darling. It is just that I was expecting another face this morning at breakfast."

"Whose?"

"Echo's. I thought she might have been the clumsy one I heard on the lower terrace at two-fifteen a.m. Her flight must have been delayed."

The last thing Venus needed was a younger sister pining over her bare ring finger, making told-you-so noises. She said, "Maybe she's not coming after all."

"Why, Venus, you are so negative this morning. No, Echo will come. She probably had publishing business to attend. You know how busy published poets are."

"So you heard me come in?"

"I'm not deaf, Venus. When you hit up against the hot tub, the collision broke the Richter scale."

"Sorry. There was this slippery slug mucous..."

"Never mind. Is that pesky Mrs. Gasgcoyne so coldhearted she won't put you up in a fresh apartment for a few days?"

"What do you mean?" Preceding the first bite of crumpet.

"You know what I mean, dear. The eviction papers. I must admit to being mortified when the gentleman came to serve the documents. Hand me the marmite, if you please."

The marmite changed hands. "I'm a little confused, Mother. I didn't go home last night. What papers?"

"Surely you knew that Mrs. Gasgcoyne issued you an eviction notice. Via my address. I don't understand these elderly eccentrics. Mrs. Gasgcoyne reminds me exactly of your grandmother. March hares inevitably loose mayhem on society. For instance, when I was a young girl, your grandmother and grandfather often threw huge parties in our home. Next morning, you never knew who would show up, and in what frightful condition, at the breakfast table. Thank you, Stephen. I'll use the gooseberry preserves today. Pass the cream, please, Venus. Are your crumpets toasted properly?"

"I haven't heard anything about an eviction."

"Tsk." Bella spread the unsightly preserves over her crumpet, on top of the marmite. Unsightly, but delectable. To her "tsk" Bella added, "Sloppy way to manage a property. Do you mean to say that Mrs. Gasgcoyne never actually informed you she was serving the eviction notice?"

"Not a word. In fact, on Friday morning, I personally handed her my rent check. She didn't mention anything about throwing me out." Venus set her crumpet down on her breakfast plate. Her small appetite had just shrunk to zilch.

Bella said, "I understand it's a fait accompli. According to the documents, your personal property has been placed in a storage unit somewhere on Mercer Street."

"That storage company near the pink neon elephant?"

"So I gather. The address places the storage company somewhere between the Opera House and Denny Way. That could be construed as near the pink elephant, I suppose. For that matter so could the wooden boat museum, but that's neither here nor there. You'll find the envelope on the front hall buffet in the salver.'' Bella patted her talented lips. ''Stephen will fetch the good news. Stephen, darling, could you manage that for us?''

Bella had Stephen mesmerized to serve her beck and call. Dutifully, he went to fetch the awful evidence. Bella sighed. ''It's for the good, you know. You really belong at home before the nuptials. Planning goes more smoothly. You may have your own bedroom back, dear, and I'll have Burden put out clean towels this morning. I'm afraid to ask what you did to inure the wrath of Mrs. Gasgcoyne before starting that fire. By all indications, you've presented a chronic problem for the landlady. That really was quite irresponsible, Venus, starting a fire in your apartment. I hope you haven't inherited any of Aunt Minnie's genes. We don't need another mad hatter on the tree.''

''Minnie Winsome or Minnie Diamond? A fire?''

''Never mind.''

Like the crumpet, Stephen's excellent soft-boiled egg had lost its allure, in spite of the perfect egg cup, her favorite, Humpty Dumpty's bottom half. Stephen might be insulted if she asked him to paint faces on her morning egg. Where was Father when she needed him?

Stephen returned with the documents, set them before Venus, went away, maybe to worry Burden. Stephen and Burden were still in the honeymoon stage of their working relationship, Bella having brought Burden on board just weeks ago. Burden's household management expertise permitted Stephen more time to dispatch his secretarial duties, and for this Stephen welcomed the handsome Englishman with open arms. The trouble was, Burden possessed a small but strong homophobic streak, and he flinched whenever Stephen came too near. This dance of the household staff occasionally loosed tension in the air, and sooner or later, Bella had confided to Venus, the honeymoon phase would give way to their first quarrel. No one looked forward to a quarrel between Stephen and Burden, least of all, Bella.

The eviction papers looked legitimate enough. The reason given; a fire, originating in the tenant's apartment, completely destroyed the apartment's kitchen, to the tune of twenty-eight thousand dollars. The tenant, claimed the landlady, had been a chronic problem since the day she'd moved in. Mrs. Gasgcoyne didn't elaborate on that part, but went on to emphasize that leaving a candle burning on the kitchen counter and going away had proved irresponsible in the extreme. Fires are nasty and expensive. The entire kitchen would have to be rebuilt.

The landlady's insurance covered the disaster, but nonetheless, the tenant would have to go.

"Fire?" Venus whispered hoarsely. "What fire?"

Bella sipped her Sumatra in cream. "The fire that started in your kitchen. Apparently you left a candle burning on a countertop before you went out Friday morning. At approximately one o'clock in the afternoon, the fire ignited the birch cabinets. Fortunately, another tenant detected smoke, thank your lucky stars, and called the engine house. Only the kitchen was damaged, I gather. That was all the six o'clock news on KIRO reported. I like that new anchorman, don't you? He adds panache to the team. I think he came from San Francisco, so of course he's very polished."

"Mother..."

"It might have made the *Post Intelligencer,* although I rather doubt the incident warranted that much attention. Why look, dear. A sun break."

"Where?"

"Right there above the Space Needle. Actually, a bit to the left of the spinning part. Honestly, Venus, sometimes I worry about your lack of swiftness. See now, you've missed it."

The sound of little footsteps interrupted Venus's suicidal musings. The patter of more trouble coming. Venus pushed back her chair, said, "I've got to go phone—"

"Sit down." Honeyed overtones laced Bella's melodious command, supreme authority in a velveteen cloak. Venus eased back into the chair and watched Timmy drag up to the breakfast table.

Timmy, the newly adopted son, was small boned, petite, like Venus, but he had Asian features and cafe au lait skin, enhanced this morning by tennis whites. He reminded her of a preshrunk Michael Chang, only more Indonesian. He was dressed neatly, his hair combed. He was too fastidious, too deft, for an eight-year-old, and far too bright.

Timmy was approximately eight years old; no one knew for sure. His hair was a chocolate brown silky fringe that Bella watched like a hawk and the barber kept neatly trimmed. He was pampered beyond any child's wildest dreams, even more so than Pansy, Bella's sharpei. Now as he came to the breakfast table, Timmy clutched a black physician's bag. He set it down with portentous care on the terrace floor beside his chair. It might have contained a bomb. Venus wouldn't put it past the precocious boy.

Timmy's eyes, still half shut, searched the breakfast table, avoiding contact with other humans. He rarely conversed before his first bowl of Cocoa Krispies. He reached for the cereal.

"What do you say, Timmy?" Bella, sweetly.

"Good morning, everyone." Grudgingly. Timmy glowered over the table, delicately poured Cocoa Krispies into a bowl, the way Betty Crocker measures flour. He reached out, plucked up the cream pitcher, poured heavy cream over the Cocoa Krispies, a junior scientist, pouring in dribs and drabs, measure by measure.

Bella didn't appreciate having two surly breakfast partners, and wisely chose to ignore all the dense emotional fog shrouding her boiled egg. Bella might have experienced the blues once or twice in her lifetime, but if she had, no one ever knew about it. Bella chirped, "Timmy, how handsome you look in your tennis whites. Are you playing this morning?"

Timmy shook his head sullenly. His thick, silky eyelashes almost concealed the embers in his clear mahogany eyes.

"Well then, young man, why in the world are you wearing tennis whites?" Bella, still chirping against the pall.

Timmy shrugged, fed his neat little mouth, chewing imperceptibly, the way Bella chews. Venus started counting. When he had chewed the mouthful seventy times, Timmy swallowed neatly and replied, "Because."

Bella's left eyebrow shot up. "Oh, so we are playing a guessing game this morning? Very well, I'll take the first turn." She set down her egg spoon, placed a slim finger against her porcelain cheek, and after a moment's musing, said, "You are wearing tennis whites because you knew Venus would be at breakfast this morning. Since tennis whites only add to your natural good looks, and since you have such a need to impress Venus, you wore them to breakfast. Am I right?"

Timmy glowered, shook his head.

"All right then, Venus, it is your turn to guess why Timmy is wearing tennis whites this morning."

Venus sat frozen to her chair, her mind two hills distant, on the crest of Queen Anne, where Clara Gasgcoyne lived, where she, too, had lived, until some time Friday afternoon. Bella's question jolted Venus out of a dull trance. "What? Oh. I think Tim's wearing the whites because he has a new girlfriend."

Venus didn't see the spoonful of Cocoa Krispies until it smacked the side of her face. Appalled but cool, Bella said, "Stephen, will you kindly bring Venus a damp cloth for her face?" And changed the subject.

Venus wiped off the soggy cereal. Timmy continued eating, as if nothing had happened. Bella chimed on about fog liftings and sun breaks, ignoring the incident until Timmy said, "May I please be excused?"

"Certainly, young man," Bella murmured. "You may be excused to your room, where you will spend the remainder of the day reading a certain book. Stephen, please fetch my copy of Emily Post's *Etiquette for Children* and deliver it to Timmy's room. And while you are at it, kindly accompany Timmy to his dungeon. Thank you, Stephen, darling."

Timmy inhaled his fury, tucking it deep into his psyche. On the way into the house, he turned to Venus, said, "I'm sorry about your broken engagement."

Venus stared. "How did you know?"

Timmy pointed at her ring finger. "Ring's gone."

Bella's pupils dilated and the eyebrow shot back up and the chime was missing from her lyrics when she exclaimed, "Timmy, march immediately to your room."

Timmy picked up his black physician's bag. On the fly, he patted Venus's arm and murmured, "It's okay, Venus. I'll take care of you." Then he followed Stephen to the dungeon. The fog was already lifting, the sun burning a hole in it, like a cigarette burn on gray wool. A patch of warm rays spilled across the terrace. That was the last sun Timmy would see for a while, but he didn't care. He'd delivered the bomb.

What followed between Venus and Bella might best be described as a regretful verbal ballet. Swan Lake in Chechnya, Onyegin on stilts. It wasn't pretty. Later, the only part Venus recalled verbatim was Bella's final remark, "Nonsense, there is no other woman. Richard isn't a gigolo. If he called things off, it can only be because you did something to provoke him. I can easily imagine your unladylike behavior as the culprit, but certainly not another woman. Poor darling. I mean, Richard. When was the last time you wore a skirt, Venus?"

She fled from the sunny terrace, from the cold, faceless Humpty Dumpty soft-boiled egg, from the half-eaten crumpet. A memory of Clara Gasgcoyne and old John flashed into her mind. She manipulated the vision until she'd placed a gun in old John's hand and made it go off, killing the landlady. That brief revisionist frolic hardly consoled, but it did remove the edge.

CONRAD AVALON awoke to a gentle breeze wafting through the Pioneer Suite's raised windows. Filtered sunlight graced a hazy blue sky. In the distance, seagulls rode the drafts over Puget Sound, mocking landlubbers like himself, music to his ears. When a ferry boat tooted basso profundo, Conrad bolted out of bed, performed ten perfect push-ups, and opening the window wider, sang out into Sixth Avenue:

> *"Love becomes a lassie*
> *When her laddie's comin' home*
> *A'pluckin' her fair blossoms*
> *O'er the heath he's bound to roam.*
>
> *Laddie's gone to Ireland*
> *Kissed Dublin's fairest Molly*
> *Traveled down in Yorkshire*
> *Where all the girls are jolly.*
>
> *Laddie's sailed across the seas*
> *Mermaids swimming round*
> *But when he heard his lassie weep*
> *He turned his ship around.*
>
> *For comin' home to lassie's arms*
> *Across the seas and heather*
> *The lad could taste his lassie's lips*
> *No others kissed him better.*
>
> *And love becomes a laddie*
> *When his lass walks round the bend*
> *He lays fair blossoms at her feet.*
> *His heart in her tiny hand."*

Which went to prove, mused Conrad, that you can't snatch the heather from a Scotsman's heath, for he'll track you into Edinburgh and clean your teeth.

Now, why did he think of that?

On his way down to the dining room for breakfast, Conrad stopped at the business desk, wrote a short note on WAC stationery, and had it faxed to a phone number in Fern, Washington. Then he strolled over to the concierge desk and asked that his luggage be brought down. He was checking out this morning, he told the concierge, going home. A businessman can't afford to leave the store for very long. The concierge said, "I thought you'd retired, Mr. Avalon."

Conrad chuckled. "I have, young man. But a family business like ours occasionally requires an old pro's seasoned nose. Besides," he added, "the poppy fields are about to bloom and I don't care to miss that brilliant spectacle." He nodded at the concierge and floated into the dining room on the aroma of poached eggs and salmon kippers. Pausing at a vase of English country garden flowers, he plucked a bachelor button, and an accommodating maître d' helped attach it to his lapel. Yes, said Conrad to himself, it is a perfect day for courting a lovely lass.

TIMMY LOOKED UP from Emily Post's *Etiquette for Children*, saw Venus standing outside his window. Whatever was Miss Trouble, U.S.A., doing in Bella's best rhododendrons? He sniffed, wrinkled his nose, went back to Emily Post. A moment later, Timmy heard a light tap on the French doors. Venus had broken through the rhododendron grove and now stood on his private terrace. She wasn't smiling. She was holding something that looked interesting in her hands, so Timmy put the book aside and went to the French doors. He opened one and peered out at her, focusing on the zipper of her uniform trousers. It's hell growing up, reaching a certain height. He said, "What's that?"

Venus showed him the striped caterpillar, now in residence in a topless Bloomingdale's swizzle sticks box, surrounded by a forest of violet leaves. The creature munched voraciously on the edges of a leaf, his forelegs serving as hands, feeding himself. She'd covered the clear acrylic box with a gold net stocking bag that provided good air circulation and hardly interfered with the observer's view. She removed the mesh bag, offered the box to Timmy. "You can pet him."

Timmy reached into the box, placed a tiny index fingertip gently on the caterpillar's smooth coat. The creature opened its jaws and bit down on Timmy's finger. Timmy jumped backward, uninjured but startled. "That wasn't nice," he said in his small, hoarse voice. "You meant to frighten me."

Venus smiled victoriously. "Now that I've had my revenge, how'd you like to baby-sit for a few days?"

"Baby-sit who?" Timmy looked dubious.

"My caterpillar. He's not just any caterpillar. He's very rare, very unique. I wouldn't trust him to anyone else but you."

Timmy folded his arms like an adult does when defenses go up. Venus said, "See, he's not biting now. He's more afraid of you than you are of him."

"I am not afraid of him."

Venus made a move to come inside. Timmy blocked her at first, then finally gave way. She came into Timmy's room, looked around. "Gad, you keep this place shipshape," she remarked.

Timmy, behind his folded arms, shrugged. "I try. Now, give me the particulars, if you please. I can't care for him if I don't know the particulars."

Venus stared at Timmy. He sounded more and more like Bella. Now that she noticed, Timmy's whole demeanor had changed in the few weeks since Venus had rescued him from the terrors of Ozone Beach and delivered him to Bella's compassionate arms. Timmy would never forget the nightmares of his early childhood, but Bella hoped that with enough affection, carefully balanced with discipline, the boy would enjoy a shred of normalcy in his life. He was catching on fast to the routine around Bella's, though, and to Bella's regal mannerisms. He'd been a frightened little snot when Venus first met him, and he was still a frightened little snot, but with this new, little prince veneer.

"All right," she said, placing the Bloomingdale's box on Timmy's dresser, "here's what you do." Timmy stepped forward to accept the assignment, cradled his little hands around the acrylic box, peered in.

"I'm listening," he said hoarsely.

"A caterpillar is the larval stage of a butterfly, or a moth," she began.

"I know that."

Venus nodded. "This very rare caterpillar is the larval stage of the Dungeness silverspot. It's been listed as extinct."

"Latin name?" Timmy raised an inquiring eyebrow. Bella personified.

"*Speyeria zerene dungenessii.* This species has supposedly disappeared from the area where it once thrived, up on the Olympic Peninsula, in a meadow, where its host plant, the western blue violet, grows. But the violet is losing ground because of so much land development on the peninsula, and now the host plant, the only food this little critter will eat, is disappearing. Then, the insects that pollinate the flowers..."

"Okay, okay," Timmy snapped impatiently. "Can we just cut to the chase? What do I feed him?"

Venus sat on the edge of Timmy's single bed. It had the same Dress Stewart bed cover that she'd used years ago, when this was her bed, her bedroom. That was before the twins, Echo and Bart, came along. Then Bella had rearranged the children's bedrooms and Venus had somehow ended up in the small sewing alcove just off the Ping-Pong room. In the alcove bedroom, Venus enjoyed solitude, and reading books. Life between the covers of a book seemed more real to her than life in the family home. You don't grow up a British peer by birth without a lot of regalia and artifice strangling your formative years.

Timmy said, "Can't you hear me?"

"What?" Venus popped out of her reverie. "Sorry. He'll only eat the leaves of *V. adunca,* the western blue violet. I'll bring you fresh supplies every day. These in the box should last until tomorrow afternoon. Meanwhile, you'll have to clean the environment at least once a day, dump out the little balls of excrement. And make sure there's a small water supply. A damp paper towel on the bottom works. Then you have to keep him in a natural light source."

Timmy looked around his bedroom. "How about over there?" He pointed to his desk. It sat in a corner near the French doors.

"Sure, that'll work."

Timmy said, "Anything else?"

"It's going to shed its skin a few times. Don't be alarmed. He'll ingest a lot of air and hold it inside until he pops out of the outer skin that's molted. He has a total of six molts, or instars. But he's probably had a few already, so maybe he'll have another three or four. Then he'll spin a silk patch on a fresh violet leaf. He'll attach himself to the patch and start to metamorphose. He'll form a chrysalis, a personal cocoon. He'll develop a cocoon and stay inside it for two, maybe three weeks. While he's inside the cocoon, he'll change from caterpillar into a soupy, juicy mass, then transform into a butterfly.

When the butterfly is ready to emerge, it will chew its way out of the cocoon.''

"Then what?" Timmy folded his arms again. She knew what he was thinking. He was thinking about investing time, possibly some emotional attachment in a relationship with another creature, and then having to let it go free. Already in Timmy's short life, he had lost his birth parents and a pair of stepparents. A lot of loss for an eight year old. Now he might get emotionally attached to this caterpillar and ultimately it would abandon him. Life was cruel that way. In Timmy's short life, abandonment had been pandemic.

Venus said, ''If the caterpillar survives, if it becomes a butterfly, we'll have to let it go free. Then you and I will go somewhere to celebrate our success.''

Timmy raised his eyes, stared at Venus. After a minute he said, ''I can take care of you a thousand times better than Richard.''

He picked up the caterpillar house, carried it over to his desk, and set it gently down in the corner nearest daylight. He didn't notice her eyes pool up, because Venus smiled and said, ''Remember, sport, this is our secret.''

Timmy touched a finger to his lips.

TWENTY

PINK ELEPHANT

CLARA GASGCOYNE wasn't answering her door. Venus glanced up at the landlady's open window. She thought she'd seen movement up there, from the corner of her eye, but it must have been a peripheral glimpse of the robin family flapping around in their nest. One of the youngsters noticed Venus, caught her eye, and cackled. Venus barked at it, but the fearless baby robin kept on cackling. Venus tried the doorbell again. Now all the little robinettes cackled in unison. Mother was absent this morning, maybe gone to market with the landlady. Or maybe landlord/tenant court. After four or five minutes of avian cacophony with no answer to the bell, Venus turned to leave the porch.

The same sprinkler made the same familiar water arc across Clara Gasgcoyne's front lawn. She was halfway across the arc's path when a high, tight voice called out, "Wait. Come back here." She turned around. Up on the porch stood old John, Clara Gasgcoyne's long-suffering husband-slave. Venus went back up on the porch. John had materialized from a rhododendron bush beside the house. His hands wore canvas gloves, and he held a pair of long garden shears. He looked tired, like someone who'd been awake for a hundred years and had seen nothing but horror and grief all that time. When she met him on the porch, old John said, "You came about the fire?"

"I didn't start it, Mr. Gasgcoyne."

Old John shrugged. "Maybe you did, maybe you didn't. But it ruined our property. My wife is very angry. Too angry to eat, or to sleep. I am worried about my wife. She has a weak heart. This might kill her. All because of you."

"But, Mr. Gasgcoyne—"

He held up a trembling gloved hand. "Please, no excuses. Nothing comes from excuses."

Venus said, "What can I do?"

John pressed his lips together, shook his head sadly.

"I'd like to speak to your wife, Mr. Gasgcoyne. Is she home?"

"She is not at home. She has gone to see her doctor. Her heart is that bad. And she doesn't want to see you ever again." He turned slowly, a thin remnant of aching bones and shriveled dreams, stepped down off the porch and disappeared around the side of the house.

She was entering Cedar Lane when she spotted Clara Gasgcoyne up in the window, watching her depart. Maybe John didn't realize she was up there, and not at the doctor's. Maybe Clara, not John, was the liar. The old woman opened the window a crack, put her siren red lips to the fresh air, and yelled, "Get off my property, you pyromaniac!"

OSCAR SUNDBORG'S penthouse condo in Belltown had a private doorman, a Zen garden, three-hundred-sixty-degree balconies, and a rooftop swimming pool big enough for water polo doubles. In fairness to Oscar Sundborg, his partner, Otto Lux, had shared the upkeep and condo fees and had done all the cooking. When it came to cooking, Oscar Sundborg knew no more than what he could measure with his little fingernail. He was in the middle of a photo shoot when Venus was shown into the maestro's studio. She sat in a canvas chair in the darkened studio, watching Sundborg photograph two overweight dachshunds eating a diet dog food called Slimdog. Presumably, they were to star in a print ad for the dog food company. The dogs didn't like the food. One walked away from the dish, his nose turned up disdainfully. The other vomited on the studio floor. Sundborg's assistants tried everything, but they couldn't lure the dachsies back to Slimdog. Finally, somebody brought in a couple cans of Friskee's Beef Chunks in Gravy. This worked, and the slop looked enough like Slimdog to avoid any retouch work. When they'd finished with the roly-poly dachshunds, they broke out a matching pair of slim dachshunds and photographed them beside the Slimdog package. Before and after, ad biz style.

Sundborg wrapped the shoot and led Venus up a spiral staircase to the penthouse living quarters. He was tall, slender. He had white-blond hair and pale skin, like a thin negative. He wore chartreuse baggy trousers and a turquoise dress shirt rolled up to the elbows. In one ear, he wore three gold hoops in graduating sizes. When they arrived at the penthouse, he snapped a finger and a latte machine started brewing. He brought the two lattes over to a pair of sliding glass doors and invited Venus onto the westward-facing balcony. From here, you could see the Belltown Marina, all the yachts. Sundborg pointed out his modest eighty-five-foot Seapalace, the *Lux*, named after his partner. He handed her a mug, gazed out over the harbor, and said, "Seattle's full of money." Then he sipped his latte.

Venus said, "You've heard about Lux?"

Sundborg squinted, nodded once, twice. Down below in the marina, a yacht named *Plaisance* pulled slowly away from its docking. Venus watched it, allowing Sundborg a moment of privacy. Then Sundborg said, "I always told Otto never to eat strange mushrooms."

"They said it was mushrooms?"

Sundborg nodded, sipped his latte. "I spoke to the coroner. The coroner said it was probably toxic mushrooms that killed him. The death's angel mushroom. But the tests aren't conclusive yet."

Venus didn't say anything.

Sundborg continued, "We were distant cousins and business partners. Otto and I were going to open a Native American restaurant here in Belltown. We were business partners and we shared this condo when he was home. I'm going to miss him."

"What about family?" Venus asked.

Sundborg shook his head. "Just me. Actually, we were fourth cousins or something like that. His parents are dead. There's no one, except for me."

"I'm sorry," she offered.

He turned, went inside. She followed him. They went into the big, modern kitchen. Sundborg went over to a bookshelf, searched, plucked out a fat spiral binder folder. He said, "I told Otto he should put this on disk. But he didn't trust computers. He was afraid the computer would lose his best recipes. So he always wrote them down by hand."

He leafed through the loose-leaf folder. It was neatly organized and tabbed. He came to a page about halfway through, opened the folder wide, handed it to Venus. "You might be interested in this," he said. "Being a nature cop."

She took the loose-leaf binder, leaned against a wall, stared at the map Lux had drawn of Yodeler's meadow. The entire meadow had been divided into harvesting plots. On the upper alpine reaches, purple camas and blue violets were indicated. In the rain forest segment, Lux had made little markings to indicate where to find woolly chanterelles, veronicas, oyster mushrooms, valerian, and chocolate tips. He had skipped over the blue poppies, down into the heart of the meadow, where he made marks to indicate locations of black caps and salmonberries, more violet clumps, blackberry vines, fiddlehead ferns, and chocolate lily. Down in the meadow's apron, he had marked more violet clumps, white-flowered camas, and finally, on the beach Lux had handwritten "Clams galore!" Lux had reduced Yodeler's meadow to a kitchen garden.

Sundborg said, "Otto always told me that map was worth ten million dollars." He laughed ironically. "That's a hell of a lot of camas cakes."

Native Americans once thrived on camas cakes. They dug the bulb of *Camassia quamash,* the purple camas, from the soil, pressed it into a cake shape, steamed it over hot flat rocks with mosses or leaves and dried grass, covered that over with earth and cooked it overnight. In the morning, they hung up the cakes to dry. The supply lasted most of the winter, kept in wood boxes. The early explorers bought camas cakes from the natives and likened them to poached pears. But you had to know the difference between purple camas and *zigadenus venenosus,* the white camas, also called death camas. It's easy to tell the difference between the edible species and the deadly species if you harvest camas before the flowers die, but after the flowers die, you might easily mistake one for the other. All camas cause great bouts of flatulence. Death camas, *Z. venenosus,* killed thousands of Pacific Northwest natives and early explorers. Yodeler's meadow was full of camas.

"But what's so valuable here?" asked Venus.

Sundborg shrugged. "I guess he meant the restaurant. He was convinced a Native American restaurant would go over in a big way. He even thought it might become a chain of restaurants. He wanted to serve authentic food, like grilled salmon with wapato, camas cakes, venison, wild berries, chanterelles, you know, all the authentic stuff."

"Whale blubber, too?"

Sundborg nodded. "Otto thought of everything."

Venus said, "Mind if I borrow this?"

"I'll make you a copy of it." Sundborg took the page out of the loose-leaf cookbook and started down the spiral staircase to his office.

Venus said, "Actually, I'd like to borrow the whole cookbook. I promise not to steal your restaurant idea."

Sundborg came back up the stairs. "Okay, I think I can trust you.

But do me a favor. Go downstairs into my office and copy it all. Leave me the original." He blinked, dry-eyed. "It was Otto's, after all."

Venus said, "He wasn't in any danger?"

Sundborg frowned. "He never said anything to me."

"Who generally sold him the produce?"

"He said he harvested most of the stuff himself. In a place called Yodeler's meadow. I gather it's a haven for herbalists and such."

"How did Lux learn about the meadow?"

Sundborg thought a minute, then said, "I think it was his homeopath. He went to a homeopathic physician for bouts of depression. The homeopath prescribed Saint-John's-wort. I think the homeopath told Otto about the meadow because he went there himself to gather medicinal herbs. Like the Saint-John's-wort."

"You got his name?"

"Let's see." Sundborg got out the Yellow Pages, leafed through, said, "Here it is. Sven Boren. A Swede, like me."

"Ballard address?" Venus took out a pen and notebook.

"Ya, sure. You betcha," joked Sundborg. "How'd you ever guess." He gave her the address.

She said, "What about a love interest?"

Sundborg shook his head. "Nothing serious."

"He ever mention anyone?"

Sundborg said, "There was a kid up in Fern. A local. Otto liked him a lot. But I don't know his name. He never said his name."

Venus went down to the studio office, copied a hundred and fifty pages of recipes and the map of Yodeler's meadow, then she left.

Pink Elephant Storage Lockers had her belongings. She paid a man to bail them out, and paid him again to have them shipped over to Bella's on Magnolia Bluff. By the time she got out of there, she was several hundred dollars poorer, but relieved to learn that her possessions were intact. Maybe eventually she'd find the charm bracelet, and a few other things she needed to return to Richard. On her way out, she asked the man, "What happened to the kitchen appliances?"

The Pink Elephant man shrugged, showed open palms. "I don't know, lady. They probably got hauled to the dump. They say that kitchen was pretty well cooked."

"What dump?"

The man stared. "How the hell am I supposed to know that?"

When she left, the man was muttering under his breath and a rain cloud burst open, spilling buckets over the glum Seattle morning.

TWENTY-ONE

LAND FOR SALE...CHEAP

RAIN BEAT AGAINST the windows. Outside, Puget Sound had disappeared beneath thundering herds of sinister buffalo clouds. Up in heaven, the angels bowled and brawled. Not her idea of Nirvana. From her perspective on the green canvas chair situated on the peon side of Olson's desk, Venus perceived raindrops pinging off Olson's bald head, then drizzling down the window panes. Olson glanced up. His Pillsbury cheeks sagged, and it looked like somebody might have smudged kohl around his bloodshot eyes. Venus wasn't sure, but she guessed the overall presentation resulted from another night of dream terror.

Ever since Regional's crackerjack agent Dave Dillon was shot down in the cranberry bogs at Ozone Beach, murdered by a gang of bear poachers, Olson had suffered horrendous nightmares. Venus had also seen Dave fall, had held him in her arms as he breathed the final breath of rotten injustice, and whenever she thought of him, which was often, a sickness filled her heart. Olson didn't have time to watch Dave die. Olson was busy shooting the poacher who killed Dave. Now, a couple months later, Olson still suffered the nightmares, but the old facade had gone back up, so you couldn't read Olson's emotions unless you knew the signs. Venus knew the signs: the certain way he white-knuckled his desktop, the throb in that one blue vein bisecting his bald egg-shaped head. Venus was fairly certain Olson had slept fitfully last night.

Olson saw him first, stood and held out an insincere hand toward the sleazy shadow now sullying the threshold. Ebert, from headquarters in Washington, D.C., the Grim Reaper in a shabby business suit. Olson somehow tricked his usual frown into a smile and ushered Ebert in. Venus had never stood in the same room as Ebert, never enjoyed the rude scrutiny of Ebert's notorious weasel eyes. He slid inside the office, grunted in a language Olson apparently comprehended, because Olson then sent out for some coffee. Ebert slithered into a green canvas chair, hefted an overweight leather briefcase onto his tight lap, and began rummaging.

Ebert had on a wrinkled blue-and-white striped seersucker suit, a dull white polyester shirt that revealed his nipples and hairless chest, a thin black tie, and scuffed black oxfords with dull white socks to match the polyester shirt. There was a thin scar over one of Ebert's beady rodent eyes, shaped like a ski jump. Rumor said Ebert got the ski jump scar shortly after selling off a thousand acres of federal wildlife preserve in East Texas, a migratory bird sanctuary that Ebert sold to tract housing developers. Ebert never knew what, or who, cracked his noggin, since it happened under darkness one night in Dupont Circle near Ebert's condo. When he came to, his assailant was gone, but later on he found a message on his voice mail warning him to cease selling off federal lands. Ebert delivered himself to the emergency room that night, got stitched up, and the next day closed a deal with a chemical manufacturer on a nice little dwarf jackrabbit preserve in Arizona. Ebert, so rumor had it, couldn't be intimidated. Ebert would sooner die than disappoint his superiors.

Olson said, "Sorry to hear that."

Venus must have missed an exchange between Ebert and Olson. Probably nothing important, just the usual verbal foreplay. Now Olson said, "Have you had lunch?"

Ebert grunted. "I don't eat on the job." From the overstuffed leather bag on his lap, he fished out a floppy disk, turned to Venus, and said, "You seem competent enough. Boot this up."

Flustered, Olson said, "I thought you two had met. This is Venus Diamond."

Ebert made a sour face. "I've seen her picture. I've read her c.v. I know who she is. Now boot this thing up."

She'd go along with a little patronizing for now. She needed time to size up Interior's own real estate agent. She went over to the main frame, fed in the floppy disk. On Olson's big television screen an aerial photograph of the Olympic National Forest popped up. After a little panning, the video zoomed in on Yodeler Preserve.

The rain beat harder against the windows, and she could hear a sou'westerly howling in off the Pacific. Olson switched off a table lamp. The video zoomed in on Yodeler's meadow. Ebert leaned back in his chair, aimed a laser pen at the screen, and slowly drew an incandescent red line around the meadow's borders. The line seemed accurate enough. Ebert said atonally, "This parcel of land is up for sale. Matter of fact, we already have a buyer. I'd like to close the deal in the next couple weeks."

Venus stared at Ebert. In the dim light, she couldn't make out his facial expression but she saw his weasel eyes glint, sparkle. Maybe he got commissions like any other real estate agent. Maybe that's all it was to him. A commission. And a pat on the tush from Congress. "Great job, Ebert. We won't forget you, buddy."

Olson leaned across his desk and snapped, "That's a wildlife preserve. We have marbled murrelets nesting in the forest up there. Spotted owls. Bear. The Roosevelt elk. We have several endangered species of plant and insect life, and dozens of species listed as either extirpated or sensitive, which we are trying to restore. You don't just go to a flower shop and order up a dozen chocolate lilies, lady's tresses, a bunch of *Viola adunca*. We're already leasing out one-third of the meadow. We can't afford to lose the remaining parcel. And we're not interested in corporate sponsorship of any of the national parks or for that matter, the wildlife preserves, in this region. Period."

Venus leaned forward and said, "Let me tell you about the western blue violet. It's an increasingly rare plant that grows only in salt-spray meadows on the Washington and Oregon coasts. *V. adunca* is the sole source of food for larvae of *Speyeria zerene dungenessii*, the Dungeness silverspot butterfly. *Dungenessii* used to be found all over the Dungeness cliffs and up on Yodeler Preserve. Now it's listed as extinct. We haven't sighted the Dungeness silverspot up in the preserve, or anywhere, for that matter, in several years. But recently, there've been a couple amateur sightings, and now we might have an opportunity to save the species. Without the western blue violet, this butterfly species can't survive. Likewise, without a salt-spray meadow, the western blue violet can't survive. Now the meadows are rapidly disappearing, as you know, victims of land development, loss of habitat. Right now, Yodeler Preserve is one of a handful of spots on the Olympic Peninsula that still has an intact ecosystem, that supports precious wildlife being threatened with extinction."

Ebert was reading his fingernails. Venus didn't like the way his small mouth pursed. She continued, trying to keep the alarm, the desperation, out of her voice.

"Because of its multitiered, very fragile topography, combining high alpine meadow with lower-tier salt-spray vegetation and the unusual climate of the rain shadow, this meadow's eco-system is unique in the world. We've got to protect it.''

Ebert sniffed. He'd heard it all before. "You guys all say that. Well, you better wake up and smell the Starbucks, folks. We no longer enjoy the luxury of a balanced budget. We can't save every little living thing in America. Those days are gone, folks, dead gone. Anyway, the meadow's as good as sold.''

Lightning punctuated Ebert's announcement. Venus counted. One hundred. Two hundred. Three hundred. Four hundred. Thunder crashed, rattling the windows. From forty-three stories above ground, it felt like riding a storm at sea. The Bumbershoot swayed in the heaving sou'wester. Olson had one hand on the Frango box on his desk. Emotional feeding. A diet shot to hell. Go ahead, chief, she urged silently. Have two or three. It's a rotten world out there. Have the whole damn box. But Olson resisted, merely fondling the smooth round carton. Gad, he must have a dynamite personal trainer, she thought.

Ebert was droning now, delivering his strong medicine in flat flavorless syrup. "Peter Avalon has made the government quite a generous offer. He wants the entire meadow to cultivate his poppies. It's a win-win situation, as I see it. Government makes a few million, cash up front, and loses maintenance costs. Land is maintained for cultivation purposes, so the ecofreaks won't go berserk on us. It's a win-win all right.''

Olson coughed lightly. Inside, he was choking on rage. Quietly he said, "The Tibetan blue poppy isn't a native. As Venus was trying to explain, Yodeler's meadow is the only known parcel of land supporting *Viola adunca* in numbers great enough to support the Dungeness silverspot. Now, apparently, there's some evidence the Dungeness is still around. In that meadow. Nowhere else. We lose Yodeler's to a nonnative species, and we might be dooming an entire species. Forever. We wipe it out.''

Ebert snickered. He might have clogged nasal passages. With the laser pointer, he drew idle circles around Yodeler's meadow. He drawled, "If we protected every goddamn weed in America, we'd go bankrupt tomorrow.''

"*V. adunca* isn't a weed," Venus interjected. "And the Dungeness silverspot is a key player in pollinating Saint-John's-wort, an herb used to treat depression. That means it's got medicinal value.''

Ebert cackled. "Not another medicinal properties defense? You know what? I'm sick of medicinal properties defenses.'' He switched off the laser pen, stuffed it in the bloated bag. He cackled again. ''That's as good as the Louisiana prickled billyboo defense.''

Olson and Venus stared at Ebert. He was going to explain. ''Down there in southern Louisiana,'' he said, ''they claimed this little piece of swamp land we wanted to sell supported the last remnants of billyboo creepyii or something, and that *B. creepyii* was the sole food source for the red-winged mosquito hawk.'' He cackled louder this time. ''You guys all come up with these fabulous crackpot defenses.''

''What happened?'' Venus.

''In Louisiana?'' Ebert shrugged. ''We ruled for sale. Sold the swamp to a tour operator. They give alligator swamp tours down there. Who'd want to tour a swamp? Look, when we want to get rid of a piece of land, we do it. Nine times out of ten, the biologists' defenses suck.''

Venus looked out the window, at a nicer view than Ebert. The storm raged on, and in the semidarkness Ebert stood, packed up his little road show. On the way out Ebert said to Olson, ''We'll run up there tomorrow, get the survey underway. Then we can pore over the fine points with Avalon. He's expecting us tomorrow afternoon.''

Olson opened his mouth to protest. Ebert ignored him. ''I'll be here at six o'clock tomorrow morning. Have the chopper ready.'' He slithered away, peeling his crooked shadow off the threshold.

Olson appeared stricken. Venus stood, fished one of the chocolate mint truffles out of the Frango box, unclenched Olson's fist, and dropped it in. ''Here,'' she said. ''I'll be back in a minute.''

Ebert was slinking into the elevator when Venus shoved her foot at the electronic eye. She stepped into the cool stainless steel chamber. They rode five floors down in silence, and on the thirty-eighth floor picked up a gaggle of stock brokers. She waited until they had reached the Bumbershoot's pink marble lobby, until Ebert felt the solid ground beneath the scuffed oxfords, then she said, ''What would it take to save Yodeler's meadow?''

''What do you mean by 'save'?''

''Keep it as a wildlife preserve, maintain its status as protected land.''

''Oh. I see what you mean.'' Ebert paused beside a marble column, rummaged through the briefcase. ''There's only one scenario I can think of, and it's too late.''

''What's the scenario? Just out of curiosity.''

Still rummaging, Ebert said, "You guys would have to prove conclusively that the parcel of land contained the only remaining individuals of some historically significant species. Or else a species of some biological value to the human race."

"Like what, for example?"

"Well, like discovering a native plant or herb or whatever that cures AIDS or dwarfism or something like that. Forget Saint-John's-wort and depression. I'm talking something really big."

Venus said, "What about the historical significance angle?"

Ebert grinned mischievously. "That's tougher." He pulled a small umbrella out of the briefcase, closed the bag, and made for the Bumbershoot's revolving doors. Venus followed him. Over his shoulder, Ebert said, "Like, here's an example of what I mean. Say you discover a species that ancient legends were based on. Like, say, the Roosevelt elk. But that's already been done. You guys already pulled that one off. And now I think you guys at Pacific Northwest have run clean out of historical significance defenses."

Ebert stepped into a segment of the revolving door. Venus took the next free segment, caught up with him on the sidewalk. Ebert stood under the Bumbershoot's green canvas awning. He popped open his umbrella and started walking. Venus dogged his heels. Ebert hogged the umbrella. In the pelting rain, she said, "The Dungeness silverspot has been declared extinct. If we find it up there, we'll actually be reviving a species."

Ebert cackled. "Nice try, agent. Extinct is extinct."

"One more thing." Venus wiped raindrops from her face.

Ebert raised his eyebrows. "Yeah? What's that?"

"I was wondering where you're staying."

"You mean like what hotel? I'm not in a hotel. I'm staying with my brother. He moved up here from L.A. a few years back. I'm parked in his condo over on Alki. That new place by the beach."

She watched Ebert set off in the rain, watched him disappear into the pedestrian traffic, where he belonged. The bureaucrat was out of sight now, but his message hung heavy on her already overburdened heart. It figured. The California connection. The trendy Alki condo. Alki Point was the birthplace of Seattle, where in 1851 the schooner *Exact* brought Captain Folger's little band of settlers ashore. Alki is a native word meaning, "bye and bye," as in, "bye and bye, Chief Sealth sorrowfully relinquished the territory to the settlers, the influxers from another, unknown territory." Somehow it all figured. Retracing her steps, she paused at a latte stand, ordered a double mocha shooter with a lid on and went back to console the boss. In the elevator, crushed against the back wall, she thought about the California aspect.

Lately, a lot of Californians who'd immigrated to Seattle were retreating southward, after noticing their hair turning brown and their moods plummeting to pre-Prozac levels. But the old Seattle was gone forever. Only a native remembered those days when Seattle stood for old salts and fresh-faced barnacles. You could take a native out of the Emerald City, but a Seattleite's heart stuck to Oz like periwinkles on a driftwood log. You can't pry them loose. Suction. You have to use a knife. And then they die.

Olson's door was shut. She knocked lightly. She could hear the storm, but not Olson. She tried the knob. Locked. She knocked harder. Nothing. She walked back to the reception desk. Dottie had phone duty. Her freckles were buried in a romance novel and one hand clutched a salmon kipper. When Venus said her name, Dottie glanced up, smiled, said, "What's up?"

The work ethic has gone to hell, Venus thought. Instead of saying that, she said, "Is Olson in his office?"

Dottie leaned forward, looked down the hall toward Olson's office. She didn't see anything helpful. Then she remembered. "Olson took off about five minutes ago. With Sparks."

"Where'd they go?"

Dottie thought it over. "I think they said something about the Metropolitan Grill. Yeah, that was it. Or was it McHugh's micro brewery? They only left about five minutes ago." She bit into the kipper. The phone rang. Her mouth was full. She let it ring a few times, chewing rapidly. On the seventh ring, she answered. She put the person on hold and said to Venus, "It's for you. It's Richard again. He's called here six times already this morning. Maybe you better speak to him, V."

Venus shook her head, walked back toward the elevator.

"Well, what should I say to him?" Dottie, over the romance novel.

"Tell him I went back to Singapore and I won't be back for a few years. Tell him I'll return his ring by courier soon as I find it."

Dottie's mouth dropped open, probably the most exercise she'd had all day. "You lost that fabulous ring?"

The elevator door opened. Venus stepped into the cold chamber.

Before the doors had completely closed, she said to Dottie, "Just tell him the part about Singapore."

At least now she had a couple diversions. There was Jonathan Willow. There was Ebert's evil crusade. No time for Richard. Too much happening. Too much on her mind. She wasn't sure which hit the ground first, the elevator or her sinking heart.

Olson and Sparks had two or three drinks on her by the time she arrived at the Metropolitan Grill. She slipped onto a barstool beside Olson. The bartender, a black Irish rogue named Jimmy whose night job was writing metafiction, saw Venus come in, brought over her usual Black and Tan, winked at her, and clicked his tongue. Venus had never figured out what Jimmy meant by this gesture. She laid her money down and Olson shoved it back at her. He was paying today. Halfway through the second Black and Tan, she said to Olson, "What are Wexler's feelings?"

Wexler, DOI's director, was once-upon-a-time a Green Party member. As Interior's chief executive, Wexler had switched over to the Republican Party. Lately, the chief had grown frustrated over federal budget cuts and symptoms that DOI was caving in to a pro-land development Congress.

Olson said, "Wexler hasn't yet formed an opinion on Yodeler's. That's Ebert's job. To convince Wexler to sell it off."

Venus felt feverish. Maybe sickness over Ebert's crusade. Maybe something more visceral, like resurgent malaria. She said, "Yodeler's isn't for sale."

Olson said, "The hell it's not."

On Olson's other side, Sparks guffawed. Venus let him have his little fun. When Sparks stopped guffawing, she told them about the caterpillar. Olson said, "What's your guess?"

She said, *"Speyeria zerene dungenessii."*

Sparks sprayed his beer out over the counter. Olson said, "So that wasn't a ruse? With Ebert? You were serious?"

Venus nodded.

Olson shook his head. "And I was going along with it just to irritate Ebert. Anyway, I'll have to see it to believe you've really got a Dungeness." He stared at Venus's fingers. "Why are you doing that?"

"What?"

"Why are you tapping your fingers on the counter like that?"

She glanced down at her hand. The index and middle fingers

tapped rhythmically on the counter about an inch from the Black and Tan. She said, "Sorry. It's a habit I picked up in Asia."

"Well, it's annoying as hell."

She stopped tapping, held up an index finger. Jimmy understood that. Nursing the bitter brew, she listened to Olson and Spark's lively conversation. They'd grown weary of the land sale subject, and now Olson and Sparks worried over the lousy salmon run on the Chinook. The hoax sighting of a marbled murrelet at Grays Harbor. The oil spill off Ozone Beach's brown pelican sanctuary. All the good news from Sparks's territory, the southern half of the Olympic Peninsula. Olson sympathized when Sparks pleaded for a few days off, from all the stress.

Through narrowed eyelids, Venus studied Sparks. Long, lanky, lizardlike. He reminded her of a chameleon, especially through the eyes. And when his wattle turned pink, like now, it jiggled. Sparks was lazy on the job, lacked ambition. He preferred reading about endangered species to defending them. If he'd been blessed with a decent brain structure, she mused, Sparks would make a crackerjack researcher. Unfortunately, chameleons possess fairly flat crania.

Olson said, "We're understaffed, remember. I can't approve more than three days."

Sparks nodded, pulled on his Oly, chug-a-lugged. Olson rolled off the barstool, dropped some bills on the counter, nodded at Jimmy, and made for the door. Sparks made no move to leave. Venus ditched the Black and Tan and followed Olson into the street. Olson aimed his footsteps toward Westlake Mall. She didn't question why, just fell in step.

At Westlake Mall, the summer carousel, antique, with fabulous painted beasts, played Bolero. The animals ran ferocious circles, their backs laden with boisterous children. Venus smiled at a little boy riding a zebra. He scowled back, flipped her off. What are kids coming to? Maybe Bella was right, after all. Maybe there were times when children should be banished to dungeons.

The kid had neatly combed hair, couldn't be more than five years old, and was impeccably groomed. She was betting he had a hidden tattoo, maybe a navel ring. He had that kind of personality. Kids these days are ruined. The whole country's ruined. The whole world is one big sourball. When your heart can be broken via e-mail, you know the world's jig is up.

Olson said, "I just need to duck in at Nordstrom's. C'mon."

On the way in, an auburn bob laden with packages knocked into Venus. The parcels flew. Venus stopped to pick them up. The auburn bob snapped, "Could you be any clumsier?" then huffed out with the goodies. Venus followed Olson up the escalator to the third floor, past some haute couture, into the gift department. Olson despised shopping, so why this detour? He walked straight to the fine jewelry section, bent over a glass display case, studied its contents. After a while, he grunted, frowned. He looked around the gift department. He took another gander at the jewelry display. Venus said, "Looking for something?"

"I'd like to find a sales clerk, just for starters."

Bad mood. Like her own. She said, "They're understaffed, too. Everybody's understaffed and overworked. Even Nordie's."

Olson jabbed a finger at the glass display case. "I'm fairly certain it was right here."

"What was?"

"Something I wanted to show you." He tried flagging down a sales clerk. She sailed past him, an obviously irritated customer in tow. Olson would have to wait. He said, "To hell with it. It wasn't that important anyway."

Outside Nordstrom, Olson said, "It was a brooch. A lady's brooch. It had four big sapphires and some cut diamonds. The thing that struck me was, it was shaped like a blue poppy. But it's gone now. Someone must've bought it. Or maybe I have the wrong store."

At the carousel, the disgraceful child now straddled a giraffe. This time when she passed him, he didn't lift a finger. He grinned menacingly and projectiled a wad of congealed saliva. It landed on her uniform near the collar.

TWENTY-TWO

FIDDLEHEADS

MISS PERKINS was filing her nails when she heard a grunting sound. Holding her downcast gaze, she completed the nail before glancing up at the rude interloper. The hand she saw was grubby, the nails ragged, unkempt, and she resented its trespassing upon her personal space when it tossed a crumpled white business card onto her desk. The object landed near a bottle of Sally Hansen's Strong as Nails. Miss Perkins glanced down at the small white interruption. People shouldn't break into other people's personal routines. Who did this jerk think he was, anyway? The business card told it all, and frankly, Miss Perkins wasn't impressed. She'd already endured one federal agent this week. That fairy-faced blonde with no sense of propriety. Now here comes Mr.—what is it?—Ebert. Now here comes Mr. Ebert, this poor excuse for a man in his wrinkled Dixie striped seersucker suit. It's hard to wrinkle seersucker, but this thin representation of male testosterone had managed it. Clueless to Pacific Northwest weather patterns, the outlander inhabited an ensemble that belonged somewhere in South Alabama, on somebody's front porch, where they served mint juleps. Not here in God's country. She'd seen a few government bureaucrats in her lifetime. Like back when she was secretary to Mayor Chin. Bureaucrats are all alike, seersucker or not. Miss Perkins gestured at the couch, rose as slowly as possible from her desk, careful not to damage her artfully painted nails, and went to fetch this Ebert person a cup of java. He took heavy cream and two Equals, and wasn't that just like a federal government bureaucrat? Once she had him comfortably ensconced, she returned to her desk, slipped the manicure paraphernalia out of sight, and turning her demure backside on Ebert, entered the boss's suite.

Ebert crossed one leg over another and sipped his coffee. The papers were all in order. They could close the deal right now, if it weren't for Wexler's final approval, Wexler's signature. He could always finesse that. Wexler had probably forgotten all about the Yodeler transaction anyway. Small potatoes in the world of federal land sales. Ebert could close this deal any time he wanted to, sure could. Head back to Washington, D.C., with a check in his briefcase. A few holes of golf over at Arlington, then on to California, to sell off a little scrap of Pipe Organ National Park.

Ebert glanced at his watch. Where was Olson? He shouldn't take so long in the can. Just as he completed this thought, Olson walked in. Ebert grunted, slurped coffee, and said, "Secretary's a little snip."

Olson didn't say anything. He didn't care about secretaries. He wished Ebert would choke on the coffee, keel over right there, the sloppy, unconscionable s.o.b. Olson went over to the window, looked out. From here he could see Yodeler Preserve but he couldn't make out the poppy field. His eyesight had worsened over the past winter. He needed to have his eyes checked. Maybe he was getting cataracts.

Miss Perkins returned, a self-satisfied smirk on her face. Olson thought her blouse seemed a bit ruffled, her makeup slightly smeared. Maybe he imagined it. She had an efficiency in her manner, a hostile efficiency that he didn't like. In fact, right now, Olson felt miserably trapped in the company of two individuals he wished he'd never met.

Ebert jerked a thumb at Olson, said to Miss Perkins, "He's with me."

Miss Perkins curled her lip and ushered them into the boss's suite. Five minutes later, she returned to her desk and called her friend Marvine over at Mayor Chin's office. This new development would fascinate Marvine. While she waited for Marvine to return from the coffee cart, she repositioned the manicure accouterment, and located the fingernail where she'd left off.

WHEN MARVINE SAW Mayor Chin coming, she quickly hung up the phone and began shuffling papers around her desk. Look busy, pretend you don't even notice him. What's this? Oh yes, the new city code, ready to be input into the system. And this? Hmmm, looks like another noise complaint against that Tiki Lounge over on the beach. And this must be—

"Miss Bobbs, I am speaking to you." The mayor, slightly impatient.

Marvine raised her head, feigned surprise. Marvine was an expert at feigning. She could feign surprise. She could feign illness. She could feign deafness, loss of vocal cords, even a chirpy disposition when the moment called for it. Marvine had a host of feignings tucked into her neat and tidy brain. Now that brain swung into full gear and Marvine said mellifluously, "Oh! Sorry, Mayor Chin. I was so caught up in all this."

"Never mind that," snapped Mayor Chin. He was five feet two inches tall, pure Chinese if you didn't count the Irish grandmother, midsixties, bald, with snow white eyebrows and Scrabble chip teeth, only white. He wore his fishing clothes, but now his mind was on town business, not the trout run. He handed Marvine a sheet of paper with something scribbled on it. Mayor Chin had the world's worst handwriting, Marvine believed, even for a man. "I need this typed and two hundred copies made by noon. Can you manage that?"

Marvine glanced at the clock on the wall. Nine-fifteen. Who was he kidding? Of course she could manage to input one typewritten page and copy it a hundred and ninety-nine times before noon. "Yes, sir." She smiled broadly, entering the chirpy mode. "Is there anything else?" She paused for effect. "Before I get back to this mountain of work on my desk?"

"Yes, there is, Marvine." Mayor Chin raised an admonitory index finger, shook it in her direction and said, "Next time I catch you gossiping over the telephone during working hours, you'll find a dismissal notice on your desk. Is that clear?"

Marvine nodded sullenly. The boss had a lot of nerve listening in to her private phone conversations. Chin darn well better watch his overworked mouth or she'd get up and walk out of here in a split second. Just watch. She made sure Mayor Chin was halfway down the street and not coming back before she touched the phone. Sherry Doolaps answered at Sigrid Chin's veterinary clinic. Sherry had bad adenoids and she always sounded stuffy. Sherry said, "Is he gone?"

"Just took off, the prickly pear," replied Marvine. "Heading your way. I think he's got a lunch date with his wife."

Sherry made snuffling sounds. "What did Perkins say?"

Marvine made a face. "She's ready. On the other hand, all she wants to talk about is Peter this and Peter that. I'm sick of hearing about Peter Avalon."

Sherry agreed. "He's an old man, for chrissake."

"Hey, did you hear what Junior Singh did over at his dad's dry cleaners?"

"What?" Marvine, barely interested in anything Junior Singh did.

Sherry said, "He put a threatening note in Peter Avalon's dry-cleaned suit pants, warning him to keep out of Yodeler."

Marvine said, "That was stupid. Junior's a dweeb. Now, listen, Sherry," said Marvine persuasively, "I want you to meet Perkins and me after work, over at the Alibi? But don't tell anyone. I'll see you there at five-thirty."

"What happened to Darin? I thought you and Darin were..."

"Never mind," snapped Marvine. "I'll talk to you later." Marvine hung up the phone just in time to answer the second line. It was Darin, who last evening had stood her up at the Alibi. Marvine gave him an earful.

MISS PERKINS WAS adjusting her pantyhose when the old woman stepped in the door. Miss Perkins pinched her nostrils together. Old people smelled. Not that she had ever noticed a strange odor on Aggie MacGregor, but better not take any chances. One thing for sure, old Aggie wasn't a Blue Poppy client. If Miss Perkins were allowed to wager an opinion, she'd say Aggie MacGregor had never worn a body product in her whole life. Now, what in the world did the prehistoric creature mean by parking herself like a piece of driftwood on Miss Perkins's couch? Just as Miss Perkins opened her mouth to object politely but firmly, Mr. Avalon buzzed her.

"Miss Perkins," came Peter's voice, "has Miss MacGregor arrived yet?"

Miss Perkins's eyes bulged. "Uh...yes, sir. In fact, I was just offering Miss MacGregor a cup of tea... Yes, I'll show her in, sir."

Aggie wore a sky blue summer dress, a deeper blue cardigan sweater, yellow-and-white striped espadrilles, and that Panama with the scary hatpin. Miss Perkins smiled sourly at Aggie MacGregor, plucked a pink Mrs. Bowser from the vase on her desk, carried it over to the old woman, and said, "Compliments of Mr. Avalon."

Aggie looked up. Her bright button eyes sparkled. She shook her head and said politely, "Thank you, dear, that's very kind of you, but you see, I don't accept cut flowers. Unless, of course, they have been cut for a purpose."

"This is a purpose," Miss Perkins insisted. "This is Mr. Avalon's way of honoring the ladies who visit his office." She thrust the rose at Aggie. Aggie held up a firm hand.

"No, no, child, put that back in its water. Might as well have its last drink in peace." She laughed, a high, melodious tinkle.

Miss Perkins marched back to her desk, returned the rose bud to its vase. Best not to argue with these fogies. They might go heart attack on you and then what? Smoothing her skirt around her perilous hips, she said, "All right then, please follow me." Under her unkind breath, she added, "You old battle-ax."

Peter Avalon stood when Aggie entered, came forward with an outstretched hand, fussed over the most comfortable seating arrangement for her, and generally made a big fat deal over her visit. Aggie might have resisted all this solicitude, but she certainly did not fall victim to its intent. Nobody, not even an Avalon, would get far with flattery. Not with Aggie MacGregor, sure and not.

Settled back behind his big desk, Peter Avalon made small talk, offered Aggie a drink of his favorite Scotch whiskey, which she declined, and a cigar, which she waved away even though she enjoyed a good rich smoke now and then, maybe once in a blue moon, and come to think of it, it's a blue moon coming out tomorrow night, now, and isn't that fine?

Peter said, "I was never superstitious, Aggie. What does it mean, 'a blue moon'?"

Aggie laughed, a high-pitched single note, and said, "Nothing superstitious about a blue moon, Peter. Blue moons are nice for lighting up the forests and fields when you're out harvesting. Some of these plants are more potent when picked by blue moonlight. It's just a simple fact of Nature. You've heard of night-blooming wapato?"

Peter squinted thoughtfully. "I vaguely recall a reference... somewhere...well, nothing I can clearly remember..."

Aggie cut off his false recollection. "There are flowers out here in the forests, and plants, too, that produce a stronger scent by night. If you harvest them by night, you can capture their scent. Being an Avalon nose," she added, "I should think you'd learned that long ago. From your uncle Conrad, sure and now, your uncle Conrad taught you about a blue moon, when that unique light opens up the sweetest of the wild..."

"Ah, yes, of course, Uncle Conrad surely, it was from Uncle Conrad that I learned about blue moons. Now it's all coming back."

Aggie nodded. "Being that as it is," she said, "why don't you come to the point? You must have a mighty big problem to summon old Aggie down from her mountain. You know I don't like it down here in town, so kindly come to the point and let me go on up home."

She didn't mince words. Peter rested his elbows on his desk, his chin on his hands, and studied Aggie. She wouldn't like what he was about to say. He had spent weeks mentally framing and reframing how he would present the issue to Aggie, in a way that would win her over to his side. Now that she sat before him, his nerves wavered and he almost didn't go through with it. But he summoned up all his courage—for it took courage to confront old Aggie MacGregor—and blurted out his proposal.

"Aggie," began Peter, "I need your land."

Aggie laughed. "What on God's good Earth would you do with my little parcel?"

"Grow poppies."

Aggie shook her head. "My land's too low on the mountain. You can't grow nonnative Tibetan blues down that low. Not in any numbers."

Peter smiled. "Ah, but that's what my family thought, too, until just recently. Just recently my brother, Troy, developed a technique for cultivating the blue poppy at any elevation. It's a delicate process, mind you, but we can do it, as long as we have a parcel of land big enough to support both seedlings and mature plants."

Aggie folded her pale, waxen hands in her lap. She wiggled her fingers to relieve the arthritis pain. Peter was going to give her planting lessons whether she liked it or not. May as well get comfortable. She leaned back in her chair as Peter stood and went to the picture windows behind his desk.

He pointed to the thick forest on Mount Pluvius. "That forest provides the seedlings with the necessary shade and moisture. When they've survived that extremely risky phase, we can transplant them in lower beds, and then once again in even lower beds, all the way down through the meadow to the highway, right down here at the beach. All it takes to be successful is the right fertilizer and constant monitoring. Troy has developed the process and come up with a powerful fertilizer formula. So now we can use the entire meadow for poppies. Your land, since it's adjacent to the meadow, would provide lateral expansion. We'll need that in a year or two."

"What kind of fertilizer?"

"What?" A hollow, echoing question.

Aggie said, "I asked you what kind of fertilizer you plan to use."

Peter rubbed an eyebrow. "It's Troy's formula. He hasn't shared it with me yet. I imagine he's applied for a patent on it. He likes to keep these things close to his chest until the patent is pending."

"Organic?"

Avalon bit his lower lip, preparing it to lie. Biting your lower lip takes the sting out of a lie. He said, "Oh, yes, of course. Organic."

"Better be," replied Aggie. "Nothing but organic is allowed on the national preserve. Anyway, what makes you think the government will lease the rest out to you?"

Peter smiled, "It's better than that, Aggie. It's not yet on the dotted line, and it's still confidential, mind you, but I'm negotiating a deal to purchase Yodeler's meadow from the Department of the Interior."

Aggie contained her surprise. Best not to show the opponent your weak spot. She said, "Uh-huh." And that was all.

"By this time next year, Yodeler's meadow will be one glorious field of rippling blue poppies."

"Had it with the Chinese, eh?"

Her candidness startled him. "Why, yes, as a matter of fact. They've cut us off, if you want to know the truth. So it was absolutely critical that we develop our own methods of high volume growth and harvest. Frankly, my family is delighted to be out from under the Chinese contract. You can only eat so many business lunches of pigeon brains and monkeys' eyes before you just gag."

"I suppose so." Noncommittal.

A brief silence, then Peter said gently, "What about it, Aggie? Will you sell me your land?"

Aggie didn't look at him. She studied her hands, the age spots, the knobby fingers. In a hushed voice, she said, "What does Conrad think about all this?"

"Uncle Conrad?" Peter shrugged. "We haven't told him. He's more or less retired, you know. Or maybe you hadn't heard."

"I had."

"We'll surprise him with the whole package. He'll be ecstatic, I feel certain."

"Will he?"

Peter folded his arms across his broad chest. What was it about Aggie MacGregor that always seemed to bring out the little boy in him? Must be something from back in childhood, something between the two of them he couldn't remember now, but which still affected him around old Aggie. He said, "Uncle Conrad really isn't that involved in the business anymore, Aggie. Things have changed a lot around here."

Aggie stood up. "They sure have," she said. She walked to the door of Avalon's suite, opened it, paused, turned to him and said, "No Himalayan poppy's going to sprout on my land, Peter Avalon. That's my final word." She walked out then, through the reception room where Miss Perkins had been secretly listening in over the telephone line, past Miss Perkins without even saying good-bye or thank you or anything vaguely polite, and left Peter Avalon to ponder his next move.

THE LAB, TINA, woke up when Aggie opened the front door, watched her carry a sack of groceries across the living room, through the dining room, into the kitchen. The cat, Pearl, on the windowsill in her favorite sphinx pose, licked her paws, preened. Aggie hummed to herself as she put away the groceries, then she fixed a pot of tea and opened a fresh box of that rich Murchie's shortbread. The evening air hung warm and fragrant, so she took her tea and shortbread out onto the front porch and watched the sun arc across the strait waters, tinting the inland passage deep strawberry pink. Red skies at night, sailor's delight; red skies at morning, sailors take warning. So then, tonight would be a calm night over the seas and tomorrow would dawn a glorious day.

A marmot darted out of the tall grass in Aggie's front yard, paused, stood erect to sniff the air. It spied Aggie's dog and let out a shrill whistle, then darted back toward the woods. Aggie had seen the marmot family around the property lately. Curious, she mused, the marmots down this low, they usually dwelt up higher, in the subalpine meadow above Aggie's land. She'd seen two or three of them just in the past week, and she guessed they might be house hunting. Aggie breathed the clean, crisp evening air, watched a long white cruise liner ply the waters heading out to sea. If she hadn't been such a landlubber, her father always used to say, he'd have sent her sailing off to all the world's exotic ports. But Aggie had never wanted to travel anywhere. She loved her world, the beaches, the mountains, the high meadow, and the way everything changed with the seasons and tides. Aggie never dreamed of discovering a better world. Her world was the best, and if only the careless tourists and the developers would go away, it would be Paradise here once again, as it had been growing up.

The phone rang, and Aggie ignored it. Probably Sigrid wanting to come over to play cards. Or watch the Canadian wrestling matches. Aggie and Sigrid loved watching the wrestlers, big greasy lummoxes throwing each other against the ring while the audience went apoplectic. Sigrid had a favorite, known as Winnipeg Fats, and whenever Winnipeg Fats came into the ring, Sigrid got hysterical and scared Tina, and Pearl, too. Speaking of Sigrid, wasn't that her car coming down the highway? Aggie shook her head, amused. Isn't that just the way life works? You get somebody on your mind, and poof, they show up in the flesh.

Sigrid parked in Aggie's front yard, hauled a can of fresh goat's milk up to Aggie's porch, set it down on the floor, wiped her brow. She said, "I'm getting too old for this, Aggie."

Aggie went indoors, got another tea cup, poured Sigrid a cup of tea and shoved the plate of shortbread at her. Sigrid didn't protest. Sigrid liked nothing better than Aggie's tea and shortbread. Sigrid had pale Norwegian hair and clear blue eyes, and she stood nearly six feet tall. This wasn't unusual, when you took Sigrid by herself. It was when Sigrid and her husband went to church, or to a town social that people inevitably raised eyebrows over what they called, "the contrast." Sigrid's husband, Fern's mayor, was a full head shorter than his wife, and standing beside her he seemed almost petite. You never met a happier couple than the Chins, which just went to prove that love is neither short nor tall. In the case of Sigrid and Harry Chin, opposites definitely attracted, and the town of Fern was better off for it. Mayor Chin kept the little town neat and tidy, virtually free of crime. Sigrid doctored all the animals, and made a crackerjack salmon soup for the autumn festival. No sir, you couldn't ask for a more upstanding pair of folks to take care of Fern, Washington. And best of all, they were natives.

Sigrid said, "I'm worried about Radio."

Aggie squinted. "What's wrong with him?"

Sigrid shook her head. "I haven't seen him in three weeks. I saw Sunbeam and the cubs over on Dungeness Spit, yesterday. Fishing. But no Radio. When was the last time you saw him?"

Aggie considered. "Maybe as far back as three weeks. Sure and now, it's been three solid weeks."

"Where was he?"

Aggie said, "Up above the waterfall. Near the cave, but above it. Like he was guarding the cave. And I saw movement down there behind the waterfall, I reckon it was Sunbeam and the cubs. This was way back in May."

Sigrid nodded. "That's what I mean. No one's seen him since the middle part of May. I think he might be sick."

Aggie nodded. "Reckon we ought to go up there, try to find out?"

"Maybe. We could tranquilize him, get him back down to the clinic. We'd need some help."

Aggie nodded and folded her slim arms around her chest. The chilly evening air sent a little shiver up her spine. She didn't mention it to Sigrid, but Sigrid noticed her friend trembling slightly and made a mental note to knit Aggie a shawl for Christmas.

After Sigrid had gone, Aggie watched until the last drop of strawberry gold liquid dropped into the strait. Darkness came slowly this time of year. It must be about ten o'clock, she thought to herself. Mercy. She'd better milk the cow.

At ten-thirty, Aggie hauled the cow's milk into the kitchen, poured it into containers, and set the containers in the refrigerator. Tomorrow, she'd take them to the fresh market in Fern. The phone rang again, and this time Aggie wiped her hands on her skirt and went to answer it. The phone was in her bedroom, right beside her fax machine, on a card table she used for a desk. She picked up the phone, but as soon as she said hello, the caller hung up. That was when Aggie saw the fax that had tumbled out of her machine onto the carpet. She bent over, picked it up. As she read it, her hands began to tremble, then a twinkle lit up her eyes, then a broad smile crossed her lips, and finally, the sheer joy of it all transformed Aggie's somber mood to sheer jubilance. She let out a whooping holler and broke into a yodel that caught the attention of a carload of tourists driving by on the highway below her land. She sat on the bed and read the note again.

My dear Agnes MacGregor,
With the utmost respect and sincerity, may I request the pleasure of your company this night at midnight exactly in our former secret meeting place? Recognizing that fifty years have passed since the last time we met in this secret location, may I be so bold as to remind you that the waterfall is especially full this time of year, so do be cautious in your steps. Looking forward to the meeting that should have been fifty years ago, I remain yours forever and faithfully, from the bottom of my heart, Conrad.

Zora met Song at the water's edge. The tide was out, and a thick belt of bright green seaweed cinched the beach. Zora wore the caftan

disguise. Only another day or two and she'd be free of all the subterfuge. Her image would be flashed across the globe: Zora, the exotic
fashion model, bathing in a field of blue poppies. She was thinking
about this when she approached Song, and the daydream put a small
grin on her lips, which Song mistakenly thought was about him. He
took her pale hand in his own, and together they set off along the
tideline, again heading west toward Pysht.

"Do you know why they call it Pysht?" Song asked her.

Zora held up a hand. "Don't tell me. I don't want to learn anything
about this soggy backwater. I'm out of here tomorrow, and that's not
soon enough."

"Back to L.A.?"

Zora nodded. Song crouched down, plucked a small stone off the
beach, played with it between his thumb and index finger. Zora said,
"What's that thing?"

"Obsidian. It's smooth." He handed over the slick black irregular-
shaped stone. Zora put it to her lips, licked it.

"I love the taste of saltwater."

Song felt a thrill pass through him. "That was pretty sexy," he
said.

Zora smiled at him. "Why do you think I did it?"

She withdrew her hand from his, slipped it under his jacket, under
his belt line, under his shirt. She let her fingers explore the small of
his back, stroking it gently. He didn't try to stop her. He couldn't,
because she had him under her spell. She said, "I love cops."

Song blinked. He stopped walking, turned to face her. "What did
you say?"

Zora stared across the strait. He thought her eyes watered up, but
that might have been caused by the breeze coming in off the strait.
After a while, she said, "I know you're a federal wildlife agent. I
wasn't born yesterday, Louie."

"Let me guess. Beatrice told you?"

Zora said, "She figured it out right away. Your Harley has a government license plate. Dead giveaway, if you ask me."

Song blanched. How had he missed that obvious detail? Did Venus
simply forget to warn him?

Zora said, "She's jealous, I think, because you're paying a lot of
attention to me. That's a problem I have with other women. They're
always jealous of me. That's why I prefer men as confidantes."

Song sighed. Busted. Busted, and maybe in love. But then, Song fell in love once every new moon in a slow year. Something about Zora, though, her stunning beauty, or some magical chemical. Maybe it was the perfume. Or pheromones.

Song said, "Am I coming on too strong?"

"You are."

"I mean," Song stumbled for words, "even if I am a cop, does that change things?"

Zora turned her back on Song, folded her arms protectively across her chest. "What things? I hardly know you. You're just another guy to me." She kept her back to him.

Song protested, "But we have this chemistry..."

"If I slept with every male that turned me on, I'd be in bed constantly."

Defensive. Cold.

Song turned away from her, faced the water, so that now they stood back to back. The wind made enough whistling noise to muffle their words, and Song didn't feel like shouting at her, nor she at him. They stood this way for a few minutes, long enough for Beatrice to come out on the inn's terrace and notice them. Long enough for the maître d' Darin to notice them out the restaurant window. Long enough for the chef Slava to glance up from his oyster shucking below the terrace and see them standing back to back. Probably long enough for a lot of people to see them on the tideline, to discern that they were obviously involved in an emotional moment. When finally Song turned to speak to her, she, too, turned to say something. Song forgot what he wanted to say, so he kissed her. She melted into him. She held onto him for a long time. On their way back up the beach, Zora said, "You shouldn't trust me, Louie. I'm an unscrupulous person. I'm only twenty-one, but I'm dangerous."

Song laughed, held Zora at arm's length. Zora, in the caftan. Song said, "You sound like a girl with a guilty conscience."

Her mouth quivered. She started to say something, changed her mind, broke away from him. She ran up the beach, into the Raven, out of sight. Song didn't follow her. Maybe he should have gone after her, but he didn't. Song never was the pushy type with women.

TWENTY-THREE

SPIKE

THE MAKOH, Hoh, Quinault, Queets, and Klallam fished, hunted, and foraged in the rain forest and down the sides of the two Brothers, where they picked medicinal herbs and camas bulbs, and on the beaches, where they found shell food and kept their dugout cedar canoes for the whale hunts. All the tribes respected the code of the territory and the rule of Tyee Sahale, the Great Chief Up Above. It is sometimes said that Kwatee's people invented Tyee Sahale to appease the white man's priests, who taught that their God was the Supreme Being, above all other spirits. But Tyee Sahale, too, was one Supreme Being, served by Kwatee the Changer and the other spirits, and Tyee Sahale always existed, long before the white man arrived. Some tribal elders said Tyee Sahale was the same as the white man's Supreme Being. This debate still rankles the people of the territory.

It is true that occasional rivalries set tribes one against the other, but everyone understood that Kwatee the Changer had created all humans out of his own sweat, and the soil from his body. Natural superiority, one over the other, never existed, although the white man sometimes fell into that dangerous way of thinking. Once in a while, there were battles between the Queets or the Quinault or one of the other tribes against the white man. The Indians, as they called the people of the rain forest, armed themselves with knives made of whale bone and guns they had traded from the white man. But even in battle, respect was often shown. Rarely did they kill one another in the rain forest, down on the beaches. And these fair conditions prevailed in the territory, throughout the forest and beaches, in the deep cold waters, for many seasons.

In those days, the natives traded camas cakes, dried and seasoned, for wool blankets. Fish for vermilion dye. Woven cedar baskets for whiskey. Native women taught the white women how to gather the wild blue violet, taught them to ease the pain of childbirth by chewing the violet's roots and leaves, and also how to apply the crushed blossoms on the chest, to relieve chest pains. According to the Klallam women, crushed violet blossoms will blister your skin if you leave the compress on too long. Once, a white man from across the ocean named MacGregor recited a poem at a potlatch. In the poem, this MacGregor compared the violet to a person's modesty, and said it was the flower of the poets. He said the violets across the ocean had a richer fragrance than those in the territory, but that the violets found on our mountainsides made better medicine.

After the chain saws came, the general harmony which had prevailed over the territory became unstuck and chaos reigned over the natural order of things. Even the climate began to change, and the very shape of the territory was unnaturally altered by the white man's steel saws. Soon logging operations surpassed natural disasters as the chief killer in the territory. White men walked around with Elk's teeth attached to their gold time pieces. They would kill Elk, leave his body to rot, just to take Elk's canine teeth. Those teeth sold for fifteen American dollars. In the logging camps, men fought over Elk's teeth.

The elders sometimes paint a rosy veneer on this time of history, but truth was, even Indians took part in the felling of cedar and fir, even Indians put silver in their pockets and spent it in the white man's camps. From then on, it seems the territory has been ruled by the sound of coins in the greedy man's purse.

An obscure nineteenth-century legend casts mystery over the whole Olympic range. In the late Victorian era, so the legend goes, a certain Seattle resident named Mr. Muscott kept a sheep farm high up in the Olympics, somewhere in the vicinity of the Brothers. The taciturn, secretive Mr. Muscott spent money recklessly in the Olympic logging camps. Whenever he went broke, Muscott would return to his sheep farm, where on the high grazing land, he prospected in a mine that was adjacent to a mountain stream. Soon he would return to town, his pockets full of precious minerals, which he would convert into currency.

Many a hopeful prospector tried to find Muscott's mine, and some even tried following the secretive miner into the mountains. Muscott would lose them in the mountain forests, protecting his precious treasure. But one day, the free-spending prospector came to a bad end.

He was high up on a mountain slope, kneeling by a stream, when someone shot Muscott in the back. Legend says the assailant mistook Muscott for a cougar, but no one ever learned the truth of that killing. Muscott had his revenge, though, for no one has ever located Muscott Mine.

THE CLOUDS PARTED, pouring milky moonlight over Yodeler Preserve. At the base of the meadow, Venus parked the Spider, got out, locked up. From the trunk she retrieved her nylon backpack, double-checked the contents. Maglite. Cell phone. Nikon with telephoto lens, loaded with infrared film. Rain gear. A bottle of spring water, a pack of Hob-Nobs to snack on. Or feed bears. Antimalarial drugs, in case the recurrent fever struck. Compass, Swiss Army knife, topographical map of the preserve. What else? Extra bullets. She reached down, felt the little Smith & Wesson holstered under her jacket. Olson called it her Cracker Jack toy. One of these days, she'd have to upgrade. Olson had already warned her. She slipped on the backpack, looked up at the full moon. A strip of haze formed a veil over its face. Mata Hari of the evening. She stepped into Yodeler's meadow, began the long climb to the top.

Halfway up, she heard a rustling in the high grass. She stopped, listened. More rustling. She flashed the Maglite beam toward the sound. The beam caught two beady black eyes and a couple long skinny ears. The rabbit froze and the rustling sound stopped. She switched off the light and the rabbit retreated, rustling, like the sound she'd heard. Twenty minutes later, she reached the base of Avalon's poppy field. Like the rabbit, she froze in her tracks.

The moon washed an ocean of fully bloomed blue poppies. A gentle night breeze rippled the vivid blue blanket. The poppies swayed, danced, electrified by the radiant light, an exotic, sensual rhythm, stimulating hypnotic trance or meditation on cosmic harmony. In the heavens, the moon blushed blue and for a few seconds, Venus stood on a Himalayan mountainside. In the distance, a deep, resonant gong, a Tibetan meditation bell struck once, twice, thrice, and on the fourth strike, a light tinkling sound accompanied the gong and lived longer, the sound of sprites dancing on flower petals, or wood nymphs singing in the rain forest. The sound faded gently. She inhaled. A fragrant woodsy low note, light mysterious top note, a transcendent fragrance. Thus transported, she stepped into the undulating blue sea, swam into the breakers, nearly drowned in sensual ecstasy. This must be Buddha's belly. A sacred womb. Transcendence of the ordinary, a sacred celebration of the senses. That fragrance, that scent of immortality, suggestive of another, previous, or future life. Nirvana. That fragrance, that fragrance.

Emerging on the other side, she entered the rain forest. Climbing slowly, her footfall soft against a rich, cedar-scented carpet, she paused once to locate the sound of the Elwha, then with her sense of direction reestablished, she headed toward the high cliff above the waterfall. Half an hour later, she stood on the crest of the granite outcropping above Sunbeam and Radio's cave and marveled at the panorama lit by the blue moon's broad beam. Outside the moonlight's range, she saw a blue velvet cosmos encrusted with dazzling stars, a night sky possible only in remoteness, like up here on Mount Pluvius. A loose diamond shot across the blue velvet, its broad tail streaking in a perfect arc. Fizzle. Below the bewitching sky, lit like a stage set, the Strait of Juan de Fuca roiled against itself, crashing waves hard and high against the rocky shores. On the straits the beaches had disappeared beneath the high tide, and if the moon's gravitational dance with Earth got much cozier, Highway 101 would soon disappear. But now the highway shone like a silver ribbon at the foot of Yodeler's meadow, dividing the salt-spray meadow from the raucous tide.

Venus read her Swatch. Eleven fifty-six. Four minutes to go. Unconsciously, she reached up, felt her shoulder holster, the neat little .38-caliber Smith & Wesson, the toy she couldn't give up. Like when her father had offered to raise her allowance from nickels to dimes. He told her that dimes were more valuable than nickels, even though they were smaller objects. But she had insisted on receiving her allowance in nickels. Size had nothing to do with it. Nickels had buffaloes and Indian chiefs. And now, whenever Olson pleaded with her to carry a more powerful weapon, she refused, because the little Smith & Wesson had character, and she valued character more than power. Besides, a .38 is more discriminating than a big gun.

Her Swatch said midnight. She gazed down into the moon-washed meadow. The gong sounded first. That Tibetan sound.

They came from all sides of the meadow into its depths, just as she had suspected they would. From the silver ribbon highway where they parked their pickups and bicycles, from the rain forest, through the poppy field and down from Aggie's land, moving in precision, soldiers on an organized mission. Tiny black specks like ants on a caterpillar's carcass, they were voracious, insatiable, greedy, an abomination of Nature, yet true to Nature's darkest side.

Most wildcrafters barely eke out a living from their harvests. They gather wild herbs, berries, flowers, grasses, and seeds that can be dried and sold at market when the harvesting is done legally. Illegal harvests of wildflowers and other vegetation—for example, harvesting on federal or state preserves, or on private property—can result in arrest and a stiff fine, even a prison term, depending on the rarity of the product harvested. Harvesting the abundant wild carrot, for example, isn't as serious as harvesting rare lady's slipper orchids. These shadows down in the meadow, what were they after?

Venus grabbed the Nikon with infrared film, fitted on the zoom lens. The camera balked at focusing in the dark. She switched to a manual setting, opened up the lens as wide and deep as it could go, and shot off a full roll of film. She hoped she'd caught them in the act, harvesting indiscriminately, stripping Yodeler's of its Van Gogh cloak, the rape of pointillism, a tragedy of evolutionary proportions. This wasn't what Aggie had predicted. Aggie had said that no wildcrafter ever came into Yodeler's meadow except herself. But now the meadow buzzed with harvesters. Aggie had been wrong, or else she had lied to Venus, maybe to cover for her friends.

They moved in tandem from all sides of the meadow, until finally, half an hour later, they met in the center of the meadow and set up an impromptu packaging industry, then hauled the harvest away in plastic garbage bags. With luck, she'd captured it all on film, including their unceremonious dispersal, their departure, and the denuded meadow, now a solid green apron grieving the violation. Interestingly, they hadn't touched the blue poppies. The poppies seemed to laugh, a rippling blue melody.

She was packing up the camera when she heard screams from inside the rain forest, piercing the night, a bloodcurdling, heart-stopping sound. Then the dull sound—of what? Like a hammer against wood. Pounding. The sound made her scalp crawl. She inhaled, breathed out slowly. She removed her gun from its holster, gripped it, listened. More pounding. Venus dropped down off the granite boulders and entered the forest.

Now the pounding was rapid, harder. The screams stopped. Then silence. Without the sounds, she lost her sense of direction. She stood in an ancient cedar grove, mystified, cold fingers squeezing her heart. She inhaled, but her breath was shallow, tight. Slowly, she removed her backpack, careful to make no sounds, set it on the forest floor, rummaged, and fished out the digital phone. At Park Service headquarters, a taped message told her that due to budget cuts, ranger service now operated only between nine a.m. and five p.m., Tuesday through Saturday. You couldn't even leave a message, and the recording ended abruptly, then a dial tone. She tried 911. No connection. Static. She tried another channel. Same. She slipped the phone into her trouser pocket, slipped the back pack over her shoulders, stood very still, listening. Total silence.

Where the moon penetrated the forest canopy, she saw a freshly carved, narrow footpath. It led uphill, toward Nine Fingers Fork, above old Aggie's property. She started up the path, walking a few yards, pausing to listen, walking a little further, again pausing to listen. Slowly, she followed the foot trail until at last the main trail, MacGregor's Trail, appeared a few yards ahead. When she reached MacGregor's Trail, she started to turn right, head back down the slopes, but the sharp, familiar scent of terror, admonished her, sent her to the left instead, heading deeper into the rain forest. She'd gone fifty or so yards up the trail when she saw Aggie MacGregor.

The scrawny body, lashed to a cedar tree, had a single spike hammered through its heart. Blood dripped from the spike onto Aggie's summer dress. Her blue eyes reflected terror. Her mouth hung open in horror, and a ball of black caterpillars poured from her mouth, crawled up her face into her cloud-white hair.

A bullet whizzed past Venus's ear. She dropped to the ground, crawled across the cedar grove into a stand of lady ferns. A second bullet struck a cedar tree, ricocheted, went astray. In the darkness, Venus felt the cool steel of her small pistol, cocked it, held her breath. No sound came from the surrounding forest, except in the distance, the rage of the Elwha. The moon slipped behind some clouds blown in off the ocean, and now a fine mist began falling and fog draped the rain forest. Blackness. She dared not flash her Maglite. Silence, except for the sound of the mist, a fuzzy white noise. She could flush the killer out. She knew how to flush a prey out of dense woods. If she fired her weapon, though, she'd only give herself away. She recalled old Aggie's horror-struck eyes, decided against provocation. Better lie still, watch, wait, pray.

Rain fell heavier now, in full-blown drops. The ground felt wet, spongy. Her rain gear was in the pack, but she dared not move. She crouched on the ground, waited some more. The fog thickened, and when an occasional rent in the shroud allowed the moon to peek through, she caught glimpses of Aggie spiked to the tree. Then the storm hit full force, the crashing lightning, rolling thunder, and Aggie's awful image lit up again and again, a flashing neon Calvary that brought her to her knees, shaking, amazed, and finally petrified. Fear transforms even the courageous, if only for a moment. Where was God when Aggie needed justice? Where was God now? She remembered the maxim, "This, too, shall pass," and she cursed the cliché and she cursed all of Nature and her elements, and the creation of humankind.

Something crashed from the tree canopy, hit the ground a few yards from where she stood. Branches of ancient cedar, felled by lightning. She stood in the rain for an hour, until the storm blew off the forest. Mellowed, the forest played a symphony of drips and drops, the fog rolled back and the moon returned to shed benevolent light across the cedar clearing, across MacGregor's Trail, across the woman spiked to the cedar tree.

His voice came from behind the tree, so that it seemed Aggie herself spoke. He said, "Here I am, ranger," and then appeared beside the big cedar, stood where she could see his silhouette. He shone a flashlight in her eyes, momentarily blinding her. She blinked, turned her head from the light. The voice was familiar, but she couldn't place it, and she couldn't see his face. "Turn around," he said. "Or I'll shoot you."

She turned around. She heard his footsteps crunching, squishing on the soaked earth, approaching her. She felt the hard barrel of his gun against her skull, just behind her right ear lobe. She felt his warm hard breath against her cheek. He breathed through his mouth, slowly, deliberately, and for a moment she had an idea he was going to spit on her. It was a ridiculous idea, inspired by the cold stark cloak that had fluttered around her heart, racked her nerves. He ran the flashlight from the top of her head, stopped, apparently studying her profile, moved down to her shoulders, her chest, her waist, and hips. At the hips, he held the light, breathed faster, harder, and then he switched off the light and grabbed her, wrestling her to the soaked earth. With one strong arm, he pinned her down. He wrestled her gun from her hand, tossed it into the darkness. She heard it land, a soft rustle, nothing more. His breath felt like a hot storm and a drop of his saliva struck her cheek, dribbled down the side, into her ear. Some distant memory from self-defense training made a pass at a brain gate but shorted out, a power failure brought on by the sheer force of his craven, primitive power. She remembered then the advice Dave had given her, when they were training together. Dave had said, "If a guy ever tries to overpower you, give him one second of slack. When he thinks you're tamed, then take him by surprise." She remembered this and let her body go limp. As he wrestled with her clothing and his own, she lay still, feigning submission. He couldn't know her inner fear, he could only suppose that she was terrified of his physical dominance. He couldn't know what she'd do next, but only guess that he had her under control. He came at her like a vulture at carrion, ravenous, violent. She'd missed the window of time. His two fists slammed into her face. She cried out and he clapped a rough hand over her mouth, fumbled with her shirt, savagely tore off a strip of cloth and stuffed it in her mouth. She could feel it against the back of her throat, suffocating her. He had her undressed now, her trousers down at her ankles, but he hadn't touched her underwear yet. She rolled over on top of her, undoing his belt, unzipping his pants. She could see his eyes flashing and barely make out his facial features. With one hand pressed hard against her abdomen, he pinned her to the earth. She struggled to breathe, realizing it could be too late to defend herself. His contorted face, his horrible strength. Her legs lay paralyzed beneath his, and now he pinned her arms behind her.

More saliva drooled over her face, and her mouth and throat felt raw pain when she fought for breath. Then her brain said, "Now," and her right leg automatically jerked up and the sheer force of her knee striking his groin sent him sideways for an instant. An instant was all she needed to free her arms, rip the gag from her mouth. He was generous, though, and gave her half a minute head start. Howling in pain, he held his wounded self as she sprang to her feet, started running, pulling up her trousers as she ran.

He came after her, thrashing through the undergrowth, cursing, shouting unintelligibly. The mucky, sodden ground squished under her feet. She skidded, fell sideways, got up, ran. She could hear his damp, powerful footfall, his cursing, and guessed he was only twenty or thirty yards behind her. The darkness confused her, but she was heading downhill, and she moved more carefully now in the soggy undergrowth, her grasping hands guiding her from tree to tree. He was gaining on her. She moved faster, taking chances with her footfall and with her sense of direction. In the distance, growing louder with each step she took, came a noise she recognized. The sound of water falling. The full moon appeared from behind the cloud cover, then disappeared, then appeared again. The brief illumination gave her a sense of her immediate surroundings, and that was lucky, since she stood now just a few inches from a cliff's ledge. By the time darkness shrouded the forest again, she knew where she was. On the rocky outcropping just above the waterfall.

She heard him sliding down the mountainside, saw his flashlight's beam. It swerved back and forth. She stood frozen on the rock ledge, and when the light struck her full beam, she nearly fell backwards over the ledge, but instead crouched and jumped sideways off the ledge onto the sheer granite cliff face and let gravity pull her down, down the rock slide until she landed on a small ledge beside the roaring waterfall. From here, she felt her way behind the waterfall, along the boulders that made the face of Radio and Sunbeam's cave. In the darkness she ran her hands over the stone face of the cave. Locating the entrance, she slipped inside. She sat on her haunches, listened.

No sound. He was probably out there thrashing in the woods, or maybe standing on the rocky ledge shining his flashlight across the mountain side. Now she listened not only for him but for sounds of bears. Maybe they were all out romping in the moonlight, feeding. She might be safe in here, at least until daylight. Unless Radio was home. She leaned up against a stone wall, consumed with more rage than fear, and waited until sunrise.

"WEXLER HERE."

"What's your stand on Yodeler's, chief?"

"Venus, is that you?"

"What's your position?"

A moment of silence. Then, "Right now, it is prone. And I am not interested in revising it."

"I woke you?"

"Venus, it's only eight-thirty here. Why do you always find it necessary to disturb me outside of office hours?"

"I can't help when things happen."

"What's happened?"

"Another murder on Yodeler Preserve."

"Just a minute."

Muffled sounds. Wexler's voice, then a female voice, a whiny high-pitched youngish voice. Then Wexler again, soothing. Then a few shrill giggles. Then Wexler, over the line. "All right. I am up and fully awake. Give me the details."

"This time it was brutal. That makes two murders in four days. Not counting the chef."

"What chef?"

She told him about Lux. When she finished, Wexler said, "Are you still on that malaria medication?"

"This isn't fever talk. Now, listen, chief. Last night, it was a seventy-five-year-old woman. He lashed her to a tree then drove a spike through her heart. After that, he beat me up, tried to rape me. He would've killed me if I hadn't struggled free and run."

"God." Then, "Are you okay?"

"Mad as hell, but yes, I'm okay."

"Did you identify him?"

"Not really. I have an idea, though. The woman he murdered was a local woman who's lived in these woods all her life. Aggie MacGregor. She was a wildcrafter."

"Define wildcrafter."

"She collects wild shoots and berries, herbs and such. Then she sells them after they're dried and packaged."

Wexler said, "That's illegal on federal land."

"She knew that. We must have talked to Aggie two hundred times over the years. But, well, her ancestors helped settle this territory, and she's elderly. Everybody left her pretty much alone."

"Including you?"

"I'm not up here all that often. But the rangers up here have cut her some slack, yes. He spiked her straight through the heart. I need your help, Wexler."

"Go ahead."

"Hold off on this sale. Don't let Ebert and Avalon close the deal."

"We already have an intent to purchase."

"Don't process it."

Wexler sighed. "It's too late, Venus."

"It's never too late. Give us a little more time. If we don't make a good case by a week from now, you can proceed. Just give us an extra week."

Wexler coughed. Something sour had caught in his throat. He said, "We're meeting with the Avalons here in my office this morning. They've flown back to D.C. to settle this deal. I can't put them off any longer."

"Are they in D.C. already?"

"I imagine so. Our meeting is scheduled for eleven this morning."

"Have you actually seen them?"

"Of course not. I won't see them until eleven. Now listen, Venus, I know how painful this land sale business is for all of you at Pacific Northwest. I feel the pain, too—"

She shouted into the phone, "What do you know about pain, Wexler? I'll tell you about pain. It's a stake through the heart of an old woman who's spent her entire life trying to keep this piece of land safe from development. And on her fresh grave, you're going to permit the destruction—the extinction—of important native species..."

Wexler came back hotly, "Don't overstate your case, Venus. And don't ever show impertinence towards me again. Do you understand?"

Silence.

Then, "Venus, are you there?"

Dully, she said, "And in her mouth, he stuffed a fistful of live caterpillars. Guess what they were?"

"Oh God, I don't know."

"Larvae of the Dungeness silverspot."

"The Dungeness silverspot is extinct."

"I disagree."

More silence. Then Wexler heard a dial tone.

TWENTY-FOUR

SUSPICION

THE SUN CREPT over the Cascades, spilling a new dawn into the valley, washing Mount Pluvius in rose crimson light. Eric Sweetwater brought the Bell Jet Ranger down high on Yodeler's meadow, the whirring of the blades sending Avalon's blue poppies into a tizzy. The team poured out of the chopper, swarmed up through the poppies into the forest, where Venus met them at the head of the waterfall. Olson, Song, and Sparks carried rifles, Sweetwater and Dottie hauled a body bag and forensics gear. Claudia carried her bag of physician's tricks and it was a lucky thing, because one glance at Venus confirmed Claudia's suspicions. Venus was injured far more seriously than she had indicated when she phoned headquarters at five o'clock this morning.

Olson covered Venus with a thick maroon blanket, held her in an embrace. Venus's body trembled, and she felt hot. When Olson placed the back of his hand gently against her neck, testing the temperature there, she broke away, turned to the team. As Claudia approached, she saw Venus seated on the rock ledge with the others crouched around her. Venus was talking earnestly, making air maps with her hands, using her fingers to emphasize a point. With the blanket on, she reminded Claudia of a miniature Indian communicating in sign language. Claudia came up, stood between Song and Dottie. Claudia could hear a small high-pitched moan coming from Dottie's throat, a reaction to seeing Venus's destroyed face. When Venus finished briefing the team, they moved single file up Mac-Gregor's Trail towards the cedar clearing where they would discover the gruesome corpse nailed to the ancient cedar.

Claudia made Venus lie down on the rocky ledge, placing her own jacket under Venus's head, covering her with the maroon blanket tucked high up under her chin. Venus threw the blanket off and said, "I'm not dead."

"Just to keep you warm," murmured Claudia, firmly replacing the blanket, "until I get this syringe filled."

"I won't have a shot." Adamant.

"You will have a shot." More adamant. Paganelli had a grizzly's grip that she only used when she had to, like now.

Venus rolled over and had a shot.

Claudia said, "There. Now, just relax."

In a few minutes, the world went deliriously adrift, Venus's head rolled to the side, her eyes tried focusing on the blue poppies in the meadow below. Full bloom, the poppies danced gracefully, a brilliant blue ballet, fantasia. That was the last thing she saw before her eyes closed. Claudia reached over, plucked the cell phone out of Venus's rear pocket.

Venus slumbered deeply while Claudia worked. The scratches on her arms and chest had been made by fingernails. Claudia scraped samples off the scratches before treating them. She bound the wounds with soft, sterile gauze. The arms were deeply bruised, but nothing was broken. Claudia examined her ribs. Might be a broken rib or two. The abdomen responded normally to her probings, and by some miracle, the rapist's attack had not been successful. Claudia paused. Rage unsteadied her hand. She sat for a while staring out at the rising sun, at the peaceful valley and the rippling saltwater strait. Calm, pristine beauty. It had no right to trespass upon her rage.

The face needed stitches on both cheeks where a hard fist or a rock, she couldn't tell which, had split the skin. Maybe the fists wore rings. She took more samples, hoping for a DNA identification of the savage who had done this. She cleaned the wounds, stitched them, covered them with sterile gauze, trying her best to be artful about the placement of the bandages. Venus despised being the object of jokes, no matter how kindly cracked. She wasn't pretty when Claudia finished her work, but she was clean, on the mend, and when she awoke an hour later, Louie Song was stroking her forehead and smiling over her like a fawning mother. Venus pushed his hand away, scowled at Song.

"Lose smarmy, Song. It kills your hipness."

"She's back," announced Claudia.

Aggie's corpse had been taken down from the cedar trunk, placed in a body bag, and loaded into the chopper. They'd found Venus's backpack, her ripped shirt. No evidence of the assailant except for poorly formed footprints on the wet earth.

"What about the caterpillars?" Venus asked.

Song looked puzzled. "What caterpillars?"

Olson said, "Weren't any."

Dot said, "You probably imagined them. It was grisly enough already. It didn't need caterpillars."

"I'm sure there were caterpillars in her mouth." Adamant again.

"Take it easy, honey..." Olson.

Venus insisted. "Her mouth was filled with caterpillars. We have to find them. They're Dungeness silverspots."

Sparks raised a finger, shook his head. "Extinct."

Venus argued. "The Dungeness has been sighted recently."

Sparks sucked on a reed. "Oh yeah?" he drawled. "Like, when?"

Claudia intervened. "Hey guys, can it, will you? Venus doesn't need excitement. She needs to go home and recover."

The team trudged down into the meadow, Song and Olson supporting Venus. When they reached the blue poppies, Song broke off a bouquet, handed it to her. "To match your face," he said and grinned. They loaded the chopper, placed Venus on a stretcher in the hold. When they had made her comfortable, Song leaned down, kissed her forehead. "You're still a knockout."

"No puns," she muttered. "Hurts when I smile."

Song nodded. "You're still in charge," he said. "But while you're recovering, I'll be your legs. Fair enough?"

Fair enough. She said, "As long as you remember who's in charge."

CONRAD AVALON moved stealthily out of the forest above Aggie MacGregor's land. When Aggie's dog barked, Conrad stood quite still for a moment until the dog paused. In a low voice, Conrad called to the dog. Tina came running up the field, barking. Conrad talked to Tina and soon built a trust. Tina wagged her tail. Conrad stepped over the barbed wire fencing around Aggie's chicken coop, sending the fancy chickens into a dither. The ground here was soft, sodden, but Conrad's favorite dress shoes had already been ruined up in the forest last night. Why hadn't Aggie come to meet him in their secret rendezvous? He'd waited all night behind the waterfall, dozing off and on, but Aggie never came. That wasn't like Aggie. And, too, it wasn't at all like Conrad to wear his best dress shoes along MacGregor's Trail, but this was a special occasion, and he wanted to be dressed for it. When a gentleman plans to propose marriage to the loveliest lady on God's fair Earth, naturally, he would wish to appear as gallant and polished as he could.

At the old shed, Conrad stopped and poked his head inside, half expecting Aggie to be in there with her plants and herbs and whatnot. Instead, he found it empty of people, but full of something else, something quite beautiful, in its own way. Here in Aggie's shed hung branch after branch of stripped willow sticks, and on the sticks were woven garlands of violets. The petals were wilting and the leaves had been chewed, still, their blue faces and soft green leaves were a sight to behold. On closer inspection, Conrad discovered there was more than leaves and flowers to these lovely garlands. First one chrysalis, then another, then another, and on and on, until he had counted eighty, and still there were more to count. So Aggie MacGregor had gone into the butterfly business, had she? Conrad chuckled to himself, leaned down and patted Tina. Women have the oddest hobbies.

As he walked through the field towards Aggie's house, Tina bouncing along at his feet, Conrad felt the bulge in his jacket pocket and smiled to himself. He might look a little grubby and warmed over this morning, after spending the night in their secret place behind the waterfall, but he still had this precious brooch to give his lady fair, and surely she would forgive the slightly rumpled condition of its delivery vehicle.

Come to think of it, Conrad had always been just that, a delivery vehicle. Not that he resented his role in life, on the contrary, Conrad had been blessed with privilege and prosperity, and too, his career had been both challenging and rewarding. Life had always been good to Conrad. Except for that brief period in his early twenties, that terrible tragedy, and the heartbreak. He didn't like to think about those horrid days, and in fact, he had suppressed the mental images that when they came, inevitably they caused a pain so sharp and so wrenching in his heart that he had actually considered patricide. But old Johnny MacGregor took care of that for him.

After Aggie's father killed his father, Conrad and Aggie had considered a suicide pact. The plan was, Aggie would first shoot Conrad, then kill herself. They met at their secret hiding place, in a cave behind the waterfall. At the very last minute, Aggie MacGregor flung the pistol into the waterfall.

"I don't kill," she told Conrad. Then she had said, "It's our families' wish that we don't marry. Your father's dead and buried. My father inhabits the grave of eternal guilt. I will always love you, dearest, but..."

"But what?"

"It's over between us, Connie."

The following year, Conrad married Dolly, much to his parents' delight. Conrad dearly loved Dolly, and he'd been a good and faithful husband these fifty years. But Dolly was gone to her grave more than two years now. Now they were all dead, except for Conrad and Aggie. The two young lovers had not met privately for fifty years, and Conrad had intended this rendezvous to rekindle the romance. But Aggie never came, and Conrad intended to find out why. And too, he had the brooch to deliver.

Her front door was shut, but the knob turned in his hand. When she didn't answer to his calling her name, Conrad stepped across the threshold into Aggie's house. The cat on the windowsill hissed at him but otherwise didn't move a muscle. Tina stayed at Conrad's heels, nipping constantly, trying to tell him something. Conrad walked into the living room, through the dining room, into the kitchen. No sign of Aggie. He turned down the hall, poked his head into the bathroom. Empty. At the bedroom door, he paused. The door was closed. He knocked lightly. No answer. He turned the knob and went in, half expecting Aggie to jump up startled out of her bed. But Aggie wasn't in bed. No one was in the bed. It was made up, neat and tidy. He sniffed. He could smell Aggie in here, Aggie's sweet scent, a scent that always reminded him of pink fawn lilies in summer, the natural scent of Aggie. He was thinking that Aggie might have gone into town, and wondering if the blue poppy brooch wasn't a mistake after all, since Aggie never wore the fragrance, when a voice behind him said, "Hold it right there. Put your hands over your head and turn around." Conrad turned around.

Upon seeing that it was Conrad, Sheriff Needles relaxed and put his gun away. "Now, Conrad, what in God's good name are you doing up here at Aggie MacGregor's house?"

Conrad lowered his hands and laughed a tight, nervous titter. "Come to see Aggie, I did. Come to give her a little treasure. But it's personal, Ned. It wouldn't interest you one bit." Conrad massaged his chest lightly with one hand. Needles had thrown him a slight scare, his nerves weren't what they used to be. "You seen her?"

Needles pressed his lips together. He'd always suspected Conrad

Avalon had a weakness for Aggie MacGregor. Of course, he'd heard stories about back in the old days, before he was even born, stories about Conrad and Aggie. The whole town knew that story, it was part of local legend. So now here comes old widower Avalon to see his childhood sweetheart. What should Needles tell him? Sometimes the brutal truth is easier to accept when you least expect it. Needles was blunt.

Fifteen minutes later, in a rain shower, Needles led Conrad to the patrol car, helped him into the passenger seat, closed the door gently. Needles slid behind the wheel, turned on the windshield wipers, and aimed the patrol car down the highway toward Fern.

TWENTY-FIVE

DIAPAUSE

In colder climates like those of Scotland, Canada, and much of North America, many species overwinter in a state of dormancy called diapause. Fritillaries of *Speyeria zerene* varieties overwinter in the larval stage, hiding in undergrowth, beneath their host plant, *V. adunca*.

— *Green's World Famous Butterfly Gardens*

TIMMY SAT ALONE in his bedroom, watching the caterpillar spin a thin silk patch on the underside of a violet leaf. Down the hall he heard Bella, Echo, and the doctor consulting in low voices. Timmy had kept his bedroom door open so he could listen to them. The doctor's voice was too low, and Timmy couldn't make out every word, but the gist was the wounds Venus had received from the attacker would heal eventually. She was weak, her system vulnerable. She was still recuperating from a bout with malaria, and that had weakened her system. The patient would be better off just resting for the next few months, until her strength came back. Meanwhile, as long as Bella retained a private nurse to administer intravenous fluids, the patient could stay at home. The hospital didn't want her until her heart stopped beating, and anyway, Bella would have more control keeping her daughter at home.

Timmy heard Bella talking to the nurse, running the sick room like a military hospital. The nurse was a sturdy, efficient Mary Poppins and Timmy thought her breath smelled like piss. She wouldn't let him enter the sick room. He hadn't even seen Venus since they brought her home and put her in the sewing room alcove. The nurse had ordered a screen placed outside the double glass doors of the alcove. The patient had a right to privacy, Poppins had snapped at

Timmy. Timmy didn't talk back to her, just sulked off to his room. Poppins had to sleep sometime, then he could make his move.

Venus had been wrong about one thing. The caterpillar had only one instar left before it started to form a chrysalis. Timmy had seen the actual event, when the caterpillar shed its skin for the last time. It had sucked in air until its body puffed up like a balloon, and then the skin broke and a thin shell dropped off. Underneath, the caterpillar was sleek, shiny. Then that very afternoon—it was yesterday afternoon—the caterpillar began weaving the silk patch on the violet leaf. Timmy used Bella's big magnifying glass to observe the caterpillar's activity. He thought he could make out the two spinnerets on the caterpillar's jaw, where it spun the silk. He fervently hoped that the creature would soon go into its chrysalis, because it had almost run out of food. He had tried feeding it some Boston lettuce and a fresh sprig of mint, but the caterpillar rejected them. It only wanted violet leaves.

Timmy sighed. Life was hard enough without Venus being sick. Somehow, Timmy thought he must have done something very bad to cause Venus's sickness. It was his fault. He wondered if he should go to Bella, confess that he was at the bottom of Venus's sickness, and take the punishment. He never liked feeling guilty. He felt guilty a lot of the time, and it wasn't at all a nice feeling. But if you tell someone that you have done a bad deed, if you confess it, does that make guilt go away? Timmy wasn't sure, and he hesitated about going to Bella. Maybe he could fix things up.

The caterpillar lay very still against the white silk patch. It might be asleep. Timmy sighed, put down the magnifying glass, and went out of his room, carefully shutting the door behind him.

Echo, Venus's younger sister, was sprawled across a chaise longue on the upper terrace. Timmy had first met Echo on the previous day, when she arrived for a visit. She had bright blue eyes, perfect skin, and blond hair, the shade of Venus's hair, only a lot more of it, and she wore it long and in her face, like all the sitcom stars. Echo dressed in black, even though it was almost officially summer. Venus dressed all in black sometimes, but in summer she wore a lot of white, and Timmy thought Venus looked beautiful when she wore white. He carried his bowl of Cocoa Krispies out onto the terrace. The breakfast table had been set, but so far no one had come to breakfast. Timmy took his place and began eating his cereal. He really wasn't in the mood for conversation, so when Echo spoke, he frowned.

"How's my new little brother this morning?" Echo chirped brightly.

"I am not your brother." Hoarsely, curt.

Echo seemed amused. She had a pack of cigarettes. She lit one, blew out the smoke.

"Pretty cool day, huh?"

Weather talk. Trying to make conversation. Timmy didn't feel like conversation. He wanted to eat his cereal in peace and quiet. Echo persisted. "Trouble will be okay, Timmy. You don't have to worry about her."

A low growl formed in Timmy's throat. He said, "Her name is Venus. And I'm not worried."

Echo laughed. She had glassy chimes like Bella's. Tinkling. She said, "Listen, Tim, I'm going to tell you something about Trouble, I mean, Venus. Venus is a hypochondriac. She imagines she's sick, she actually makes herself sick so that she'll get everyone's attention. She's done it all her life. Trust me." Echo leaned back and puffed on the cigarette.

Timmy watched a Boeing 777 fly over Puget Sound, headed toward Boeing Field. Timmy knew all the Boeing airplanes by sight, even from a far distance. He wished he was on that airplane going back to Singapore with Venus. That trip had been fun, and Timmy liked Venus's friends in Singapore. But then Richard had shown up and spoiled everything. He winced thinking of Richard. Echo saw Timmy wince and said, "Bit down on a Cocoa pebble, huh?"

"No. I did not." How dare this girl interrupt his private thoughts. He turned his back to her, hoping she would get the hint. She didn't.

"Timmy, how'd you like to go sailing this afternoon? My friend Fred has a really cool sailboat. Actually, it's a small yacht. We're going out on the Sound this afternoon. Wanna come with us?"

Timmy hadn't expected the invitation. He had to admit it sounded like fun. He turned it over in his mind. What was there to do at home anyway? Venus didn't need him. She had the Poppins woman and besides, she was always sleeping. The caterpillar didn't need him, at least he didn't think so. Bella had her hands full balancing a garden party and Venus, and she wouldn't care if Timmy went out for the afternoon. Best of all, it seemed to Timmy, a sailing adventure would help get his mind off the guilt, the terrible, nagging guilt. He said, "I have a program to download from the Internet." Playing hard to get.

Echo nodded. "Too bad. We're sailing over to Vashon, to a fab beach party."

Timmy shoved his cereal bowl aside, stood up, and walked across the terrace to the open French doors. "Sorry," he said. "Maybe some other time."

He was already inside the house when Echo yelled, "We'll run the ferry wakes, like, really up close."

Timmy popped his head out the door and said, "Okay, okay. Just let me change my clothes first."

He didn't notice Echo roll her eyes. He probably never knew that Bella had commanded Echo to get Timmy out of the house for the afternoon. Timmy might be a sour little albatross, Echo told herself, but hey, it's a big sailboat. Practically a yacht.

Timmy changed into his best white jeans and a striped navy shirt. He combed his hair, watched his reflection in the mirror for a moment, and was on his way upstairs to meet Echo when Bella appeared at his bedroom door. Her razor vision immediately spotted the Bloomingdale's box.

"Why, what is that, Timmy?"

"What? Oh, that's a Bloomingdale's swizzle stick box. I like them because you can look inside from any angle. And those are pansies inside. I really shouldn't have picked them from your garden bed, but..."

"Timmy, don't look now, but there is an odd creature lurking in among your pansies. I don't believe I have ever seen such an ugly creature." Bella called out down the hall, "Stephen, please come here. We need you."

"Mother, that is the larva of the—"

"I won't have larva in my home. Place it outside, if you please. Preferably in the garbage."

"But Venus gave it to me, to take care of."

Bella rolled her dazzling eyes and spoke out loud to herself. "Honestly, will Venus ever stop bringing strangers home? This is proving a lifelong pattern, and I don't approve at all."

"I was one." Hoarsely.

"One what, darling?"

"A stranger. When Venus brought me home."

Bella smiled and gently tweaked Timmy's nose. "You're different, Timmy. You're very, very special."

"So is the caterpillar." Not whining, just a statement of fact.

Bella sighed and pointed her finger at the French doors. "Very well, darling, you may keep the creature. But place it outdoors, if you please, and when it dies from neglect, I don't want to hear sobbings and remorse."

"You won't," he promised, but she hadn't heard him. She was chugging down the hall toward the caterers, who had just arrived with the garden party chow.

DARIN WAS serving luncheon when Slava put his florid face to the round window and mouthed a word. It had three syllables. Fid-dle-head? No. Chan-te-relles? Maybe. Darin finished what he was doing and went into the kitchen, where Slava had a prep cook named Alice up against a wall and was shaking a finger in her face, yelling something about confusing avocados and poached pears. Alice's lower lip trembled, but Darin knew the girl, and he knew her acting talents. Once she'd faked something with Darin, and now he was sure this trembling lip was pure hoax, faking her fear of the Russian prima don. Snooty Alice could fake anything. Slava noticed Darin, released Alice from his grip, and said, "The telephone is for you." Then things returned to normal in the kitchen, at least as normal as Slava's kitchen could be. Darin went over and picked up the phone. It was Marvine.

"We're meeting at six o'clock this evening. You know the place. Be there, Darin. You're in this just as much as we are."

"What? Oh, oh sure, Marvine." Darin rubbed his scrawny beard. "I'll be there. Who else is coming?"

"Everybody. I mean, all the key players. It's a dress rehearsal. We need to role-play the event. We don't want anything to go wrong, you know."

"Like what? What could go wrong?"

Marvine considered for a minute, then said, "You know what I'm talking about."

Darin pressed her. "No. Tell me."

Marvine made an impatient sound. "Like, things getting, you know, like, out of hand."

"Like violence?" Darin picked his teeth. A chanterelle slice had caught between two rear molars.

"Yes," spit Marvine. "So we need everybody there tonight." She hung up.

Darin finished picking out the chanterelle, rinsed his mouth at the sink, washed his hands with antibacterial soap, and returned to work. On his way out of the kitchen, he passed Alice and said softly, "You coming tonight?"

Alice made an O with her mouth. "Where?" she said through the O.

"Dress rehearsal."

The girl's eyes flitted around the kitchen. Slava couldn't hear them. She nodded at Darin and whispered, "I think everybody's coming, don't you?"

Darin smiled and put a palm against the cool silver door.

OLSON HAD Ebert on one line and Wexler on the other. Claudia Paganelli and Sparks sat in Olson's office, listening in on the rancor. Ebert had just said something that ticked him off, and now Olson was shouting at Ebert. Ebert was laughing raucously and Wexler was pleading with the two of them. Claudia shot Sparks a bored look and stood up, walked to the windows, peered out at the gray gloom. She couldn't recall a summer this gray and gloomy. She'd lived twenty years in the Pacific Northwest, and still she couldn't adjust to the climate. In Norway, where she came from, the skies produced fewer clouds, less rain. Less gloom.

Half an hour earlier, Claudia had brought Olson the evidence. It didn't take Olson long to digest the material and posit a theory on how things happened up on the mountain. Clearly, whoever had nailed the old woman to the tree was the same individual who attacked Venus. Claudia could prove that beyond a doubt. She had the DNA, she had fingerprints off Venus's gun. Claudia could also prove that the old woman had mercifully died from a heart attack before she was nailed to the tree. She probably died when her assailant was beating her. Yes, they had DNA evidence that linked both crimes.

Claudia could confirm that scenario, based on the evidence. Beyond that, Claudia knew little about what happened to Aggie MacGregor and to Venus last night on the mountain. Why had Venus gone there in the first place? What reason had she for hiking up that trail all the way to the waterfall in the middle of the night? Furthermore, why was the old woman up along the trail so late at night? For a minute, Claudia tried imagining that Venus and the old woman had made a plan to meet up there. But why? Claudia shook her head. No, that didn't ring true. Venus would never have asked the elderly woman to climb that steep trail so late at night. So even though she knew how the old woman died and how Venus got three broken ribs and the scrapes and bruises, she still didn't know why it all happened, or who did it.

Now Olson was shouting. Claudia turned from the window, stared at the boss. His face glowed beet red. Even the top of his bald head beamed crimson. Olson might be a curmudgeonly boss, thought Claudia, but he could move heaven and earth when one of his agents was attacked. She had never seen him this angry. Now, he shouted at Ebert.

"There's no deal, Ebert. I don't care whose signature you have on what document. That land cannot be sold."

Ebert chuckled into the phone. Claudia and Sparks heard it on the conference speaker. Sparks raised his eyebrows, triggering a nervous tic. Claudia sighed, walked over to the sofa, slumped into it, folding her hands in her lap. How much longer would this go on? She heard Wexler's voice, calm, cool, almost detached. Didn't he care about his own staff? Didn't he even care that Venus had almost been killed, that she had been savagely attacked in the course of her work? If only Wexler would shout the way Olson did, she'd respect him more. She was about to lose every shred of respect for him when suddenly Wexler's voice came booming across the speaker, silencing both Ebert and Olson.

"Shut up," he bellowed. "Shut up, both of you, and listen!"

Claudia sat up straight. Sparks leaned forward toward the phone speaker. Olson fumed silently and listened. Ebert, wherever he was, had quit his sadistic chuckling. Wexler took a deep breath and said, "As it stands, the land still belongs to Interior. I haven't signed anything, and I haven't asked the President to sign anything. What Ebert has is an intent to purchase signed by Peter and Troy Avalon. I understand they require a third signature on that paper—"

"Right," Ebert cut in, "the uncle's signature. Piece of cake."

"I said shut up," Wexler growled. "Furthermore, I will not tolerate any loose lips around this deal, and I will severely reprimand any Interior employee who tries to interfere with a closing on the sale—"

"But..." Olson broke in, "you just said..."

"I just said that we haven't closed the deal yet. I did not imply that we weren't going to sell the land. Unless something drastic happens, I foresee the sale going through in the next few weeks."

Olson exploded. "So you're selling out, Wexler? And you're taking us down with you, is that what you think? Well, I'll tell you something. You can have my badge and my pension. I'll quit before I participate in the reckless sale of a fragile ecosystem to a private corporation that wants to plow under a virgin meadow for its own financial gain. You've got my promise on that, Wexler.''

Silence. Claudia realized that if she were going to speak up at all, it had to be now. She cleared her throat and spoke in her even, slightly accented voice. "I don't know about the rest of you," she began, "but right now I am thinking about a murder victim. The old woman who was nailed to the tree last night deserves justice. My opinion is that right now, the department should concentrate on bringing the killer to justice. That same killer nearly murdered one of our agents as well. It's my opinion that before we argue the pros and cons of a land sale, we should be using our energy toward finding the killer. When we have brought the killer to justice, then maybe these other issues will solve themselves.''

Olson shot Claudia a hard glance. "What's that supposed to mean?''

Claudia shrugged. "I haven't any specific ideas," she said calmly. "But it has occurred to me that the sale of the land and the murder of the old woman might possibly be connected. Even the murder of the man, Jonathan Willow, might be connected. We don't know anything for sure. I think we owe it to ourselves to investigate this possibility.''

More silence. Sparks sniffed loudly, wiped the tic. Claudia played with the folds of her skirt. Finally, Wexler spoke.

"We'll find the killer. After that, we'll talk about the sale.''

Claudia glanced over at Olson. He winked at her.

TWENTY-SIX

FRAGRANCE OF TIBET

ZORA SAT horrified before the dressing table mirror. First of all, no hotel, no matter how quaintly chic, ought to place lilacs on a dressing table, especially not purple ones. Didn't anyone around here realize what dreadful tones the color purple can cast across an alabaster complexion? Zora summoned the housekeeper, who came swiftly and removed the offensive florals, and only then did Zora proceed with her makeup routine, a ritual she adored almost as much as her own reflection in the mirror.

This morning marked the dawn of destiny. Zora's destiny. If these images of Zora amidst a field of blue poppies turned out the way everyone hoped, soon all the world would be privy to her special beauty. Granted, blue poppies might cast an offensive tint, but she had tricks to deal with blue, like the slightly yellow-tinted ivory foundation she applied to her flawless skin. That would counterpoint—or was it counteract?—every hint of blue. She was applying false eyelash fringes, her fingers steady as steel girders, when Shelby's voice in the foyer startled her and a lash fringe ended up on her eyebrow.

"Go away," snapped Zora. "Come back in fifteen minutes, and when you do, bring me a margarita." Shelby fled. Zora sounded awfully bossy this morning.

When she had finished the creative work, Zora flitted around her bedroom like a dragonfly in tropical heat. From her dressing table to the breakfast cart, from the breakfast cart to the window, then back again to the dressing table where the phone should be ringing right now but wasn't. When Shelby finally entered the room, Margarita first, Zora had made it halfway from the bedside table to the window.

"Settle down, honey," drawled the Warlock. "It's your big day. Why are you so jumpy, darlin'?"

Zora slinked over to the dressing table, wiggled onto the satin bench, and peered into the mirror. Even after the cosmetic artifice, her eyes looked all wrong this morning. That new bag-reducing cream had utterly failed. "I need tea bags," Zora announced. "Call the kitchen...no, better not do that. I don't trust that chef. Call the front desk and tell them to send over tea bags."

Shelby sashayed over to the bedside table, parked languorously on the unmade bed, and picked up the telephone. While she waited for an answer, Shelby said, "Cookie's out there in the lobby. She's going along for the show. Maybe to put a distance between you and Peter." At the mirror, Zora peeled down a lower eyelid and studied a road map of bloodshot veins.

"Gawd, I hate her accent. She sounds like a four-year-old sucking her thumb. Now, where did these things come from?" Referring to the tattletale veins. Shelby, speaking to the front desk, didn't hear Zora's question. "Anyway, I despise Peter. Doesn't Cookie understand that?" A whiny lament that went unanswered.

When Shelby hung up the phone, it rang immediately. "It's for you," said Shelby. "Troy-boy."

Zora cradled the phone, purred into it, but Troy wasn't in the mood for patty-cake. "The car's waiting," he said. "There must be a dozen reporters and cameras outside. Even Fox is here. And there's a lady with *Vanity Fair* credentials."

"But how in the world," purred Zora, "did they ever find us?"

Troy, speaking from the house phone in the lobby, turned his back on several reporters. Sarcastically, he said to Zora, "Well, somebody must have tipped them off."

"I wouldn't do that." Zora, hotly.

"Of course, they won't be allowed near the poppies. And you'll be secreted out through the kitchen. They mustn't identify you until the ads come out, remember. Are you ready?"

Zora lit a cigarette, blew smoke, winked at Shelby. Into the phone, she murmured, "For you, darling, I'm always ready." Lying through her teeth, but what did she care? Zora held the world in the palm of her grasping hand, and if she really wanted to, she could squeeze it dry.

THE ROLLS-ROYCE Silver Cloud floated regally down Highway 101, a media cavalcade in tow. Zora, her face cowled in black silk, sat beside Cookie Avalon, across from Troy and Peter, while Shelby slow-burned in the jump seat. If Cookie hadn't imposed herself upon this festive foursome, Shelby would be seated across from Troy right now, rubbing knees. Of all the dumb luck.

Troy popped the cork on a champagne bottle, poured, passed glasses around. Zora couldn't resist. A few sips wouldn't hurt. Shelby guzzled, and Cookie abstained. Over his champagne glass, Peter studied Zora. How could he ever have made such a regrettable mistake? Maybe something in the Roman light had fooled his eye. Nothing about Zora was compatible with the Blue Poppy image. He should have listened to Cookie after all. She'd been right about Zora's harsh face and grinding voice, her brash hair, clawlike nails. She reminded Peter of a Senegalese parrot. Thank God little Lily had come along. Thinking of Lily, Peter sat back and relaxed. Let Zora have her fun, he told himself. Because she would never, as long as Peter Avalon was alive, under any circumstances, be publicly connected to Blue Poppy perfume. Peter noticed Zora scowling at him, maybe reading his mind. She looked the type. He smiled bravely and sipped champagne.

Cookie took all this in, her own mental exercises consisting of suspicion and a hyperactive imagination. Why was Peter staring so appreciatively at Zora? Hadn't he told Cookie just last night that he thought Zora was a cheap little thing? Now Peter was all over Zora with his eyes, drinking her in like so much cheap swill, feasting upon her like a crow on trash. He should be ashamed of himself. Peter knew better than to fall for this face-injected, breast-enhanced, bottled-jet tramp. If Uncle Conrad were here, he would stop this nonsense. Where was Uncle Conrad when she needed him? Did she have to do everything by herself? Honestly, how did she ever get connected to the Avalon family?

Troy nattered on about the ad campaign. When he had exhausted that subject, he commenced gushing over Mother Nature. "Wait till you see the field," he said to anyone who was listening. "I drove past it this morning just after dawn. Magnificent. Truly magnificent. Our best crop ever. Won't last long, though. Harvest begins day after tomorrow. It's fleeting beauty, but Gawwwd, when that field blooms, it's like one long ocean wave crashing into the mountainside. Just wait until we have all of Yodeler's in poppies. Then you'll see fantasia. And the MacGregor land, once we get our hands on the MacGregor land—"

"Shut up," snapped Peter.

Troy, reddened slightly, shut up, turned his back on Peter, and stared sullenly out the window. He had the distinct feeling that Peter was about to pull a fast one, and yet he couldn't say for sure. There was no evidence. The party rode in silence until just as they reached the meadow, the telephone jangled. Troy answered, then handed the receiver to Peter. Peter's confident voice said into the phone, "Yes, we've just arrived at the meadow. Give us about half an hour. Then bring around the cargo. No, wait. Give us an hour." Peter rang off.

"What cargo?" said Troy.

"Never mind," snapped Peter.

Gawwwd, he's in a prickly mood this morning, thought Troy. One of those walk on eggshells days.

Peter helped the women out of the Silver Cloud. Troy could help himself. As Zora exited, she shot Peter a triumphant glance. Shelby followed, muttering under her breath. Last of all, Cookie exited in a huff, her flashing eyes slicing her husband into tiny pieces. As Peter expected, Cookie performed her usual security guard maneuvers on the way up the green meadow, placing her body firmly between Zora and himself, sticking to his side like a fly on marmalade. They hadn't gone far up the meadow when Troy remarked, "Wildflowers have such a short life span, y'know? I mean, a few days ago, this meadow was just covered with wildflowers. And now look. Nothing but grass and weeds."

Peter pointed up at the poppy field. "Now there's beauty."

Zora sneezed. Something flew at her face, a nasty winged insect. She tried batting it away, but the insect persisted, fluttering very near her creamy white neck. At her ankles, the sawgrass irritated, itched. She slapped at her neck, stooped over, and scratched her ankles. Bucolic just wasn't Zora's idea of a fun time. As far as she was concerned, the insects could have this rural aspect. Right now, all Zora wanted was a good dose of Rodeo Drive and a few other comforting signs of civilization. She called to mind the purpose of her sacrifice, and steeled herself for the next torturous couple hours of work, promising to reward herself that night. Right now, Troy seemed the obvious candidate, but you never know. At this point in her life, Zora had trouble remembering whether or not she'd slipped around on the present boyfriend, or even who the present boyfriend was, or had been. She was pretty sure she hadn't cheated on him, whoever he was, had just imagined doing so with Troy and a few other hunks, like that cute wildlife cop. What was his name? Sun? Chin? Oh well. What's this? Troy reached out, took Zora's hand with the parrot claws, squeezed it. Now, what's that supposed to mean? Zora smiled. With nooky on the horizon, the next couple hours should be a piece of cake.

The film crew had arrived at dawn, hauled their equipment up the meadow, set up the cameras and lights, baffles and backdrop, so that when the star arrived, they were ready for her, and, God willing, a cooperative sky. The next half hour passed swiftly for Zora as a makeup artist preened over her and the film crew held light meters up to her pale skin, measured reflections and generally fussed over her. This was where Zora, the hope of Hollywood, had always belonged. This was her destiny and from now on, nobody would ever speak the name Zora without visualizing her face, her body, her glorious being. Zora, the household word. Zora, the legend had finally come to pass.

In all the fuss and excitement, Zora didn't notice Peter disappear from the scene. She had metamorphosed into a sort of living modeling clay, leaving the tricky angles and other decisions to the creative director and his crew. Ten, maybe fifteen minutes passed, and then, on cue, Zora dropped the black cape. Clad now in a tiny bright blue bikini, the pale Zora swayed nimbly into the full blown poppy fields, her skimpy bikini blending perfectly with the flowers. She turned to face the legions. Gawwwd, I must look ravishing, she thought. Now, if these pesky mosquitoes would just drop dead...

Troy shouted, "Squat down, honey. Spread your arms like wings. That's it. All I want to see is your head and neck, and maybe a little arm, a few fingers. Down, down, turn to the left, down about two more inches...there. Hold it."

From Troy's perspective the composition appeared almost perfect. He shouted, "Lick your lips. I want to see that sexy mouth. I want those eyes to make love to me. You're a flower, making love to the sun. Wet your lips again... Hold it."

Troy saw the blood before his brain registered the gunfire. Zora's forehead split open when the bullet entered from the rear of her skull. The bullet lodged in the frontal lobe, a bloody knob on the beauty queen's once snow-white forehead. She fell forward into the poppies, her arms and legs akimbo. She'd never be bored again.

BY THE TIME Song arrived, Needles had already sent a small search party into the forest. The camera crew and makeup artists hovered together beside a silver spruce tree. The Avalons and Shelby Warlock sat in the Silver Cloud, Shelby guzzling champagne. Peter was smoking, and Shelby had taken two tranquilizers. Troy was too dazed to be of use. Needles hitched up his trousers and left the ticklish situation to Song.

Zora's body was taken to the county morgue. Olson sent the team up to assist Song. Even Dottie. Song had Eric Sweetwater and Dottie take statements. Claudia and Song worked over the evidence. There wasn't much, just the bullet in Zora's forehead and the position of the body, the way it fell all akimbo. She'd been relaxed when she was hit, unsuspecting. The bullet had come from above the poppies, from the forest. The forest where so many nightmares are born, thought Song as he and Claudia climbed up MacGregor's Trail searching for signs of the killer. They found nothing. When they got back to the meadow, the sun's angle had changed, and the meadow swam in deep shadows. The search for the killer had to be called off. Song double-checked Dottie's notes before he released the witnesses. He wanted to be sure Dottie's mind was on her work. Apparently, it was. The notes she and Sweetwater took seemed thorough, along with addresses and phone numbers. Everyone told the same story. They were filming the last shot. Zora stood alone among the poppies, clad only in the thin poppy blue bikini. Suddenly, a gunshot sounded and Zora lurched forward, then fell to the ground. It was only then that anyone noticed she had been shot through the back of the head. Except for Troy. Troy had noticed the blood on her forehead even before she fell. Troy emphasized this point to the agents. The blood, and the bullet poking out of her skull. The killer had hit the proverbial bull's eye.

On the way back, in the car, Troy turned to Peter. "Where's Cookie?"

Peter looked around. Shelby on his left. Troy across. No Cookie. Peter shrugged. "She probably went back with Jacob."

"The camera man?"

Peter nodded, picked up the phone, dialed. When Miss Perkins came on, he said, "Get ahold of Anson Budge. Tell him I need to reschedule with his daughter."

"Mimi?"

"No." Tersely. "I mean Lily."

Silence in the Silver Cloud. Uncomfortable silence. Finally, Shelby piped up, "Someone called Cookie should be grateful for all her freckles. At least they distract from her stupid name."

Anxiety humor. She poured out a trickle of flat champagne, used it to chase a Valium. Who wouldn't, after all?

TWENTY-SEVEN

LOVE KNOT

COOKIE CHARMEAUX AVALON stood naked before the Yocum mirror. The four-by-five-foot beveled plate glass, shaped like a queen's tiara and enclosed in a golden gilt frame, had been in Cookie's family since before the War Between the States. Whenever she gazed into the Yocum mirror, she could see the Yankees bearing down on her family's plantation. But the mirror held wonderful images, too, and Cookie loved nothing more than gazing into its magic depths.

According to Cookie's great-great aunt Clydia Louise, the Yocum mirror had returned the proud gaze of Colonel Elderbright B. Yocum, just after Yocum met the Yankee warship at the river bend above Natchez. Yocum was on shore, his men tattered and exhausted, with few firearms, no cannon, and nothing to eat. Still, Yocum and his men managed to hold off the Yankee warship for three solid weeks until reserves came up from Baton Rouge with enough firepower to send the Yankee boys aflyin' back upstream. In the end, the Yankees came back and captured Natchez, and then Aunt Clydia Louise had been just a baby in the arms of her colored nanny when the Yankees marched Colonel Yocum up the front lawn of the family plantation home and there exiled the colonel until the war was lost. That was when Aunt Clydia Louise was just this little infant child, and she could barely recall the old colonel, but one thing Aunt Clydia Louise always recalled was a memory of the colonel watching himself in this gilt mirror.

Ever since Cookie could remember, she had checked her physical progress in this mirror. From earliest childhood Cookie had peered into the Yocum mirror to check on her hair ribbons, her lace collars, her private school uniform skirt, to see that it hung properly at mid-knee length. When Cookie had started to grow little bumps on her chest, she used to sneak out to where the Yocum mirror hung in the rear hall near some French windows and stand naked before this mirror, studying her progress. This habit continued all through school days, through deb season and graduation, even through college. In summertime, when Natchez alternately baked in sweltering heat and reveled in afternoon rain showers, Cookie would wait until her mama was napping, then slip down along the hall to the Yocum mirror, strip off her thin summer dress and check her progress. That's how it came to be called in her own mind, checking her progress. This remained Cookie's secret, a sacred pact with her own reflection.

Other things happened before the Yocum mirror. Like the debutante party, when Jason LeBlanc kissed her in front of it. She peeked and saw him kissing her. Then there was the time that nasty girl from down in New Orleans came to Natchez and Mama hired her to polish silverware and she caught Cookie standing stark naked at the mirror. Cookie had let out a scream to raise the dead, and the girl ran downstairs hooting with laughter. Cookie had to pay the nasty girl ten dollars to promise not to tell Mama. And, too, the wedding picture Cookie and Peter had made before the Yocum mirror. Lord knows, Cookie had been the season's most beautiful bride. Everyone in Natchez said so. The girls were all so jealous of Cookie's big catch, thinking Peter Avalon utterly charming and too sexy. Not only her sisters, but all the girls in the wedding party had agreed that given the chance, they would change places with Cookie on her wedding day. In the picture, Cookie and Peter gazed at each other's reflections in the Yocum mirror. What a portrait that had made. Now that portrait hung over the family fireplace in this godforsaken cold-hearted, clammy mansion in Fern, Washington. And across from it, reflecting itself, hung the Yocum mirror today.

Imogene was out on errands and it was the houseman's day off. The girls were off in Europe and Peter was at his office, at least he said he was. Cookie was alone this afternoon, standing almost naked before the Yocum mirror. She gave herself a quick once-over, made a semidisgusted face, then began studying her progress area by area.

Her sisters had called her "flamingo legs." They were as long and lean and pearly white as ever. No cellulite, no extraneous fat. No gravity pull. Not yet anyway. The stomach lay flat and hard between strong hip bones. Her waist was still her best feature, nineteen and one half inches if she held her breath. Her skin was the exact shade of Mikimoto pearls, as Peter had once told her, back in their romantic period. Smooth, creamy, inviting. She had small breasts with tiny shell pink aureoles and nipples like baby pearls. Her shoulders were narrow, perfectly formed, like her other features, but her arms... Cookie held out one arm to the side. A slab of flesh drooped down from the bone. She moved her arm. The flesh wiggled back and forth. She lowered her arm and raised the other one, repeated the exercise. More flab swung. Cookie said, "Damn Aunt Clydia Louise," for family portraits proved that she had inherited this slack upper arm feature from the Yocum side.

Cookie had boxes full of old tintypes of Clydia Louise and her husband and their children. It was around the birth of the second child that Clydia Louise began developing the slack upper-arm flesh. Cookie saw it on the tintypes. Same with Cookie. After the second child was born, Cookie's arms went to hell and never came back. She'd tried everything from a personal trainer to these rah-rah video-tapes, everything short of liposuction, but nothing had worked. Now, as Cookie stood before the mirror naked, watching her upper arms swing flab back and forth like porch swings, Cookie decided the time had come. If her modeling career was to be revived, she'd have to do something about her arms. They wouldn't get better by themselves, and anyway, didn't she owe herself a present after Peter denied her this year's Miss Blue Poppy title?

Once the tough decision had been made, finalized with a nod to her own reflection in the Yocum mirror, Cookie slipped her summer dress back on and went back into her private study. Rain fell outside in the garden, and as she got comfortable on her pink satin chaise longue, she wondered if the garden soil would wash away, so hard did the rain fall. But what was this? Imogene coming back already. Thank goodness she hadn't caught Cookie at the Yocum mirror. Imogene wore a rain slicker with a hood over her head. In one arm, she carried a bag of groceries. Her other hand held a garden trowel. Cookie watched as Imogene set the groceries down on the covered terrace, then went into the garden and started digging. Right in the middle of Cookie's foxgloves. In spite of the rain and the runny garden mud, Imogene dug furiously. Like a dog burying a bone, or digging it up again.

When she glanced up and saw Cookie glaring out the window, Imogene stopped digging. She tossed the muddy trowel into the garden, stood up, retrieved the sack of groceries, and entered the house. Whatever Imogene had been digging for in Cookie's foxgloves, she hadn't found it.

Cookie dismissed garden matters and picked up her daily journal. She was halfway through the list of lovers she suspected her husband of entertaining, and she wanted to finish the list by this evening, before Peter came home. Now that Zora was out of the picture, Cookie crossed her name off the list, a gesture she performed with supreme satisfaction.

MIMI BUDGE possessed the unladylike habit of throwing things when she lost her temper. Cleo couldn't have known this when she accepted employment at Chrysalis. The Budge could throw a box of bobbins across the full length of the studio, send a pair of scissors sailing swift as a saber toward the furthest mannequin. In this case, the bobbins and the pair of scissors weren't aimed at anyone in particular, at least not anyone who was there in the room. The object of Ms. Budge's rage wasn't so much Cleo as the small blond spy girl who had duped Cleo into thinking a wedding was imminent, when all along spy girl was after information about Jonathan, heart of hearts, barely cold in his grave. Didn't Cleo know any better than to ask for the name of the church, the location of the reception, the honeymoon plans? To verify the client's credentials? Cleo might have seen through the shallow subterfuge if she weren't so dense. And the worst part was, Cleo had almost shown spy girl the butterfly collection. My Gawd, is nothing sacred anymore? No, Mimi wasn't planning to fire Cleo, so Cleo could just stop bawling into her skirts. But on the brink of her fashion debut in New York, Mimi was not anxious to get busted for illegally obtaining rare butterfly specimens. A jail term wouldn't look good on the resumé.

"Yes, Cleo, they do send people to prison for poaching butterflies," Mimi told Cleo. "One guy had the stupidity to brag over the Internet how he'd captured all these fabulous endangered butterfly species? They traced him, raided his house, and packed him off to prison for a couple years. I won't let that happen to me."

"Golly," said Cleo, "I hope she doesn't find out about that Dungeness silverspot you're planning to sell to her neighbor."

Mimi squinted. "Spy girl lives on Magnolia Bluff?"

Cleo nodded. "Their addresses are practically identical."

Mimi the lioness roared, grabbed the closest object, and threw it across the studio. The portfolio landed splat against a wall and broke open. Wings and bodies flew out. Her butterfly collection lay in ruins on the studio floor. Cleo grabbed her purse and fled out the front door, leaving Mimi to clean up the bodies.

AN AFTERNOON cloudburst pummelled Victoria, B.C. On a hill over-looking the Strait of Juan de Fuca, in Victoria's public cemetery, Jonathan Willow's grave, marked by a small, white marble slab, glistened in the rain. Besides his name and the dates of his birth and death, nothing had been engraved on the headstone, because no one knew what to put on the scientist's grave. He wasn't a religious man, so proverbs were out. He wasn't famous for any scientific discoveries, so attributions weren't befitting. For now, just a name and significant dates would have to do.

Lily felt the first heavy rain drops and pulled her rain hood up over her head. Kneeling, she placed a small bouquet of wildflowers on Jonathan's grave. The tears running from her eyes fell heavier than the raindrops, more forlorn. With a chilled hand, wet from rain, Lily wiped off the tears, but more came, and then more, until she gave herself up to sobbing, weeping over Jonathan's remains. Nobody could ever understand her love for Jonathan, least of all her family. No man could ever take Jonathan's place in her heart. Such a short romance, so swift and fleeting, yet so true and intimate. Too late, they had discovered their mutual attraction, something more than chemistry; the bond they shared so briefly born of love. So suddenly had he come to her, so suddenly had he parted. If only she could share her grief with others who loved Jonathan, maybe she would find solace. But she dared not tell her sister, or anyone else in the family. Budges don't betray one another, and with Jonathan, Lily Budge had betrayed her sister.

Mimi never knew that Jonathan and Lily had met secretly, had been together just moments before he died. Or did she? Lily hadn't told anyone about being with Jonathan in Yodeler's meadow, about taking Jonathan's hand and walking beside him up through the poppy fields into the forest. Jonathan had a special place he wanted to show Lily. He had come to the inn on Thursday night, called Lily on the phone, asked her to meet him the next morning at sunrise. He had made her promise not to tell Mimi or anyone else. He wanted to talk to Lily, he said, and show Lily something in Yodeler's meadow. She trusted Jonathan after all, and so she agreed. Slipping out of the inn just before sunrise, Lily took her father's BMW, drove to the high-way, and met Jonathan.

Up along MacGregor's Trail, the rising sun burnt off the dawn mist with warm pink rays that flooded the forest canopy in soft, mysterious light. They walked up the trail in silence, Jonathan holding her hand. She liked the feel of his flesh against hers, his smooth, warm hand held hers gently, like a brother holds a sister's hand, she had thought at first. When they had climbed for half an hour, they came to the pool below the waterfall. Jonathan pointed up at the crest of the waterfall and said something to Lily, but she didn't hear what he said because of the noise of falling water. She stood on tiptoe, put her ear near his lips, the better to hear him speak. What she heard completely surprised her.

"I love you, Lily."

Then he kissed her, and she didn't resist because she had always loved him from a distance. Until now. Entwined, they slid to the ground, and there beneath the forest canopy, pierced by the dawn's sun, they made love. She kept whispering, "I love you, Jonathan. I love you, Jonathan," and he answered her with protestations of desperate love for her. They joined together not just physically, but as soulmates, careening through space and time, finding each other in a blazing collision of spirits. The forest seemed to bless their union as they lay in each other's arms listening to the waterfall and the song birds. On the way back down MacGregor's Trail, he told her of his plan to chase butterflies, in hopes of capturing a rare specimen. He told her about his work with the Avalons, and they laughed together over the notion that an exotic floral blend to which alcohol was added could be construed as sensual. He explained about pheromones, how, for example, certain species of butterfly employ scent to attract a mate. Jonathan was halfway through a research project funded by his work for Blue Poppy Perfumery that he hoped would apply the insect pheromone strategy to a human pheromone strategy to attract mates. Grant money is hard to come by these days, and Jonathan couldn't resist Peter Avalon's offer of financial support.

When they reached the poppy field, they clung to each other for a few moments, as if sealing their joint destiny. Then Lily left him standing in the high meadow with his butterfly catcher's gear. She ran all the way down the meadow to her father's car. She streaked down the highway, returning to the inn just in time to see her father and Mimi emerge from the lobby with their golf clubs. She'd made some excuse about driving into Fern for breakfast, and they didn't seem at all suspicious.

Lily's raincoat was made of poplin, not really meant to repel rain this long. But she couldn't tear herself away from Jonathan's grave just yet. She wanted to feel their bond, in memory if not in the flesh. She remembered how Jonathan felt, how he breathed, how he looked when they made love. She could remember his scent, too, and that memory seemed the strongest, the most enduring. He'd only been buried two weeks, and already Lily feared her visceral memories were fading, but each visit to his grave brought back waves of feelings that fed her grieving heart. Her fear, though, never abated, and she woke up nights calling out his name. Had anyone heard? Lily dreaded the thought that Mimi would figure out what happened between her and Jonathan. More than anything, Lily was afraid that Mimi had some-how learned about the secret rendezvous, had followed her to the meadow, up along MacGregor's Trail, had watched them making love, and then after Lily fled, had shot Jonathan. Had killed Jonathan. But that was impossible, wasn't it? Didn't Lily see Mimi and her father coming out of the inn with their golf clubs? Mimi couldn't possibly have left the meadow after Lily and reached the inn first, in plenty of time to meet Lily at the front door, golf clubs in hand. Unless, thought Lily grimly, Mimi knew some shortcut between Yo-deler's meadow and the inn. Then, too, the authorities were saying that whoever murdered Jonathan might also have murdered two other people in the wildlife preserve. Mimi had no reason to murder that old woman, nor had she anything to gain from killing Zora. Then again, Mimi had always been competitive, chronically vicious, and she never thought of anybody but herself. She had a wild temperament. And she owned a gun.

She was turning to leave the grave site when a man walked toward her, appearing out of nowhere. He had dark hair and wore sunglasses that covered his eyes. He wore jeans and a leather jacket. She thought he was Asian but wasn't certain. He walked respectfully between the rows of gravestones towards where she stood. Lily's first instinct was to run, but her feet were frozen to the ground. When he got closer, just a few yards off, he smiled and waved. She liked his smile, wanted to trust him, but lately Lily couldn't trust anybody. She wanted to scream, but couldn't. He might be the killer, coming after her. Why wouldn't her feet move off the ground? The man nodded at Lily. He came over to Jonathan's grave, stood beside Lily. He shoved his hands in his pockets, stared down at the grave stone, as if communing with the dead man, as if she weren't standing there at all. Then it came to her in a rush. My God, she told herself, he's a policeman. He knows about me, and he's going to arrest me. At that instant, her feet came unstuck and Lily took flight, swiftly across the gravestones and rain-soaked grass to the parking lot. She jumped into her car and drove off. In the rearview mirror, Lily saw the man turn and watch her flee.

TWENTY-EIGHT

SLUGFEST

VENUS STEPPED gingerly over the gray-green slug on Bella's lower terrace. *Ariolimax columbianus*. The grooved olive slug with a vestigial shell beneath its mottled mantle had wormed a path from the coral rhododendron towards the white espaliered camellia, and now threatened the hot tub. A slug has a mind of its own. A slug is stubborn, determined, rarely detoured. She let it continue on its way, its mucus membrane laying down a slimy iridescent trail across the patio's damp terrazzo tiles. She dropped a bath towel and cell phone on a cedar bench and stepped into the hot tub.

What's this? A sun break. Lowering herself into the blessed churning waters, she felt the heat invade her aching bones, shut her eyes and let out a grateful sigh. A moment later, she opened her eyes to see the slug staring at her from the terrazzo tiles.

Slugs and Seattle are synonymous. Slugs go back to the origins of the phenomenon called Seattle. Nobody "gave" Seattle its cachet, its verdant, morose character. The California immigrants of the 1980s like to claim credit for bringing progress to Seattle, and perhaps they did inject a spurt of commerce and oddball ambition. But they didn't invent Seattle. Seattle sprang from the womb of a great gray cloud, fully realized, its low blood pressure and fogbound personality built in. Slugs included. They came with the original package. A native respects this. One rainy morning in the not-so-distant future, Seattle's come-lately neo-pioneers will awake in their beds to the maulings of mucous-coated banana slugs and if they remain in Seattle after that, the immigrants will never again blaspheme against Oz's origins, because the truth, straight from the slug's mouth, is that nobody created Oz, it burst from the gray cloud fully intact, its psyche developed. Forget that, and you'll discover slugs in your bed.

Two weeks of bone mending had taken its toll on Venus, physically and mentally. The worst part had been staying in bed, being unable to move because even the slightest gesture caused her ribs excruciating pain. She remembered little of the past two weeks, only snatches here and there. She had a foggy memory of the rescue, when Claudia gave her an injection, when Song promised to find Aggie MacGregor's killer. She recalled the nurse's face popping in and out of her fever-seared vision, and the nurse's gentleness. As she recovered, the nurse had grown tougher, though, even threatening to tie her to her sickbed if she continued trying to get up. Today, the nurse went home. Venus smiled to herself. Free at last.

She recalled Echo entering the little alcove, pulling a seat up beside the bed, reading to her. She couldn't remember a word of it, but thought it might have been Echo's latest tone poem. Under normal conditions, you couldn't pay her enough to listen to Echo read her poetry, but she'd had been a captive audience. Besides these dim memories, she had scattered recollections of Bella appearing at her bedside, but couldn't recall anything specific, except that Bella always looked fresh and beautiful, and not at all distraught. Maybe she had worried over Venus, but Bella rarely exhibited her emotions, so how would Venus know?

Slugs and mold. Venus looked up. The big sun break had ended. Now grayness recaptured Oz, rolling in off Puget Sound. One way to distinguish influxers from true natives was how they referred to Puget Sound. Influxers usually added "the" before saying "Puget Sound," as in "the Puget Sound." Natives rankle at this blasphemous faux pas. Puget Sound doesn't need an article to distinguish it. Puget Sound might be "the Sound," or "the saltwater sound," but it was never, ever, "the Puget Sound." This is one way a mosshead separates the worthy neo-native from the dross.

Slugs and mold and rust. All by-products of Pacific Northwest weather. You don't tan here, remember. You rust. Your vehicle better have fins. And don't forget Seattle manners. Open displays of affection, laughter before or after noon, a beaming smile, all these clash with the city's character. Got a problem with that? Then go away. If you aren't willing to grow webbed feet and shod them sensibly, then go back where you came from. If dampness irritates your arthritis, scram. Seattle doesn't need foreigners coming in here grousing about the weather. Natives might act morose, but few grouse about weather because they know it's a futile exercise, and it's rude. Speaking of natives, if you can't identify the origin of the following secret password, then don't go near Ballard. Here goes: Zero dockas, mucho crockas, Halla-balloo-za-bub. This isn't native snobbery. This is pure, unadulterated native fact, the stuff of rich legend, like Louie-Louie, Bigfoot, and geoducks. So here's a clue about surviving Seattle and its environs: Respect Oz, never pose as a native, and shut up about the rain. Other than that, welcome to the Emerald City.

A drop of water struck Venus's nose. She didn't bother wiping it off. She let it drip down the bridge, roll across her cheek, slip into her ear. Gad, she thought to herself, the simple sighting of a slug conjures the most hostile emotions. Seattle natives are a snooty bunch, Venus concluded. Maybe all humans, no matter where they hail from, carry that clannish gene. Maybe Cookie Avalon, being from the South, held the same attitude toward Yankees.

Now why did she suddenly think about Cookie Avalon? Probably the idea of lolling around in a hot tub in the middle of a weekday reminded her of the Cookies of the world. Then there were the Budge sisters, privileged women from coddled backgrounds. From Song's report, she knew Lily Budge had been in love with Willow. That gave Mimi a fairly solid motive to kill him. While recuperating, she'd read over Song's reports, which didn't tell her much but included the Lily factor and supported some of her earlier theories on Willow's killer. Now she believed that more than one killer was involved in the Yodeler murders.

But why Lux?

The chef, Lux, as she had guessed, died from consuming death camas. The toxins in a white camas plant cause violent vomiting and diarrhea within hours of consuming the plant. Death's angel mushrooms take much longer to kill. Accidental? Surely, Lux knew his camas plants. Lux's death had already been ruled accidental, and although she could request exhumation and a second autopsy, it probably wasn't necessary. The chef's cookbook was the key to his death. He had developed an appetite for camas cakes, and it seemed likely that Lux had died the way thousands of early Native Americans died in the Pacific Northwest, by confusing purple and white camas bulbs. In early spring, when the camas flowers bloom, it's easy to tell the difference between purple camas plants and the death camas variety. Death camas have white flowers. Purple camas are distinguished by their purple blossom. But later on in the season, mid-June, some of the early bloomers lose their flowers. The remaining stems and leaves would have shriveled, so that you could still identify the camas bulbs but you couldn't tell if they were purple camas or a white, poisonous variety. In his wildcrafting, Lux may have come across a leafless death camas plant and mistaken the bulb for the edible plant. He might have dug up the bulb, taken it back to the restaurant to test out a new recipe, with unfortunate results. Then again, someone might have placed the death camas in Lux's purple camas supply.

Even if Lux's death was accidental, that meant three murders remained unsolved. Jonathan Willow died from a bullet wound to the chest, inflicted by a .38-caliber weapon. Aggie MacGregor had been pummeled to death, then nailed to the cedar tree. Some DNA evidence from Aggie's remains matched DNA material found on Venus's clothing. They had Venus's vague description of her assailant and the DNA material. That was all, no other real evidence, not even stray hairs or threads of clothing. Nothing to connect Willow's killer to Aggie's killer. Except the one fact; they both occurred on Yodeler Preserve.

Zora's murder presented a new twist. Lab tests on the .38-caliber bullet casing found in the poppy field suggested that the same weapon used to kill Zora had killed Jonathan Willow. Both murders occurred in the vicinity of the poppies. In Willow's case, the bullet had come from somewhere in the poppy fields. Zora's killer fired from the forest edge. Same vicinity, and probably the same killer. The news media was speculating that a crazed stalker had murdered Zora. A Hollywood gossip columnist reported a litany of Zora stalkers. Zora's mother verified these reports. You couldn't eliminate the stalker angle with a looker like Zora. But why Willow? And Aggie?

The three murders had only one certain connection. They all happened in Yodeler Preserve. Then again, there was Lux. Lux's death might hold the key to the other deaths. Venus made a mental note to read the cookbook manuscript again.

Could there be any connection to Lux and Willow? Lux and old Aggie MacGregor? Lux and Zora? What about the Avalon brothers? They had a stake in the preserve, they wanted to own the biggest part of it, to expand their poppy cultivation. They might want to scare other interested parties away from the meadow. It wasn't unheard of for a corporate officer to hire out thugs to do their dirty business, keep their own hands immaculate.

Three deaths in Yodeler Preserve, and a fourth that might possibly be connected. Maybe the preserve's jinxed, she thought, maybe some vengeful ancient spirits live among the verdant moss-draped cedars, the alpine meadow, the salt-spray apron.

She hadn't heard from Olson in two days. Maybe something was wrong. She reached for the phone, careful not to drag it through the frothy bubbles, punched in the office number. Dottie came on the line.

"How are you feeling?" Spoken too compassionately for Venus's tastes.

"Okay, Dots. Olson around?"

"Yes, but he's in a foul mood."

"Put him on anyway."

Dottie hesitated, then said, "Well, good luck with Mr. Crankhead."

Olson might have been out of sorts, but when he heard her voice, he turned soft and gooey. She said, "Cut it out, sir. I don't need sympathy."

"It's not sympathy, it's compassion."

"Well, it makes me uncomfortable. What's happening?"

"Regarding...?"

"Yodeler."

"Oh, that." Olson cleared his throat, buying time. "Actually, you would probably do better discussing that with Louie."

"Would you put him on?"

"Ah... Actually, I gave him a few days off. The Zora thing really tore him up. He kept running into dead ends, so I gave him a short leave. He's gone up to his cabin near Gold Bar. He doesn't want to see anyone or talk to anyone for a while."

"You reprimand him for the personal involvement?" She was direct.

Olson sighed. "No. And I don't plan to. He wasn't really 'involved' with Zora, in the true sense of the word."

"What's the true sense of the word?"

Olson got tongue-tied. "They never actually, er, compromised themselves. I mean, it was strictly business, at least that's what Song told me, except for the one embrace on the beach... I don't need to explain to you why he wasn't reprimanded. Also, I might point out that drinking alcoholic beverages while on duty is strictly forbidden."

"Except when you join us?"

"That was an exception. That whole thing with Ebert just rankled me."

"He take the Harley?"

"Who? Song? Now, how the hell am I supposed to know that?"

"So, if Song is incommunicado, how am I supposed to get an update?"

Olson groaned. "Obviously, the task is left to me. All right, here it is. Are you ready?"

"Go." She adjusted the thermostat on the hot tub. In her peripheral vision, the slug's shadow appeared, moving closer.

Olson said, "Nothing's really new since Zora's murder. You got the lab reports, right?"

"Check."

"We sent the team up, of course, and took statements from everyone who was there. Nothing suspicious from that angle. Claudia performed the autopsy on Zora."

"Cause of death?"

She could see him smiling sarcastically when he said, "Bullet wound to the brain. Claudia ran the bullet through tests. Thirty-eight caliber. I've already told you this. Don't you remember?"

"Sure. I just like the sound of your voice. Go on."

"Maybe the same weapon used on Willow. We need the weapon, though. It's got to be the same weapon."

"Claudia said that?"

"Everyone down at the lab agrees."

"What about Aggie? Any hard evidence yet?"

"Negative. We have DNA samples, no suspect."

"No one's come forward offering information?"

Olson said, "Afraid not. But I'll tell you one thing. That Mimi Budge bothers me. When I interviewed her, the day after Willow was shot? She was clearly withholding information. Anyway, it boils down to this. We don't have a clue who committed these murders. And the only thing that ties them together, apparently, is the preserve, they all happened on the preserve, within a short distance from each other. So, soon as you're feeling up to it, I'd like you to pull together a report for Sweetwater."

She sat up straight in the hot tub. "What are you trying to tell me?" A single raindrop landed on her nose, dribbled down the smooth, flat bridge, clung to the tip. She wiped it off.

"That I am turning the case over to Sweetwater. It's too dangerous for you to go back up there. I mean, being a... It's just too dangerous for you."

"Eric won't get anywhere up there. He's still wet behind the ears. Anyway, it's my case."

Silence. Maybe he was mulling it over. Or maybe mollifying his jaded tongue with a Frango Mint. She could imagine that. Or maybe he was just picking his teeth. Whatever he was doing, he was taking a long time. Finally she said, "You still there?"

Olson grunted into the phone.

"Talk to me, chief."

A long, heavy sigh, then, "All right. But only if you take another team member along. Otherwise, I won't allow you back on the case."

Venus smiled. "Fair enough. Claudia free?"

"Negative. Claudia's on the poaching case in the Dalles. That's still top priority here. Cougar poachers. I can't pull her off that case unless we have an emergency."

More heavy raindrops plunked into the hot tub, mixed with the froth and steam.

"This isn't an emergency? Three killings in the same wildlife preserve isn't an emergency?"

"Two weeks have passed. No more killings. No, it isn't an emergency."

Venus said, "I don't want Sweetwater up there. He's too inexperienced."

"How about Sparks? I can spare Sparks for a few days."

"Gad, no. Sparks doesn't move fast enough. What's Dottie doing?"

Olson laughed ironically. "Right now, she's sitting at the switchboard reading one of her romance novels. She hasn't exactly been highly motivated lately. Anyway, it should be a guy. You need a guy to back you up."

"I'll tell you what, chief," she said, "let me go up there just until Louie comes back. Then Louie can do the backup."

Reluctantly, Olson said, "Okay, but you've got to promise you won't do anything very stupid."

"Such as?"

"Such as wandering around that preserve by yourself. In fact, I don't even want you going up there without Needles or one of his deputies along. Is that clear?"

She raised her right hand, like he could see it. "On my honor." Two fingers crossed.

Olson said wearily, "We're too frigging shorthanded around here.

Why can't Wexler understand how shorthanded we are?'' Rhetorically.

Venus said, "It's Congress, chief. Wexler's hands are tied.''

"The hell they are,'' snarled Olson. "Wexler's gone off the deep end. That's what's wrong in Washington, D.C. He's frigging gone off the deep end.''

"He sold the meadow?'' Alarm.

"Negative. But he's going to approve the sale.''

"When?''

"Soon as you've brought in the killer. Or killers. That's when.''

Olson hung up. She heard the line go dead. She felt the rain, falling harder now.

The slug had finally reached the hot tub. Venus cupped some warm water in her hand, leaned over the side, poured the warm water over the slug. The slug reared up on its hind quarters and cast off in the direction of the lush, manicured lawn. Fortunately, this was Mr. Satori's day off. Mr. Satori bore no real malice toward slugs, but he didn't tolerate them on the lawn. A slug belonged in the compost and to the compost went all the slugs on Mr. Satori's green velvet turf. A banana slug is a gardener's worst foe.

The rain drenched the lower terrace, Venus in the hot tub, and the intrepid slug bearing down on the lawn. She got out, switched off the hot tub, toweled off, pushed open the recreation room door, entered the Ping-Pong area, passed through it to her little alcove bedroom, into the bath. The phone rang just as she was stepping out of the shower. It was Dottie.

"I have a woman on the line who wants to speak with you.''

"What's her name?'' Venus emerged from the hot steam.

"Imogene something. Imogene Donner, I think she said. She's sounds pretty nervous. Says she's a maid at Peter Avalon's home. Should I patch you in?''

"Go ahead.'' The steam burned off. She saw her reflection in the mirror, the remnants of bruises, the stitches, the wreck that was her face.

Imogene Donner came on the line, a high, thin voice, shaky. "My friend Beatrice Yamada at the Raven Point Inn said I should contact you,'' she explained. "I have some information. Maybe it's important, or maybe it's nothing at all, but Beatrice thinks you will be interested.''

Venus said, "Where are you now?''

Imogene coughed self-consciously. "In the kitchen of the Avalon home. I can't talk very much longer. Could you meet me tomorrow, somewhere in Fern?"

"Tell me where and what time." Venus rubbed lotion on her face. It stung.

"I don't want anyone to see us talking. I go to the fresh market tomorrow at noon. Can you meet me at the fresh market in Fern?"

"Sure. Tell me how to recognize you."

Imogene said, "I'm just an ordinary old woman. I'll wear my red dress so you can recognize me. And I know what you look like."

Venus frowned. "How do you know what I look like?"

"Because I saw you up in the meadow. The day they found—I have to hang up now."

The line went dead. Venus went into the little alcove, lay down on the bed, on cool, crisp sheets. Ironed Egyptian cotton sheets, the only kind Bella allowed on her beds. The last thing she needed was more sleep, but in the comfortable bed, exhaustion overcame her and she fell off into a deep slumber, lulled by the rhythm of the afternoon rain.

STEPHEN CLEARED his throat tactfully. Venus opened her eyes. Stephen held a small tray with a cup of tea and some Hob-Nobs. She said, "What time is it, Stephen?"

"Six o'clock. You missed tea, so I thought I'd bring you down a cup." He cleared his throat. "I should add that Timothy is missing. I have been all over the house and I cannot seem to locate him."

Venus sipped the tea. "Maybe he went somewhere with Bella."

Stephen shook his head. "Your mother drove off an hour ago with Woofy Benson. They were going to your sister's rehearsal. Timmy was standing right beside me when they left."

"Rehearsal for what?"

"Echo's poetry reading. This evening is dress rehearsal. They postponed the reading until you recovered."

"A dress rehearsal for a poetry reading?" Venus stared.

Stephen shrugged. "But back to Timothy—"

Venus said, "Timmy's an elusive kid, Stephen. He's probably around somewhere." She stood up. "Come on. I'll help you find him."

Burden was on the front lawn, bending over the reflecting pond, feeding the goldfish. He hadn't seen Timmy for more than an hour.

Venus and Stephen went out into the street. No Timmy. On the way into the house, Stephen said, "What really bothers me is the boy's emotional state. Something's bothering him, I don't know what. Something is on his mind, and he refuses to share it with your mother, or with me. I'm afraid he might—well, perhaps I shouldn't say this, but I am afraid Timothy might try to hurt himself."

"Why would he hurt himself?" Dubious.

Stephen said, "Maybe your mother didn't tell you."

"Tell me what?" Impatient.

Stephen grimaced. "A week or so ago, I found a rope in the boy's bedroom closet. Fashioned into a noose."

"Aw, come on, Stephen, he's a normal kid. He's just experimenting with knots or something."

Stephen shook his head. "There is nothing normal about that boy."

"His bedroom closet?"

Stephen nodded. "And now his bedroom door is locked. And I can't find the master key."

Venus said, "Let's go." She ran down the long hallway, down the stairs, across the landing, down the next flight of stairs to the house's lower level, down another long hall, a seemingly endless hall, toward Timmy's room. Stephen and Burden followed close behind.

At the door, Venus knocked and said, "Timmy. Timmy, are you in there?"

No response. Venus tried the knob. Locked.

"Timmy, open up. It's Venus."

Still no response. Venus knocked louder, harder. Stephen said, "He isn't allowed to lock his door."

Venus ran back down the hall, through the garden room, opened the French doors to the lower terrace. The rains had let up, and the lower terrace was almost dry, just a few puddles remaining on the outdoor furniture, on the cover of the hot tub. A terrifying thought struck her. She ripped off the hot tub's cover, looked in. Burden and Stephen peered over her shoulder. Nothing but still water.

She slipped through Bella's thick rhododendron grove, reached Timmy's private terrace, the French doors leading to his bedroom. She pounded on the glass, peered through a crack in the drawn curtains. She couldn't see much, just a sliver of the bedroom, a corner of his bed, part of a closet door, part of his computer screen, the keyboard. She was breaking the French door glass with a rhododendron branch when a small voice said, "Why are you doing that?"

From the depths of the rhododendron grove, Timmy appeared. He was holding the Bloomingdale's swizzle stick box carefully between his palms. Venus dropped the rhododendron branch, went over to Timmy, crouched down to his height. She put her hand on his shoulder, squeezed it, just to be sure he was real. She took a deep breath, exhaled.

Timmy's nose twitched, but otherwise he appeared calm, relaxed, as if nothing were wrong. In Timmy's opinion, things were quite all right. He held the Bloomingdale's box out to Venus and said in his tiny, hoarse voice, "I was just looking for you, to show you this."

Venus looked inside the Bloomingdale's box. A perfect chrysalis hung from the dried violet plant. The chrysalis glinted slightly in the daylight, iridescent.

"Now what?" asked Timmy.

Venus grabbed Timmy's hand. "Come on, sport. We need to find some nectar for this little guy. He'll be thirsty soon."

TWENTY-NINE

HUFF

THE MIST BURNT OFF early on a promising July morning, and over Fern the skies exactly matched Avalon's blue poppies. Or was it the other way around? Pacific Northwest summer was just reaching its peak. From now until October, you could expect glorious, languorous sun-kissed afternoons, and up here on the sunny side of the Olympics, you might actually enjoy a full day of pure celestial harmony. But soon as the sun sets, the air turns cold and damp, and you need a sweater or jacket even on the most mild summer evening. Venus had remembered to bring along a sweater and a few other things, like hiking clothes, boots, a backpack full of gear. She was ready for anything, at least she thought so.

Romeo purred along Highway 101, zoomed downhill into Fern, finessed a left turn at Orcas Lane, and came to a graceful stop. The security guard studied Venus's badge, then said, "We're not open yet. We don't open for visitors until ten a.m. Nobody's in there this time of morning."

"What about Conrad Avalon? He lives here, doesn't he?"

The guard nodded warily.

Venus said, "He up at this hour?"

The guard nodded again. Warily.

Venus said, "Maybe you could phone him and say Lady Bella's daughter is calling on him."

The guard's eyes toured her face. He knew who she was; he recognized her from television coverage of the Aggie MacGregor murder. This was the federal agent whom the killer had attacked. She wore white jeans, a white T-shirt, a thin gold necklace that flirted with sunlight. She didn't wear makeup, as far as he could tell, and the way she wore her hair reminded him of Sharon Stone, only not as sexy. If you ignored the facial scars, she was pretty in a fresh-scrubbed way, and she had nice teeth in a beguiling smile. The smile was the only part he didn't fully trust as genuine, and he hesitated before picking up the phone, mentally composed what he'd say to Mr. Conrad, then punched in the elder Avalon's code. A minute later, he bent over the Spider, said, "Mr. Conrad asked me to direct you to the rose garden. He'll meet you there."

He opened the gate, waved the Spider into the property. Venus glided slowly along the elegant drive past the formal English garden, the employee tennis courts, the employee swimming pool and health club, and pulled up at the rose garden just as an elderly, dapperly dressed gentleman crossed the drive from the estate's main house to the rose beds.

His cloud white hair was neatly combed, his face cleanly shaved and shiny, as if polished with Windex or car wax. When he shook her hand, she noticed his fingernails wore a perfect manicure, the tips white, impeccably clean, buffed. He led her into the garden to a frilly wrought-iron bench beneath a high trellis profusely draped in climbing roses. The blossoms were pale pink and cream, with a tinge of yellow in the centers, fat, blowzy blossoms with an intoxicating fragrance. She sat down on the bench and he sat beside her. He said, "We include this flower in our perfume formula. It balances the poppy scent."

"Do all poppy species have a fragrance?" she asked Conrad Avalon. For openers.

"Some do, some don't. This species of *Meconopsis, M. betonicifolia,* produces a fine, light top note, which is enhanced by careful fertilization and meadow cultivation. You can't get a decent fragrance out of hothouse plants, no matter how you treat them."

He seemed depressed, she thought, not really in the mood for conversation. She said gently, "I miss Aggie, too."

Conrad nodded, pressed his thin lips together. In his lap, his age-spotted hands flinched. He took out a clean white linen handkerchief, held it, wrung it, maybe to divert his energy from his tear ducts. His chin trembled slightly, rhythmically, and he struggled to keep his emotions under control. He didn't speak, and she almost regretted she had come, had disturbed the elderly gentleman in his grief. They sat side by side in the rose garden, silent, listening to the song birds, inhaling the sweet, heady fragrance. Out on the drive, a few vehicles glided past, heading for the employee parking lot. She saw a late-

model Ford minivan, a Jeep Cherokee, a couple pickup trucks, and
the Rolls-Royce delivering Peter Avalon to his offices.

The Silver Cloud pulled to the curb across from the rose garden
at the main building, the elegant Victorian mansion. The driver got
out, swished around to the curb side passenger door, opened it. First
out came a man she didn't recognize, about Avalon's age, dressed in
golf clothes, a pair of golf shoes dangling over his shoulder. Next
came a young woman, familiar looking. Was that Lily Budge? Yes,
it was Lily, but she wore her hair differently, big and poufy, and it
was blond now, instead of light brown. She wore makeup that made
her look glamorous and silly at the same time. Last out of the Cloud
was Peter Avalon, also dressed for a round of golf. The three walked
up the front steps and entered the house. The Silver Cloud drifted
away. Conrad laughed ironically and said, "Those boys are going to
ruin everything."

"What boys?"

Conrad said, "Peter and Troy. My nephews. All this commercial-
ization is destroying Blue Poppy's tradition. The perfume is fast becoming just another commercial product drowning in media hype."

Venus said, "The new, improved Miss Blue Poppy campaign?"

Conrad nodded, twisted the handkerchief. "Now they've got this
new girl, Lily Budge, and I liked her at first. But already they've
corrupted her. Already, she's becoming a celebrity, and she's too
young, too naive to handle the attention. So it's ruining her. I hate
watching it happen. I tried talking to her, but she's on my nephews'
team, not mine. We don't need celebrity. We need innocence, purity." He shook his head. "That other one, that Zora, was all wrong.
I'm sorry she died, but for Blue Poppy, she was all wrong. This girl
Lily, now she might have worked if they hadn't gone and ruined her
natural beauty with all that artifice. The ad campaign is doomed.
Women shouldn't dye their hair."

Venus opened her mouth to speak, caught herself just in time. She
wanted to say a lot of things about exploiting people for profit, about
media hype and greed. Instead she said, surprising herself, "Why
didn't you marry her in the first place?"

If Conrad was surprised at her abrupt segue, he didn't show it. He
said, "Families. Our families have been bitter enemies for centuries.
Clan wars. When Aggie's father heard that I wanted to marry her,
he shot my father, killed him. That was up in Yodeler's meadow.
They never arrested him. Called it self-defense, and it might have

been. My father had a mean streak as wide as the Strait of Juan de Fuca. He might've tried to kill old MacGregor first. I wouldn't put it past him.''

Venus touched her cheek. The stitches there burned. To Conrad, she said, "So you decided not to pursue Aggie anymore?"

Conrad laughed bitterly. "It was she who decided to drop me. Said we shouldn't go against our families' wishes, said we should respect our elders. She knew my mother and father didn't like her."

A sparrow hopped across the rose garden, pecking at the rich soil. Overhead, the sky was Dutch blue, the clouds brilliant white, torn, like gauze, wispy. A breeze encouraged the scent of roses. Venus inhaled the fragrance. Then carefully, she said, "Why didn't they like her?"

Conrad winced, shook his head. "Just old family rivalries, that's all. She was a MacGregor, so they didn't like her."

Venus looked up. One of the blowzier rose blossoms had attracted a bumble bee. The bee buzzed softly inside the flower's sensuous petals. She wanted to be inside there, too, trade places with the bee. She said, "What started the rivalry?"

Conrad sniffed. He put the handkerchief to his nose, turned his head, blew slightly. "It goes way back to Scotland. Both families hail from the Highlands. Clan rivalry goes back hundreds of years. But I don't agree with that. I think people who leave their homeland for another land should leave behind all those old rivalries, those clan wars. Old MacGregor should have welcomed my father into this territory. Instead, the whole MacGregor clan up on Mount Pluvius treated my father as an outsider, never accepted us as neighbors. Aggie and I were doomed from the start."

Gently, she said, "Do you know what happened to her?"

He nodded. "It was my fault, too."

"Why do you say that?"

"I asked Aggie to meet me up on the trail that night. I had something for her. A little bauble. A silly brooch of blue sapphires and diamonds, a blue poppy. I was going to give it to her that night, up where we used to meet as young lovers. I wanted to start courting Aggie again."

"Don't be so hard on yourself. If she hadn't been up there that night, the killer would have gone to her home and murdered her there. It wasn't your fault."

Conrad looked at her. "How do you know that?"

"Aggie was murdered because she witnessed something the murderer did. He or she had to get rid of her before she told someone what she saw."

Conrad seemed interested, perked up a little. He said, "What did she witness?"

Venus said, "Maybe a murder. Maybe something else."

"Whose murder? Are you talking about that man Willow?"

"Aggie might have seen it happen. I think she saw who killed Willow. She could identify the murderer. I think she even knew the killer."

Conrad's face went pale. "You don't think I killed him?"

Venus laughed. "Mr. Avalon, the thought never crossed my mind. Well, it crossed my mind, but it never actually made any sense. That is, I didn't consciously include you on my list."

"Thank God." Conrad sighed. Sardonically, he added, "Wouldn't that be a blot on the Avalon name?"

The bee had a fickle side, and now it zoomed out of the blowziest blossom toward a newer, fresher, younger blossom. A Richard kind of bee, Venus thought dejectedly. What ever happened to commitment? To Conrad, she said, "You've heard about the land deal?"

"Which one?"

"Your nephews want to buy Yodeler's meadow, to expand the poppy cultivation. At least, they say that's why they want the land."

Conrad shook his head. "Acquisition's all they ever think about. If it isn't another piece of land, it's a new house, a new car, a new girlfriend. I don't know what's happening to our young people today. Their priorities are all akimbo. Now, in my youth I concentrated on learning the perfume business from my father and on being a good citizen. I never had children of my own—we weren't blessed that way—but if I had, they wouldn't be spoiled rotten like Peter and Troy were. They haven't any real values. All they think about is their own comfort and prosperity. They're as shallow as the women they keep company with. It's a shame to have to admit that my own nephews are greedy lads, but it's true."

"Change is unavoidable, Mr. Avalon. Business is different today than it was thirty or forty years ago."

"And that's what's wrong with this country." He stood up. He wanted her to leave. She stood, shook his hand. Near his head, the poufy, unkempt blossom hung, beckoning, tempting. She resisted an urge to bury her face in its petals, its fragrance. At the garden's edge, standing beside the Spider, she thanked him, repeated her condolences. He shrugged, started walking away.

"Mr. Avalon," she called out. "Wait."

She ran back to him, threw her arms around the old man's neck, hugged him. They didn't speak, just held each other for a long time. He watched her turn the Spider around. Just before she drove off, she said, "I think you have something else to tell me. Only you're not ready yet."

He smiled grimly, waved good-bye.

BEATRICE WAS checking in new guests when Venus arrived at the inn. It was Friday morning in the first week of July. This group Bea was registering probably wasn't prepared for an Olympic Peninsula summer night. The inn's gift shop would do a brisk business in windbreaker sales. Venus strolled into the Oxygen Bar, ordered a Lemon Arrowroot Bubbler, sucked it while Bea finished up with the tourists. When Venus caught her eye, Beatrice slid out from behind the registration desk into the Oxygen Bar.

"What are you doing back here?" she asked, only half friendly.

Venus disentangled the oxygen tube from her face, smiled at Beatrice. "Work."

Beatrice made an impatient tsking sound. "Well, I didn't think you were on vacation. You're not the vacation type."

Venus placed a hand on her chest, looked down at her civilian clothes. "Oh, I guess I am. On vacation, I mean."

Beatrice shook her head. "You're weird," she said. "So what can I do for you this time?"

"I was wondering what you've heard about the murders up on the preserve."

Beatrice folded her arms. "Not much," she lied. "I don't have time for idle gossip."

"Idle gossip? There's a killer loose around here. Doesn't that disturb you?"

Beatrice shook her head. "He hasn't struck in weeks. Anyway, as long as you stay out of that meadow, you're safe. That's how I see it."

"What about the spa's clientele? What has management told them?"

Beatrice read her watch. "Mr. Price has issued a notice that goes in everyone's suite, requesting that guests keep clear of the meadow."

"He tell them why?"

"He just said that it is a wildlife preserve. That trespassers would be severely punished." Bea studied her fingernails. Today they were Fourth of July red.

Venus said, "Nothing about the murders?"

Beatrice sighed impatiently. "We don't want to alarm the guests. It wouldn't be very relaxing for them, would it?"

Venus nodded. "I see what you mean. So what do you think?"

"About what?" Beatrice read her watch again.

"About the killer. Any ideas who it might be?"

Beatrice winced, like someone had just stabbed her. Her eyes traveled around the lobby. Her arms tightened around her small chest and Venus thought she shivered, but that might have been an illusion, misconstrued body language. When Beatrice's long glance had traveled the full breadth of the lobby and returned to the Oxygen Bar, it eventually alighted on the bar table, about six inches west of Venus's left hand. Bea opened her mouth, started to speak, but something caught in her throat and she collapsed in a fit of coughing. Pure subterfuge. She coughed her way out of the Oxygen Bar, waving apologies to Venus, coughed her way behind the registration desk and into the manager's private offices, where she took refuge against blistering questions and Nosey Parkers. Venus had wanted to ask her about Imogene, the Avalon's housekeeper, but Bea didn't come back out so she left the Oxygen Bar, walked across the lobby to the Fiddlehead.

In the restaurant, Darin was supervising the wait staff and breakfast buffet. She caught a glimpse of Slava through the round windows in the stainless steel doors. His face looked flushed. She slid over to the buffet, filled a plate with fresh blackberries and papaya, plopped a butterhorn on top, and went over to a table by the windows. The strait was mildly choppy this morning, the skies alive with sea gulls, shearwaters, and a few birds she didn't recognize, migrating flocks up from the Equator for a taste of Pacific Northwest salmon and sunbathing on nearby federal bird sanctuaries. A bird's-eye view of this territory, thought Venus, would reveal a plethora of secrets.

A bird's-eye view would see the clear-cut bald mountainsides hidden behind their narrow fir outer edges, left standing to create the illusion of forests, if not the reality. A bird's-eye view would see the state and federally protected rain forests, now threatened with intrusion by logging concerns pressing Congress for permission to take old growth timber. A bird's-eye view would reveal the comings and goings of boat traffic along the strait, some less legal than others, smugglers, bringing illegal immigrants, shipments of endangered species, and refined heroin for sale on the black market. A bird's-eye view, constantly vigilant, might reveal the secrets of Yodeler National Wildlife Preserve, stories of love and death played out in the idyllic sanctuary, and the identity of a brutal murderer. Or murderers.

A hand held a pot of coffee before her eyes. She followed the hand to the arm, the arm to the shoulder, shoulder to the face. Darin grinned. "Back again, huh?" She nodded. Darin said, "Coffee?" She shook her head. Darin said, "How about tea?"

"No thanks," she said. "I'm already overcaffeinated this morning."

Darin nodded. "Can I get you anything else, then?"

"How about a camas cake? You have any camas cakes?"

Darin rolled his eyes. "We don't serve camas cakes. Since Lux, you know."

"Yeah," she said. "I know."

"He was a great chef," Darin added. "We miss him."

"I'll bet." Noncommittally. "How's Slava working out?"

"He makes a mean blini." Darin smiled, held the pot out again. "Sure?"

She shook her head and Darin went away.

Where was she? Oh yes, the Willow aspect. Jonathan Willow's specialty was pheromones, and his doctoral dissertation was on fragrances derived from insect pheromones. Which explained the golden brown dusty substance Venus noticed on Willow's fingertips. DNA tests proved the dust was scales from the wings of the Dungeness silverspot, now classified as extinct. But when Willow's body was discovered, the butterfly was missing. If the butterfly hadn't been destroyed, if the killer had taken it off Willow's dead body and kept it, like a collector would, it might prove who killed Willow. For all she knew, the killer might have been a professional rival of Willow's, someone doing the same insect pheromones research. And the bouquet of blue poppies in the corpse's hand? Needles had conjectured that Willow was stealing blue poppies from Avalon's field. Peter Avalon told authorities the bullet that killed Willow had been meant for him. Avalon had implicated Zora because they had recently quarreled, but Zora's murder might put a damper on that conjecture. Had

Zora been intimate with Peter Avalon? Troy-boy? Song? All of the above? Did it even matter?

Then, too, there's Lux. The logical scenario was Lux had been up in the meadow gathering mushrooms and camas bulbs, when he came across the death camas, mistook it for purple camas. He might also have come across Willow in the meadow and seen the killer. She doubted Lux had shot Willow. Are rare wildflowers, edible plants, or butterflies, for that matter, really important enough to incite murder? Or did Lux have another reason to shoot Willow? But she couldn't realistically place these two victims at odds with one another. Why?

The accordian file Professor Burke had given her containing Willow's Blue Poppy invoice still puzzled her. She had gone over those few notes again. Those and Lux's recipe book manuscript. Nothing popped out at her. Right now, she was more concerned about Willow's fiancée, Mimi Budge.

Venus and Mimi Budge shared one important quality: a passion for rare, extraordinary species. The difference was, Venus wanted to preserve their habitats, while Mimi Budge poached rare specimens for her own profit. Venus had known a few other wildlife poachers like that. Willow's practice had been in line with his profession; it is generally accepted that entomologists and other scientists may capture rare insects for study. But he shouldn't have been harvesting on a federal preserve; that was illegal, and Willow no doubt knew he was violating the law. Budge's apparent practice, on the other hand, was blatant harvesting of species; like a shopping addict in a mall, Budge probably harvested everything she saw. Amateur butterfly collectors aren't always this ruthless, she reminded herself. Still, Budge's paranoia over her specimen collection suggested an indiscriminate, almost obsessive passion for rare species.

Mimi Budge was as transparent as Saran Wrap; beneath the thin veneer of the Daddy's girl with a bad case of nearsightedness and deceptively splashy appearance, beat a heart of solid stone, a heart to fear more than love.

Venus read her watch. Nine-fifty a.m. She was thinking about going up to the meadow when Miss Perkins came out of Fiddlehead's kitchen. She had on a peppermint pink flowered dress with a full skirt and matching pink high heels. When she walked across the dining room, she swayed, rolling her pert, tight hips, her head tilted high, aloof, a tiny, self-satisfied smile pasted on her lips. Venus watched her go into the lobby, got up, followed her at a discreet distance.

Perkins crossed the lobby to the Oxygen Bar, went up to the bartender, whispered something in his ear. She then swiveled over to the registration desk, where Bea had reappeared. Perkins and Bea spoke in lowered voices, like conspirators. Venus stood by the house phone, her back to them, pretending to use the phone. Darin came out of the restaurant, crossed the lobby, went over to the registration desk, joined in the hush-hush conversation. Venus turned halfway around, focused on Bea's rapidly moving lips, and made out three words, "It won't work," before Bea noticed her and looking at Perkins, nodded toward Venus. They all turned, stared at her. Darin patted Perkins's shoulder, swept back across the lobby, nodding to Venus and smiling his most charming smile as he passed. Bea made some loud remark about having to make out a registration schedule, and Miss Perkins started toward the door. Venus followed her outside, caught up with her at the shrieking geraniums.

"Remember me?" she said.

Miss Perkins turned around, stared, crushed her lips together, and nodded once.

Venus said, "So, what's up?"

Miss Perkins opened a tiny handbag, fished out a set of keys. She looked Venus straight in the eye when she said, "I don't talk to the enemy," then swiveled off toward a beat-up Mazda, got in, drove off in a cloud of huff.

Slava and Alice were flirting in the kitchen when Venus ambled in. Casually, like she belonged there. Slava didn't notice her, his eyes were focusing down the front of Alice's food service jacket. She had opened it so that Slava had a cinemascopic view of what she had there. Venus went over to the fridge, opened it. Slava whispered something down Alice's exhibit. Alice giggled. Venus rummaged in the fridge until she located the remaining camas cakes. Deftly, smooth as silk, she pulled her arm out of the fridge, and the camas cakes came along. She slipped the small package under her T-shirt, nodded once to Slava just in case he had peripheral vision, and ambled toward the kitchen door. Her palm could feel the cool stainless steel when Slava called to her.

"Looking for something, miss?" He said "meese."

Venus turned around. "Actually," she improvised, "I'm looking for the time clock. The employees' time clock? I can't find it."

Slava smiled, unhinged his eyes from Alice's movie. "Over there." He pointed to the wall beside the door.

Venus paid a lot of attention to the spot. She flipped through the time cards. They still used the old-fashioned written method, clocking in and out on individual cards. Over her shoulder, she said, "Hey, thanks. It's my first day." Under her breath, she whispered, "Of the rest of my life." Then she left. When you need to infiltrate a kitchen, it helps if you're wearing solid white.

By eleven o'clock, the package of camas cakes was on a chopper flight to southeastern Washington, where Claudia, still in the field, would run the ingredients through tests in her makeshift lab. By noon, as Venus parked in the lot of Fern's fresh market, her phone rang. Claudia said, "You're right again. Death camas. The weird thing is, it's all death camas. Somebody really wanted Otto Lux to die. But just think, it could've killed a bunch of customers, too."

Venus said, "I think the killer planned to ditch the leftovers, but forgot to. Fingerprints?"

On the highway, a couple logging trucks screeched downhill. Venus couldn't hear Claudia's answer. She repeated the question. Claudia said, "Two sets."

Venus smiled. "See if you can match one set with Lux."

"And the other set?"

"Match them to the fingerprints you took off my gun. I have to meet somebody now, Claud. I'll ring you back shortly."

"Okay," said Claudia. "Be careful, will you, for God's sake?"

THIRTY

FRAGILE

THE OLD WOMAN stood at the entrance to the tented fresh market, near the wild berry stands. Shifting from one foot to the other, she kept her eyes focused on the parking lot. The person Imogene Donner was meeting would come from that direction, and she wouldn't recognize Imogene, so it was up to her to make the contact. True, she had worn her red house dress as a means of identification, the one she always wore on marketing days, but when she arrived at the fresh market, Imogene realized to her dismay that several women wore red dresses. So, when Imogene spotted the Fish and Wildlife agent, Venus Diamond, stepping out of a fancy sports car and walking towards the market entrance, she stepped forward.

Venus stopped walking, squinted. The woman walking towards her had on a red dress that was the same shade of red she'd seen—where? Then it came to her. The woman's red dress matched the red thing she saw up in the poppy field, on the day Jonathan Willow was shot dead. The woman was about sixty-five, with fluffy gray hair and a wan smile. She carried a picnic basket on her arm. This was Imogene Donner, Peter and Cookie Avalon's housekeeper.

Intimately acquainted with the market's nooks and crannies, Imogene led Venus past the berry stands, through the rows of fresh turnips, rutabagas, and Walla Walla onions, the first of the season, past the herb stands, and around a corner. At this end of the tent, Imogene guided Venus through an exit. They stood in the rear of the market, where vendors dumped their refuse. Venus wrinkled her nose against the stink of rotting produce. Imogene pointed to a stone bench beneath a Douglas fir. They sat down, and Imogene fumbled for words.

"It all started on that morning the young man was killed up in the meadow," she said. "Then yesterday I put it all together, after that odd woman came to the door. Oh, I don't know where to begin."

Venus held up a hand. "Start from the beginning, Ms. Donner."

Imogene set the basket down on the ground beside the bench. Trembling, the old woman related her dark tale:

On the morning Jonathan Willow was found murdered up near the poppies (said Imogene), Cookie and Peter Avalon quarreled at the breakfast table on the terrace, just outside the kitchen windows. A frightful quarrel, with harsh accusations made on both sides. Imogene, in the kitchen, covered her ears, trying not to hear the exact nature of the quarrel, but she knew what it was all about. Once again Cookie suspected Peter of philandering, when all along, everyone, even Imogene, knew that Peter wasn't at all the philandering type. If he didn't come home at night, he was sleeping over at the office. He often slept over, especially in peak production season.

They quarreled at the breakfast table, didn't touch the breakfast Imogene had fixed. But before Peter left to check his poppies, which he did most every morning, he managed to calm Cookie down, to reason with her. He even took her in his arms, held her, kissed her sweetly, the way he always did when she flew into one of her snits. That was Imogene's term, not Mr. Avalon's. Then Peter went up into the woods toward the poppy field to check on his flowers. He did that nearly every day, Imogene knew, like clockwork. Cookie went into the house.

A few minutes later, Imogene went out to the garden shed, to repot a root-bound dwarf Japanese maple. Some gardeners, like Cookie, like to keep dwarf Japanese maples in pots, placed indoors. It works, if the indoor climate is carefully controlled.

The first thing Imogene saw was Peter Avalon coming back toward the house. The shed's window was open. Peter walked passed, leaned in, smiled at Imogene. "I completely forgot," he said. "I have a meeting this morning." Then he went to the wide driveway, got into his Silver Cloud, drove off. "That car is so quiet, it barely makes a purr, and Cookie must not have heard Peter drive away," said Imogene.

A few minutes later, Imogene saw Cookie come back outside. Now Cookie was dressed in a lovely summer frock and she carried a picnic basket. Through the garden shed window, Imogene saw Cookie trip off into the forest toward the poppy fields.

Imogene had just finished repotting the little tree and was on her way into the main house when the gunfire sounded. She ran into the house, and from the safety of locked doors, peered out through the kitchen windows. If a killer was on the loose, Imogene didn't want to be seen, so she closed the louvered blinds in a way that allowed her to see out without the killer being able to see in. She watched and she waited.

Before long, she saw Cookie come running back down the forest path into the rear garden. She was carrying the picnic basket. She went into the garden shed, came back out with a trowel, a plastic trash bag, and a pair of garden gloves. In the garden, she fell to her knees, just at the foxgloves, and began digging, digging with the trowel. Cookie was a devoted gardener, sure, but Imogene had never seen Cookie dig so close to her prize foxgloves. That close, she might sever the roots, kill the plant.

Imogene couldn't see distinctly what Cookie removed from the basket and stuffed into the plastic trash bag, but she did see the revolver, or pistol, or whatever you called it, the gun, that Cookie slipped into her dress pocket. And what went into the trash bag, into the ground? A net. Maybe to catch butterflies. And something else Imogene couldn't describe clearly.

"A piece of cardboard. That's what it looked like. Just a piece of cardboard. She buried all of it in the ground behind the foxgloves, toward the rear of the planting bed, where nobody ever goes, except herself, when she weeds.

"She filled in the hole with dirt, tamped it down with her hands, then gathered some twigs and other garden refuse. She sprinkled that over the top. When she finished, you'd never guess a hole had been dug there. She stood up, brushed off her dress, looked around. She didn't see me through the kitchen louvers." Then she came indoors with the picnic basket, set it down on the kitchen counter. By that time, Imogene had run off to her room, where she collapsed in a chair, her heart pounding.

"When they found the man up in the meadow, near the blue poppies," continued Imogene, "I was quite certain it was Peter who'd been shot. I saw the helicopter circle, then land, people trudge up into the meadow. I saw it all from the kitchen window." Imogene hand's began shaking slightly. "I have an awful guilty conscience," she confessed. "But I can't hold it in any longer."

Venus nodded. "It's okay, Ms. Donner. I know it's hard, but what you tell me may help stop another murder. Please, I beg you, continue your story."

The old woman steeled herself against the harsh truths that

wounded her heart and continued, "Then I sneaked out through the garden, up along the forest path, hiking all the way to the poppy field. I wanted to see if Mr. Avalon was still alive or not. I crouched down in the poppies, hiding, trying to see what happened without being seen myself. I was just so confused, so fearful for Mr. Avalon. And for Miss Cookie."

Venus nodded.

Imogene said, "That's when I saw you searching the poppy field. And I wanted to come forward then, to relate what I had seen earlier that morning, from the kitchen window, from the garden shed. But I was too frightened, understand?

"I could hear you people talking about the dead man. When I heard someone say his name, 'Jonathan Willow,' I almost fainted with relief. Mr. Avalon was safe, he was safe after all. I rose up then, out of the poppies and I saw you. And you were looking in my direction. I got such a fright, and so I ran into the forest..." Imogene put her head in her hands. "I just feel so awful about all that's happened. I hate to suspect my Cookie of doing wrong. She's a pitiful girl, really. She's always been pitiful. See, I've been her nanny since the day she was born. Even as a child she didn't laugh much or play like other children. Always depressed, always complaining. It got worse when she moved up here, up to Fern. The Northwest doesn't suit her at all."

A yellow skipper fluttered past the two women seated on the bench. A brilliant sun washed the fresh market, bleaching out the produce's vibrant colors until they became ghost vegetables, ghost fruits, ghost legumes. Food for the dead.

The yellow skipper landed on the picnic basket, spread its wings, basked. When the sun beats down like this, some humans complain. Not butterflies. Butterflies thrive on light.

Venus said, "You did the right thing, Ms. Donner, sharing this information with me."

But Imogene wasn't finished. "Then yesterday," continued the housekeeper, "that odd young lady came to the door. And ever since, Miss Cookie's been in a kind of rage, and now I'm really frightened."

Venus could see fear in the woman's eyes, and something like disappointment or sorrow. Gently, she said, "What happened yesterday?"

"Well then," said Imogene, sighing, "it was about ten o'clock yesterday morning..."

Imogene's strong hands were knuckle-deep in a sourdough knead when the doorbell rang. She almost lost count of her turns and folds. She leaned into the dough, kneaded harder, as if that would answer the door. On the second ring, Imogene heard Cookie call from her bedroom. "Answer the door, Imogene. I can't have all that noise."

The housekeeper slapped the dough ball onto the floured kneading board, wiped her hands on her apron, and went to answer the door. Who in the world would ring so insistently? Some people have no patience. Imogene opened the front door.

The young lady was a stranger to Imogene. Eccentric creature with big, flowy clothing, a red Dutch bob, eyes made up like a Mardi Gras queen. Lips as black as coal that curved up into an expression Imogene couldn't read. A sneer or a smile, Imogene wasn't sure. Imogene said, "Yes, what is it, miss?"

The visitor said, "Is Mrs. Avalon in?" A whiskey voice.

Imogene nodded. "Is she expecting you?"

"Not really. I mean, she may be, in some vague sense of the word, expecting me, but I don't actually have an appointment." She handed Imogene a small engraved card.

Imogene studied the card, glanced up at the stranger, said, "Come in, please, Miss Budge." She ushered Mimi Budge into the foyer, down a short hall, around a corner, into the huge living room. She pointed to a sleek couch beneath a massive mirror with an impossibly baroque frame. The Yocum mirror. Been in Cookie's family for eons. Mimi Budge sat down, and Imogene went to find Mrs. Avalon.

Cookie let Mimi Budge wait for a solid fifteen minutes. Whatever she wanted couldn't be more important than what Cookie was doing now. What Cookie was doing was a yoga routine, a very complicated, deeply engrossing contortion of the legs and arms that required every ounce of Cookie's concentration. The Om always took precedence over the ordinary, that's what Cookie had explained to Imogene about yoga.

When she finished, Cookie untangled her legs, wrapped a slinky sarong around her leotard, and after freshening her lipstick and brushing her luxuriant hair, she went to meet Mimi Budge. On the way past the kitchen, Cookie mumbled out loud, and Imogene heard her say, "What could the little twit want, anyway? Probably an introduction to my friends. Don't they all?"

They met beneath the Yocum mirror, Cookie all smiles and full of social grace. They occupied the same couch, face-to-face like old friends, and made small talk. Imogene, knowing her duties by rote, brought coffee and little cookies. She poured the coffee, passed the cookies, then left the two women alone. But she didn't go far. She slipped behind a Greek column, where she could see the two women and hear their conversation.

"There now," chirped Cookie cheerfully. "What can I do for you?"

Mimi laughed hoarsely. "It's just a small thing, really."

Cookie smiled, waited.

Mimi said, "I'd like the butterfly."

Cookie blinked. Her stomach churned. She said, "What butterfly?" Like she didn't know what Mimi was talking about.

Mimi stood, walked up to the big mirror, checked her black lips. With one finger, she pushed her lipstick around her mouth. "You know," she said, watching Cookie in the mirror. "The butterfly Jonathan caught just before you shot him."

Cookie inhaled deeply. Exhaled. "Just why, exactly, did you come here?"

Mimi turned around, faced Cookie. "I want to make an exchange."

"What do you mean?" Cautiously.

Mimi said, "The butterfly you took from Jonathan after you shot him in exchange for my silence."

Cookie's mouth worked. Otherwise she appeared calm. "Silence about what?"

Mimi shrugged. "It's kind of embarrassing, really. I shouldn't have been spying on Jonathan and my sister. But I was in a rage, I couldn't help it."

"You couldn't help what, Mimi?"

Mimi shrugged. "It's bizarre. Really bizarre. I mean, here I was following Jonathan, suspecting him of collecting butterflies worth thousands of dollars behind my back, in the meadow I discovered first. I go up there to catch him in the act. I'm mad as hell at him anyway, for breaking our engagement. I was pretty sure that's what he went up into the meadow for that morning, for butterflies. And I was partly right. Only partly. Jonathan went to the meadow to meet my sister, Lily. When I saw them together, coming down from the forest, I waited until Lily left and then moved up into the meadow, hid in the grass."

"He didn't see you?"

Mimi shook her head. "I brought my gun. I was planning to kill him. After I saw him with Lily, I was determined to kill him."

Cookie's small dog pattered into the room, circled the stranger, sniffing. Mimi nudged it with her vamp shoe. The dog whimpered, ran to Cookie. Cookie picked up the ball of fur, her precious, carried it over to the terrace door, opened the door, tossed it outside. She went back to the couch, sat down. She said, "Go on."

Mimi frowned. "I'm not sure you want to hear the rest."

"I want to hear it," snapped Cookie.

Mimi fidgeted with her billowy clothing. "You killed him for me, Mrs. Avalon. You shot Jonathan. Maybe you thought that was your husband up there, with Lily."

Cookie stared.

Mimi said, "I saw you fire the gun. I saw Jonathan fall. Later on, when I found out how jealous you are of every female who comes near your husband, when I got a good look at your husband, I figured out why you shot Jonathan. You mistook Jonathan for your husband."

Cookie said, "What exactly do you want?"

"I have a buyer for the Dungeness silverspot, a collector who's willing to pay a fortune for a specimen. Now, I happen to know that Jonathan captured a Dungeness silverspot just before you shot him. I saw the autopsy report. There was butterfly DNA found on his fingertips, from a Dungeness silverspot. I also know that Jonathan always immediately preserves his specimens when he captures them. That specimen should have been in perfect condition when you removed it from Jonathan's hand and put the poppies in its place. What did you do with it?"

"I buried it. I slipped it into a plastic bag, and I buried it."

"Now, why would you do that, I wonder?"

"I buried the whole thing. The net, the board with the butterfly on it. I wrapped them up in a garbage bag and buried them. I don't know why. I guess I should have burned them."

Mimi smiled sympathetically. "I know why you didn't destroy them. You thought you might use them later, to implicate someone else."

Silence.

Mimi said, "Do we have an understanding?"

Cookie nodded.

Mimi followed Cookie Avalon through complicated architectural curves and turns, down various atriumed hallways, through a massive kitchen, through a sliding glass door, into the rear garden. A lovely English garden, with rows of antique rose bushes, cheerful birdbaths, a boxwood topiary maze, and of course, the prize-winning digitalis plant. Cookie went into the garden shed, came back with a trowel and a pair of garden gloves, went over the beds where the foxglove grew. She knelt on the ground, reached behind the foxgloves, started turning over the moist earth. Mimi watched Cookie dig.

In a few minutes, Cookie unearthed the plastic trash bag. She dumped out its contents at Mimi's feet. Mimi announced the contents article by article. "Jonathan's butterfly net. Jonathan's butterfly board, with his name written on it. Jonathan always wrote his name on his butterfly boards. It was an old schoolboy's habit. Now, see this board, Mrs. Avalon? See how Jonathan protected the specimen with a formaldehyde-treated Mylar sheet?" Mimi peeled back the sheet and gasped. "The exquisite corpse. It's extraordinary. Simply extraordinary."

Cookie wrinkled her nose. "It is?"

Mimi nodded. She held the butterfly gently up to her breast. "I should keep it for myself. I really should. But this collector is offering an amount I really can't refuse. Do you realize that this single specimen will completely pay for my Paris launch?"

Cookie sniffed. She stood up, pulled off the garden gloves.

As Mimi departed, the net, the board, and the butterfly securely in her possession, Cookie leaned against the door. "Call me, sometime," said Cookie cheerfully. "I have some friends in retail who are absolutely dying to meet you."

Mimi smiled, waved, drove away. When she was gone, Cookie shouted, "Imogene! Imogene, where are you?"

Imogene stood by the open kitchen window. Cookie hadn't seen her in there, hadn't realized that Imogene heard every word Cookie and the Budge girl exchanged. Imogene hated spying on Cookie. But when you've seen certain things, overheard certain things, when you know the intricate machinations of your employer's troubled mental state, you just can't go about your chores as if nothing's wrong. After Cookie showed the Budge woman out, she shouted across the house, "Imogene, I want my lunch! I'm famished!"

Imogene sighed, signaling the end of her tale. "That's what I had to tell you, miss. It breaks my heart, but I can't live with this any longer. I love little Cookie like my own child, but what's going on is all wrong."

She leaned down, picked up the picnic basket, placed it in her lap. She opened a flap of the basket, peeled back a linen towel, reached inside, and fished out a small .38 pistol. She said, "Lord have mercy, I'm a bad nanny."

Venus took the lethal toy from Imogene Donner's hand, placed it back in the picnic basket. "You can't go back there."

Imogene smiled wanly and said, "She won't hurt me. She'd never hurt me. I've been her nanny all her life. Miss Cookie won't lay a hand on me. And by the way, Miss Cookie and I come from Hoboken. That Southern belle never existed, except in Miss Cookie's imagination. And all these years Mr. Avalon has kept her secret. About her mind, her sick mind."

When they parted in the fresh market, Imogene stopped to buy fresh raspberries. Venus carried the picnic basket to the Spider, got in, called Claudia.

"We've got a match," said Claudia. "Fingerprints on your gun match prints taken from the camas cake wrapping. Now what?"

"I need Song up here. Send me Song."

Smugly, Claudia said, "I'm way ahead of you. Louie should be there any minute now. He said to tell you he'll meet you at the ranger lodge up near the park entrance."

"Gad, you're swift, Claud."

She spun out on Highway 101, floored the gas. Come on, Needles, come and get me.

THIRTY-ONE

METAMORPHOSIS

EBERT SPED ALONG Highway 101, the radio in his Budget rental car tuned to a local country and western station. Ebert hated music of all kinds, but he liked background noise, especially when he was thinking. At a steep hairpin curve, he braked, coaxed the Dodge Shadow through the dizzying loop. When he came out on the other side, Ebert pulled the Shadow over on the highway's shoulder, parked, looked up at Yodeler's meadow, then down at his Timex. Four-fifty p.m. He got out, went around to the back, opened the trunk. He dragged out a pile of wood stakes, a hammer, a fat staple gun, and some FEDERAL LAND TRANSFER, SALE PENDING signs. He'd start at the bottom and work up.

Ebert had planned to reach the meadow at eight o'clock that morning, but got detoured when at six a.m. he boarded the wrong ferry boat in Seattle. Before realizing he'd flubbed, he was on Vashon Island. Then he had to take the next Vashon ferry back to Seattle, drive up Interstate 5 to Edmonds, wait for the Kingston Ferry, cross Puget Sound again, then drive from Kingston up the Olympic Peninsula to Fern. A trip that ought to have cost him two hours turned into an odyssey of navigational errors, lasting eight and a half hours. That didn't count the stop at Peter Avalon's office in Fern, or the meeting time with Peter and Troy Avalon. That tacked on another forty-five minutes, and now here it was nearly five o'clock and he was just getting started. He'd have to work fast to get the job done before nightfall.

The only way to cut through government red tape is not to cut it at all, but to slink around it. That's how you accomplish things in a bureaucracy, you just do them, and to hell with the consequences. If Wexler didn't like Ebert taking the initiative, then he could transfer him out of Interior's land sales. But Wexler couldn't fire Ebert. Once a federal bureaucrat, always a federal bureaucrat. It's maybe the only job left with tenure. Anyway, Ebert was the best land sales officer in Washington, D.C., so people expected him to take liberties now and then. He could afford to take premature steps like this one to close a sale.

The hysterics he anticipated from Olson and his staff were nothing to sweat over. Ebert had weathered other emotional monsoons from other livid conservationists over other federal preserves. Ho-hum. Just get it over with, go on to the next job. Ebert's Way. After the hysterics, Ebert would come back up here, go around putting up little sold signs over the SALE PENDING signs. Maybe he should make some EBERT'S WAY signs, post them, too.

Ebert loosened his tie, slung the stakes over his shoulder, and set off on foot. Working his way up the meadow's western perimeter, he pounded a wood stake into the ground every five hundred yards, using a little pedometer he wore on his belt to pace off the distances. The rich earth, soft, moist, easily accepted the wood stakes with the signs on them, but when he reached an elevation high up in the meadow, near the edge of the Avalon poppy fields, he hit some hard, resistant ground underneath the peaty topsoil, and had to work harder, pounding with all his might. The pounding felt good. Ebert needed a physical challenge after those long hours behind the wheel of the rental car. He leaned into the stake, was about to pound it again, when behind him, a female voice said, "Who are you? And what are you doing up here?"

Ebert straightened up, turned around. The woman stood just a few yards from him, knee high in the tall grass. She had long red hair that billowed. A sultry face with boudoir eyes. She wore a revealing green leotard with green tights. She parted her lips and smiled, and Ebert involuntarily swooned. Of course, he recognized her from the picture in her husband's office. Cookie Avalon. And what a cookie.

When autumn arrives, nothing is more spectacular than a falling leaf that captures sunlight, wrapping itself in a dazzling death robe, a last-ditch attempt to suffuse life into a corpse. Ebert's heart usually felt as dead as a fallen leaf. For whatever reason, Ebert lived like a monk on skates, skimming life's safe top layers, celibate, without a passion for anything. Rarely was he moved by emotion or by beauty. Now his heart suddenly felt bright and vibrant, full of borrowed energy drawn from the brilliant creature in the leotard. For a fleeting moment, Ebert glowed. Then he blinked once or twice, and the swoon passed.

She came over, held out a delicate white hand. "How do you do? I'm Cookie Avalon. Peter's wife." She cocked her head to one side. "Are you working for the government or for my husband?"

Ebert's wiped his hand on his trousers, took hers, a dead fish in his own limp, sweaty paw. He told her his name and what he was doing in the meadow. He rested a black oxford on the bundle of stakes, said, "Where you're standing is government property. If you step backwards about two feet, you'll be back on your own property."

Smirking, Cookie plucked a piece of long grass, twirled the blade around her index finger. Her hair moved softly in the breeze. The diamond on her ring finger caught the sun, nearly blinding Ebert. He averted his eyes.

Cookie could play his little two-step game. She stepped back two feet, not an inch more. "Is that better?"

Ebert nodded.

"Does this mean they found the killer?"

Ebert cocked his head, like he didn't understand. Cookie reframed her question. "Have they caught the person who murdered those people up here?"

Ebert shrugged.

Cookie said, "Well, I understood the land sale can't be finalized until they close this murder investigation. Did you hear about the young model who was shot to death a couple weeks ago?"

Ebert nodded.

"Well, that happened right here, in this very meadow. You're practically standing on the spot. No, wait a minute. That was Jonathan Willow, the other one. The model was shot over there, in the poppies, when the poppies were in bloom."

She pointed at the poppy field, now a mass of withering stems, dead leaves turning rapidly to mulch. She'd almost forgotten an important part of the story. "There've been other killings, too," she added. "At least one that I know of, up in the forest."

Ebert said, "I heard about that."

Cookie persisted. "So, if you're up here placing all these SALE PENDING signs, they must have arrested someone. Am I confusing you?"

Arrogantly, Ebert said, "I'm never confused. I don't have time to be confused. To answer your first question, I'm up here expediting the land sale. So that when my boss in D.C. gives the green light, I can cinch this deal in five minutes flat.''

Cookie twitched her nose. ''Oh? Does that mean we're definitely acquiring this land?''

''Within the week, it's yours. You can quote me on that.''

''How can you be so cockeyed sure of that?''

Ebert smiled. A little ruse never hurt. He lied, ''Because we now know who committed the killings, and we're making an arrest today. Actually, any minute now. Then the Department of the Interior will release this land for sale. Soon as we close the investigation.''

Cookie scowled. ''I don't believe you.''

Ebert shrugged. ''Just watch.''

''I mean, about catching the killer.''

''Oh, we know who it is, all right,'' Ebert lied again. ''Now it's just a matter of arresting the person.''

Cookie blinked. ''Do you know who this—person—might be?''

Ebert shook his head. ''Naw. Not my department.''

He picked up the stakes and the hammer, tipped his vestigial hat. Resetting his pedometer, he took off uphill. He didn't turn around, didn't look back. He just climbed to the next spot and pounded in the next stake. Some things take more energy than one man can spare.

FREUD SAID that man, if left unfettered, has a primary need to destroy himself. If he'd lived in the present era and been politically correct, Freud would have included women in that pronouncement. Freud was also addicted to cigars. Sucking. And he called women ''the dark continent.''

Cookie, the dark continent, drank her afternoon herbal tea before the Yocum mirror, staring deep into the glass, beyond her own reflection. Something, or someone seemed to beckon her from deep inside the mirror. She had heard the voice many times over the years, ever since she was just a young girl. Each time she heard the voice, she tried following it into the mirror, but it never worked. Until now. Now, the voice called Cookie and Cookie's fixed gaze penetrated the glass, traveling backwards in time, to the image of the little girl with flowing red hair, no more than four years old. A very fragile, very frightened child, dressed in a white lace flower girl's gown with a blue ribbon sash and blue satin slippers. She's a precious, delicate child, with wide blue eyes, an angel's radiant smile. She lives in a world of plantation homes and live oaks dripping Spanish moss, a world of privilege and comfort, surrounded by servants, her nanny, Imogene, never very far from her side.

Aunt Mignon's wedding. Cookie, the youngest member of the wedding party, stood shyly, trembling, in the middle of a huge ballroom floor. The adults, hundreds of them, stood far back against the walls, clapping their hands, exhorting her to dance, to perform for them. The orchestra struck up "Le Waltz des les Enfants." Little Cookie, painfully shy, caught her father's stern eye, heard her mother's haughty, insistent voice, calling, "Dance, Cookie, dance for the people. Dance, Cookie. I said dance."

Over and over, until Cookie, mortified, obeyed. Holding her gown slightly off the ballroom floor, she bent and swayed, bent and swayed, but she couldn't catch the music's rhythm, couldn't twirl and step like her mother did. She really couldn't dance at all, and so she bent and swayed, and the orchestra kept playing and playing. Tears rolled down her rosy cheeks, while all around her people laughed, howled, made fun of her. The little girl who couldn't dance. The orchestra kept on playing, and Cookie thought she would faint from embarrassment. Suddenly, she turned and ran out of the ballroom, ran, ran, down a long hallway, around a corner, ran, ran, until she came to the end of the long hall. There, for the first time in her life, Cookie ran smack into her own reflection in the Yocum mirror.

Tentatively, the child moved forward, touched her own image, the face, where tears rolled over her cheeks, the dress, the beautiful dress, her little feet, encased in the pretty blue satin slippers. Cookie smiled, curtsied to the reflection. It smiled and curtsied back. She stuck out her tongue, and so did the little girl in the mirror. The image was friendly, and not at all demanding. She had made a friend in the Yocum mirror, a friend for life.

The next part was sketchy in her mind. A woman's figure loomed in the mirror behind her new friend. The woman grabbed Cookie, shook her hard, slapped her face over and over again. Cookie cried and begged the woman to stop, but the woman kept on hitting her until Cookie couldn't defend herself. The woman swept her up off her feet, carried her like a bag of laundry down the long hall. They came to a tall cupboard. The woman stopped, opened the cupboard door, stuffed Cookie into it.

Cookie heard the woman breathing hard, her angry voice, the words flying from her mouth on sour spittle. "How dare you make a fool of me?" the woman hissed. "How dare you behave like a stupid little moron." The woman pushed her, and Cookie fell, tumbling over herself down a long, dark shaft.

The next thing Cookie remembered was the huge, greasy rat chewing on her satin sash. Then more rats, moving in from the dark shadows, crawling across her body, over her face and hands, up her arms and up her legs, underneath her gown. She was too frightened to move. She screamed, but no one came.

She must have fallen asleep, or passed out. The next thing she recalled was a shaft of light falling across her. Daylight, streaming through a small window. Now she could see the walls of the room, could see where she lay. She lay in a pile of fertilizer, or peat moss. It stank, and it was damp, and the room was hot, steamy hot. The rats had retreated from the light, but she knew they lurked nearby.

She whimpered at first, then called out, "Mother, I'm sorry. I'm sorry, Mother. Come and get me now."

The old houseman had come around the side of the house to fetch a garden hose when he heard the child's pleas leaking from a basement window. He quickly located her, carried her outside into the morning sunshine, laid her on a bench inside a white gazebo. He called for help, and help came.

The family doctor pronounced the child physically unharmed, except for some bruises and the rat bites. Those would leave scars, and she had to take a tetanus shot. The doctor said the real problem was her psyche. Trauma in a child this age could leave deep, permanent psychic scars. It would help, said the doctor, if the child's assailant could be identified. Unfortunately, no one ever came forward to confess, and Cookie could never decide if her assailant had been her mother or her nanny, Imogene.

BY SIX O'CLOCK, Ebert had the meadow staked out, from the Avalon property on the west to the MacGregor land on the east, from the highway's shoulder up the meadow to the poppy field. The legal requirement prematurely satisfied, Ebert tossed a few surplus stakes, the staple gun, and the hammer into the rental car's trunk, slammed it shut.

Walking around to the driver's door, he noticed something moving down near the ground. At first, he thought it was a yellow jacket aiming at his left ankle. With his foot, he kicked the air. The thing swooped upwards, where he could see it, and it wasn't a yellow jacket at all. It was a butterfly, orange and black, translucent, backlit by the setting sun.

Ebert stood still, watched the butterfly flit over to the rental car, land on the hood, pose, like a fancy hood ornament. He didn't know anything about butterflies. He didn't even care about them. Why would anyone make such a big stink about endangered butterflies? If all butterflies became extinct, would anyone really notice? Would the world come to an end?

An Earth First! demonstrator once told Ebert that butterflies are crucial pollinators of plants that are critical for the survival of certain other fragile creatures, which are critical for the survival of other creatures, and so on and so forth, ad nauseam. Besides, the demonstrator said, butterflies are like canaries in coal mines; they're fragile harbingers of ecological imbalance, trouble in the planet's environment, danger. To convert Ebert. But Ebert wasn't convertible, not then, not ever.

The butterfly didn't move. Then Ebert got a clever idea. He reached into his pocket, fished out a paper tissue. He always carried tissues. For allergies. Holding the tissue in cupped hands, he moved in slowly, stealthily. He pounced, taking the butterfly by surprise. "Gotcha," he cracked triumphantly. As if a butterfly understood bureaucratese.

The creature struggled. Ebert held it by the body, squeezed his fingers into a vice, tighter and tighter. The creature's internal organs, its juices, came squishing out all over his hands. When it was dead, he dropped it on the ground, cleaned his hands with fresh tissues, then gingerly plucked up the butterfly corpse, inspected the wings. Perfect condition. He couldn't ask for a better trophy, a more befitting souvenir from this latest, potentially most lucrative land sale. He tossed the dead butterfly in the glove compartment and turned on the ignition, but in a split second, Ebert's plans changed.

They came from every direction. From both ends of the highway, up from the beach, from the meadow itself. Ebert counted ten, fifteen, twenty people, then lost count as their numbers grew. He gripped the steering wheel, felt his stomach churn. Now there were over a hundred of them, and more coming, pouring off the highway like swarming bees. Now Ebert's rental car was surrounded. He couldn't move an inch. He checked the locks on the doors. Ebert's scalp crawled and the hair on his forearms bristled.

A long line of people formed at the base of the meadow, unfurled a banner. Ebert strained to see past the crowd surrounding his car. The banner said, THIS LAND NOT FOR SALE. As the banner billowed in the breeze, the crowd cheered. Ebert let the car window down a couple inches and shouted to a woman standing nearby.

"What's this all about?"

Beatrice Yamada peered into the car window, said, "Oh, hi there. Who are you?"

"Never mind," snapped Ebert. "What's this all about?"

"Oh. Well, the people of Fern are fed up with all this landgrabbing around here. We're going to prevent the sale of this wildlife preserve."

Ebert stared. He couldn't suppress a laugh. "You people think you can stop this land sale?" He laughed again. "You guys are nuts."

Beatrice shrugged. "Maybe. But we're not leaving this meadow until the federal government withdraws its plan to sell it."

Ebert shook his head in amazement. What a bunch of dodos. He turned on the car's ignition, shouted at Beatrice, "Tell those jerks to clear out of my way."

Beatrice went over, spoke to the people blocking Ebert's path. A few of them turned, peered into the windshield at Ebert. He felt like a caged animal, a zoo display. The people broke out laughing, and Beatrice held up her hands helplessly.

"They won't move."

"Why not?" Ebert. Outraged.

"See that lady sitting on your hood? She says you're the federal land agent. She says you deserve to be tarred and feathered. But don't worry. It's just rhetoric. Anyway, they won't let you out of here until this issue is settled."

"The hell they won't." Ebert put the car in drive. "Tell them if they don't move now, I'm going to plow them under."

Beatrice went back, spoke to the hood ornament and her entourage. The hood ornament shook her head adamantly. Then she turned around and stared at Ebert through the windshield. Ebert almost fainted. Miss Perkins raised a stiff finger and shook it in his face.

Up in the meadow, the crowd had grown to hundreds. They undulated in the twilight, a sea of bodies, swaying, chanting, making an awful racket. Ebert shook his fist at Miss Perkins. She slid off the car's hood, came over to the window. Through the two inch slit, she said, "If it isn't Mr. Decaf-with-Cream."

"Where's your boss?" Ebert demanded.

Miss Perkins said coyly, "I'm my own boss. You got a problem with that?"

Ebert growled, "Get these people out of my way."

Miss Perkins shook her head.

Exasperated, Ebert searched the car for a cellular phone. No phone. To Miss Perkins, he said, "Have you got a telephone on you? I'd like to call Mr. Avalon."

Miss Perkins smiled. "Mr. Avalon can't come to the phone right now."

"Why not?" Shouted.

"Mr. Avalon is being held hostage in his office until he agrees to drop his offer on this land."

Ebert's eyes bulged. "You're joking."

Miss Perkins gestured at the crowds. "You call this a joke? I don't. I call this a concerned community. We're sick and tired of developers barging into our territory with their bulldozers and their sleazy shopping malls. And now the federal government has joined their ranks, trying to sell off a precious piece of our Paradise. This is God's country, Mr. Ebert, sir, and just in case you hadn't noticed, the natives here take their stewardship seriously. So you can drop your plans to sell off this preserve, because we'll fight you, Mr. Ebert, sir. I don't care if you are a federal agent. We'll put you in the ground if you ever come back to the Olympic Peninsula. Now, we're going to help you turn your car around. Then a couple of our citizens will escort you down the highway. You better not turn around. Don't even think about turning around. Go back where you came from, Mr. Ebert. Get out of our lives. And, God bless you, Mr. Ebert, sir."

Ebert felt the Dodge Shadow rock slightly, felt it turning, rocking, until it faced the opposite direction. Goddamn beefy rural machismo, that's what it is, Ebert grumbled to himself. When they set the car down, Ebert was facing east, toward home. The crowd parted. Ebert hit the gas. He'd never had a motorcycle escort before, and when the bikers finally set him loose on 101 South, at the Kingston ferry turn-off, Ebert didn't bother waving good-bye. He just drove onto the ferry ramp, onto the ferry, and sailed across Puget Sound slumped over the steering wheel.

"LOOK UP THERE."

Song was driving. He steered the Spider around the hairpin curve outside Fern. He pointed toward Yodeler's meadow. Venus squinted through the windshield. "Candles. They lit candles. Hey, that's neat, isn't it? How they're twirling them around like lassos?"

"But why?"

"I don't know, but we're probably going to find out." She took out her phone, called the office in Seattle. Dottie answered.

"They're all in the field," said Dottie. "Except me. I'm holding down the fort."

"Where are they?" Venus almost shouted. "We need the whole team."

Dottie sniffed. "Well, you can just forget that fantasy. Everyone's still in the Dalles. I don't expect them back until tomorrow."

"What about Olson? Did Olson go, too?"

"Yep. And Song and Sparks and Claudia and Eric. Even Marla went. She abandoned her new baby. It's that serious over there."

"Like I said, I'm all alone. What's up?"

"Song's with me, Dottie. We need backup." Venus heard the futile intonation in her own voice.

Dottie hooted. "Better call the local law, toots. That's always the last resort. Call the sheriff, why don't you?"

"Sure," she answered dully. "Why don't I?"

When they reached the preserve, Song parked on the highway shoulder, behind a slew of trucks and vans. They got out, walked over to the demonstrators. Venus looked around for a familiar face. Then Darin emerged from the crowd, an officious, bloated ego propelling him. When he saw Venus, he smiled, waved a hand, and called out, "Welcome to our demonstration."

"What's it all about?" No harm in asking.

Darin pointed up at the sign in the meadow. Spotlights illuminated the message. They read the sign. Song said, "Who are you? Che Guevara?"

Darin didn't appreciate the humor. He sniffed, turned to walk away. Venus reached out, touched Darin's shoulder, said, "How's the spelunking business?"

Darin paused, turned around. Evenly he said, "Spelunking isn't a business. It's a sport."

"So, how's it going? Find any new caves lately?"

Darin narrowed his eyes. "No. I haven't. Why do you ask?"

Venus shrugged, showed empty palms. "Just making conversation."

"Well, I don't have time for conversation. I have a job to do here."

Song said, "You must really want to protect this meadow. I mean, organizing a big demonstration like this."

Darin nodded, walked away, started hiking up into the meadow into the sea of candlelight. Venus and Song exchanged a glance. They let Darin walk a few paces, then Venus caught up with him. "I just wanted to tell you that I read Lux's manuscript. The cookbook?"

"Yeah?" Coolly. "So what?"

Venus said, "It took me a while to find it on the map Lux drew of the preserve. Finally I found it, on the very edge of the paper."

Darin looked at her, frowned. "What are you talking about?"

"The cave. Lux had marked out a cave up behind the waterfall. I don't know if you're familiar with that cave. It's a hibernation den for a family of bears."

Darin nodded. "Sure. I know that cave."

He quickened his pace up the steep meadow. Venus had to run to keep up with him. "On Lux's map," she continued, "he drew a treasure chest inside the cave. Any idea why he did that?"

Darin stared at her, or possibly through her. "What's this all about, anyway?"

Venus glanced over her shoulder. Song followed them, a few paces behind, watching, waiting. Venus said to Darin, "It's like this, Darin. Lux drew this treasure chest icon on his map. Then I discovered that Jonathan Willow, the fellow who was killed up here in the meadow? Willow had made a similar notation in his files. Actually, it was just a reference to a mineral. Gold is a mineral, isn't it?"

Darin stopped walking. "I suppose so, yes."

Venus spread her hands. "So I figured out that Willow and Lux both had a mutual interest in the preserve. Something more valuable than the wildflowers and butterflies. At least, they considered it more valuable. They might have been friends, sharing their knowledge, or they might have discovered a treasure separately. Either way, I think they both knew about some treasure stashed on the preserve. In the cave under the waterfall."

Darin rubbed his sparse beard, considered what she had said.

Venus added, "I figured that since you're a spelunker, you'd have been inside that cave. Maybe you discovered the same thing. It's probably too big, too heavy for one person to haul down the mountainside. Unless you were pretty muscle-bound, you know?"

Darin stared at her. She pressed on. "Then this morning, I had the opportunity to check out the employees' time clock at the Fiddlehead.

The day Lux was poisoned by death camas, you checked in early. You probably helped Lux sort out his fresh produce."

Darin's body twisted awkwardly, his mouth contorted. Venus continued, "I also checked out the fridge at the Fiddlehead. And way in the back I found this package of camas cakes. Only they were made from death camas. They'd kill you within a couple hours if you ate them. And guess what? The package had fingerprints on them. Oddest part was, Darin, those prints matched the prints on my gun, after someone attacked me up there not far from the waterfall and the cave. After Aggie MacGregor was spiked to that tree." Venus felt her body shaking, the rage of recognition. She fought against it, she had to stay cool, calm. Now she delivered the punch line. "I'm betting those are your fingerprints on the death camas package. You poisoned Lux because he knew about the cave, about the treasure. Then when Aggie MacGregor caught you up there near the cave, you panicked. Had she seen you go under the waterfall into the cave? And since the treasure belonged to Aggie, and you knew that, you decided to kill her right then and there. You spiked her to the tree, to make it look like some angry lodgers killed her."

Darin looked around. Miss Perkins stood a few feet from him. He grabbed her by the hand, started running. Miss Perkins argued with him at first, but she trusted him, ran with him, up into the high meadow, up where no candles glowed, into the darkness, disappearing from sight. Venus's ribs ached and she was miserably out of shape. Song had outpaced her and now was a few yards behind Darin and Miss Perkins. But Darin was fast and so was his hostage.

People noticed the commotion, but they had more important business. The crowd kept singing, chanting, their faces glowing in the candlelight. At the edge of the forest, Song stopped, waited for Venus to catch up. She crouched over, held her rib cage, fell to the ground. "I have to rest. I have to."

"Don't move. Stay there. I'll be right back." Song disappeared in the dark shadows.

WHEN FULL DARKNESS cloaks the rain forest, shadows beget shadows, and only a benevolent moon permits the human eye to see. Song's penlight was worthless in the vast darkness. A pale thin moon offered little benefit as he crept up along MacGregor's Trail. He moved slowly, as much by feel as by sight. Every few paces, he stopped, listened. He heard the raging Elwha River. He heard an owl hoot.

And he heard Miss Perkins's insistent voice suddenly escape from Darin's hand.

"Keep your paw off my mouth, Darin, or I'll bite you again."

Bingo. They were closer than Song thought. Very close. He could hear Darin's loud whisper.

"Shut up, will you? Just shut up and nothing will happen to you."

Then Miss Perkins's lowered voice. "I don't like it up here, Darin. Let's go back down. Anyway, I'm not having sex with you, if that's what you think."

"Shut up!" Whispered violently.

Song's eyes grew accustomed to the darkness, and now he could see the trail leading up the mountain, and he could see the waterfall glinting in moonlight. It wasn't the Elwha, after all. It was a tremendous waterfall careening down a high cliff. Underneath the waterfall was a pool of light, of water, and beside the pool of water, Darin and Miss Perkins stood side by side. They had paused in their flight so that Miss Perkins could have a drink of water.

Song took a single step forward, toward the voices. Underfoot, the soft, moist mossy carpet gave silently. He took another step, placing himself behind a cedar tree. From there, he had a good view of them. He reached inside his jacket pocket, curled his hand around the butt of his pistol, pulled it gently out of the holster. It felt good in his hand. Better than any handgun should against flesh. A gun just shouldn't feel this good. He'd kill the bastard.

Darin was sweet-talking Miss Perkins. He wanted to show her something. "You won't believe your eyes," whispered Darin. "Come on, it's not far from here."

"Oh, all right," muttered Miss Perkins. "But if my shoes get ruined, you're going to buy me a new pair."

Darin took Miss Perkins by the hand, led her back onto the trail. Song, having missed his first opportunity, followed them. In a few minutes, they reached the top of the waterfall. Darin started climbing the rocky outcropping. He helped Miss Perkins across the boulders, ignoring her constant crabbing. She slipped and slid but finally made it to where Darin stood. Miss Perkins looked around.

They were behind the waterfall, looking out, facing the pounding water curtain. Miss Perkins gasped. Darin said, "Like it?" Miss Perkins nodded slowly. Darin said, "Now, turn around." Miss Perkins turned around. Darin pulled a candle from his pocket, lit it, held it up.

Miss Perkins said, "There's a cave back here. I never knew there was a cave back here."

Darin grinned. "You can go inside. Go ahead."

Miss Perkins wrinkled her nose, shook her head.

"Go on," Darin urged.

"There might be bears in there."

Darin laughed. "It's totally safe, I promise. I go in there all the time. The bears come here in winter. It's too early for them now. Come on, I'll go in first."

Song put the gun away, climbed onto the boulders, worked his way over the expanse, slid down behind the waterfall. Darin and Miss Perkins were stepping into the cave. He let them go inside, listened, then followed.

At the entrance, the cave was thirty feet wide and high enough for a tall person to stand comfortably. Song could hear Darin's voice from deep inside. He followed the narrowing passage, guided by the dim light from Darin's candle. Now he could see them standing in a corner. They were standing over a pile of something. What?

Miss Perkins said, "Would you look at this? An old boom box. You think it works?"

"Sure. I found it in here yesterday. I just put new batteries in it."

Miss Perkins fiddled with the boom box. Song heard static at first, then music. Country and western music. A latter day Hank Williams wannabe wailing about empty hearts and empty promises. Miss Perkins did a little dance.

She said, "Fabulous reception up here. I really like this song. Hey, how'd this boom box get up here?

"Bears. They bring stuff in here all the time."

Miss Perkins stopped dancing. "You mean, there's been a bear in here?"

"I told you, they only come in winter."

"But you said you come here all the time, Darin. And now you just said you didn't bring this boom box in here, that a bear must have brought it. But you didn't see it until yesterday. So a bear must have been in here recently."

Song felt his scalp crawl. Then Darin spoke again.

"Don't worry. We'll leave in a minute. I just want you to see one thing."

"Well, hurry up, Darin. I'm already having a hissy."

Darin walked to another spot in the cave, Miss Perkins at his heels.

In the candle glow an old steel trunk appeared. Darin flipped open the top. "Now, this is what I really wanted you to see."

Song heard Miss Perkins gasp. He strained his neck to see what she saw. Miss Perkins said, "Darin, is this stuff for real?"

Darin smiled triumphantly. "It's gold bouillon. Worth a few million at least. I'm going to be a wealthy man, honey."

"But—but, where did it come from?"

"You ever hear that legend about old man MacGregor?"

"Aggie's father?"

Darin nodded. "They said he put all his gold into a bank down in Seattle. But he didn't. He hid it in here. And I found it."

"Really?" Amazement. "Did Aggie know it was here?"

"Sure. That's how I found it. I followed Aggie into the cave."

Silence. Then, in a tiny voice, "Darin, you didn't kill her, did you?"

"What if I did?" Miss Perkins backed up slowly. Darin moved toward her. "It's okay, honey. I just want to feel your tush."

"Don't touch me, Darin." Sheer fright.

Song moved fast, grabbed Miss Perkins, pointed the gun at Darin. Startled, Darin dropped the candle. He lunged at Song, shoved Miss Perkins aside, and ran, fumbling against the walls, out of the cave. Miss Perkins screamed and fainted.

IN THE COOL evening moonlight, Radio and the twins, Berry and Roe, were wallowing in the upper meadow, feasting on a cascade of blackberry brambles, when they heard a noise. The great male bear paused, sniffed the air. What rude interruption was it this time? Radio grunted at the twins, sent them flying back into the forest. He bounded down off the brambles, sat hunched in the grass, waited.

Breathless, Darin slid down a short embankment, paused in a clump of tall grass, spotted some overgrown brambles. A perfect hiding place. He could leave later, when no one was around. He sucked in a deep breath, paused midair. What was that noise?

From the opposite side of the brambles, Radio growled.

A chill ran along Darin's spine. The moonlight shone on the great black bear. Darin froze. Radio reached out a paw, batted the air near Darin's trembling hand. In all his spelunking, Darin had never actually encountered a bear. He didn't know how to act. Should he stand still, or run?

Radio growled again.

Slowly Darin shrugged off his leather jacket. He tossed it into the meadow, momentarily diverting the bear's attention. In that split second Darin turned and ran back into the forest, as fast as he could go. Radio watched him go, then picked up the leather jacket and lumbered off toward home. Later that night Berry and Roe met Radio at the pool beneath the waterfall. The twins had enjoyed a lovely repast, as evidenced by their bloodstained paws. Radio grunted. He'd never tasted human flesh. He wasn't interested.

THIRTY-TWO

THUNDERBIRD

THUNDERBIRD CAME FROM the sea, fully formed, three canoes long, with feathers the size of oars. When Thunderbird flaps his wings, the winds blow and the sky growls. When he blinks his eyes, lightning flashes. His home is a deep cave high in the Olympic Mountains. He guards the cave jealously, destroying anyone he deems unwelcome. Thunderbird and Killer Whale struggled through many wars; each time Killer Whale tried to invade Thunderbird's cave. Finally, Killer Whale fled back into the sea and Thunderbird ruled the land and the air. The legacy of their battles are the prairies that formed where their struggles had uprooted trees. The prairies are where camas bulbs grow and are harvested, mountain prairies, foothill prairies, all made from the struggles between Killer Whale and Thunderbird.

Today, Killer Whale is called Orca. But Thunderbird is still called by his original name, because it suits him. If you ever see Thunderbird circling over the mountains, you can be sure he's guarding his home from invaders. If you listen, you can hear Thunderbird's warnings. Thunderbird always warns the creatures of the land and sea before he ushers in a storm, and his great booming voice is respected throughout the territory.

This particular Thunderbird didn't roar. It buzzed. It wasn't very dangerous, unless the wrong person took the pilot seat. This Thunderbird was bright yellow with black trim and resembled a bumblebee more than a bird. You could hear it coming from a great distance, and when it flew overhead, it didn't fly as high as some airplanes. This Thunderbird preferred the lower vapors, swooping and soaring quite close to the mountain meadows.

When dawn came, a brilliant orange ball rose out of the east, burned off the night chill, poured across Yodeler's meadow. The sky was a turquoise dome, and for all it knew, clouds had never been invented.

In the meadow, a hundred human bodies lay prone against the moist earth, some wrapped in sleeping bags, others in thin blankets, or down comforters. When the dim sound of buzzing filled the air, Sigrid Chin opened her eyes. Beside her on the meadow grass lay Bea Yamada. Sigrid sat up, nudged Bea.

"What is it?" Beatrice, yawning, stretching.

"Up there." Sigrid pointed to the sky, just left of the rising orange ball.

Beatrice fumbled for her glasses, peered through them at the perfect sunrise.

"Beautiful," she said, and lay down again.

Sigrid nudged her again. "I mean that."

Bea sat up again, put the glasses back on, focused on the sky. The fat black-and-yellow airplane was heading straight for the meadow. Beatrice gasped. "They're going to bomb us."

"I don't think so, dear. That is Lady Bella Winsome-Diamond's airplane."

"Oh, yeah. Now I recognize it. But what's it doing?"

The women rose, stepped over several neighbors, walked into the meadow away from the sleepers. But some of the sleepers had also heard the buzzing sound, and now they rose, and as the buzzing grew louder, as the plane came closer, all of the people woke up and scanned the skies.

The yellow plane made two low swoops directly overhead. From the crowd came exclamations of wonder, of irritation, of amusement. On the third swoop, the crowd saw Conrad Avalon lean out of the plane's window. He was holding a big boxlike thing. He opened the lid, and the skies went dark for a second. Beatrice blinked. Now the darkness shattered into tiny patches, thousands of golden wisps floated, swooped, soared above her head. All around her people cheered.

"Butterflies," shouted Beatrice.

Sigrid sighed, said softly, "Too bad. They're the wrong subspecies. These are silverspots, but not the Dungeness variety."

"Who cares what species they are," cried Bea. "They're beautiful!"

The giant bumblebee circled the meadow one more time, then

winged off into the sunrise. Beatrice folded her hands against her chest. "Did you catch a look at that pilot?"

Sigrid shook her head. She wasn't thinking about pilots. She was remembering Aggie MacGregor. How when Aggie and Sigrid were just little girls, they would frolic right here in this meadow, and Aggie would yodel down into the valley while Sigrid chased butterflies. Back then, it was the Dungeness silverspot. Today it was a more common species of butterfly. Still, Aggie would be happy to see them fill the meadow like this.

"Gad," sighed Bea, stuck on the pilot's good looks. "He had black hair. In a pony tail? I could see his teeth when he smiled. Big, white, flashy teeth. And gorgeous eyes."

Sigrid ran after a butterfly. Not to capture it, just for the memory. Beatrice called out, "I'm serious. I really saw his face. I'm totally in love."

VENUS MET SONG on the highway below the preserve.

Song said, "Are you all right?"

"Why didn't you come back last night?"

"I had this albatross to contend with."

"Darin? You caught him?"

Song shook his head. "Couple bears beat me to it. Miss Perkins. The future Mrs. Avalon."

"Get out."

Song chuckled. "No joke. When I got out of there with Perkins in tow, I couldn't find you in the dark. I knew you'd be okay, with all those people in the meadow. I mean, it was pitch dark. I couldn't see anything."

"Get to the point, Song."

"The future Mrs. Avalon." Song relished her impatience. "So I went with her over to the Blue Poppy factory."

"It's not a factory. It's a perfumery."

"Perfumery. She sweet-talked her boss into signing an agreement."

"What kind of agreement?"

"To leave Yodeler's meadow alone."

Venus stared. "She did that?"

"She pulled out her trump card. And it worked. Apparently, Peter Avalon has been in love with Miss Perkins for a couple years."

Venus opened her mouth to say something. Song placed a gentle hand over it. "Let me finish. Miss Perkins obviously has the hots for her boss, but they didn't pursue each other. At least she claims there hasn't been any hanky-panky between them. He's been a faithful— if miserable—husband to Cookie. But one thing was obvious. As soon as Miss Perkins entered his office, the energy between those two was hot-wired. They made me leave the room. Then, a few minutes later, Miss Perkins came out of Peter's office with the signed agreement in her hand."

"Was her blouse ruffled around the buttons?"

"What?"

Venus's phone rang. She reached into her pocket, pulled out the phone, clicked on the receiver.

Wexler. "Venus, where are you?"

"In a state of confusion. Where are you?"

"I'm at the office. I just had a fax from the Avalon brothers. They've dropped their offer on the meadow."

"Really?" Acting surprised.

"They mentioned a demonstration out there, in the meadow. I want you to accompany the Avalon brothers out to the meadow this morning. Peter Avalon will hold a press conference. He wants to face the demonstrators straight on, tell them his decision."

"Sure. I can do that."

Wexler rang off. Venus felt a hand on her arm. A familiar, steely grip. Bella's hand. Bella's grip. Here, Bella, there, Bella, everywhere, Bella Bella.

"Did you see Thunderbird, Venus? What a spectacular sight."

"Mother, what in God's good name are you doing up here?"

Bella smiled a bit secretively, Venus thought. "Connie needed to borrow Thunderbird. He and the veterinarian up here were named as old Aggie MacGregor's executors. A fine choice, in my opinion. Conrad needed Thunderbird to carry out a task for poor Aggie."

"The butterflies?"

Bella smiled. "Look, darling, down in the water. Thunderbird is waiting to take us all to breakfast. Louie, you must join us, dear."

Quizzically, Venus looked across the highway at the saltwater strait. Thunderbird, Bella's six-passenger amphibious plane, sat in the water.

"They're waiting for us." Bella made a quick phone call. A minute later, they saw Stephen open the cargo hold. A neat little skiff popped out, Stephen at the helm. He hummed toward the shore, waving at them. They watched until the little skiff pulled up a few yards off-shore.

Bella called to Stephen, "Here we come now."

Venus said, "Mother, I can't join you. Louie and I have to go somewhere."

"Nonsense, darling. I came all the way up here to the end of the world with the sole purpose of aiding you in your endeavors. The least you can do is join us for breakfast. Besides, Connie would enjoy seeing you."

"I thought you came up to help Conrad release Aggie's butter-flies."

"That was only part of my motivation." Bella reached into her handbag, fished out a carefully wrapped package. "Here, darling." She pressed it on Venus. "I have something for you. It's quite small, but I do think you'll like it."

Venus unwrapped the package, Song peering over her shoulder. Jonathan Willow's butterfly board. Pinned to the butterfly board was a perfect specimen of the Dungeness silverspot, beautifully preserved between a sheet of Mylar and the board, so perfectly displayed that you couldn't even see the pinhole where Willow had stabbed it. It still had its eyes, its brilliant green eyes.

Bella said, "I bought it from a dealer. She sells butterflies to all the best collectors. That's illegal, isn't it, darling? It was the Budge girl, Mimi Budge? Do you know her, dear?"

Bella didn't wait for Venus's reply. On her way to the skiff, Bella turned and said, "Oh, and by the way, the secret's out."

"What secret?" Venus held the butterfly board to her chest.

"The secret ingredient, dear. Connie decided it was time to confess all. The secret ingredient was Yodeler's meadow, every flower, every grass. Since the first batch of perfume, the majority of ingredients has been the flowers and grasses of that meadow. The blue poppy simply added the panache. But the fragrance should really be called Meadow, don't you think?"

A seagull touched down on the beach, pranced over to a clump of dried seaweed, picked at the translucent green strips. Salad. Venus watched the gull. A few yards down the beach, at the tideline, Bella's chimes went off. "Come along, children. We'll miss the omelet chef."

Venus studied the Dungeness silverspot, its exquisite orange-and-

black checkered wings, and the iridescent silver spots on the underwings, the lime green eyes that reminded her of her own.

Bella, in the skiff now, called out, "Children, I am going to leave
you on this beach unless you come right this minute."

Stephen piloted the skiff across a calm saltwater strait to Thunderbird, where Bella's pilot was even now revving up the propellers.
The skiff disappeared inside the cargo hold, swallowed up by Thunderbird. When the plane had taxied out of sight, Venus turned to
Song.

"Let's go."

Song felt the gun in his shoulder holster and nodded.

COOKIE HAD PACKED UP all her jewelry, removed all the cash from
the safe. She had another suitcase crammed with clothes. In her purse
she had a passport and the address of a tony Brazilian health spa.
Passing the Yocum mirror, she paused, twitched her nose at her reflection.

She should have shot Mimi Budge. If she'd had her gun handy,
she would have shot her right here, right on the spot. Then claimed
self-defense. It was, wasn't it? People barging into your home like
that, uninvited, and making threats? Where was that gun anyway?
And where was Imogene? Cookie had a sick feeling about Imogene
and about the missing gun.

No one would be surprised that Cookie just up and flew off to
Rio. She did things like that often enough. She wouldn't be gone
long, though. Just a few weeks, until things calmed down. Hopefully,
they would arrest the wrong person. She'd be home free. Then she'd
deal with Imogene.

Cookie sat down on the couch before the Yocum mirror. Just for
a moment. Just to clear her head. The terrace door on the beach side
of the house was open and a cool breeze wafted through the louvered
blinds. Cookie stared at her reflection in the mirror, concentrated,
trying to get past the gorgeous face and figure, the knockout eyes,
trying to find the child again, her little friend who curtsied when she
curtsied, giggled when she giggled. She tried and tried but couldn't
break the surface.

As if by magic, another woman's face appeared in the mirror. A
ghost? No. That woman. Vanna. She saw Vanna's reflection in the
Yocum mirror. She saw the gun in Vanna's hand, pointed at her. In
one swift, spontaneous motion, Cookie leaned over, pulled off a

chunky shoe, threw it hard at the Yocum mirror. The mirror shattered, raining ancient glass tears.

She stood up, walked over to the shoe, slipped it back on her foot. She licked her lips. Fluffed her hair. She rested her hands on her hips and said, "There was a man here a minute ago, trying to kill me, but he seems to have disappeared."

Disappeared had five syllables.

"You're that Vanna woman, aren't you?" Cookie pretended the Smith & Wesson didn't exist.

"Venus."

Cookie slapped her forehead. "I am so bad with names. Venus the planet, Venus de Milo, Venus on the Half Shell, Venus the Goddess of Love. There. That should be enough visual association."

Venus said, "You're under arrest, Mrs. Avalon, for the murders of Jonathan Willow and Zora."

Cookie got huffy. "You are trespassing on my property. Get out of here this minute or I'll call the police."

Venus explained how that wouldn't be necessary. Cookie made a few shrieking protestations, but Venus was firm, insistent. Cookie agreed to go, on the condition that she could change her clothes. They walked across the house to Cookie's dressing room. Cookie took a long time deciding what to wear to jail. When she finally had it all figured out, she had on a white linen suit and beige pumps. A lot of jewelry. The handbag with her credit cards, her passport, and some cash, and a makeup case the size of a Southern belle's hope chest.

She was still fuming, threatening lawsuits as Venus guided her out the front door, across manicured lawns to the driveway. Song stood beside Needles's patrol car, Needles in the driver's seat. Venus helped Cookie into handcuffs, Song helped her into the car. Needles leaned out the window and said, "That damn bunch of demonstrators has ruined my day."

Venus said, "What's wrong with them demonstrating? They're not harming anything."

"My wife's in there among them," said Needles dully. "And my two sons. Everybody I know is in that meadow. What the hell do they think they're doing up there?"

Venus smiled. "They won a big battle today. You should be proud of them."

Needles snorted, mumbled to himself.

Venus and Song watched Needles drive away, Cookie sitting stiffly in the backseat of the patrol car. When they disappeared from sight, Venus went back indoors, looked around. She found the little Pekingese whimpering and shivering, hiding under the kitchen table. She picked up the froufrou pet, held it in her arms as she walked through the big house.

Imogene's quarters had been cleared out. Maybe this had been Cookie's first sign that her time was up. Forty years of loyalty, and suddenly her nanny deserts her. Venus would never see Imogene Donner again. She had fled the scene, was probably headed back home, to Hoboken, where she understood the people, and too, the reasons why Cookie Charmeaux had finally resorted to murder. Imogene might know more than she told, but there are certain things nannies will never reveal about their charges, or confess about themselves. It's the nanny's code. Imogene was bound to flee.

On the way out of the house, Venus caught a glimpse of herself in a surviving corner of the big mirror. Startled by her own reflection, she didn't recognize herself at first. Then Song walked in, sauntered up to the mirror, peered at her reflection, and said, "Who's the babe?"

THIRTY-THREE

MEADOW LARK

THE RICH HARVEST of blue poppies lay piled upon stacked perfume dryers, awaiting the rude crush of the presser's vice. In the poppy field, nothing remained but a dark brown stripe of dead plant refuse and loamy earth, a dull remnant of glory stripped. Below the denuded poppy field, Yodeler's meadow had emptied of demonstrators. The deserted meadow wore its summer cloak, a deep, rich fabric of late-blooming purple asters, veronicas, deep yellow Saint-John's-wort, tawny roseroot, bleeding heart, arnica, and golden fleabane. Here and there clumps of squaw carpet and pink heather wove the tatters of its last blooming into the meadow's fresh apron, and Venus had to search to locate the clumps of wild violets. She found them still blooming, but on the wane. No more signs of Dungeness silverspot larvae.

Venus stood up, stretched. Her rib cage hurt, but the fever had subsided, at least for now. She started climbing the meadow, her eyes like jumping jacks flitting from one colorful bloom to the next. Enveloped in this fragrant patchwork quilt, she felt strong, somewhat victorious, though she hadn't saved Yodeler's meadow. The people of Fern had saved the federal wildlife preserve from ruination. And Bella had sealed its fate by recovering the specimen of Dungeness silverspot from Mimi Budge. Jonathan Willow's catch. She wished it had been her catch, her discovery. Lepidoptera envy. That single specimen proved that *Speyeria zerene dungenessii* still existed, at least in this meadow, on this preserve. Now if only the little caterpillar she'd found on the violet leaf would metamorphose into another dungenessii specimen...

Halfway to the top, she paused, sat down to rest. Her mind felt clear, her thoughts organized, fitting together like a pair of folded hands. Now it was time to move on. Wexler had plans for her. What plans? In a couple days, she'd find out.

A seagull flew low across the meadow. Venus watched it glide, heard its shrieking lament. Her eyes followed its airborne path, but she was distracted by something in the lower meadow. A little troop heading up the meadow, heading towards her. She squinted, blinked, shaded her eyes, stared. When they got closer, Venus saw the group's leader. Bella. The nonpareil queen of cinema waved up at Venus. Behind her trudged a small figure whose identity she could only guess, until he came a few yards closer and shouted, "Hey, Venus! Here we are!"

What in God's good name did Bella and Timmy think they were doing? And here came Burden, along for the country air. But it was the last person in the group, the man walking beside Burden, who caused her heart to somersault down the mountainside. He looked the same as the last time she saw him. He was smiling, his white teeth flashing. Even from here she could see his eyes twinkling, and she could almost, but not quite, read his lips. Whatever he said made Burden laugh uproariously. But then, Richard had always been able to coax a smile onto Burden's dour countenance.

"Richard. My God, it's Richard, and just look at me," she whispered. Jumping to her feet too fast, she doubled over in pain. She took a deep breath, straightened up, and before she could focus, she felt his arms surround her, felt his breath on her face. He drew her close and her ribs might have shrieked but she didn't notice because now he was stroking her hair, whispering in her ear.

"God, Venus. Oh my God." He said it over and over, like a broken record, like a man desperately in love.

She was melting into the embrace when an alarm went off in her head. First of all, people were standing around. She wasn't about to make a fool of herself, especially in front of Bella. Secondly, what right did dastardly Richard have to touch her? She was filling out these thoughts when Bella cried, "Come Burden. Come along, Timmy. I see a lovely patch of gooseberries."

They were alone. Richard took her hand in his. With his other hand, he slipped on Count What's-His-Name's pear-shaped diamond ring. He said, "Mrs. Gasgcoyne found it in the refrigerator that used to be in your apartment. In the freezer section. She brought it to me. She's a sweet old bag."

Trapped in his energy field, she had trouble acting standoffish. She said, "What's this supposed to mean?"

Richard smiled. "Maybe Timmy ought to explain." He called to

Timmy and the boy came running back. "All right, Timmy, tell Venus. Everything."

Timmy hung his head, stared at his feet. Richard prompted him. "Go on, Timmy. Start at the beginning."

Timmy drew a deep breath, exhaled, and said, "Okay, okay, but don't let her hit me or anything."

"I won't hit you, Tim."

Timmy spread his hands, showed empty palms. "It was only a joke."

"Tell me the joke, sport."

He shifted on his feet. "All right. I sent you that e-mail and signed Richard's name. I sent another one like it to Richard and signed your name."

"What? Why in the world...?"

"Because I can take care of you better than he can."

He was almost shouting, tears welling in his eyes. She crouched down to his height. He probably despised people who did that, but now that they were face-to-face, she reached out, pulled him to her. "Sure, I believe it, Tim. I believe you could take care of me." He sobbed quietly in her embrace.

"I don't want you to go away," he said softly.

She crooked her finger under his chin, said, "What if you came to live with us?"

Timmy curled his lip. "All three of us?"

Venus nodded. Richard said, "Sounds good to me."

Timmy growled, "I'm not talking to you, Richard."

"Oops." Richard.

Venus said, "What about it, Tim? We can all be a family. Even Bella can be part of the family."

"Sure, like the Dowager Empress." Richard. More handsome than ever.

Timmy looked thoughtful. "Are you two moving in with us?"

"Richard and me, move into Bella's?" Preposterous.

Timmy nodded. "There's enough room for all of us."

She said, "I had another scenario in mind."

"Like what?" Sullen, suspicious.

"Like, you and Richard and me getting our own place."

Timmy screwed up his face, thought about it, then said, "Nope. Won't work."

"Why not?"

"Because for one thing, Mother would never agree to give me up. And for another thing..." He paused. He couldn't say it, so she said it for him.

"You could never give up Bella?"

Timmy nodded. "She's my new mom. I can't desert her." He kicked at a clump of Saint-John's-wort. The sturdy plant sprang back defiantly. "Will you visit a lot?"

She smiled at him. "Promise."

Richard cleared his throat. "Maybe you'd like to tell Venus about the fire?"

Timmy shook his head vehemently. "I don't ever want to tell her."

Gently, Richard said, "Better get it over with, Timmy. You'll feel much better afterwards."

The boy collapsed to the ground, buried his face in the grass, cried softly. Venus and Richard sat on either side of him, waiting for the tears to subside. But they only increased and his body started shaking, heaving. Venus rubbed his back gently. Timmy growled, "Stop that." She stopped, waited. More sobbing, then, "I didn't mean to make trouble. I wanted to give you a gift."

Venus looked at Richard. Richard nodded. Timmy blurted out the rest. "I took a taxicab over to your apartment, see? You gave me a key, remember? I left you a note. Okay, okay, a love note. And a candle. It was that eucalyptus scent. You told me you like eucalyptus. So I lit the candle and left. I thought you'd be home pretty soon after that. Because you said it was your day off. So I guess that's what started the fire." He swallowed back some tears. "I didn't mean to start a fire. I only meant to surprise you. I wanted you to come back and live with us. Now I'm really in trouble. They might send me to prison."

It was Richard who spoke next, softly, soothingly. "Hey, sport, you're not going to prison. You're staying with Bella and you're going to grow up like a regular kid."

Timmy stopped sobbing, listened. His body still heaved. He lay on the sloping meadow, face to the ground, but he listened. Richard went on, "You'll have to see a shrink for a while. And Bella will probably dock your allowance, but it's over now, Timmy, and we all understand what you were trying to communicate to us."

"What?" A hoarse, curt, typical Timmy intonation.

Richard said, "You're having a tough time right now, sport. Your life's been turned upside down, you're confused about all the people around you, all the grown-ups. Do they want you? Or are they just pretending to want you? Will they abandon you? And too, you probably have a lot of emotional stuff stuck inside you, stuff you need to get out. The shrink idea might be for the best.''

Timmy turned over onto his back. His face was swollen from crying, his eyes red and puffy. He said, "Is it a kid's shrink, or what?"

"Probably a kid's shrink." Richard smiled. "Maybe you'll like him. Or her."

Timmy waved a hand. "No females. I won't talk to a female. I don't care if she is a doctor."

Venus opened her mouth to say something, but Richard stopped her. "We'll take that into consideration. Now, I think Bella and Burden could use some help with the gooseberry harvest."

Venus said, "That's illegal."

Richard rolled his eyes. Timmy got up, ran across the meadow toward Bella and Burden. Over his shoulder he shouted to Venus, "I have a surprise for you. Don't go away. I'm going to get your surprise."

He ran to Burden. Burden swung his backpack to the ground, unzipped it, fished out the Bloomingdale's swizzle stick box. Timmy grabbed the box, ran back to Venus, held it up to the sun. The violet leaves had completely shriveled, the stems dried up. In their place appeared the most glorious golden butterfly she'd ever seen, more brilliant for its distinctive black chevron markings on the upper wing surface, the iridescent silver spots on the under wings. It was perfectly formed, still damp from its metamorphosis. A perfect specimen of the Dungeness silverspot.

The sun illuminated its golden wings, warmed them. Timmy set the box on the ground. She was leaning forward, reaching for the box when Timmy yanked off the net covering. The never-quite-extinct Dungeness silverspot fluttered out of the clumsy box, its wings already spread and warmed. Venus's fingers were half an inch from the precious creature when it lifted off, sailing into the air. Venus jumped up, chased it, zigzagging across the meadow, around in circles, until at last she fell to the ground defeated. They watched the silverspot flutter up to the high meadow, toward nectar, and hopefully, but not likely, a mate. Timmy shrugged, as if dismissing yet another loved one from his life. He didn't show any feelings one way or the other, just shrugged. Then he turned and ran back to Burden and Bella.

Venus punched the air, shouted at the butterfly. Apparently it didn't hear her. It didn't come back.

"Rejection's hell," Richard joked innocently. "Especially from a butterfly."

"You have no idea how important that little insect was." She lay back on the sloping meadow, closed her eyes. When she opened them a moment later, Richard held out a bouquet of white flowers. "I picked this down at the bottom. For you," he said. "A wedding bouquet."

"That's real nice, Richard," she said, accepting the showy nose-gay. "Only I don't think death camas are really appropriate for a bride."

AN OWEN KEANE MYSTERY

The Ordained

Terence Faherty

LOST IN RAPTURE

Ex-seminarian Owen Keane returns to Indiana to attend the parole hearing of a killer he helped convict. Here, in the isolated town of Rapture, Owen is drawn into a bizarre mystery.

Three people have disappeared. But stranger still is the legacy of the town, a place populated by a religious sect who believed the world would end in 1844. Has the prophecy come true 150 years later…or is there a more sinister explanation?

Available January 1999 at your favorite retail outlet.

A NOAH RICHARDS MYSTERY

WILLFUL

NEGLECT

DEATH OF INNOCENCE

Attorney Noah Richards finds himself taking on a case that's both a legal and emotional land mine: medical malpractice.

Moved by the sad circumstances of a young boy's death in the local hospital, Noah begins probing the bizarre events that led to the tragedy. The attending nurses are terrified and closemouthed, and one has disappeared.

Noah soon discovers that the truth is as elusive as people willing to talk.

MARY MORGAN

Available January 1999 at your favorite retail outlet.

Look us up on-line at: http://www.romance.net   WMM297